POLAR HORRORS

POLAR HORRORS

Strange Tales
from the World's Ends

Edited by
JOHN MILLER

This collection first published in 2022 by
The British Library
96 Euston Road
London NW1 2DB

Cataloguing in Publication Data
A catalogue record for this publication is available from the British Library

ISBN 978 0 7123 5442 4
e-ISBN 978 0 7123 6825 4

Frontispiece illustration drawn by Captain John Ross from John Ross, *A Voyage of
Discovery ... enquiring into the Possibility of a North-West Passage*, John Murray, London,
1819.

Illustration on page 352 by Manuel Orazi from *The Sphere*,
23 December 1911, London Illustrated Newspapers.

Cover design by Mauricio Villamayor with illustration by Sandra Gómez

Text design and typesetting by Tetragon, London
Printed in England by CPI Group (UK) Ltd, Croydon, CRO 4YY

MIX
Paper | Supporting
responsible forestry
FSC
www.fsc.org   FSC® C171272

CONTENTS

INTRODUCTION

There is a longstanding conception of the Earth's polar regions that there is nothing much there but vast expanses of featureless ice, fearsome weather, a few solitary wandering bears in the Arctic, huddles of penguins at the other end, above them the glorious Auroras (Borealis at the north; Australis at the south) and very few—if any—signs of human culture. The poles in this tradition represent the absence or even negation of civilisation and politics: the last great wildernesses where nature continues in its purest form. It's an alluring narrative, even if (as we shall see) it isn't true.

When Mary Shelley's *Frankenstein* (1818) reaches its climax among the far north's "eternal frosts" with the angst-ridden scientist pursuing his creature on an "almost endless journey across the mountainous ices of the ocean", the Arctic setting is an exploration of intensities of the heart and mind as much as it is an account of a physical place (which Shelley in any case never herself visited). The same pattern holds at the far south. Edgar Allan Poe imagines a similar landscape to Shelley's in his 1833 Antarctic tale "MS. Found in a Bottle". As Poe's unnamed narrator takes refuge on the ghostly vessel *Discovery*, he records the ship running further and further towards "stupendous ramparts of ice, towering away into the desolate sky, and looking like the walls of the universe". The narrator experiences a deepening sensation of horror at what might await, but nonetheless acknowledges that "a curiosity to penetrate the mysteries of these awful regions, predominates even over my despair, and will reconcile me to the most hideous aspect of death". At Poe's historical moment in the early nineteenth century, when little was known of the Antarctic

7

continent (and like Shelley, Poe was writing about a place he'd never seen), the narrator's horror is balanced by the glamour of the unknown, the apprehension that he is "hurrying onwards to some exciting knowledge—some never-to-be-imparted secret, whose attainment is destruction". The Romantic imagination of the poles works through an intriguing mixture of emotions: the dread and the desire which reinforce rather than oppose each other, and which together emphasise the dual function of extremity as existential as much as geographical.

Shelley's and Poe's early depictions of polar regions remain influential, even after two centuries of Arctic and Antarctic exploration have threatened to bring such flights of literary imagination back to the ground of sober fact. Conventionally, the poles remain the blank space on which literary and cinematic fantasies—some of which are very odd indeed—can be imposed. H. P. Lovecraft's formative version of weird fiction draws on polar regions to a significant extent, mainly the Antarctic world which in "At the Mountains of Madness" (1931) appears as a "frightful gateway into hidden spheres of dream". Dan Simmons's *The Terror* (2007) shows the allure of Arctic horror lingering into the twenty-first century, even if the novel's supernatural elements rely on a historical setting in one of the far north's great mysteries. The disappearance of Sir John Franklin's 1845 expedition to navigate the Northwest Passage—the long-sought sea route between the Atlantic and Pacific Oceans—was a real-life Victorian horror story. What dire fate befell the crew after the two ships, the *Erebus* and the *Terror*, were abandoned in the ice in 1848? The evidence of cannibalism that was presented by an 1854 search party was rejected with jingoistic indignation: British gentlemen do *not* eat each other, not even the common sailors (though actually they probably did, even if scurvy, cold and poisoning from canned food played their part in the crews' demises too). Simmons inevitably throws a monster into the dramatic mix to hammer home the Arctic's Gothic credentials. The historical setting—think too of Michelle Paver's 2010 Arctic ghost story *Dark Matter*, set in the 1930s—distances the strange happenings from the rationalising gaze of modern science. Fiction reveals a consistent longing to hold onto the poles' otherness, even if it has to go back in time to do so. It's not enough for the poles to be colder and further away than other places (though that of course depends where you are to start with); there needs to be some deeper weirdness at work in these extreme latitudes.

In the literary history of the Arctic and Antarctic continents there are some striking motifs, some of which seem curious today. For a start, the weather at the poles isn't always what you would expect. Shelley's narrator in the opening sections of *Frankenstein*, the pompous Arctic adventurer Robert Walton, can't help but wonder if the expectation of "frost and desolation" will turn out to be misguided and that instead he'll discover a place where "snow and frost are banished; and, sailing over a calm sea, we may be wafted to a land surpassing in wonders and in beauty every region hitherto discovered on the habitable globe". The idea that the poles may—contrary to expectation—contain open seas and a tropical climate has a long history and takes its place among a variety of eldritch geographical speculations. In one tradition, dating back to the fourteenth century, the poles are sites of whirlpools that lead down into a hollow earth: a serious hypothesis that was embraced enthusiastically by novelists, to the extent that hollow earth fiction comprises its own subgenre. Lost races and civilisations abound, both within the planet's imagined interior and on the surface of the poles. Poe's 1838 novel *The Narrative of Arthur Gordon Pym of Nantucket* is one influential example of a curious polar population. As Pym and his companion Peters head further south they arrive at the island Tsalal, home to a stereotypically savage Black tribe from whom the adventurers escape only to disappear down the Antarctic plughole.

It is fitting, perhaps inevitable, that the weird worlds imagined at the poles should be the home to a parallel natural history of fantastic, and in many cases paranormal, creatures. Some of these beasts spin off from a recognisable polar zoology. The "limitless void" of Lovecraft's subterranean domain in "At the Mountains of Madness" contains a population of penguins, those familiar Antarctic denizens, though these are "of a huge, unknown species larger than the greatest of the known king penguins, and monstrous in [their] combined albinism and virtual eyelessness". Other creatures of the polar imagination are more outrageous. I'll save for now the creatures that make it into this volume, but here are some examples from the wider ecosystem of the polar and subpolar weird. Abraham Merritt's 1918 story "The People of the Pit" follows a group of gold prospectors in Alaska as they reach as lost city of reptilian trees and "monstrous slugs". Jim Kjelgaard's "The Thing from the Barrens" (1945) pits a remote community of trappers in the far north against an invisible predatory duck monster. Prehistoric creatures linger in confirmation of the tendency to fix the poles into a perpetual past. James de Mille's Antarctic novel *A Strange Manuscript Found in a Copper Cylinder* (1888) is perhaps the classic of the sub-subgenre of polar dinosaur fiction. The most prominent creatures in the story are the athalebs, "of portentous size and fearful shape... with rows of terrible teeth like those of a crocodile [and] vast folded leathern wings... like some enormous bat".

Given the strangeness of the imagined lifeforms of the poles, it is no surprise that the literary history of the far south and the far north is swarming with aliens. Again, Lovecraft has got a lot to answer for here: behind the secret Antarctic world of "At the Mountains of Madness" are the Elder Ones who "filtered down from the stars when earth was young". John W. Campbell Jr's 1938 novella *Who Goes There?*—later the basis of the movies *The Thing from Another World* (1951) and *The Thing* (1982)—is premised on the depredations of a shape-shifting alien monster, unleashed from the ice by a crew of researchers at an Antarctic outpost. Back in the (ostensibly) real world, ufologists have often looked to the poles. One of the most strange and remarkable cases is the 1946 Hefferlin Manuscript, based on information communicated telepathically to Mr. and Mrs. Hefferlin of Livingston, Montana, that tells of Rainbow City, an alien metropolis thriving under the Antarctic. There are so many stories of aliens at the poles that you could be tempted to conclude—as Arthur C. Clarke does in his Lovecraft spoof "At the Mountains of Murkiness"—that the aliens themselves have got their tentacles mixed up in them somehow. As Clarke has the extra-terrestrials reflect, "We started writing stories about ourselves, and later subsidised authors, particularly in America, to do the same". With everyone adamant all these tales of polar aliens are just part of the sci-fi publishing boom of the early twentieth century, the aliens are "quite safe" from human interference. They're pleasingly polite in Clarke's story, but don't let that fool you. Their secret plan is found in a scrawled note: "Destroy human race by plague of flying jellyfish".

The key point then is that the poles seem destined to be other in time, space and in the beings that inhabit them. In effect, the polar regions are as close to outer space you can get and still be on the planet (though the deep sea has a similar function in sci-fi too). Yet behind the monsters and the aliens, in the vast sublime void, among the fantasies and speculations are very real places with very particular histories. For sure, it can be hard to disentangle fact from fiction: Shelley and Poe both drew on nonfictional accounts of polar exploration and their versions of them are recycled back in later exploration narratives. There is an important point here.

Although they seem beyond the tawdry world of colonial expansion and consumer culture, the poles have long been economically significant, primarily in Poe and Shelley's day (and for a long time afterwards) for the animal bodies that were harvested in vast numbers, mostly for oil, with serious consequences for whale and seal populations. Skipping ahead two centuries, it's hard to avoid the conclusion that a rapidly heating world signals the start of another polar resource rush. When Donald Trump announced in 2019 that he was pondering a "large real estate deal" to buy Greenland, his seemingly eccentric claim made a certain horrible sense in the logic of global capital. Greenland's extensive mineral deposits are quickly becoming more accessible. It's hard to imagine they'll be left in the ground. And while commercial exploitation at the south has been off the table since the 1959 Antarctic Treaty, an astonishing number of countries are laying claim to parts of the continent: from China to the US, from Venezuela to Turkey, Iran, India, Pakistan, Chile, Argentina, Australia... There is no pure wilderness anywhere now.

Far from the fanciful otherworlds of the gothic imagination, the poles are in many ways the front line of economy and ecology. Today they are intensely politicised zones and real places of enormous significance. After all, their ice is what keeps much of the world above the waves. It's worth remembering too that despite the cliché of the Arctic as an empty space, it has been continuously inhabited since around 2500 BC by Indigenous peoples, whose cultures and cosmologies involve deep connections with the environment and the creatures who live there. There are Indigenous traditions in the Antarctic too. Tales of the southern continent appear in Māori mythology; there is even a hypothesis that Māori explorers discovered Antarctica as early as the seventh century.

So while the tales of *Polar Horrors* incline in many cases towards the fantastic—there are ghosts and monsters here, curious minerals and surprising topographies—there is also a consistent attention to the profit motive that drew many to the far north and south. The heyday of whaling in the nineteenth century is an important context for many of the stories. The volume moves from 1837 until more or less the present, with a slightly skewed chronology between Arctic and Antarctic: the northerly tales are by and large earlier than the southerly, reflecting the earlier arrival of the Arctic than the Antarctic into European and American writing. There are real animals in these pages (real-*ish* at any rate) as well as mythical creatures. These are stories, then, in which imagination and history are mixed up together; in which the lively worlds of the Arctic and Antarctic can be discerned among the psychic projections; and ground and ice (as well as sea and outer space) exist in tense equipoise with the strange interior worlds of weird fiction.

JOHN MILLER, 2022

FURTHER READING

Hill, Jen, *White Horizon: The Arctic in the Nineteenth-Century British Imagination* (SUNY Press, 2008).

Leane, Elizabeth, *Antarctica in Fiction: Imaginative Narratives of the Far South* (Cambridge University Press, 2012).

Loomis, Chauncey, "The Arctic Sublime" in *Nature and the Victorian Imagination, 1818–1914*, edited by U. C. Knoepflmacher and G. B. Tennyson, 95–112 (University of California Press, 1977).

McCannon, John, *A History of the Arctic: Nature, Exploration and Exploitation* (Reaktion Books, 2013).

Poe, Edgar Allan, *Selected Writings* (Norton, 2004).

Price, Robert M. (ed.), *The Antarktos Cycle: At the Mountains of Madness and Other Chilling Tales* (Chaosium, 2006).

Shelley, Mary, *Frankenstein* [1818] (Oxford World's Classics, 2001).

Spufford, Francis, *I May Be Some Time: Ice and the English Imagination* (Picador, 1999).

A NOTE FROM THE PUBLISHER

The original short stories reprinted in the British Library Tales of the Weird series were written and published in a period ranging across the nineteenth and twentieth centuries. There are many elements of these stories which continue to entertain modern readers; however, in some cases there are also uses of language, instances of stereotyping and some attitudes expressed by narrators or characters which may not be endorsed by the publishing standards of today. We acknowledge therefore that some elements in the stories selected for reprinting may continue to make uncomfortable reading for some of our audience. With this series British Library Publishing aims to offer a new readership a chance to read some of the rare material of the British Library's collections in an affordable paperback format, to enjoy their merits and to look back into the worlds of the past two centuries as portrayed by their writers. It is not possible to separate these stories from the history of their writing and as such the following stories are presented as they were originally published with minor edits only, made for consistency of style and sense. We welcome feedback from our readers, which can be sent to the following address:

British Library Publishing
The British Library
96 Euston Road
London, NW1 2DB
United Kingdom

NORTH

THE SURPASSING ADVENTURES OF ALLAN GORDON

James Hogg

James Hogg (1770–1835) was among the foremost authors of Scottish Romanticism. Born into a poor farming community in Ettrick in the Borders, Hogg continued the family tradition, working as a shepherd even after he began to publish poetry that drew the attention of some influential literary figures, most notably Sir Walter Scott who became a keen supporter of his work. Hogg eventually turned to professional writing aged forty; today his best-known work is the 1824 theological murder mystery novel *The Private Memoirs and Confessions of a Justified Sinner*.

"The Surpassing Adventures of Allan Gordon" was published posthumously in 1837. Behind the fantastic, hallucinatory ambience of Hogg's Arctic tale are two pieces of historical fact. Firstly, the whaling vessel the *Anne Forbes* was wrecked near Greenland in 1757. Secondly, Greenland had for many centuries been home to Norwegian colonists and, although these settlers had all perished in the fifteenth century (probably as the result of an outbreak of the plague), an expedition by Hans Egede in 1732 aimed to revive Norwegian interest in the area. Some literary elements of Hogg's story are familiar too. The story of the shipwrecked sailor evidently owes a good deal to Daniel Defoe's *Robinson Crusoe* (1719) and the depiction of the Arctic world draws on Romantic conceptions of the sublime poles in Samuel Taylor Coleridge's and Mary Shelley's writing. What is most distinctive about Hogg's weird tale is his depiction of the polar bear Nancy. While polar writing of the period usually focuses on animals as monsters and/or commodities, Hogg's bear is a compelling creation and one of the great—if lesser-known—non-human characters of nineteenth-century literature.

Humbly and most respectfully inscribed to
SIR DAVID BREWSTER

I t is well known that the ship, Briel of Amsterdam, took up a Scotsman from the ice of the Polar sea, in the year 1764, and set him ashore at Aberdeen, from whence he had sailed seven years before, in the whaler ship, Anne Forbes. His name was Allan Gordon, and his narrative, as taken down by John Duff, schoolmaster at Cabrach, is now in my possession.

I, Allan Gordon, was the son of Adam Gordon, a hind, or farm servant on the banks of the Bogie, and I was born in a small cottage three miles above Huntly. My father learned me to read, but never to write, and when I was eleven years of age, he bound me apprentice to a tailor in Huntly, a little crooked wretch, who, whenever any body offended him, always wreaked out his ill nature on me. I bore with him long, not daring to break my apprenticeship for fear of the fine that would fall on my poor father, although many a thrashed skin I got, and every time my knuckles itched to be at this tailor's ugly face. I was always obliged to *sir* and *master* him, and if by chance I called him by any other name, I got the length of the needle in my flesh instantly.

This was not long to be borne by a lad of any spirit. One time we were sewing on a board together at the manse of Auchindoir, and the minister and his wife were sitting by the fire in the same apartment. It was Saturday evening, and my master was anxious to have the job done that night, and kept urging me to ply and make long stitches. This last injunction he durst not give openly, but there was an understood term which conveyed his meaning. This was, "sit yond, boy, sit yond." This he kept repeating and repeating that evening, and at every hint, gave me a pradd with his needle, until in a fit of impatience I returned, "the deil's i' the bodie, for I can sit nae farther yond unless I baiss." He gave me such a look! I regarded it not, but laughed, and joked, and crooned, "Cauld kail in Aberdeen, an' sowins in Strathbogie," and, "The Tailor fell o'er the bed, needles an' a'." But the minister said, "Aha, William, so the secret is out regarding the order to your lad always to *sit yond*, therefore, give up, and go your ways home, and come back on Monday morning, for I will not have my clothes or my boy's clothes spoiled by your long stitches." "But tell me this, sir," said my master, who wanted to put the matter off as a joke, "whether do you think long stitches or short sermons are the worst."

"William, I want none of your profane and homely jests," said the parson, "therefore keep them to yourself, and give up my work; I can have another tradesman to finish it."

"Yes you can, sir," said my master, "and so can I go and hear another minister. I have the advantage of you there, for you cannot have a tradesman like me in Aberdeenshire, whereas I can have a far better minister. For I maintain, that in short sermons often repeated, there is greater blame than in long stitches on new ground."

Thus parted the parson of Auchindoir and my master in high chagrin, the consequences of which I was doomed to abide. No sooner were we beyond the glebe lands, than he said with ill feigned civility, "Well, you have behaved yourself like a sensible young man and a gentleman tonight." I was going to say, that I had spoken rashly and unadvisedly, and was sorry for it, but that it was the severe prick with the needle that caused it. Before I got my answer arranged, he struck me such a blow above the right eye, that made the blood to stream. I chanced to have the lapboard carrying in my right hand, a substantial plane-tree deal more than two feet long, with which I gave him such a knap over the head that I made his skull ring again, and his eyes to stand in back water. "How dare you for your saul, sirrah, lift your hand against your master," said he.

"I'll not be struck like a dog in that manner by the king, or the duke of Gordon," said I, "and far less by a bowled tailor."

This answer, put the creature perfectly mad, for he valued himself greatly on his personal appearance, and he flew on me like a tiger. My spirit of resistance was fairly up. I returned blow for blow, and there as desperate a battle ensued as ever was fought. In a few minutes he began to quail, and, though his lip quivered with rage, he was rather frightened, and wanted to call a parley. "Come, come, this will never do," said he, "down on your knees, and beg my pardon."

"I'll be d—d if I will," said I.

"You, sirrah, you'll be d—d if you will! Do you say so to me," said he, in a loud majestic tone, for two masons appeared coming toward us. "Then, sir, know that your life is in my hand, and I will chastise you until you be no more." He threw off his coat and waistcoat, and fell to me like a day's work. I held down my head, and took a tempest of blows on my shoulders and neck. I then ran with my head full drive on the pit of his stomach, which made him stagger and fall backward. I gave him just one fundamental kick, and then turned and laughed aloud. He flew after me in desperate fury, striking both with feet and hands, fighting in glorious style, for the two masons were now close at hand. I could fight none, save as a bullock or ram, but having frequently seen these fight desperately, I followed their example instinctively, and ran always against my dumpy misshapen master with my head full drive. He tore out my hair, and cursed and swore most manfully, but I regarded not these, giving him always the other dunch, and whenever I hit him fairly, whether on the face or breast, I knocked him down. The two mason lads rolled on the green with laughter, for, to make the thing the more ludicrous, whenever I knocked him down with my head, I turned round and flung at him with my heels like a horse, thus in my warfare imitating the beasts only.

I soon mauled him so, that he could not rise, but there he lay, threatening future vengeance, and cursing me most emphatically. He threw first the goose, and then the lapboard at my head, which I eschewed and then ran up and flung at him like an incensed or vicious horse, giving him some good hard kicks, and then went off and left him. Instead of going home, I went straight to Aberdeen, where I could have procured work as a journeyman, but durst not remain for my late incensed master; so I went on board a Hull coasting vessel, and continued in her five years as a cabin boy and sailor, and by that time, had become quite attached to the nautical life. I went one voyage to New York, and another to Lisbon, but the description of these voyages would only delay the narrative. I now sit down to relate, only I thought it behooved me to tell how a man of Bogieside chanced to become a sailor.

In 1757, I entered on board the Anne Forbes for the Greenland whale fishery. Our captain's name was John Hughes, an Englishman, a drunken, rash, headlong fool, and one with whom it was impossible for any seaman to have the least comfort. As there had been some excellent fish taken the preceding summer in the Spitzbergen seas, we had instructions to proceed thither. Accordingly, we parted with the rest of the whalers off Cape Farewell, and stretched away to the north-east. We had fine weather and an open sea, save that there was a girdle of ice of from ten to thirty miles broad, that belted the whole coast of east Greenland, the mountains of which country were frequently in our view. We sailed between that and Iceland, and about the seventieth degree, came frequently in view of some tremendous fish, all of which appeared to be journeying rapidly northward. We captured one, and continued our route straight on for a fortnight, although our mate, who was an old experienced hand, represented to our captain, again and again, the danger of penetrating so far into the polar seas; but he was an absurd and obstinate mule, and only laughed the good old man to scorn, pretending that he was making some curious observations on the dipping of the needle, whereas he never dipped the needle at all, it just stood where it was, only it gave over pointing. He then told us we were at the pole, and afterwards that we had sailed round it. He gave us a treat, and plenty to drink on this joyful occasion; but we only laughed in our sleeves at him, for in fact there was no pole nor pillar of any kind to be seen; neither was there any axle-tree or groove, which there behooved to have been, had we been at the pole of the world. There was nothing but a calm open sea, and the sun beating on us all the four-and-twenty hours. There were plenty of fish. We loaded our vessel; but yet the absurd monster would not leave the ground, but continued exulting and filling himself drunk on the merits of his grand discovery, and pretended that he could sail to China as soon as to Spain. For my part I believed then, and believe still, that it was all nonsense, though there was certainly something peculiar in our situation, for the needle had no power, not a grain. It stood where we put it, or kept whirling and wheeling as if it had been dancing a Highland reel.

For two days the mate kept pointing out to the captain some brilliant appearances at a great distance, which he said he suspected were immense floes or fields of ice, and if the wind should chance to rise in that direction, we should to a certainty be enclosed. But captain Hughes answered him with the greatest contempt thus: "Why, you old grovelling ass, you have not half the science of a walrus, nor half the ambition of a lobster. You do not perceive, and not perceiving you cannot estimate, the value of the discovery I have made; a discovery which will hand down my name to all generations, and not only my name, but the very name of the vessel, and every one on board of her, will go down to posterity. Therefore, tell not me of your floes and your fields, your rainbow colours and cowardly surmises. Am I not resting on the pole of the world, and can run from hence into any of its divisions I choose. I am like a man on the top of an hill, who, if the storm approaches on the one side, can take shelter on the other."

"Why it may, it may a'be true that ye say, captain," said old Abram Johnston, the mate; "I may hae little science an' less ambition. But I hae that muckle science as to perceive that you are detaining us in a very critical and perilous situation, for no earthly purpose that I can see; and my ambition is all to save the ship and cargo of my employers."

"Say, rather, to save your own mean and despicable life," retorted the captain. "I am answerable to my employers for the ship and cargo, not you. And think you not the value of the discovery I have made to be of more value than any ship or cargo that ever sailed the ocean?"

"Perhaps it may, captain," said he, "that point I shall not dispute with you. But if we lose the ship, we lose ourselves and the grand discovery into the bargain."

"There you said true, old foggie!" said the captain, "and it is the first word of sense you have spoken. Come and let us have one bottle together on the head of it. Who knows what you may yet be. You can box the compass. Now tell me which is north and which south?"

"What o'clock is it?" said he.

"Aha, catch me there, old foggie."

"Then in fact, captain, I do not know, for this place is like the New Jerusalem, there is no night here, and no star to be seen, and glad would I be to be out of it."

"Better and better, old Abram. Well, then, we shall sail southward with the first breeze to give you peace of conscience, and I'll take you half a dozen we be the first of the whalers on the coast of Scotland."

The captain filled himself drunk as usual; and in a few hours afterwards, from some unaccountable current, the mate perceived the vessel to be drifting with great rapidity: and not knowing in what direction, he called up the captain. I shall never forget how blue and confounded like he looked that morning; but he instantly commanded all sails to be set; and after he had taken the sun's altitude, he actually knew where we were, put about ship, and sailed in the contrary direction from that in which we had been drifting for the last eight hours. The current was strong against us, with a light breeze on our starboard bow. The ice approached us on all sides, and, what was worst of all, a whitish fog covered us. The captain was now manifestly alarmed, for he kept close on deck, and gave his orders with impatience and surliness, cursing and thrashing us as we had been beasts. I confess I enjoyed his dilemma somewhat, and would almost have run the risk of shipwreck to have seen his big lobster snout cooled on an iceberg, for I hated him most heartily.

When our needle became once more fixed in the same direction, I never was so glad, as I then knew what we were doing and whither sailing.

But sailing was soon out of the question. We were completely involved in broken floating ice, while an interminable field appeared following us behind. In the midst of this confusion, we continued drifting swiftly toward the south-west with reefed sails, sometimes finding a little opening and making some progress. We passed what I took for a huge iceberg; but I heard our captain say it was one of the seven sisters, off the coast of Spitzbergen. That was the last land we were doomed to see. After struggling on for four-and-twenty hours longer, we perceived another field of ice before us, which likewise seemed approaching us, for the floating ice was crushing up before it, and rolling over it. But whether it was floating or fixed I know not; the consequence to us was the same, for the field behind coming on us with great velocity, while we were fixed on the one ahead, I saw what was likely to be the issue. I ran up to the topmast, while our captain cursed me and ordered me down; but I regarded him not. In an instant crash went the masts and bulwarks of the goodly Anne Forbes like egg shells. I was swung from the mast by the concussion I know not how far, and landed on one of the fields of ice. I saw the captain and William Peterkin struggling to reach one of the floes; but they were instantly swamped and crushed to pieces. The whole perished in an instant, except myself, and the ship went down; but in less than half an hour, by some extraordinary operation of the iceberg below the water, she was thrown out on the ice, keel uppermost, a perfect wreck.

There, then, was I left on a field of floating ice on the great polar ocean, without one bite of food. I had nothing in my pocket save an Old Testament of very small dimensions, which my mother gave me when I went to my apprenticeship. It wanted both the prophecies and New Testament, but had the psalms, and with it I had never parted, having lost the fellow of it. I saw at once the necessity of trying to reach the hulk, which was beset with danger, for the broken ice towered up in heaps, and I had no doubt there were great gulfs between them. But life was sweet, and hunger hard to bide, so it behooved me to try. It is impossible to describe the perils I underwent in this attempt; for when climbing over mountains of ice as firm as rocks, I came to other parts which had little more consistency than froth, and there I slumped over head and ears into the sea. But the sea was so terribly compressed by the weight of the ice that it always balked me up again fairly above the ice. Then the ice was so slippery I could get no hold, and I knew if I sunk among the rubbish into the water gradually, I was gone; therefore, when I found that I was going, I jumped in, and then I was sure to come up again with a bolt. At length, when beginning to despair, I reached a splinter of a boat-mast, and then it was wonderful with what safety I proceeded, though on the very point of being totally exhausted with cold, hunger, and fatigue.

But, behold, when at length I reached the wreck I could not get in. Her keel was right uppermost; but all the other parts were so jammed in among ice, that I could find no ingress, and, moreover, I was completely exhausted, and had nothing to dig with save the mast splinter. The hulk, as far as above the ice, seemed nearly complete and unbroken; but within I could not get. Perceiving a number of things scattered here and there at a little distance, I took my splinter and made toward them in hopes of finding something to allay my hunger and thirst. I suffered far more from the latter; for all the ice which I tasted was salt, and my heart was burning with unquenchable thirst. I found nothing save scraps of sails, cables, boats, and things that had been smashed on deck when the ice closed on us; but by the clearing up of the fog for a little, I perceived a mountain not far from me beyond a level plain of ice. I hastened to it, supposing it to be an island; but when I went it was a tremendous iceberg, so steep and slippery, that I could not climb it; but, to my agreeable astonishment, I found the ice was fresh. I kneeled and blessed my kind Maker for this relief, commended myself to his mercy and pity, in that my perilous situation, and there I sucked and sucked till I could hold no more.

My strength was now renewed, and my eyes enlightened; but the throes of hunger were increased. I went once more among the wreck, looking for something to eat; but in fact with the hopes only of finding some one of my dead companions, on whom I had made up my mind to prey most liberally; but I found none; so that the Almighty preserved me from cannibalism. I however found, among other things, a small boat-hook used for the yawl, and a harpoon fastened to a part of the shattered long-boat. These were prizes not to be despised by a man in such circumstances; so returning to the wreck with the boat-hook, I easily cleared away the ice astern, and reached the cabin window, by which I entered; but found a dreadful cabin, full of ice, and all turned topsy turvey. I made my way to the biscuit bunker, which, being inverted, I broke up at the bottom, and found it crammed full of biscuit. Although it was steeped in salt water, I thought I never tasted any thing so delicious; so I eat and eat till I grew as thirsty as ever, and was obliged to betake me to my iceberg again; but this time I was so provident as to take as much of it with me as I could carry; and now having some prospect of protracting existence for a while, I felt rather happy and thankful that I alone was saved from such a sudden and dreadful death. I had likewise rather sanguine hopes that the Almighty had something farther to do with me in this world, and might preserve me to mix once more with my fellow creatures, though by what means I could not divine.

There was one phenomenon here which to me was incomprehensible. Perhaps not more than a month before, (for there being no nights I could not exactly tell) we had sailed along that sea without once perceiving ice, excepting that which girded Greenland, and now there was nothing to be seen but solid ice all around as far as the eye could reach on the clearest day. Where could this ice have come from? for a part of the day was still very warm. It must have shifted from one side of the polar sea to the other till it rested on some island. If I had not seen this I could not have believed it; but there are currents, tides, and workings of nature or of God in that sea, that man comprehends not.

To return to my narrative; I continued clearing away the rubbish from the cabin, for I could not be idle; and on reaching the captain's secret store closet, I broke it open in hopes of getting something to drink; but the wine bottles were all overturned and smashed, at which I was exceedingly grieved, for I felt a violent inclination to drink of something stronger than ice-water. I got knives and forks, however, a cork-screw, and many other things that would have been of great use—had I had any use for them. At length, below all the rubbish, I came upon a whole cask of spirits unpierced, and certainly never man made a more joyful discovery, not even my late captain, when he absurdly supposed he had discovered the north pole. My desire was that it might prove ale or porter before opening it, for there was a feeling within me that whispered these were greatly wanted. The cork-screw was instantly put in requisition, out flew the bung, and down went my nose to the hole. It was either rum or brandy, I could not tell which, indeed I believe it was a mixture of the two; so taking the tube of the old ship bellows, I put in the wide end and sucked the small one. The liquor came liberally. Never was there such nectar tasted! But I was little aware of its potency, having never drunk any thing so good before, and besides, my stomach and whole frame was out of order; of course I was overcome in an instant, grew dizzy, and persuaded that the hulk was turning up, I catched at the closet shelves to support myself, but down I went beside my cask, and I remember of laughing and trying with my whole might to rise, but could not; and there I lay till the wheeling of the ship, which run round swifter than an upper millstone, twirled me into a profound sleep.

The most singular thing now befell to me that ever befell to a man, and I cannot explain how I outlived it. I had actually lain in a trance, for at least a month, in that closet, in utter darkness, the door having been closed, no doubt, by myself, but how or when I knew not. The first thing that brought me to my senses was the discovery that my tube would no longer reach the brandy, and that my supply was cut off for the present. This was a grievous disappointment at the time; but it proved a lucky and providential one, for if my tube had been long enough I had never risen from the ceiling of that inverted closet. I put up my hand by chance, and feeling that my beard had grown to an enormous length, I began to consider where I was, and by degrees was enabled to trace myself all the way from the minister's glebe at Auchindoir to Aberdeen, and then away to the north pole, and back again to my deplorable habitation. My body was all so benumbed that I could not rise, which gave me still more leisure to reflect, and reflection sobered me apace. The whole of the time I passed in this oblivious state appeared to me, on reflection, as only a few hours, if I say a day and night it would be the most, that was left impressed on my memory. I recollected of taking some merry and liberal sucks; but the intervening time was wholly lost.

Still I lay quiet and dormant, except that I occasionally tried to rub my limbs, to bring them in play. At length I conceived that I heard a great number of people busily engaged and muttering round the vessel. I listened and listened, and became certain of it; and never can I describe the terror that came over me. One would have thought the conviction that I was surrounded with human beings would have brought me joy, as it gave hopes of the possibility of escape. But I assure you the reverse was the case; for my body being in a nervous state, I was seized with the most dreadful horrors. I supposed they were some sort of polar demons, or, at best, savage cannibals; and at length I heard one of them enter the cabin at my hole astern with apparent difficulty, and soon after began a munching at my salt biscuits. I lay long; but at last was seized with irresistible curiosity to see what kind of mortal it was, and how dressed. I therefore rose up and cautiously opened the closet door, and when I looked by, I saw what I supposed was a naked woman escaping out at the cabin window. I was sure I saw her bare feet and toes, and from her form, she appeared altogether without clothes. This in the middle of the frozen ocean was altogether unaccountable; but having now my cabin to myself, I seized my boat-hook in the one hand, and my harpoon in the other, and went cautiously to my cabin hole, for window there was none; it had been knocked out altogether during the ship's temporary dive among the ice. Horrors multiplied upon me! When I peeped from my hole, judge of my feelings on perceiving a whole herd of white polar bears prowling around the ship, and all busy digging and eating. Whether a distant view of the hulk, or the smell of the blubber and carcases of the fish had brought them, was the same to me; there they were, and all busily employed; and it was amazing what holes these powerful persevering monsters had dug in the ice, and were preying on the fish that had been in the ship, and on the bodies of my late companions. There were two bears within twelve yards of me rugging and riving at the body of my late captain, which I knew to be his from the shreds and patches of his clothes that were strewed about, and a part of his deck hat, such as is worn by English coasters—and there was the end of his grand discovery, poor infatuated wretch! From this fatal catastrophe I have often thought the north pole would never be discovered, or that the discoverer would never return with the tidings, for none could have a finer or opener passage than we had northward, which was soon obstructed in such an extraordinary manner.

Not knowing what experiment to fall on to drive this herd of monsters away, I took a speaking trumpet and shouted through it with all my might, "Avast, brothers!" on which they sprung all up on their hind feet, standing as straight as human creatures; and I am sure there were some of them that stood at least ten feet high. As they were all sleek, fat, and plump, they appeared very like naked human creatures with long brutal heads. Such a fearful sight I never had seen. They listened and stared about them for a space in this position; but showed no inclination to fly, sensible, I suppose, that they were the lords of these regions. They again fell to munching their grateful repast. I tried them with various kinds of sounds; but instead of flying, they began to congregate and draw nearer me, to reconnoitre what it could be, expecting, I was sure, some fresh prey. I now began instantly to barricade my only place of entrance, putting the fire-grate into it, which was now of no use, the chimney being turned downward. I then took all the knives and forks I could get, and every sharp instrument, and tied them to the bars with oakum, putting their sharp points outward; and conceiving myself in perfect safety, I retired to my closet, drew off a tin tankard of the grand elixir, took the blankets from the cabin beds, which were hard frozen, and making myself a bed in the closet, I locked the door inside, took a composing draught, wrapped myself up in my frozen blankets, and, like other polar animals, once more betook me to a state of torpidity.

But let no one think I was utterly abandoned and hopeless. I knew and believed that wherever I was, God was there also, seeing every one of my actions, and hearing every word that I spoke. So before I set my lips to my beloved and intoxicating potion, I sung a great part of the 107th psalm, and was rather proud to hear the white bears gather around the hulk to listen. I then read two chapters in Genesis, and prayed every sentence of prayer kind that I could make out, some of it very ill expressed, but perfectly serious. I then laid me down, after taking a potent draught of spirits, as happy and careless as the king on the throne, and slept until my tankard was out, which I think could not be above two days; and as it required both light and strength to renew it, I was obliged to sober myself before I could effect this. I arose again; but the nights were now setting in, and the bears prowling all about, though rather in a more listless manner, as if gorged. I thought, too, there were not so many of them; but then I could only see in one direction. I eat a good deal of salt biscuit at that time; and I could now reach plenty of hoar frost, which lay nearly two inches thick, to allay my thirst. I am, however, quite certain that I could live for months and years, if not centuries, on good rum and brandy mixed, without tasting any thing else.

I was now quite sure, from the invasion of the bears, that there was a communication from my abode with some country. I knew not which; but I thought it would most likely be with Spitzbergen. I was sure I had passed it far to the southward, and had a particular aversion to returning north. I imagined I was somewhere about the middle of the sea between Greenland and the North Cape; but I was wrong, as will eventually appear. I could not think of parting with my half hogshead of precious spirits in such an inhospitable climate; and I knew there was plenty of stuff of all kinds within the hulk if I could reach it; and about this period I more than half determined to attempt wintering on the ice. On pondering over the possibility of this, I plainly perceived that the first thing it behooved me to do was to drink in moderation, and the next was to work my way both into the hold and the forecastle, at whatever labour, where it was likely plenty of coals and stores of various sorts would still remain. I did not understand the geography of the ship very well, every thing being reversed, and the companion door down among the ice. This I judged it necessary to gain, and then work my way between the deck and the solid ice below; and many a day's hard labour I spent in vain upon this; for when I at length arrived at the valve of the hold, I found the whole weight of the cargo tumbled over and lying above it, so that to open it was not only impossible, but if it had been practicable, would have been attended with certain suffocation to myself. I marvelled at my stupidity in not perceiving this before; and rather suspect, that what with horror and drinking I had not all my senses about me.

In the course of my excavations, however, I found the captains wardrobe, consisting of plenty of shirts and clothes; but all steeped with salt water, and frozen. I found his shaving utensils, too, and his flint and prizel for lighting his pipe, the far greatest treasure of all. I reached likewise the coal-bunker, behind the flue, containing a few coals and an old axe for breaking them. Among the rubbish of a boat that had been fastened on deck, I likewise groped out a square sail and some smaller ones, which I had put there below cover with my own hands. I likewise recovered a gallant hatchet, and many other things of value; and notwithstanding my disappointment in not gaining the hold, I was a happy man.

I next made haste to kindle a fire, which I easily effected; but the success was premature. From my inverted grate no smoke finding egress, I was in a short time nearly quite suffocated, and was obliged reluctantly to extinguish my fire. Before doing so, as the ice below the door of the hold, and all about, was loaded with blubber, I cut a part of my shirt into candle wicks, and making a lamp of a broken bottle, I kindled that, which was of itself a great comfort. My whole wits were now put in requisition how to make a vent. I durst not break open the rigging of my house in the keel. No, no, that would never do. If I had had a hearth of any sort, to prevent my house taking fire, I could have made a fire astern, and a vent of the cabin window; but then I had no hearth, unless I could have reached the gridiron in the forecastle, which at that time seemed impracticable; and besides, if I made a chimney of my only door of access, I could neither get out nor in. Another plan behooved to be contrived; and I did contrive one which I had very nearly effected with great ease, but was too little of a philosopher, till experience made me one. I took a goat skin, which had long been used as a hearth rug in the cabin, and putting that next to the fire, I made a funnel of that and sailcloth along the roof of my inverted cabin, and out at the cabin window. I did it simply by pinning the cloth along the roof on each side, and always as I proceeded I put in a piece of stick, those next the fire being six inches long, and those at the outer end only three, so that I had a nice funnel of a triangular shape. I kindled my fire with a heart full of hope. No! The devil a piping of smoke would go out at the end of my grand flue! I was terribly cast down, and knew not what to do next, till at length it struck me, as I lay on my bed, that perhaps smoke would not descend. I had never seen it do so, and people made their chimneys always on the tops of their houses, never either at the bottom or through the gable like mine. I could not think of breaking up my keel, in which I might yet be obliged to trust myself on the ocean, and therefore I longed ardently to preserve it as a forlorn hope. Fire was now the only thing I wanted to make me exceedingly happy. I wanted it for melting snow or ice, for cooking, and for drying my clothes; but without a smoke-vent I could not use it. So the next day, as an easy experiment, though one of which I had little hope, I carried my flue up to the hee of the keel, and kindled my fire once more. There was not a vent in all Aberdeen, no, nor in London, drew better. I clapped my hands, and screamed and danced for joy; but bethinking what better behooved me, I kneeled down, and blessed and thanked my kind Maker and Preserver most heartily; and I always reflect on those ardent devotions on the ice of the northern ocean with great delight. I was then only in my 21st year strong, agile, and so healthy, that I never in my life had had any ailment; and I cannot describe my exultation that night, as I sat by my blazing fire drying my new stock of shirts, bedclothes, and clothes of all sorts. It was a night to be remembered as long as I live, and shall be so most gratefully.

It was plain that winter was now set in. The calls of the swans and geese journeying southward no more reached my ears. A few bears were occasionally prowling about; but they neither troubled me nor I them and as I now had to use my grate, I merely stuffed up my entrance with a large snowball, which I shaped in it, of wet snow, and suited it, when frozen, to a hairbreadth. It pushed outward; and as I had a piece of cable through it, I pushed it out or drew it in as suited my convenience; but my employment and enjoyment being all within doors, I went out only once a day to gather snow, look about me, &c.

Well, just when the days were beginning to fade altogether, it came one night a terrible storm of wind and snowdrift. I peeped out several times at it, but it was dreadful; so I drew in my snowball, stuffed the hole doubly, and retired to rest, after singing a psalm, reading, and praying. About the middle of the night I was awakened by some noise inside my cabin. I was frightened beyond measure, for I had no conception what it could be. I conceived that the bears had all retired to their dens long ago, and were lying in a state of torpidity and an absurd terror took hold of me that it was the ghost of captain Hughes. The conviction that I was sleeping in his shirt and bedclothes, and drinking his beloved beverage nightly, made me feel very uneasy. I had likewise seen him perish among the broken ice; and though assistance was out of my power, I had never proffered it; and, finally, I had seen the bears grubbing up his flesh and bones without greatly regretting it. In short, the meeting with my late commander's spirit, at this time, I found would be any thing but agreeable. It came to my closet door and rapped; I held my breath, for I was unable to speak with terror. It tried to wrench open the door, and a terrible effort it made; but it failed for that time. I was by this time on my feet, with a large carving knife in my hand, as sharp as a lance in the point, which I kept always on a shelf beside me; but presently I heard the ghost go away and attack my biscuit bunker. I then knew it was my former visitor, the bear, and kept quiet. She did not stay to eat any; but immediately drew herself out at the window again with much difficulty.

I lay still, though the cold from the open window was terrible; but having nothing wherewith rightly to shut it, I lay still, hoping the danger and spoliation, for that time, was over, and resolved to secure my premises better in future. In about half an hour I heard the creature dragging itself in again. I arose with great quietness, and listened, and heard it take bread from the bunker, and immediately depart. I was now sure that it had come to steal for its winter store, and that it would leave me destitute; for though I knew that there was plenty of provision in the hulk, I could not reach it; so I instantly struck a light, which (having made tinder) I could now do in a moment, and keeping close within my closet, I awaited the return of this foraging monster with a palpitating heart; for whether or not it was from having been bred a tailor, I cannot tell, but I certainly had something rather cowardly and timorous in my nature. In about the same space of time, half an hour namely, I heard the creature enter once more and attack the biscuit. I flung open the closet door, and bolted out, having the light in my left hand, and the long ship carving knife, for cutting up beef, whales, and porpoises, in my right. This apparition, particularly, I supposed the light, which in all probability the creature had never seen before, frightened it so dreadfully, that it dashed out at the window with more precipitance than prudence; for not taking leisure to put out its forefeet first along with its head, it stuck fast, and could not move. I ran forward, and with my long knife gave the animal two deadly stabs below the fifth rib, toward the heart. The blood gushed out, and nearly filled my cabin; and the creature very soon gave over struggling.

I had no intention of committing this murder on the poor animal. It was wholly an accidental act. When I struck it, it was merely with a sort of vague intention of frightening it that it might not come back; but when I saw it stretching out its limbs in death, and its feet and thighs so like those of a human creature, I could not help feeling as if I had committed some enormous crime. I am ashamed to own this now, but it is the truth; and all that I can say for myself is, that I was bred a tailor, and was often ashamed of that which other men would have been proud of, and proud of that of which they would have been ashamed.

Be that as it may, I left the huge animal sticking in the hole to keep out the cold, and retired to my couch, locking and bolting my closet door, but not to sleep. I was in a quandary, and was afraid of something, I knew not what; but I took a good dram, which warmed and cheered my heart considerably. I lay long in a sort of feverish state without repose; and at length I arose and went to examine my prey. It was stiff, and beginning to grow rigid in the flank; yet, strange to say, I heard it munching the biscuits outside, and making a sort of grumbling noise over them. I was more frightened than ever, and began to think that nature was all reversed in that horrible clime; for how a creature could be dead and frozen in its hinder parts, and munching and eating with its fore parts, was to me quite inconceivable; yet I was sure of it. What does any body think I should have done? Certainly just what I did—I ran once more into my closet, and locked myself in.

This state of things could not last. I could not remain shut up in my cabin without water, by a huge monster half dead and half living; so as I could not push it out, I resolved to pull it in, and abide by the consequences. I did so. The animal was stark dead, and its tongue hanging out at its mouth hard frozen. I was, you may be sure, glad to find it so; yet how to account for my former impressions was above my calculation.

I turned my prey on its back, to begin the operation of flaying and cutting up. The animal was a huge she-bear, with milk in her dugs, which had manifestly been newly sucked. If my heart smote me before for what I had done, it smote me ten times more intensely now, when I had taken a mother from her starving offspring; and when I thought of her having been stealing bread to preserve them from famishing amid the storm, I not only shed tears, I wept like a repentant sinner, and begged forgiveness of Heaven.

What could be done? I had taken a life which I could not restore; and thinking it might be a prey sent me by Providence to preserve my own life, I skinned the animal with great difficulty, chipped it into neat square pieces, and spread it on the ice below the inverted deck to freeze. I calculated that I could not have less than twenty stones' weight of good wholesome fresh meat. I then cleared out my cabin, washing it all with hot water, and spread the bear's skin on it for a carpet. I then took a modicum of warm punch, went to my bed, and slept most profoundly.

But new adventures still awaited me, even in that solitude, where any one would have thought I was abstracted from every thing that had life. On awaking, I heard a noise at my window, and instantly recognised the sounds as the same which I had heard before when the dead bear was sticking fast in the window. It was a sort of plaintive grumbling. I had fearful misgivings, guessing too truly what it was, and, without hesitation, opened the window. It was a bear cub, just apparently starving to death of hunger and cold, and asking its mother of me with such pitiful whines, looks, and trembling gestures, as I never in life witnessed. It raised its forefeet to the window, as if entreating to be taken in. I helped it in, and I am sure a more affecting sight never met the eye of mortal man. When it found its parent's skin, it uttered a bleat of joy, and the tears actually streamed from its eyes. It went on uttering the same sort of joyful sounds that a foal does which has been long kept from its dam. It went round and round, and licked the skin for very fondness; but, alas! it was always looking for what it could not get, the mother's exhausted dug. Poor object! When I thought of its having come to the very spot where it had last seen her, and where it had been fed with bread from her dying mouth, I felt as if my heart would break.

At length it seemed to comprehend something of the matter, that a rueful change had taken place; for after long pauses of stupid consideration, its mutters of joy gradually changed into moanings of heart-rending pathos. It showed neither hostility to, nor fear of me; its mother was its home, its guide, and director, and it had no other. So after going several times round, with the most hopeless looks that I ever witnessed, it laid itself down in a round form to die contented; but its groans were not to be borne. I proffered it some biscuit; it looked astonished and rather afraid, having assuredly forgotten, in its agony first of joy and then of sorrow, that there was any other creature present to witness these. It received the first small piece shily and timorously; but the rest it ate so voraciously, that it scarcely took any time to masticate it, and I was afraid it would choke. It had been clearly on the very point of famishing. I knew that was not its natural food, and I had little to spare; but what could I do? I had not the heart to offer it a piece of its parent's flesh, and I had no other.

In casting about in my mind how I was to feed this poor forlorn object, I recollected with joy, that on the ice which I had cleared below the deck of the hold, there were huge heaps of frozen blubber lying. Forthwith I crept away with my old coal axe and a light, and brought plenty of rigid blubber, which I brake into small pieces and fed it from my hand, patting it every time, and speaking kindly to it, calling it Nancy, after the only girl I had ever loved, for it was a female; and if ever I witnessed looks of gratitude, it was from that helpless creature, thus cast friendless and destitute on my protection. I patted it and fondled over it; and when it licked my hand in return, my heart bounded with delight. Our friendship was formed with a resolution that it should never be broken on my part.

No one can imagine who has not, like me, been left all alone on a wide, wide sea, the interest that I felt in this young savage of the desert. I have no expression for my feelings otherwise than to say, I loved it. Yes, I felt that I loved it for its misfortunes, for its filial affection, and for thus confiding in me. I fed it slowly and liberally, until I began to dread I was giving it too much, and took the remainder away back out of its reach. I then sat down beside it, gazed fondly on it, patting it all the while, and repeating its name, "poor Nancy, poor Nancy." She licked my hand again, and then rolling herself up once more on her mother's skin, after a few occasional heavy moans, fell sound asleep.

Out of this sleep she did not waken for I know not how long, for I lived a strange sort of life, having lost all reckoning of months, weeks, or days. The only regulator that I had of time was by the length that my beard had grown; and I think the length of this first sleep of hers was at least three days and nights, and she might probably have slept as many months if I had not, with great difficulty, awakened her for the sake of her society, which I could not live without.

In the mean time I was not idle, having now a new motive for exertion; and it was amazing how easily I effected my object when once I fell upon a right plan. I cannot imagine how I should have been so stupid; but the truth is, that never having passed from the cabin either to the hold or forecastle save by the companion door and the deck, so even now, when the ship was turned with her keel right uppermost, I never had once thought that any other way was practicable, whereas, in the present position of the vessel, it was utterly impracticable. But the road I now discovered was this: In the floor of the forecastle there was a trap-door, communicating with the bilge water, into which we emptied foul water, without being obliged to run up to the ship's side every instant. There was likewise one in the cabin; but that being carpeted, was seldom or never opened. These floors, be it remembered, were now my ceiling, a circumstance which seems, till then, never to have been thoroughly comprehended by me. Thus on pushing aside the latch of the trapdoor above, which I easily effected with a table knife, well knowing its simple structure, the door fell toward me, and hung by the hinges. On entering this hatch-hole, I found myself in the keel of the vessel, among the pig-iron, which, having fallen downward, I had a free passage, first into the hold, where I found abundance of: coals and casks of fresh water, or rather of fresh ice, and the carcases of five or six whales; so at all events I had plenty of meat for my new companion for many

44

years to come, and plenty of blubber to burn; but all was in a state of perfect rigidity. Over this I passed into the forecastle, and in the larder found a large barrel half full of beef, and another more than half full of pork. These were turned, of course, with their bottoms upmost; but the lids being locked, I had no other thing to do but to turn them the other way, and then they were just as at first. I found, likewise, bacon, mutton, and deer hams, and about half a cask of Highland whisky; so that no man could have a better provisioned house than I had, if its foundation had been upon a rock, save on the ocean ice, which, in the event of any great storm from the south or south-east, was liable to be broken up. I had, however, a strong trust in the mercy of God, who had hitherto preserved and provided for me in such a wonderful manner; and great as my dangers and difficulties have been, my trust was not placed on a bruised reed.

I now went back rejoicing to my sleeping partner, taking a good whang of solid fish with me, with pipes, snuff, and tobacco, all which I found nicely packed up in boxes. I had found the captain's store before; but now I had the greatest abundance, for every one of our crew had been smokers, and some of them took snuff. I tried to waken Nancy, but tried in vain. She was quite dormant. I lifted her up in my arms, shook her, and boxed her on the ear; but her head hung down. When I boxed her she uttered sometimes a sort of sleepy "humph;" but would not open her eyes. At length I held burning tobacco to her nose, which made her sneeze violently, and wakened her up somewhat. I then held a piece of fish to her nose, which slowly and carelessly she devoured. In a little time her eyes lightened up, and she looked for more; I fed her, and she awakened, and her eyes lighted up; but ever and anon she smelled on the skin, uttering a mournful mutter over it. I wanted her to lie beside me, and carried her into my room, closing the door; but she would not settle nor rest from the skin of her mother. I then arose, and bringing the skin, I spread it above my blankets; she then came in of herself, and lay down on it, uttering the same kind of sounds as before.

My only difficulty now was in keeping her from sleeping, which I could only effect by constant and gentle feeding; for it seems to be inherent in the nature of the great white polar bear only to burrow in their dens and sleep when they can find nothing more of any kind to eat. In short, I got her learned, by degrees, to follow me out and in. When out, she was never weary of rolling among the snow; and she often scraped bitterly at the ice, as if longing to get into the sea. But as she now lay in my bosom, I did not encourage this propensity, especially as she continued to thrive and grow amazingly fast, and was as plump as a small fatted calf. Yes, she lay in my bosom; and though certainly a most uncourtly mate, she being the only one I had, I loved her sincerely, I might almost say, intensely. She never once showed the least disposition toward surliness; but having transferred her love from her mother to me, her only protector, she was all affection and kindness, seeming to consider me as a friend of her own species. She answered to her name, and came at my bidding; and when we walked out upon the ice, I took her paw in my arm, and learned her to walk upright. A pretty couple certainly we were, I dressed like a gentleman in my late captain's holiday clothes, and she walking arm in arm with me, with her short steps, her long taper neck, and unfeasible, long head; there certainly never was any thing more ludicrous. I often laughed heartily at the figure we made; and as she tried to imitate me in every thing, so she did in laughing; but her laugh was perfectly irresistible, with the half closed eye, the grin, and the neigh. It was no laugh in reality, and such a caricature of one never was exhibited. There was a fine echo proceeding from some caverns in the huge iceberg which rose immediately in our vicinity. There was something exceedingly romantic in the voice of this spirit of the iceberg; and I often amused myself by shouting to it, and listening to the distinct repetition, which I persuaded myself was louder than my own voice. But how was I amused one day with Nancy, who had been gambolling and rolling on the ice at a great rate, when she all at once, of her own accord, stood up on end, and putting a paw to each side of her mouth, as I was wont to do, she uttered such a tremendous bray to the echo, as was enough to have split its parent iceberg. The shout was returned with increased energy, while Nancy was standing with her nose towards it, listening with the most intense admiration. Then turning round her grinning snout, and perceiving that I had fallen down in a convulsion of laughter, she too threw herself down on the snow, and laughed, kicked, and spurred to admiration. I laughed until I was weak, and then went up to her and caressed her, saying many kind things to her. After that she shouted every day to the echo, until I gave over laughing at it, and then she gave it up.

From the time that I got possession of Nancy and the whole ship, I never spent a winter so uniformly delightful; and long as it was, the only thing I was terrified for was its coming to an end, for then I knew the ice would, break up, and God only knew where I might be driven. I never understood aught about the seasons, nor troubled myself calculating about them, which I knew would be to no purpose; for suppose the winter is all one night, yet the fact is, that there is no night at all in these arctic regions, at least on the blazon of white ice where I was. There is no pitch-dark winter night such as I have often seen in Strathbogie. I never went out that it was not quite light, though I knew not one time of the twenty-four hours from another. There was often a white frost fog brooding over the ice, through which I could not see objects at any great distance; still it was quite light where I stood. The darkest time I ever chanced to be out, was like a winter twilight in Scotland an hour after the sun goes down. Neither was the cold at all intolerable. Loud stormy winds came but seldom; and if it had not been for my nose, I could have wrought at hard labour in the open air a part of almost every day; but the frost raised such a smarting in my nose, I could not suffer it.

The sun at length made his appearance above the southern horizon; and though I felt no symptoms of instability in the foundation of my abode, I began to have many anxious thoughts, for the snow with which I had covered the hulk to a yard in thickness, began on some days to melt and run down on the one side, forming huge icicles. The first thing I employed myself in, after the appearance of the sun, was to go daily and labour at cutting out a regular stair to the top of the iceberg, in order to make what discoveries I could. This I was not long in effecting, and found it a huge mountain of solid ice, as high as North Berwick Law, but more irregular in its form, having creeks and ravines innumerable. I felt greatly exhilarated on feeling myself on such an elevation; and as for Nancy, she was perfectly mad with delight, for her spirits always rose and fell with mine. She ran round and round the top, making many acute wheels, and cutting the most ludicrous capers, till coming inadvertently on a steep place, she missed her feet, and went to the bottom as swift as an arrow. The hill was so high, and she so white, I could scarcely discern her trying to climb it again; but she could not, until she came round by the stair. Then seeing that I appeared amused at her adventure, she took another scamper, threw herself on her hams, set her fore feet wide, and down she went again. This was an amusement of every day's occurrence, until I gave over being amused with it, and then it was given up. I often persuaded myself that I perceived hills sometimes in one direction, sometimes another; but they were never to be seen again. These were singularly illusive scenes. I could fancy I saw hills and glens, with wreaths of snow here and there, and yet I could never see them in the same direction again. It is a strange unearthly climate thereabouts, and has no congeniality in it with human nature.

At length the swans came north over my head, shouting day and night, and the voice of the wild gander from the breast of the sky was rarely silent. This, I thought, boded bad things for me, for it told plainly that the polar seas, beyond this great land of ice, were open. I therefore judged that if the ice broke up, I was sure to be carried northward, no man knew where, among unknown seas and frozen coasts, and perhaps be frozen to one of the latter, to remain till I suffered a miserable death.

The truth is, that I felt myself a very helpless being. I had no compass, and not the least notion where I was. I thought it behooved me, at this time, in order to endeavour the preservation of my own life, to set out in search of some country; but I knew not where to go, or where to find either continent or isle. I had still plenty of victuals, such as they were, both oatmeal, rye, and flour. I had a fowling-piece, and had contrived to dry a box of gunpowder, which had all run into one lump; but when scraped down, fired middling well. I had beef and pork; but for the longing desire I had for fresh meat, I had devoured a good deal of my bear's flesh, though I never let Nancy taste it, nor yet the soup it was boiled in. She liked the whales better, and lived most sumptuously, better than ever a bear lived before; and I never saw an animal thrive so well. She rolled and tumbled among the snow often for hours at a time.

I climbed the iceberg every tolerable day; and at length formed the resolution of digging a cavern in it, as it was impossible, I thought, that it could sink, nor could it melt for ages. I began, accordingly, with axe and shovel, and high up, I am sure three or four hundreds of feet above the level ice, I opened my cavern. The task was a delightful one. It was very easy, the ice coming off in great splinters. I made great progress; and when I had finished my anteroom, it was like a crystal dome, perfectly brilliant and beautiful. When the sun shone, it had all the colours of the rainbow. I liked the employment, and persevered on till I made several neat apartments, and one with a chimney, which I made with great labour with a bar of pig iron. I gloried in this achievement, feeling as if I were in a castle, where no polar bear or enemy of any kind could approach me without finding out my stair, which, on such a large mountain, was quite improbable. There was one of my apartments allotted for a pantry; and here I carried, with great toil, a part of my provisions, a part of spirits, meal, and, in short, every thing I had; but the carrying of them up that perpendicular stair was a very severe job. I resolved, if I saw the ice breaking up, to trust myself on the iceberg as my best resource, and leave the rest to Providence, which had hitherto been so kind to me.

Had the hulk of the Anne Forbes been situated in the middle of a floe, I would have trusted myself in her with perfect security; but I knew she was on the verge of a fissure, in which she had first been swallowed up, and then, by some extraordinary operation in the meeting of the ice below water, was shortly tossed up again with her keel uppermost.

Now, I must let the friends that read this see exactly how we were situated. When the ship went down, I was at the top of the mast. I was swung off a great distance to the south. In a short time, by a tremendous convulsion of the meeting of the two fields, the ship was tossed up again. That fissure between the fields, in which the ship was swallowed up, was between me and the ship, as the reader will recollect, and the difficulty I had in crossing it to the wreck. The iceberg arose straight to the north-west, and the base of it only about the distance of a hundred and forty paces; the ice between being all level, while that to the south and south-east was all broken and raised into ridges. This engendered a hope in me that the floe on which the hulk rested was attached to the mountain iceberg. There was likewise a sloping declivity all round the southern base of the mountain, as if part of it had been melted and frozen again; and I therefore considered myself perfectly safe in it from any danger but starvation, and could not but deem it eminently sublime for me to be living in a crystalline palace on this elemental mountain, which, for any thing I knew, might have brooded upon the shores of the polar sea, or traversed its lonely depth for ages.

For the space of two months, I daresay, I spent all my waking hours on the top of this romantic mountain with Nancy, for she was as constant to me as my shadow; but we still continued, at some risk, to sleep in the cabin, it being so much more comfortable than sleeping in a bedroom of ice. Then every morning when I went up to my crystal palace I sung a psalm, read a chapter, and prayed; and every day my hope was strengthened that God would not forsake his poor outcast from humanity, who thus trusted in him. The whole of those two months passed in our common routine manner; so that I do not recollect any thing worth relating.

I can give no dates; but one morning, which I supposed from the height and heat of the sun was about midsummer, on going to the top of the ice mountain and looking round, the whole sea to the northward was clear of ice to within a mile of us, while there was at the same time manifestly a strong current running northward, as I perceived pieces of broken ice, &c., running rapidly in that direction, and I hourly expected some great revolution. It was to me like the subverting of a kingdom, or the breaking up of a world.

Every thing remained as usual for several days longer, only I and my companion slept in our crystal chamber, and continued carrying necessaries to it the whole day; for I had a wallet with which I loaded Nancy, and she could carry more at a time than I could. But there was one time that would have been about midnight, if there had been such a thing, for the sun was north, that I was awakened from a sound sleep by the tottering motion of the iceberg. I was astonished and frightened, for it was not like the motion of a ship getting under weigh, but that of a cart over great stones. I then became convinced that that huge mass of ice rested on the bottom of the ocean, and I thought it would certainly split into shivers. The motion, however, ceased in the course of a minute, by which time I was up and out on my platform, from whence I saw that the iceberg had moved a small degree round to the west. It had separated from the interminable field of ice on the east, leaving a gap there about a bow-shot over, and on the west that gap not only ran to a point, but south-west from that, the ice of the field was crushed up in a crooked ridge. From this it was quite evident that the bottom of the iceberg rested and swung on some point from which it could not get free.

As the wreck remained on our side of the opening, I hasted down from the mountain to see how matters stood, and view this mighty phenomenon, for so it appeared to me. But it was a far greater phenomenon than any man can conceive, for it is impossible to describe it in any words that I have. The place where I stood, and where the hulk of the Anne Forbes rested, was only on one of the shelves of this mighty mountain. The sea in the opening was as bright as a mirror, nay, it was as pure as ether, and through it I could see the ledgins of this amazing cone spreading away shelve below shelve into the channels of the ocean.

I now understood perfectly well the whole circumstances of our wreck. This huge mass had been coming from the north with an under current, carrying all before it. The field of ice that encountered it had been going in an opposite direction with a surface current; then, when the collision took place, this great surface field, heaved up by some of the downward shelves of the mountain, had rushed over the Anne Forbes, smashed her gunwale and masts to atoms, and laid her over. This sudden pressure of the great field had put the iceberg a little off its equilibrium, making the forepart to dip, when the revulsion had tossed the wreck backward on the mountain's own base. Nothing could be more natural or evident; indeed it could not have happened otherwise.

As soon as Nancy saw the water, she rushed into it, and swam about in perfect delight—vanished in below the ice for a space that frightened me for her safety, although I knew it was the nature of that species to fish for their food even in the channels of the ocean. She at length appeared with a fish in her mouth, something like a large hirling. I was glad of it, regarding it as a feast, and caressed and commended her for it. No sooner was she sensible of my approval, than away she flew again to the verge of the opening, peeping along its margin with a most knowing turn up of her cheek. Whenever she dived she brought up a fish of some sort; but that day, I think she only got three. Every day thereafter the fish grew more plenty, the light having brought all the fish in that channel to enjoy its influence; and day after day Nancy had the verge of the opening bedded with fine fish, so that I had a treasure in value far above what I had calculated in that singular animal. These fish were all unknown to me nominally, except the cod; but there were some of them of a very rich flavour. I cleaned them carefully, washed them with salt water, and spread them among ice in the heart of the iceberg, in case of future exigences. These fish, before the end, would have loaded a cart.

I often reflected with wonder and admiration on the extraordinary kindness of Providence to me, that I should have been left alone in the midst of the frozen ocean without lacking one of the necessaries, comforts, or even luxuries of life. I wanted nothing but the society of my species, which was half and more compensated by that of the most docile and affectionate of all animals. I hope I was duly grateful to my Preserver; I meant to be so, and expressed it as well as I could, always before I lay down to sleep, and immediately after I arose. I was glad that Nancy, who was such an irresistible mimic, did not begin singing psalms with me, for she would have made a very bad business of it; but the poor creature had the good sense never to attempt it. She uniformly lay down with her head on her fore paws, closed her eyes, and looked very devout, without any caricature.

Perceiving the strong foundation on which I rested, I again slept in my old birth in the closet of the cabin; and one morning when I arose (I must call it morning, though there was no night), our beautiful crystal gap of water, I observed, was gone, and we had set off on another polar voyage, and left the interminable field of ice behind us as far as the eye could reach. Soon did I lose sight of it, and then all was again sea, nothing but sea; and that we (by *we*, I mean the iceberg, Nancy, and me) were generally going on an under current, was quite evident from the swiftness with which all other floating substances past us in the contrary direction.

O that I had been a man of science, or that I had had a compass or any kind of instruments with me, that I might have noted down marks that would have kept things in my memory, for write I could not. But of all expeditions, next to that of Noah, I consider this of mine as having been the grandest ever accomplished by man. There was I reposing at my ease, or walking in awful sublimity on the top of a lofty mountain, moving on with irresistible power and splendour. Without star or compass, without sail or rudder, there was I journeying on in the light of a sun that set not, solely in the Almighty's hand, to lead and direct me whithersoever he pleased. The fowls of heaven occasionally roosted in thousands on my mountain, and regarded me only as a fellow creature. I rejoiced in their presence, and loved to see them so beautiful and so happy; and, moreover, they assured me of the presence of the Deity, for I knew they were all his creatures, a portion of his limitless creation; and as a sparrow could not fall to the ground without his permission and decree, so I knew that all those lovely creatures were living and moving in him; and that I was there in his benign and awful presence, in that sublime tabernacle of the ocean, as immediately as in the grandest temple of worship that the world contained.

I never lacked amusement long at a time, when abroad on that wonderful hill. There was a broad field to walk on all round the ledges of it, except on one place where it rose perpendicular from the sea. On these ledges the uncouth and lazy walruses were frequently to be seen resting and rolling themselves; and the seals would have congregated on it had it not been for Nancy, between whom and them there was a perpetual and bloody warfare carried on, and many of them were forced to give up the ghost to her indomitable spirit and prowess. I was grieved at these encounters, thinking my favourite and only companion would be disabled or slain, for they often went below water, while the sea would become all red with blood. But so keen was she of the sport, I could not restrain her; nor could I make any use of the carcases, for cook it as I would, the meat was bad. Nancy was fonder of it than any other. She did not catch very many fish in the open sea, although constantly on the look-out for them; yet it was very rare that I had not plenty for my table. There were some times that she catched great numbers of herrings of the very finest quality; and there were other days that we fell among great shoals of gilses, or small salmon, as I thought.

For the space of six months, at least, must I have traversed these polar seas without ever knowing where I was. I knew the main points of the heaven for a while, by accounting the point of the sun's highest elevation above the horizon, south; but at length I lost myself, and this rule proved of no avail. The hulk, which, for a long time at first, had always been astern, became at length the prow, and I knew not where I was going. I several times saw mountains on my larboard bow in the early part of my tour, and twice, in particular, quite distinctly. They were all speckled with snow, and very like the Grampian mountains of Scotland in a day of spring.

At length I saw a headland or island straight before me, and my resistless vessel bearing straight upon it. I was all anxiety, of course; and though I believed I was not in Europe, I was anxious to see what kind of country it was, and was on the top point of the iceberg on the watch. It was very rugged, rocky, and steep, and at least one-third of it covered with snow. I was even so nigh, that I saw a being moving about on the shore, staring at the floating mountain. I saw, or at least believed that it was a woman, while my bosom dilated, and my heart beat hard with joy, at coming once more in contact with my fellow creatures. I thought what countries and continents I was willing to traverse, what seas to cross, and what hardships to endure, to reach my dear Scotland again. I put my two hands to my mouth in place of a speaking trumpet, and hailed the female stranger with my whole strength of lungs. But ere ever I was aware or could prevent it, Nancy did the same, and sent forth such a bray, that made all the rocks of that unknown country ring. That being a voice the most dreadful of all others to these polar inhabitants, the poor frightened native fled with the swiftness of a roe, and vanished among the rocks. I was for the first time provoked and angry at poor Nancy, who having perceived my elevation of spirits, thought it incumbent on her to have the same. I threatened her angrily; but the poor creature first prostrated herself at my feet, and then turning up her four feet, she kicked and writhed as if begging pardon in the most repentant manner; on which I caressed her and said, "Never mind, dear Nancy, only you are never to do the like again." She never caricatured me all her life again.

I had observed a good while before, that there was a stripe of something on the surface of the sea before me, like a line of broken ice; but I regarded it not, for my glorious vessel ploughed through all such like foam-balls. But when I drew nearer, I perceived that it was a current running through a strait, from one ocean to another, and at such a rate as I had never seen a current before. I am sure, at the lowest calculation, that it was running at the rate of sixteen knots an hour. The broken ice, driftwood, and something like large morsels of moss, were running by me with a swiftness quite incalculable. Still I regarded it not, seated on my invincible mountain. But before I came into this stream by a quarter of a mile, I got into an eddy, which actually rolled my mountain almost completely round. In this gyration some of her projecting under shelves had got into the stream, which sucked her in, and away I went exactly at a right angle from the course I was journeying on before. This stream came through a strait, between steep and rocky mountains, and, by my calculation, was running from the south-west to the north-east; but this is not to be relied on. The current was running at such a rate, that among the floating ice it was white with foam, and roaring like a flooded river. For a space of time that may have amounted to weeks, I ran on with this stream; and at length I landed in another eddy, on a far larger scale, in which I floated round and round I do not know how long, within a diameter of about two miles. Having seen nothing like any of these phenomena the preceding summer, I am persuaded I was then in the northern seas of Asia; and though I saw nothing like a pole, I must have been far beyond it.

All this time among those rapids and whirlpools, I got no fish. I had still plenty preserved in ice; but I began to long for them, fresh out of the water. Nancy never looked for them. From some singular instinct she seemed perfectly to understand that it was in vain. At length I saw her one day diving very often. I was on the height; and being persuaded that we were off on another tack, I did not descend, but continued on the hill until I went to sleep, making observations, and at length was quite convinced that we were moving straight on at a steady pace, and, as I judged, in a direction between south and south-east, so that I became convinced I should rest or be frozen still on the coast of Siberia, or Nova Zembla. I sailed on and sailed on, in utter uncertainty, but without one symptom of despair in my heart. I sang praises to God, and worshipped him before I went to sleep; and as soon as I awoke, I cast myself entirely on his protection, and was all submission to his will. I still wanted none of the conveniences of life. With Nancy and an open sea, I could never want fish; and I was occasionally laying by what I could spare for the approaching winter. I had been saving my spirits all summer; but I was ashamed on calculating how much I had drunk in less than a twelvemonth. I could not have had less than forty gallons at first, of the very best, which was enough in all conscience for three years; but I had been rather reckless on it at first, which now I sore repented.

I spent a part of every day teaching Nancy to understand and obey every one of my commands; and though not a very apt scholar, she was an attentive one. When she found that she had done any thing that drew forth my approbation, she never forgot that again. She swam for every thing I threw into the sea, carried burdens cheerfully, while her sagacious looks proved an agreeable conversation to me in absence of all others.

I came once more in sight of land, still on my left hand, so that it behooved to be another continent, as I was passing to the north before, and southward now. On the third day I came very near the coast, and saw high rugged shores, tall, precipitate mountains, which reminded me of sugar loaves in a grocer's shop. The narrow valleys between were nearly free of snow, and the perpetual sunshine on the country gave it rather a pleasing and interesting appearance. The current was prodigious. I was going at such a rate that the mountains appeared changing their relative situations in constant succession. When I next awoke from sleep, I found that I was off at a tangent with another current, and had lost sight of the country for ever.

About this time the fogs began to brood over the face of the ocean, the sun to wear toward the horizon, and from that time forth I saw no more around me, sun, moon, nor stars, but journeyed on I knew not the least whither. During this period Nancy added materially to our stock of fish, many of which I had never seen before. I suppose they were dog-fish, and cat-fish, and sea-wolves, &c.; however, I cleaned them all in the best manner I was able, and laid them up in a state where I was sure of their perfect preservation. Unless when employed with some little thing of this nature, I either lay and dozed, read my bible, which I got mostly by heart, or conversed with Nancy. She was not only a most useful slave, but a social and agreeable companion. The only thing that I regretted, she was growing far too big.

The hulk of the Anne Forbes still continued in the same position without the least alteration; and though I often slept in my crystal cave in summer, I drew into my old cabin as winter approached, for my anteroom at the cavern had been all melted away during the summer months, and it was grown quite imperfect.

The next change I met with was the hearing of a great rushing noise like a tempest, which astonished me not a little, as the frost-fog was sitting as dense and, calm as ever. I could not even perceive a movement in it, nor any alteration of the ocean. I climbed the mountain; but there all was dense and calm, and the roaring sound not nearly so palpable to the sense. I descended again, slept, and wakened, and still the sound grew louder and louder. This to me being quite incomprehensible, I was bewildered in undefinable terror, not knowing what phenomenon was next to overtake me. It was in vain that I climbed the hill and came down again, I could see nothing, and still the sound increased. Nancy never regarded it, but watched for fish always when not asleep; and numbers boiling up in our wake, she did not miss to improve her chances, never, I believe, letting one escape that once came fairly in view.

Not so with me. I was utterly dumfoundered, till at length I resolved to walk round my huge mountain as far as I could get, one side being perpendicular and impassible, and when I reached that, to return. But by the time I got half way round, that was to the prow of the mountain, the mystery was cleared up. The new ice had commenced, and a strong under current bearing this irresistible mass with its broad base previously on it, it was breaking it up with tremendous violence, louder than the loudest thunder. The conflict was so fierce and awful, I was glad to retreat astern in trembling amazement, and commit myself once more unto Him whose mighty arm alone can control the elements.

On my next awaking, the constant thundering sound was changed into loud crashes, like discharges of artillery. I was almost resolved not to go and witness the turmoil, for I was aware how awful it would be; but I am glad that I went and witnessed a scene with which I shall never see any thing again to compare. The ice had thickened to a board, several inches in thickness; but the form of this huge mountain, with its broad shelving base, running in below the ice with the current, heaved up the field into broad crystal flakes, which gradually rising to a perpendicular position to the height of an hundred feet and more, they then fell backward with a crash that made the frozen ocean groan and heave. The attack and resistance continued. Again and again was the great frozen space broken up with crashes not to be equalled by any thing in nature, and therefore incomparable, unless we could conceive the rending of a sphere to pieces.

The ice continuing thus to be rolled up like a scroll before the mountain, was heaped up before it to such a height, that it at length became once more immovably fixed, and all the turmoil was still. Here was another instance that a kind Providence watched over me for good. Had my valuable hulk of the Anne Forbes been in front of the mountain at this time, it would not only have been smashed to atoms, but covered ten feet deep beneath shoals of ice; while there on the stern, and lee side of the mountain, it stood all unskaithed and snug as ever. I was exceedingly thankful for this.

I had now nothing before me but a life of monotony for six months, and I made up my mind to it. I took a thorough review of all my store, and perceived there was no danger of starvation for a time, but how long I could not calculate, and from the calculation, indeed, my mind revolted; for O it is true that the Almighty once said, "It is not good for man to be alone."

However, as usual, I was not suffered to be long without some incidents of thrilling interest. An intense frost set in, the fog cleared away, the stars appeared in the zenith, and a beautiful blue twilight sky fringed the horizon. It was so light, that I could have perceived objects at a greater distance than in sunshine. I was on the top of the mountain, looking all abroad, and persuaded myself that I saw land right ahead, and at no great distance. My heart palpitated with anxiety, joy, and fear, and I could scarcely sleep or eat, but kept constantly on the watch at every bright interval, and still the form of the hills continued the same; so I became assured they were not clouds, such as often had deceived me.

While sitting contemplating this scene with the deepest interest, judge of my excitation when the report of a gun reached my ears, and, as I conceived, from the same direction; at least I was sure it was not far from it, either to the one side or the other. I took it for a signal gun from some ship; but what it was, or whence it came, must ever remain a mystery to me. There is no doubt that the interminable field of level ice would conduct the sound unimpaired from an immense distance; but to my ears it sounded as quite nigh, not more than two miles. I hasted from the height, seized my fowling piece and some of my powder, little otherwise than a stone in hardness and consistency, and as fast as I could scrape it down, I charged, and, again ascending the height, fired. After my third shot, the salutation was returned with a roar louder than before. I tried as well as I could to imitate the signal of distress; but judging that there was no time to be lost after my first signal had been answered, I hasted down once more, packed up some powder and shot, victuals, and a bottle of spirits, and posted off in the direction whence I deemed the sounds proceeded and the land lay.

I had to take a circle to eschew the heaps of broken ice before me, which put me a little off my aim; but before I went away, I had lighted a lamp in the cavern, which I knew would burn for a long time, and which could not be seen from any point save one, being that from which the sound proceeded, and, as I thought, due south. The wind was perfectly calm, the cold intense, and a thick hoar frost covered the ice to the depth of about three inches. Yet, though at that time the sky was perfectly clear, and the stars visible in the zenith, the hoar frost, or rime, as it is called in Scotland, was falling very thick, the aurora borealis made it nearly as bright as day, and the scene was truly beautiful, the silvery rime that quivered in the atmosphere being all spangled with pale rainbows, much more beautiful than a lunar one. Although the falling rime was so light as not to be perceptible to feeling, yet my budget and hat were soon loaded with it.

Well, I kept looking back to my light, and firing my piece all the way, posting on with what speed I was able; but a life of almost complete idleness had rendered me soft and lumpish, and instead of being frozen by the cold, I felt myself getting much too warm, and then I took a sirpling of rum-brandy and a lick of snow alternately. I lost sight of my lamp, and then had no other guide save to look behind me at my track, and see that I kept always on a straight line. No answer being made to my signals all this time, I found I had embarked on a voyage of great uncertainty; but at length I fairly discovered a hill right before me, something like Arthur's seat, and, as I thought, other subjacent ones, so, laying other hopes and uncertainties aside, I made straight for that.

I was calculating that by this time I had travelled from sixteen to twenty miles, from the length of time I had taken and the fatigue I felt; and while still making straight for the hills, which I thought were not above half that distance from me, I perceived Nancy a long way to the right, seeming greatly interested about something, and as if following a track. I turned in the same direction, and to my joyful astonishment, found the traces of a company amounting to from thirty to forty individuals, all journeying on the same path straight for the land. I had some scruples at following and joining so large a body of savages, who might be cannibals for ought I knew, and might flay and eat Nancy and me, even without the ceremony of letting out the life blood. I knew not what country I was in, whether in Europe, Asia, or America. I had a sort of conviction, that after going the round of all the transverse currents of the polar ocean, I was again fixed on the same ground, and against the same field of ice that had opposed me the preceding year; but as I had no data to go upon to ascertain this, it must be viewed for the present as mere conjecture. Yet this conjecture, vague as it was, encouraged me to proceed, as I knew to a certainty, the year before, from the mountains I had seen on my tour, that I had been off the coast of Greenland, where I had heard there were colonies of Christians.

Well, on I went on the track of this colony of sincere and simple Christians, as I weened they must be returning from their summer stations of hunting and fishing to their winter abodes, with their families and spoils. The traces of their steps were partially filled up with the falling rime; yet still I could perceive that there was a mixture of large and small footsteps, of full grown and young people; and thus encouraged, I posted on for many miles. I had for a good while imagined that the interest Nancy was taking in the pursuit was greater than could well be accounted for. She was constantly standing and walking on end, holding out her long nose as if scenting something of mighty concern to her, and turning first up the one ear and then the other, as if perceiving something through the gloom. At length I came upon some marks that were rather equivocal, on which I stood still to consider a little. I went on. A man hotly engaged in any pursuit does not like to turn from it all at once. I stooped down, and took the light hoar frost carefully from several of the footmarks. O, they were the steps of human beings, there was no doubt of it. There were the five toes, the ball of the foot, and the heel, all as apparent as the sun at noonday. But then I thought again, that that inapt simile might have been suggested by divine Providence; for, in the first place, there was no sun and no noonday there; and, moreover, how was it possible the people of that country could travel over ice and snow barefooted? That *certainly* was impracticable; for their toes would be all frost-bitten, and their journeying quickly at an end. Still I went blindly on, hardly knowing what I was doing, thinking, or where going, till I perceived that Nancy had run off and left me on the track; and then straining my sight forward, I perceived on a rising ground, that must have been a shore, a whole herd of white bears, all turned with their faces towards me, waiting her approach with the news. I saw some of them standing upright, larger than the largest giants; and certainly I never got such a fright since I was born of my mother. I durst not run for fear of being pursued by the whole herd, and torn to pieces. I durst not call on my favourite and best friend, for fear of being discovered, in case I was still undiscovered; and as I dared not either advance or retreat, I squatted down on the ice, and wished myself under it.

There I lay for a considerable space, peeping over my hands like a setter on a dead point, and my heart beating against the ice with audible thumps, till at length the monsters came all off in a body toward me. There was no more time for me to lie praying there, so I sprang to my feet, and ran. Yes, I ran with a swiftness which the extreme of terror only could have impelled me to effect. I flew without looking behind me, and actually thought I was outspeeding the best polar bear, till a certain noise that I heard behind me compelled me to look over my shoulder, when I perceived two bears in close pursuit of me. I flung my wallet of provisions, and my remaining bottle of rum, from me, and held on, having then nothing but my gun, which was loaded, and my long dirk. The two bears seemed to be quarrelling; but whether quarrelling or junketting I had not time to distinguish, till they came to my wallet, at which they paused, and tearing the wallet, they soon devoured my victuals. I then, with the most extravagant joy, perceived that the lesser one of the twain was Nancy, and my terror greatly was abated; for I thought, with her and my loaded gun, and long knife, I was a match for this single monster at any rate.

Still I durst not call on Nancy; but being quite out-spent with running, I paused to gather breath, and look at the two. The large wild monster took up the bottle of rum, smelled it, and turned it over, seeming greatly taken with it; when Nancy, with perfect *sang froid*, snatched it from him, drew the cork with her teeth, and setting the bottle to her mouth, took apparently a long pull of the spirits, and then handed it to her travelling companion. He took the bottle, set it to his mouth, and, as I thought, drank about the half of it. To describe his motions and looks, at that stage of his progress, is impossible. He held up his nose at an angle of forty-five, shot out his long red tongue and licked his chops, and ever and anon cast the most eloquent looks to Nancy. He seemed both delighted and astonished, and would not part with the bottle again, although Nancy tried to attain it by every wile and quirk she could invent. No, he would not part with it; but wheeling always round with his back to her, took another pull, till he finished it; and many a turn up he gave the empty bottle before he threw it away in a rage, because it would not produce any more.

He then fell a dancing and bobbing on his hams most potently; and never was drunkenness better portrayed. He nodded his head from side to side, and cut capers innumerable, while Nancy, exhilarated by the novelty of the scene, stood straight up on her hind feet, and waltzed around him. He would needs do the same; but then, at every whisk and every embrace she gave him, he tumbled over at full length, till, finally, after several ineffectual efforts to rise, he groaned, stretched out his limbs, and lay still. I had easily foreseen what the consequences would be, knowing the potency of my liquor from experience; so I kept my station, determined to kill the monster as soon as he grew incapable of defence.

Nancy manifestly anticipated this. She came running to me, fawned, and led the way back again; and to show me that he was incapable of moving, she scraped him with her foot, and then jumped upon him; but all that she could elicit was a groan. I had my gun loaded with two balls; but for all that, when I saw the inordinate size and strength of the monster, I took fright, and durst not fire. I paced his length as he lay stretched. I declare, with perfect seriousness, he was within a foot of four yards, and his body as thick as a two years' old bull. I durst not shoot for my life, though I had the muzzle of the gun twice at his ear, for I knew not what such a monster might do in a last struggle. One blow of his paw, or one craunch with his teeth, would have finished my course; so upon the whole, I thought my safest plan was to leave him asleep, and make my escape; which I did. I have often thought it was a cowardly action; but I did it, and lived to repent it.

My situation was now any thing but enviable. I had fled with such precipitancy, that I had lost all traces of my path back to my castle. My own track would have been a sort of guide to me; but I knew not where to find it. Besides, I had neither meat nor drink, and was still uncertain about the pursuit of the bears after me. I had no dependence save on Nancy, who was so much taken up with the drunken monster we had left behind, that I could scarce make her attend to any thing else. Although it is very unnatural to suppose it, I am certain she wanted me to kill him; for when I left him whole and sound, her looks of disappointment were quite manifest. After travelling several miles with me in gloomy discontent, she returned and hastened back again; and as she and I had been accustomed to kill every thing that came in our way, I had no doubt that she was gone back to worry a monster three times as large and strong as herself.

I was now in a most woful case, having lost my only guide, who I knew could have led me home as easily as I could have gone from Huntly to the carse of Strathbogie. I was hungry, I was thirsty, and overcome with sleep and fatigue, yet was still speeding on I knew not whither. I had only one stay wherein to trust; but it was the best, and one that never yet had failed me, even in perils of shipwreck and death. I kneeled on the snow-covered ice, and prayed to God to direct and save me. I did this shortly, for I was afraid of falling asleep, in which case I was gone; but the moment I rose, I found myself strengthened and revived. More than that; when I rose I was a little jumbled about the line I behooved to pursue; and examining the one I had come, I had a strong impression it was not the right one. This irresistible impulse was, I am certain, impressed upon my heart by a divine Providence; for though I almost went off at a tangent to the right, I had not journeyed an hour ere I came on my own backward track, which, though a little filled up with hoar frost, was still visible. I never was more happy at any relief than this; and I did not fail to testify my grateful thanks to heaven for the happy deliverance. O let never mortal man despair, for he may depend on this, that whether in the noisy crowd or on the lonely waste, he is in the hands of the Almighty, who can direct or leave him to himself as he sees meet. For me, in all my perils, and they have been many, I have ever trusted in the Lord, and have never trusted in vain.

I now hied me on with a cheerfulness and eagerness that were too much for my ability, hungry and fatigued as I was; but I knew where I was going, and had hopes that I was near my secure but solitary home. The want of Nancy preyed heavily on my heart. No man alive could miss a partner more than I did, for I found I could not subsist without her. If I had had her that night to have spoken to and leaned upon, I felt how happy I would have been, and how helpless I was without her. I grew exceedingly fatigued, and began to eat snow incessantly. This did me ill, for my joints lost their power, and sleep quite overcame me; and though I knew that to lie down on the ice was death, I felt an irresistible inclination to do it. I actually laid me down, though I knew it was the sleep of death; but a better resolution aroused me. I stood on my knees, and leaned my head and arm on the muzzle of my gun, thus getting some momentary sleeps; and then, whenever I was getting too sound asleep with the benumbing frost, I fell over, which wakened me.

These temporary restings refreshed me. I could walk three or four hundred yards after them at first with considerable agility; but then I could not give over eating snow, and my stages continued to become shorter and shorter. My track was still visible, and that was all; and I now came to some broken ice, which raised my spirits, as I remembered of none save that ploughed up by the prow of my ice-mountain. At that very time I heard a sort of noise coming along the ice; but although it was very light for that region, I could see nothing, owing to the frost, rime, and the dazzling whiteness. I heard it approaching still, like the galloping of horses, accompanied occasionally with a growling murmur. I made all the speed I could; but, alas! I fear I made but poor progress, for my strength was gone. At length, hearing the sounds close behind me, I looked back, and beheld a bear coming on me full speed. It was soon kneeling at my feet, and licking my hand. It was Nancy bleeding. She instantly turned about, set up her angry birses, and went slowly and doubtfully back, as determined on an unequal battle. After straining my sight through the rime, I perceived a gigantic bear standing on end, like a tall obelisk covered with snow. Any one may guess how my heart fainted within me; but I cocked my gun and tried to run on. My power was exhausted; I could do no more. Nancy tried to oppose the monster by throwing herself always in before him; but she durst not apparently seize him. He was a male, and partly a gentleman, for he would not bite or tear her; but he sometimes gave her a cuff with his paw to make her keep out of his way. I tried several times to take aim at him, but found it impossible without shooting Nancy; so that all I could do was to run on, until fairly exhausted, I fell flat on my face. The strife continued, and approached close to my heels, and instantly I found myself grasped, and one of the bears above me. I could make no exertion; but I soon discovered that it was poor Nancy trying to cover me with her own body from the dreadful death that awaited me. The monster struggled to reach my neck, while my defender clung to me so closely that I was nearly strangled. His strength was overpowering; he forced his head in below her, and I felt first his cold nose and then his warm lips close to my throat. I called out, "Seize him!" the words that I used for baiting on Nancy, and which she always promptly obeyed, on which she gave him such a snap, that not only made him desist; but growl like a bull. Still he would neither lay mouth nor paw upon her, one of those rare and beautiful instances of the sublimity of natural instinct, of which there are so many among the brutal creation.

The monster growled, and went round and round, and at length made his attack at the same point again; and in trying to reach my neck, he seized me by the left arm, close below the shoulder. I called out furiously to Nancy, who that moment seized the gigantic monster by the throat with her teeth and paws at the same moment. He flew away from me, and swung her round and round like a clout, bellowing fearfully; but quit her gripe she would not. He seized her with his paws, hugged her, and threw her down; but all this while never made a motion to tear her. He squeezed her so strait that I saw the white of her eyes begin to turn up. I then, with all the speed and precision my wounded arm would admit of, held the muzzle of the gun to his ear and fired; and yet, owing to the violent motion he made, none of the two bullets went through the brain, but one at the root of the jaw, and the other between that and the eye. The shot took away the power of doing any hurt with his mouth; but his paws continued to embrace Nancy with a deadly grasp, she still keeping a fast hold of his throat. I then stabbed him to the heart again and again; and though the blood streamed through the snow as if a sluice had been opened, it was amazing how tenacious the monster was of life. But at length he slackened his hold, and rolled over and over on the ice. Still he was not dead; but as soon as Nancy got free, I embraced her, and feeble and overworn almost to death, with her at my side to lean upon, I made my escape to my old hulk, the welcomest sight I had ever seen.

I barricaded my entrance-window, fed Nancy, eat some raw frozen fish myself, drank a little rum-brandy, and then took a short and troubled sleep; but before I did any of these save the first, I kneeled down and thanked my kind Maker and Preserver for this most wonderful deliverance. I then kindled a good fire of coals and driftwood, of which I had collected great store during summer; and having plenty of ice in the hold, I warmed a pot of water, bathed and dressed my arm, which was sore lacerated; I then washed and bathed Nancy all over. Her shoulders were a little lacerated and swelled from the grasps of the monster's paws; but saving that, there was no wound upon her. I dried her with a cloth, combed her, and made her as clean as a bride; and though she licked my hand and my wound, and was as kind and gentle as ever, I could not help observing, with pain and a share of terror, that there was a gloomy gleam in her eye which I had never witnessed before. Her look was quite altered. It was heavy, sullen, and drowsy; but when she looked up, there was something like a glare of madness in it. This was the most distressing circumstance of all to me; and though I suspected it was from the heat of irritation to which she had been driven by the deadly combat with one of her own species, and one that had followed her too for love, still it was the same to me, who was obliged to abide by the consequences.

We had slept in the same bed ever since we met; but gladly would I have dispensed with her company that night. Still I had not the heart to separate her from me per force, as she sat nid-nodding and casting imploring looks for me to go to bed; so we went into the closet together, as usual, although I was not at all at my ease. Nancy was in the same state; she tossed, and tumbled, and groaned, whereas she was wont to lie as quiet as a lamb. At length she laid her left paw over me, above the clothes, and seemed to fall sound asleep; but in about ten minutes after she gave me such a hug, that it had nearly deprived me of breath. I made no motion, no resistance, but suffered patiently, though in agony both of body and mind; and I acted wisely, for in a short while after her hold relaxed, and she again tossed herself over, and fell asleep.

I then rose as quietly as I could, stole out to the cabin, and locked the door, and making myself up a bed in my late captain's hammock, I slept apart, though ill at ease. I heard no more noise or disturbance, all remaining quiet; so I lay and rested myself I know not how long. When I next arose, urged by hunger, I peeped in to Nancy, after much fear and solicitude, thinking she was dead. She had taken the round form, and was lying with her limbs folded, and her nose in below her flank. I at once perceived, that with the late exertion and a hearty meal, she was falling into the torpid state; and that the hug of the preceding night (which I am always disposed to call the time allotted for sleep) had been the result of a disturbed dream about her late combat; so I heaped clothes above her, of which I had plenty, and left her to her repose; and if I calculated any thing aright from the sleeps I took, each one of which I estimated as a night, she lay snug in that state for three months.

I visited her once or twice every day; and though I could not distinguish her breathing, nor feel the play of her lungs, the dull heat of her body continued the same, which assured me she was not dead, but sleeping. That was a wearisome time for me, and save the skinning and cutting up of my great white bear, absolutely void of adventures. He was as fat as a fed bullock, and his flesh tasted very much like that of a he-goat; having been completely blooded, it was white and clean, and a great treat. He had as much tallow as loaded me for one jaunt; and I judged his carcass to be about thirty stones, Aberdeen weight.

It proved a severe winter, much stormier than the last; and there was one morning I perceived that my smoke would not vent, and, behold, on opening up my window, I found myself covered up with snow to a depth of which I could form no calculation. It had been a great snowdrift, and the hulk having been on the lee side of the mountain, I was completely covered in. I soon, however, opened up a vent for the smoke, and then I had a snug warm abode for the remainder of the winter.

I read much on my bible during this lonely season, and got a great part of it by heart. By that, I mean the historical parts. I could name to myself all the kings of Israel and Judah, how long each of them reigned, and all the battles they lost or won. I could go over the judges of Israel, in the same way, with the twelve tribes and the numbers of each. I had, besides, particular favourites, and could recite every word concerning them. Benjamin was my favourite tribe for spirit and bravery, and Jonathan my favourite character of the whole scripture catalogue.

But if I read much, I thought more of my singular destiny and condition, and what it behooved me to do. Was I to try once more to reach the abodes of humanity, see my own species face to face, and enjoy that social intercourse for which the human heart and affections are so peculiarly framed? Or was I to remain there where I was, and traverse the arctic regions on an iceberg all the days of my life, subjected, without remedy, to all the caprices of the elements, the storms, and the currents of the ocean? After balancing these things in my mind for months, I could not decide which to fix on. My present life was one of such romance, that if I could have been certified that at any future period I should escape to give a relation of it, I would have chosen to remain for the present. I was far from being unhappy, and I had no dread of a shipwreck, believing my floating mountain impregnable against all shocks, currents, or tornados. I had, moreover, a companion, which was really of more value to me than any one of my own species could have been in such circumstances, as well as more attached and subservient; and, altogether, I considered that I had more real enjoyment than the one half of mankind. There was only one thing that distressed me; should I chance, by accident or disease, to be deprived of Nancy, then I would be left helpless and stayless, and likely perish of hunger. This was a terrible prospect; so by the time the sun began to show his disk above the horizon, I had half and more resolved to make a pilgrimage over the ice in search of some inhabited country.

My next great concern was to waken Nancy; but that for a long time I found quite impracticable. She continued not only sound asleep, but perfectly rigid. At length, by blowing tobacco smoke into her nose, I awakened her. She fell into a violent fit of sneezing; and then I took care not to let her fall asleep again. She was perfectly weak and tangle,* her limbs being scarcely able to bear her weight; and when she first went out to roll among the snow, her favourite exercise, she could not turn herself round. But she increased in strength and spirits not only every day, but every hour, and was soon as frisky, as gentle, and kind as ever. I am almost ashamed to acknowledge how much I enjoyed the society of this devoted and delightful creature; for though she could not speak, there was a language in her eye that told every thing, and she knew every word that I said to her. I looked on her as a treasure sent me by Heaven in a most wonderful way, and really loved her.

My thoughts were now employed night and day about my journey; for though I knew the ice would not break up for a long time, I thought it best, now that I had daylight all the twenty-four hours, to perform my journey before there was even a chance of the ice breaking up; accordingly, I made preparations for many days, washing, drying, cooking, and packing up. It is needless to enumerate all the miscellaneous things that I thought necessary to take with me; but, in short, I loaded myself and Nancy heavily, very heavily, knowing that our loads would constantly be turning lighter, and then I left my old comfortable cabin, and my mountain of ice, with many bitter tears, all uncertain whether or not I should ever see it again, or any other home in this world. I never had wept so sore all my life as I did on setting out that time, while Nancy went rock rocking with her load, and ever and anon casting the most piteous looks at my face.

* Lank.

Away we jogged in this manner, holding our course, as nearly as I could guess, to the south south-west. The mountains towards which I had journeyed before were quite visible; but I called that land, in my own mind, The Bear Island; and believing it inhabited by a whole colony of bears, I left it on the left hand, and held on. It seemed to be a long rugged island, stretching from west to east, but not very wide from north to south, for, as nearly as I could judge, I had passed it in the space of three days.

But new adventures still awaited me, and, all at once, I met with one of the utmost consequence. Having, as I said, just passed the south-west corner of this country, which I had named, in my own mind, The Bear Island, I unexpectedly came upon the traces of three men and a number of dogs. Their footmarks were so large that I believed them to be giants, and, at first, knew not what to do; but perceiving that their steps were not longer than my own, I was convinced they wore snow shoes, took courage, and determined to follow them; which I did, and in a few hours reached the shore. There I came to a spot where the men had rested, and fed themselves and their dogs, and my heart lightened with joy. I now knew not what to do, but, in order to overtake them, it was necessary to leave my luggage, or the greater part of it. But what I was to do with Nancy, that puzzled me worst of all. She was an indiscriminate destroyer, and I knew all the dogs would suffer first, and, in all probability, the men next; so that, in fact, with her I was not fit to approach the walks of humanity. Something behooved to be done; so I made a muzzle for her of strong cord, and taking a bottle of Highland whisky with me, and some provisions, I set out on the track of the three men, and followed most eagerly; but all that I could do, I could not restrain Nancy from leaving me on the scent of their track. I durst not let her go muzzled, else they would worry her, and kill her at once, and she was the whole of my world's inheritance. I durst not let her go unmuzzled, lest she might devour them all; so I was obliged to fasten on the muzzle, put a cord to it, and lead her. She liked this very ill, and even tried to get loose by pulling the muzzle off with her paws; but my commands restrained her, although she continued to look at me with apparent astonishment and dejection. I said all the kind things to her that I could, told her she was still my own dear Nancy; but added many a time, "O you must not, must not." She cowered in subjection, and walked peaceably by my side.

I soon came to a place where the three men had all separated. I followed the steps of the middle one; but these were so irregular, up hill and down hill, that it was a most fatiguing task; and, besides, all the snow on the south sides of the hills was becoming softened with the sun, and there were here and there small black patches from which the snow had melted altogether. These I found to be mostly rocks or precipices. I was obliged to rest often, and slept several times in the sun; but I always fastened Nancy to my arm, for fear of her making her escape.

After I had travelled about fourteen or fifteen hours, I came to a place where the three men had all met again, rested, and refreshed themselves; and there was a great deal of blood upon the snow, from which I concluded they were hunters, and had killed some game; and, moreover, I perceived, from some herbaceous garbage scattered about, that they had been feeding their dogs on the nombles of a deer. Here I took a short sleep and some refreshment, there being a spring gushing out of a rock like a mill-lead, and likewise fed Nancy, who was always going scenting among the blood and offal. At length she fixed upon a spot between two rocks, and fell a scraping, where I soon discovered a store of venison, covered over with snow, which was trampled firm over and all about it. From this I perceived that this spring was the rendezvous of the hunters, and to meet with them I had only to remain where I was. With what anxiety of heart did I pass these few hours, all uncertain as I was whether I stood on the shores of Asia, Europe, or America; or whether I would fall among savage cannibals or civilised Christians. Sometimes I laid me down, seeking in vain for some repose; and sometimes stalked about, looking all around me.

Perhaps I did not wait there many hours, but they seemed to me like as many days, such a feverish anxiety had taken possession of my mind. It was at length relieved by the approach of six strong dogs coming all up hill, baying upon me in the most furious manner. This was a trying situation, as I was desirous of neither suffering skaith nor giving offence. But an expedient struck me in a moment, one which I had often amused myself with in youth, and never knew it fail, not even with a chained mastiff. I drew my coat tails over my head, stooped, and ran forward to meet them. The scheme succeeded like a charm; for after uttering a few short barks of terror, they all turned tail and fled as the devil had been chasing them. These canine hunters had left their masters a little astern, in order to have a rummage among their precious fragments, when they were thus discomfited, and chased back faster than they had advanced.

The astonishment and terror of their masters may well be conceived when they thus met their dauntless assistants retreating with looks of such wild dismay. They knew there were no herd of bears yet awake on the island, and they could form no conception of any thing else save some supernatural being of horrid presence. The flying dogs vanished over a sharp ridge of the hill; and as I conceived myself still only waging war with them, I hasted over after them in the same attitude. I was clothed in my late captain's Sunday, or best suit, and had the tails of my superfine blue coat drawn over my head, which was bowed nearly as low as my knees, and my hat I held out from me with my left hand, and led Nancy with the right. In this mode was I first introduced to my new associates, and that too without knowing it, till hearing the frightened bark of the dogs once more close below me in the ravine, I peeped through the cleft of my coat, and perceived masters and dogs flying amain, the latter leading the way, barking in downright terror, and the men cocking their heads and brattling after them. I instantly assumed my natural shape, and hallooed out after them to stop and take a friend with them. They turned round, gaping and staring, but durst not wait the encounter; and although they called something in return, which I believed was my own native tongue, yet as I approached, they turned and fled once more. The seeing of a human creature coming on them in the company of a white bear, the only creature of which they stood in perpetual dread, was too much for their comprehension. But the terror of the dogs was that which most of all convinced them that I was not an earthly creature; so they took to their heels, and I had no other shift but to pursue.

This made matters still worse; for their snow shoes kept them above the snow, whereas every step that I took I sunk at least half a foot, the surface being thawed on all the south sides of the hills. I lost ground, of course, terribly, and was obliged to give up the pursuit and return. At the place where they took first to flight, they had dropped a bear's hide and some wallets of bear's flesh and grease. On these I made seizure, and carrying them piecemeal to the spring, deposited them with the rest of their spoil. Assured, then, that they would come back to that place, if not through hunger, at least for the fruits of their severe labour, I hid myself among some rocks hard by, from which the sun had melted the snow, to watch their motions.

They were long in returning, at least I thought so, for I slept twice with Nancy in my bosom. Having become inured to the climate, and having, likewise, a bearskin jacket, and drawers next my flesh, I could now sleep any where without inconvenience or danger. I was at length awakened by Nancy struggling to get away, and on coming to my senses, I heard people speaking; and on peeping over the rock, I saw the three men standing over their prey, in earnest conversation, and apparently astonished at finding all their prey carefully deposited together. The dogs still kept at a due distance, the only thing I saw which kept them still jealous. An effort behooved to be made. I drew myself up to the verge of the cliff over which I was peeping, and at once, on my knees, implored them, for Jesus Christ's sake, to take me under their protection. They knew the name, and each of them took off his fur cap and kneeled on his right knee. Whenever Nancy appeared on the cliff, the dogs once more took to their heels. The men were just about to follow, when I called out again, naming the same sacred name with great emphasis. They paused, and pointed to the bear, saying something. I held up the cord to show them that she was muzzled and chained; and ordering her, she cowered at my feet, and kissed my hand. In all my life I never saw three such statues of astonishment as these three men were on seeing this. They gaped and stared on one another, spoke a few words, and then prostrated themselves on the snow, taking me for a divine being. I saw this manifestly, and resolved to keep up a sort of dignity, as far as I was able, for my own behoof. They lay on their bellies wallowing in the snow, until I came to them, when, perceiving one of them with grey hairs, I lifted him up first to his knees, and laying my hand on his crown, I blessed him in the name of the Holy Trinity. He seemed to understand something of the import of the blessing, for he embraced my knees. I blessed the other two in the same manner, and then lifting up my eyes and hands to heaven, I prayed fervently that God would bless and sanctify our meeting, and our communion and fellowship with one another while it continued. I then showed them my half bible, and made them look on it; but they shook their heads, and did not comprehend the meaning of it. But when I named Moses, and David, and Solomon, and Jesus Christ, they held up their hands in admiration, named them after me, and then took the book, kissed it, and pressed it to their bosoms. We were now friends; and they seemed, from the deference they paid me, to consider themselves as my sworn subjects. I then took out my brandy bottle, and a small crystal glass without the shaft, that I carried in my pocket, and filling it, I drank to their good healths, and then gave each of them a glass, which they all emptied. They then smacked their lips, and stared at one another in astonishment, till one of the young men, feeling its salutary effects on his cold stomach, screamed and jumped for joy.

We were now friends, and sat down to eat together, I of some potted bear's flesh, which I carried, and they of some haberdine and raw flesh. We then packed up for our departure, they having secured as much food as they could convey, although they took care to carry no bones. They gave the dogs these for their share, after having sliced the flesh neatly off them, which they stuffed into sealskin bags, and then yoking the dogs to these in pairs, they trailed them with great swiftness over the snow. While the dogs were gnawing at their bones, one of the largest and fiercest flew at Nancy, who was muzzled; but with one blow of her paw, she made him tumble heels over head, roaring like a bull. One of the men bent his bow, and was going to shoot the dog; but I interfered, and made signs for them to muzzle the dogs, which they did, and then we journeyed together in peace; I likewise having Nancy well loaded with their provision, which they admired exceedingly.

My great anxiety now was, to learn what country I was in; but it was long before I could understand this. I was sure I had fallen among Christians, but where I knew not. I was very ignorant of the polar countries; and though I knew some of their names, I knew nothing of their inhabitants. When these three men spoke to one another at a little distance from me, I could not believe my senses that they were not speaking broad Aberdeen, or rather Shetland Scots, the tone and manner were so exactly the same; and yet, when they spoke to me, I could not understand them, though convinced it was a dialect of the same language. The only country which I could name that seemed to impress them, or that they understood, was Norroway. At the name of that country, which they repeated, calling it Norgeway, I observed that they sometimes crossed their hands and looked up to heaven. I believed then that I was on an island, somewhere off the coast of Norroway, and that these three men had come from that country to hunt. I made them repeat the name of the place where we were again and again, and the name they gave it sounded to me like "Jean Main's Land." Having never heard of such a place, I remained in the dark.

When we came to my luggage, the sun being warm, we rested long, and slept; and the men let me understand that we had to provide for a long journey. Accordingly, we set out on the ice once more, and the dogs easing us greatly of our baggage, we travelled at a great rate; yet, as nearly as I could guess, we journeyed for a space of time equal to three days and three nights, without a change of scene, straight along the level surface, the dogs knowing the road perfectly well, and always running on before us. I at length beheld the open sea, and marvelled greatly, thinking our journey was now coming to a very abrupt and woful termination. The men, however, seemed nothing daunted, but, as far as I could judge, were getting rather into better spirits, and were occasionally pointing out some place, of which I saw nothing but a blue calm sea, basking in endless sunshine for the present. We at length came to two canoes and a boat, lying on the ice near to the verge of the open sea. The boat was for carrying the dogs and one man, and the canoes for a man each. The latter were covered with sealskin, which belted round the occupier's waist that no water could touch him, neither could the canoe sink. I had never seen one before, and wondered that men could go into an open sea in such trifling little things that one might carry below his arm. There was a good deal of demur how Nancy and I were to be accommodated among the dogs; but as the dogs were perfectly obedient, each of the men took two dogs below the leather of his canoe, and I was deposited in the bottom of the small boat made of skin, driftwood, and bones of fishes; and there, with Nancy in my bosom, I was forbid to move for fear of oversetting the frail bark. The sea was as smooth as a mirror; and I am convinced that we glided over it with great celerity. The canoes kept ahead, but they were always hailing one another in a cheering strain; and at length I perceived mountains spotted with snow straight before us. We had been journeying, as well as sailing, nearly south-west; and how to reconcile this country with Norway I could not divine. Yet I had hopes that it was Norway, and that I was among the native simple Christians of that country, and would soon find a conveyance from the southern parts of it to my dear native country.

We at length arrived on another coast, and were met upon the shore by twelve young people, which turned out to be women, though I could not distinguish at the time to which sex they belonged. The greyheaded man first kissed them all, and then harangued them, introducing me to them, on which every one of them came to me, the eldest first, and apparently all the rest in succession, according to their ages, kneeled to me, embraced my knees, and received my blessing and a kiss; and, in fact, never was poor forlorn stranger made more welcome. The two eldest women gave me each a hand, and with six on each side, the youngest outermost, they conducted me to their habitation, the elderly hunter walking before us, and the two younger behind us; and at the entrance to their habitation we were received by an old man, with hair and a beard as white as the driven snow. He was the patriarch of the little colony, and their priest; and I was instructed, by signs and words, to kneel and receive his blessing, which I did, and was then conducted in, and welcomed by many tokens of veneration.

It was a strange place. The outer apartments were built and vaulted with snow; but, besides these, there was a long natural cavern stretching under the rocks, that seemed once to have been a seam of limestone from roots of large stalactites that appeared on its roof; but time, and thaws after frosts, had wasted it away. There were, beside this, many irregular side apartments, in one of which my bed was made, which was a good one; and there Nancy and I were left to our repose, and a more sound sleep I never enjoyed.

The colony consisted of thirty-one women and ten men, including the aged father; the rest of the men had perished at sea, or in bear-hunting. Beside these there were seven children, two of whom only were boys; so that a stout healthy young man, such as I was, certainly was as high a boon as heaven could have sent them in one individual, though a whaler's whole crew would doubtless have been more welcome. There were other three men arrived at the settlement that night, who brought a seal and some sea lions for the general good; but all were alike kind and civil to me.

I have not yet told in what country I was, for I did not know myself until a good while after the period of which I am writing. But it may be as well to let the reader know, that I was in Old Greenland,

and among a remnant of a colony of Norwegians, a race of simple primitive Christians, whose progenitors had occupied that inclement shore for centuries, and once, by their account, amounted to many thousands; but, strange to say, if these people's accounts were at all to be credited, fell by degrees a prey to the irresistible invasions of the great polar bears. All their traditional stories were about these ferocious animals, and such stories for horror never characterised the legends of a country. They were described as having made frequent inroads in the month of October in such force, that no single settlement could cope with them, nor yet escape to seek help from others. And when once they beleaguered a settlement or tribe, they never left it while there was a bone of the inhabitants remaining. All their songs and ballads related to those heart-rending scenes of ravage and blood; and they had a prophecy among them, and a firm belief, that the bears were one day to devour the last of them.

The people were much like ourselves, but of lower stature than Scotsmen; and their fur dresses made them appear as square creatures, very near as broad as long. The women had mild simple faces, all of one weather-beaten hue, very like the women of Lewis and Harris. I was so delighted to be among females of my own species once more, that I thought some of the young ones the most bewitching creatures in the world. It was amazing how soon we understood one another's language, for we conversed without ceasing; and I had soon taken up the laudable resolution of marrying three of them. I tried several of them on that point; but all that I could make out of any of them was, that I would be allowed but one; and though I say it who should not, there were plenty of competitors for that distinction. But persuading myself that I perceived symptoms of there having been some departures from this rule in the community, I applied to the old father for satisfaction on this head, who informed me, that as Christians we were only allowed one wife; but owing to the depressed state of the colony, and the great shortcoming of men, every man was allowed one or two handmaidens, like the patriarchs of old, that every woman among them might have the chance of becoming a mother, if desirous to be so. But it was very customary for their women to decline all advances save by lawful marriage; and, in that respect, they were virtuous to a failing, and to the great detriment of the colony.

I felt that in my heart I had no such scruples, and that I should like very well to act the part of old Jacob over again; and I judged such scruples in a woman quite unnatural in a state of society such as this, in which she was sequestered from all others of her species; so having made a choice of three, I determined on marrying one of them, and keeping the other two for mistresses. And in making my choice of a wife, I did rather an ungenerous thing, for I took her who I thought was most indifferent about me, and I chose her that I might make sure of the others afterwards, who were rather overfond.

But there was one great obstacle to my enjoyment, which I could not see a possibility of overcoming, and that was the jealousy of Nancy. I knew she would not leave my apartment while I slept, and I knew as well she would not suffer another to lie in my arms in her presence. I felt that I was so much subjected to her, that I could not have answered for the life of a girl whom I was caressing, no not for a day; for though Nancy had been close muzzled, she could have killed her rival with her paws in a few minutes. I often saw the gleam of jealousy and proud offence in her eye, and dreaded the final consequences; but these poor innocent maidens perceived nothing of the kind. Moreover, Nancy soon became a favourite with the whole tribe, owing to her expertness in fishing, which was altogether unrivalled, and held out a prospect of greater plenty to the clan than it had ever experienced. Her success was so astonishing, that in narrow creeks she would often catch more in one day than all the fishermen of the tribe could do in ten. In fact she was worth us all for laying in a stock of provisions; and to think of injuring, parting with, or even offending Nancy, would have been a dereliction from nature. She had been the preserver of my life and the supporter of it, and never was affection more ardent or disinterested than hers was for me; it was therefore that I felt a reluctance in forfeiting it, by exciting her jealousy. Accordingly, I resolved on taking a stolen kiss with one or all of my charmers, and put off my nuptials until the winter months, when Nancy would be asleep, and we confined to our cabins.

In the mean time, we were busy preparing for that period of rest, devotion, and festivity, and our success, especially in fishing, was consonant to our utmost wishes. There is a curious phenomenon which I conceive to be peculiar to this country. It is, that all along the coast the sea is open for seven or eight months of the year, while farther out at sea, where there are chains and ridges of rocks and islands, the ice frequently remains unbroken through the whole year. And what is more, there are no regular tides, these degenerating all into irregular currents, which seem to be affected by the prevalence of certain winds, but not the least by the tides. There is a regular ebb and swell, and sometimes a very high swell, but no turn of the tide and alternate current as on the shores of Britain. I have often wondered that the tides were not perfectly understood. I have understood them since ever I went to sea, when merely a boy; at least I believed I understood them, which was the same thing to me. I believe in my theory still, and the study of this northern or frozen ocean has completely confirmed me in it.

It is astonishing that neither natural philosophers nor accomplished navigators, of which there have been so many, ever perceived that the earth, in its diurnal motion, rolled with a swing from north to south, and *vice versa*, every five hours and so many minutes, and that this swing was caused by the influence of the moon upon our planet, which, at full moons, is stronger, and at certain other full moons acts with double force; and this at once accounts for all the phenomena of the tides, which, ere they reach the equator, being opposed by others, run all into currents, and ere they reach the poles, the same. And, moreover, this lunary swing of the earth accounts for the tides rolling past the mouths of the cross seas, such as the Baltic and the Mediterranean, whose only tides are a gentle alternate swell from shore to shore occasioned by this swing. The thing is so apparent, that no man sailing on the British seas can help perceiving it. I remember that there was one year I was on board the Hawk of Liverpool, which brought a deal of uncustomed wine and spirits for Glasgow and the towns on the Clyde. We durst not enter the outer frith, where a strict watch was kept, but stretching away to the west, we came at length into a creek in Argyleshire, called Loch-Tarbet, where we carried all our smuggled goods across a narrow neck of land. Here, to my astonishment, I found that it was high tide on the one side of the isthmus, and ebb at the other, and scarce a bow-shot between them. The cause was manifest. Here was an estuary, taking Lochfine and the frith, an hundred miles and more in length; before this was filled full by the one swing, the tide had turned, and the ebb below it brought it roaring and foaming backward; and this continued, I was told, the whole year round, flood tide on the one side, and ebb on the other. Not being able to describe this power that the moon has over the diurnal motion of the earth scientifically, I merely mention it to put men of science and experience on a right basis, because, without adopting it, they will never account logically for the tides and currents of the ocean.

The only extra expedition which we had this summer was one to the hulk of the Anne Forbes, my old habitation, of which I was very fond. I had described to them the riches that I left there in oil, spirits, iron, &c. These two last were so highly estimated, that the desire for the expedition grew irresistible. Accordingly all things were prepared for the adventure; but as canoes were the only vessels chiefly used, we had a terrible business before we got our dogs and sledges across the open sea, and placed fairly on the ice. One woman and one dog were drowned in this expedition across, and we were very near losing two men besides; but the greatest exertions imaginable were made for their preservation, a man's life being a thing of high estimation there. We at length set out with eight light sledges, drawn by one-and-thirty powerful dogs, and the whole conducted by four men, of which number I was one, while poor Nancy accompanied us on foot. We had likewise a light canoe lashed on one of the sledges, for fear of meeting with open fissures in the ice. The snow having been mostly from the ice, it was blue and keen, and once the dogs were fairly set a going, they ran on with amazing swiftness. I never saw any journeying half so quick; for there was an emulation among the animals who to be foremost, the whole journey was actually one pitched race after another; so that, with the delay of only one sleep, we arrived at my glorious crystalline mountain, beaming in the sun with prismatic and dazzling brightness. But still, before we reached it, the chasm in the ice separating it from the main field had begun, and it was only by going round to where we saw the ice crushed up, that we succeeded in getting on to the mountain and the wreck. I found every thing as I had left it, and still plenty of stuff useful for the colony. Had we had fifty sledges we could have loaded them all; but so intensely fond were my three associates of iron, that they would have loaded almost wholly with it. We still found plenty to eat and drink, and plenty for our dogs, so we were in no hurry in loading and departing; but here we were guilty of an oversight fraught with great danger, for the mountain, already affected by the great under current, was just in the act of wheeling and moving off.

All was now bustle and confusion, in order to get as much removed on to the firm ice as possible, before the final separation took place; and we did succeed in bringing a very miscellaneous cargo, though not half so much as we wished; and at length the great mass went off with a roll, that made a concussion in the ocean that would have swallowed up a whaler of the largest size. Two men and several dogs were still by the wreck when the iceberg separated; but they were on the other end from the great turmoil. The men threw themselves into the sea, leaving the canoe behind them, and then calling on the dogs, they all followed, and we got them safe on the ice, and away went the splendid meteor mountain once more on its voyage round the polar regions. A more glorious sight I never beheld in nature than this. The steep side of the hill being toward us, it reflected the rays of the southern sun in a thousand dazzling hues, too brilliant for the eye to look on. It was an illuminated phenomenon fading gradually from our astonished view on the far surface of the ocean. That was the last sight I saw of my old and sublime habitation; and as it was still increasing by the alternate rains and frosts of autumn, I have no doubt that it is roving about among these interminable shoals and currents to this day, unseen by all of existence save the walrus and the wild swan, and haply the whale from his window of foam.

We now loaded with all diligence, and returned home; and during our stay Nancy, as on the former year, had furnished us with an immense heap of excellent fresh fish, which were a great treat to us, and formed a good part of the carriage of two sledges. We brought also the remainder of the spirits, bags of blubber, bear's flesh, iron, and a great number of miscellaneous articles. I likewise loaded Nancy, and every man carried some loading, as our progress was now necessarily slow. There was nothing remarkable happened on our return, save a great confusion in getting our goods from the ice to the land. The men and dogs returned for the remainder; but I had no heart to go again, so another returned in my stead, and I went home with the baggage.

After this we had a grand fishing expedition, about a hundred miles to the northward, in which we took tents and the greater part of the women with us, as also canoes and all our homely fishing tackle of nets and lines, spears and clubs. We had excellent sport and fair success; but our lodging accommodation was very bad, for we lay in tiers above each other, and the abundance of bad breaths from foul feeding was disagreeable to me, I would rather have lain beside poor Nancy by herself than in this mixed multitude; but here she was very cumbersome to me, for not being able to get in at my side, she often lay with her head across me, and she was grown so heavy, I could scarcely bear her. I once awakened in a state of absolute suffocation, and found her lying straight across my face. She was still, however, the queen fisher, and catered for us most abundantly; but she would not suffer any one to lift the fish that she caught but me. She was fond of salmon, and when she fell in with them would eat till I was often afraid she would kill herself.

At length the thin ice began to cover the creeks, and we were obliged to return to our winter settlement, which was now well stored with every production of that inclement coast. Fish was our great staple; but we had part of rein-deer and bear's flesh beside. As soon as the snow came on, we fortified our dwelling by triple walls of half melted snow, which afterwards freezing, grew as firm as adamant.

It is amazing how much driftwood comes annually to that coast and all along the edges of the ice. Of this we had a considerable hoard; but we trusted much to the blubber both for light and heating our water. We merely thawed our meat, we seldom boiled it; and some crumped it up frozen as it was. I even had grown that I preferred the fish in a raw state.

The sun went down, and our long night at length commenced. Nancy fell asleep, so I left her my apartment to herself, covered her well up, and took another bosom partner, Lefa, a young maiden about her prime. The old father Herard joined our hands, prayed over us, made us kiss, and then pronounced us married persons, with a benediction on us, which, as far as I could understand, was very nearly the same as that generally used in Scotland. I had reserved a part of my Highland whiskey for my wedding, and a merrier night I believe never was in Greenland. They know nothing about ardent spirits there, and are naturally a sedate, simple set of people. I speak of this tribe, a remnant of an old Christian community, for any other human being I never saw so long as I was there.

What a strange life we led during the dreary and darksome winter months! We were actually little better than the bears lying in a torpid state. The air being closed out as far as possible, we were drowsy, insipid, and almost incapable of moving. I am sure that after I was married I was not twelve hours out of my bed for three weeks. It was very difficult to get out to the open air, the entrance was so shut up with fagots of seaweed and furze; and unless one went at the hour of public egress, when the shell was sounded, to get out was next to impossible.. We had plenty of meat, but we could not eat it. We had neither air nor exercise; and the three months in the depth of winter passed over like a drumly confused dream. They pretended always to keep the Sabbath, though I daresay as distant as could be from the real first day of the week. They however kept a portion of their time; and on that day I uniformly sung a psalm, and read and prayed with them. As for old father Herard he prayed every day; and as I came soon to understand it, a very original prayer it was, different altogether from any in use in my native country. He prayed always for "the life of men and the death of fish," and "that angels of God might pitch their tents near our happy home, to guard and defend us against the great enemies of human nature, *the white bears!*" Many other sentences beside had allusion to them; and, moreover, he prayed for "the blessed and happy communion between the sexes of their tribe, that all their maidens might become mothers, and bear men children like the young of the dolphin in abundance, healthy as the eagle, and strong as the bear of the lands of snow." For strange to say, they accounted their own country a terrestrial paradise, although the bleakest and last abode of living men.

The spring months at length returned, and daylight appeared, bracing our nerves and cheering our hearts. But now a great and irretrievable misfortune befell me, and one which I fear led to the most dismal of consequences. With the spring, Nancy awoke, and, as soon as her lethargy wore off, was kind and affectionate as ever; but when the poor creature found that she was debarred from sleeping by me, and watching over me in the night, her unhappiness was extreme. Her moans by night disturbed the whole community and kept them waking. There was, moreover, a gleam of jealousy in her eye toward some of the women which frightened me, for I was afraid some one of them might be torn to pieces, her whole savage nature being apparently roused up to brutal revenge, though she luckily could not recognise at that time on whom her vengeance was to fall: I caressed her more than usual during the day; but when she always found that she was expelled from me at night, her chagrin increased to utter misery. I was now in a sad dilemma. I could not leave my wife, to sleep with a huge white she-bear; and yet I had resolved to do it rather than drive her to desperation. Several of the men advised it, she being the great support of the colony by her profound art in fishing; but I put it off from day to day, well knowing that she would never suffer one to lie on the same bed with her and me; and so, after she had spent a part of one night in such groans, as if each were to be her last, in the morning she was missing.

Great was the alarm and intense the sorrow at the loss of Nancy; but as the snow was by that time beginning to soften on the surface, we could trace her foot marks from the door of our retreat, and we set out in pursuit. We found that she had taken to the ice at once, there being still no opening in it, and had made straight toward the Bear Island, where she met her first lover, whom, for my sake, she cruelly murdered. There were two men went with me. We soon lost the track by reason of a shower of wet snow that had fallen; but we followed to the mountains, where I called her name from hill to hill, but all to no purpose; so we were obliged to return home, weary and broken-hearted. We had a tichel of dogs with us, and from their marking on a snow wreath, we digged and killed one sleeping bear with great difficulty, as she awoke partially before we got her wounded. Had it not been for the dogs, weak as she was, she would probably have torn us all to pieces. With this prey we returned; but a very poor prey it was, the flesh of the bear being very bad at that season.

I felt now that I was reduced below the greater part of the men of the colony, whereas before I was rather viewed as their chief, next at least to the patriarch; but my indefatigable provider was gone to mix with her own species, taking the pattern from me, who had deserted her for mine, and I was left untutored and uninitiated

to the strenuous means necessary to be used for existence in that
inclement shore, from whence I had slender hopes of ever making
my escape. It is impossible for me to describe how inconsolable I
felt for the loss of this invaluable animal. No man could have felt the
loss of any worldly substance so much; for when I thought of her
boundless affection and kindness, the tears always rushed to my eyes.
I was like a heart-broken being, taking no interest in our hunting and
fishing expeditions, save the providing for mere animal existence;
and I found that I had actually been happier traversing the frozen
ocean on my iceberg, with one faithful and obliging animal for my
companion, than I was now with an amiable wife.

The rest of the time that I remained here was a mere blank in
existence, and to recount every action minutely would be a weariness to the spirit of man, and far more so to that of woman. It was a
repetition of the same Scenes over and over again; of dozing, and
tanning leather all winter beneath the snow; making nets, spears,
and canoes, all the spring; and fishing and hunting all summer and
autumn; and thus we went on from year to year.

But in 1764, just as we were repairing our snow ramparts around
our cavern, on rising one morning we found ourselves invaded by
a horde of white bears, and our ice-roof penetrated in two places.
The colony now consisted of about sixty men, women, and children;
but only one-third of these were efficient men, capable of standing
any deadly struggle. True, the women assisted in all employments,
however dangerous; but in a bloody battle with a brutal horde, they
were not to be counted on. Such a scene of consternation I never
witnessed, and may never Christian view such another as was that
time among the simple inhabitants of our lonely abode. There was
nothing but weeping and wailing, and every one lamenting the day
that he or she was born. I tried to comfort them; but comfort was out

of the question. Man and woman continued to aver, that these animals never yet invaded a settlement in that country without devouring every bone of its inhabitants before they left it. Then the horrid descriptions followed, drawing pictures of what the bears had done, what they would do. They represented them as liking best to eat the children alive; and that, in order to enjoy such a meal with perfect zest, they always held children down with one paw, and began at the feet, and eat upward, and that the poor things would be crying and trying to creep away even when the monsters had proceeded leisurely with their meal nearly as far as the heart. In short, the people were all seized with a mania of terror; and it was agreed, without a dissentient voice save my own, that they would barricade the cavern that no bear should be able to enter, and sleep all together in death, which the want of air would soon procure to them insensibly.

This resolution was hailed with joy, and even the old patriarch approved of it. I alone withstood it with all my eloquence and with all my energy, declaring, that if no one would join me, I would stand in the breach myself, and defend our women, our children, and our provisions, to the last drop of my blood; but if they would all join me nobly, and exert themselves in the same sacred cause, I would answer with my life for the ultimate success of our defence. "The bears cannot keep their eyes open now," I added, "for more than a week or two. In less than a month they will be all sound asleep, and lying torpid beneath the snow. Why, then, throw away our lives without an effort to preserve them? And worst of all, if we immure ourselves up in our inner cave, and smother ourselves to death, do we not every one of us, save the babies, commit suicide; and with our blood upon our own hands, how shall we ever appear before our Maker, or expect mercy at his hands, who durst not trust to it here below?"

This argument prevailed with the simple Christians, who could not bear the thought of losing their immortal souls. But they assured me that, let us do what we would, the herd would not leave a bone of us, for what they never had done, they would not now begin. Nevertheless, if I would be the responsible captain, and take the whole charge of the defence, they would take an oath to stand by me to the last in defence of the lives that God had given them. This they did, man and woman, in the most solemn manner, kneeling, laying both their hands on the bible, and then kissing it.

I then undertook the defence of the settlement, not only with high hopes, but perfect assurance. Never was there a commander undertook the defence of a fortress, however strong, who was as confident of wearing out his enemy as I was; and I really accounted the danger rather a slight one. We had plenty of spears, both of bone and iron, some bows, and arrows in abundance; but these last could only wound the bears, not kill them. Of powder and lead we had only a few charges remaining. Had we had plenty of that, some of our men were such excellent marksmen that we might have shot the whole herd one by one; but, alas! that resource was no more. We had, moreover, to do with an enemy which every defeat, every life taken, and every wound given, only tended to exasperate, and to determine them the more on our total subversion.

Our cave under the rocks I deemed quite impregnable; but then there was no water in it, and snow would not keep within it if unmelted; so that we were obliged to keep possession of a part of our snow fortress, which was no easy matter, for the strength of these animals, and the power they have in their paws is so prodigious, that when left at liberty to work, they could dig almost through any thing. They soon had our snow roof riddled by several windows, although, whenever we were apprized of their attacks, we could drive them off with our long sharp spears. In fact they did not seem peculiarly voracious or outrageous; a united shout from us, joined to the baying of dogs, made them always scamper off, and keep at a good distance for a space afterwards.

The frost now set in with all its usual intensity, the weather grew calm and clear, and we thought, if we could drive the bears from our habitation, they would soon be seized by a hopeless apathy, dig holes for themselves, and fall into the torpid state. Besides, from any late glimpses we had got of them, the herd seemed not nearly so numerous; so we concluded they had separated, and we would needs become the assailants in our turn.

Accordingly, early one morning of the then short day, we sallied out on the bears, not only every one who could bear arms, but every one who could bear a red clout for a flag, for which colour the bears were said to be frightened. Man, woman, maid, and stripling, sallied out, with all our dogs and all our sounding shells; and such a deafening noise I believe never was raised in old Greenland. The bears durst not once stand before it, they fled before us in a body, and we pursued with cheerful hearts, shouting on the dogs in the van, the men next, and the women last. But before we were aware our ears were saluted by some piercing shrieks behind, and on turning round, we perceived with horror, which may easily be conceived, that another powerful body of bears had attacked our rear, and having already seized on a number of the women, they had them carrying here and there clasped in their paws, and then stretching them on the snow, they embraced them to death, and sucked their blood. We ran to the rescue, and attacking such of the bears as had not yet seized a victim, we drove them back. But, alas, our efforts were powerless and vain! for we were instantly attacked again behind by those we had been chasing, and there being more of the bears than of us, our case was desperate; for a man was no more in the paws of one of these monsters than a babe is in the hands of a man. The women were all seized first, particularly the young ones, prostrated, and devoured. The short stifled shrieks of these hapless wretches, and the apparent joy and triumph of the bears over their prey, will haunt me to my dying day. I fought with blind fury and desperation, and a few of the Greenlanders still stood by me; but many prostrated themselves on the ground, whether to implore mercy from Heaven or of the bears I could not tell; but there was no mercy shown to them.

I was at length seized by an immense powerful bear round the arms and the breast, and borne off with great rapidity; but I neither cried nor prayed. I struck with my heels, and tried to wound with my weapons; but my arms were held so strait, they were void of power. The huge animal never once stopped until it had me at the door of our now nearly desolate habitation, where it set me down uninjured, kneeled at my feet, and licked my hand. "Nancy! My dear, dear Nancy, have we two met again?" cried I, embracing her, "Then we shall never part again in this world."

The generous animal whined and whimpered her joy, grovelled on the snow, and licked my feet, my knees, and my hands. I was now sure of protection, this being a friend in need, whose prowess in my defence had never been baffled; and I was so overjoyed to meet with her again, and at having found protection when I expected every moment to be torn in pieces, that I was never weary of caressing her, and saying kind and endearing words, every one of which she seemed well to remember.

The cries of death, and the growls of voluptuous joy continued to come from the slaughter-field, and some grovelling sounds seemed approaching nearer, on which Nancy seized me by the robe, and drew me into the recess, where she and I had had our abode for a season; and leaving me to my repose, she returned and kept watch in the inner door of our tent.

I heard no more, and I think I had a drumly and dreadful sleep, from which I was awakened by Nancy pulling once more at my clothes. I saw she wanted something with me; but for a long time I could not conceive what she wanted. I brought her meat, but she would not taste it, and I could not read her looks nor her whimperings; till at length she seized a sealskin wallet, and laid it on her back. I then knew at once that she wanted me to load her with provisions and fly, which I effected with all speed; and we issued from the cave, Nancy leading the way with great caution. All was quiet. The bears were gorged, and fallen into their repose; and I believe a fitter time could not have been chosen to make my escape. There were several children and two old frail people in the cavern when I left it, wholly unprotected. Some of those children were my own, or supposed to be so; and when I came away, I heard one weeping and calling for its mother. But what could I do? I could do nothing but shed tears, and leave them to that mercy which I prayed and hoped might yet be extended to save them.

Away then I went once more to push my fortune I knew not where, with Nancy trotting loaded by my side. She led me straight to the sea side, to the very spot at which she and I had first landed in Greenland, and there she threw my load from her back, kneeled, licked my hand, and then scampered off at full speed to share the prey with her associates.

There were plenty of canoes lying at the spot, and some fishing boats; but choosing the best canoe I could find as the safest vessel, I stowed my victuals in about my feet and legs, bound the doughty sealskin cover around my breast, and away I set on my perilous voyage. The sea was still open all along the coast, and I plied my voyage night and day along a weather shore, going merely to land occasionally to take a short sleep. I got some distant views of Iceland, but could not get near it for ice; so I held on my course until fairly hemmed in with ice, that I could get no farther. I then drew my canoe ashore, and climbed a hill, from which I saw the open sea at no great distance, and several ships all apparently bearing southward. Many an anxious day had I spent in my life, but never one so fraught with anxiety as this. I posted on, running without intermission in the direction of the ships; but before I reached the verge of the ice, they were all gone beyond hail. I set me down, and cried one while, and prayed another; but in less than twelve hours the Briel of Amsterdam hove in view, beating up, and as in one of her tacks she came close to me, I was taken on board, and safely landed in Scotland.

THE MOONSTONE MASS

Harriet Prescott Spofford

Harriet Prescott Spofford (1835–1921) was a prominent and versatile American novelist and short story writer whose writings included Gothic romances and science fiction along with tales in a more domestic, sentimental style. After falling out of favour in the twentieth century, Spofford's work has been subject to renewed critical attention, much of which focuses on her extraordinary 1860 story "Circumstance". Here an unnamed protagonist wandering the woods of Spofford's native Maine finds herself "instantly seized and borne aloft" by a panther. Caught in a "lithe embrace" and faced with "streams of his hot, fetid breath", she is able to win her safety by soothing the beast with song. The strange encounter foregrounds two of Spofford's most conspicuous themes: the struggles of women in a patriarchal society (she identified as a suffragette from the age of fourteen) and the meaning and experience of wilderness. Both of these motifs are reprised—albeit in subtler form—in "The Moonstone Mass", published in *Harper's Monthly* in 1868.

The 1860s were an important decade for America's Arctic interests with the launch of two notable expeditions. Isaac Israel Hayes and Charles Francis Hall left the US in 1860 on separate missions to reach the North Pole; neither would succeed. The 1867 publication of Hayes' account of his travels, *The Open Polar Sea: A Narrative of a Voyage of Discovery towards the North Pole*, establishes the Far North as a part of the cultural scene at the time Spofford was developing her writing career. While Arctic narratives are characteristically brimming with machismo, Spofford's approach is more attuned to the poetics of male failure, the frustration of the profit motive and the mystical power of the landscape (a topic she would return to in the 1897 poem "The Story of the Iceberg", in which the narrator recounts the journey of a berg sailing away from its "mother glacier").

There was a certain weakness possessed by my ancestors, though in nowise peculiar to them, and of which, in common with other more or less undesirable traits, I have come into the inheritance.

It was the fear of dying in poverty. That, too, in the face of a goodly share of pelf stored in stocks, and lands, and copper-bottomed clippers, or what stood for copper-bottomed clippers, or rather sailed for them, in the clumsy commerce of their times.

There was one old fellow in particular—his portrait is hanging over the hall stove today, leaning forward, somewhat blistered by the profuse heat and wasted fuel there, and as if as long as such an outrageous expenditure of caloric was going on he meant to have the full benefit of it—who is said to have frequently shed tears over the probable price of his dinner, and on the next day to have sent home a silver dish to eat it from at a hundred times the cost. I find the inconsistencies of this individual constantly cropping out in myself; and although I could by no possibility be called a niggard, yet I confess that even now my prodigalities make me shiver.

Some years ago I was the proprietor of the old family estate, unencumbered by any thing except timber, that is worth its weight in gold yet, as you might say; alone in the world, save for an unloved relative; and with a sufficiently comfortable income, as I have since discovered, to meet all reasonable wants. I had, moreover, promised me in marriage the hand of a woman without a peer, and which, I believe now, might have been mine on any day when I saw fit to claim it.

That I loved Eleanor tenderly and truly you can not doubt; that I desired to bring her home, to see her flitting here and there in my dark old house, illuminating it with her youth and beauty, sitting at the head of my table that sparkled with its gold and silver heir-looms, making my days and nights like one delightful dream, was just as true.

And yet I hesitated. I looked over my bank-book—I cast up my accounts. I have enough for one, I said; I am not sure that it is enough for two. Eleanor, daintily nurtured, requires as dainty care for all time to come; moreover, it is not two alone to be considered, for should children come, there is their education, their maintenance, their future provision and portion to be found. All this would impoverish us, and unless we ended by becoming mere dependents, we had, to my excited vision, only the cold charity of the world and the work-house to which to look forward. I do not believe that Eleanor thought me right in so much of the matter as I saw fit to explain, but in maiden pride her lips perforce were sealed. She laughed though, when I confessed my work-house fear, and said that for her part she was thankful there was such a refuge at all, standing as it did on its knoll in the midst of green fields, and shaded by broad-limbed oaks—she had always envied the old women sitting there by their evening fireside, and mumbling over their small affairs to one another. But all her words seemed merely idle badinage—so I delayed. I said—when this ship sails in, when that dividend is declared, when I see how this speculation turns out—the days were long that added up the count of years, the nights were dreary; but I believed that I was actuated by principle, and took pride to myself for my strength and self-denial.

Moreover, old Paul, my great-uncle on my mother's side, and the millionaire of the family, was a bitter misogynist, and regarded women and marriage and household cares as the three remediless mistakes of an overruling Providence. He knew of my engagement to Eleanor, but so long as it remained in that stage he had nothing to say. Let me once marry, and my share of his million would be best represented by a cipher. However, he was not a man to adore, and he could not live forever.

Still, with all my own effort, I amassed wealth but slowly, according to my standard; my various ventures had various luck; and one day my old Uncle Paul, always intensely interested in the subject, both scientifically and from a commercial point of view, too old and feeble to go himself, but fain to send a proxy, and desirous of money in the family, made me an offer of that portion of his wealth on my return which would be mine on his demise, funded safely subject to my order, provided I made one of those who sought the discovery of the Northwest Passage.

I went to town, canvassed the matter with the experts—I had always an adventurous streak, as old Paul well knew—and having given many hours to the pursuit of the smaller sciences, had a turn for danger and discovery as well. And when the *Albatross* sailed—in spite of Eleanor's shivering remonstrance and prayers and tears, in spite of the grave looks of my friends—I was one of those that clustered on her deck, prepared for either fate. They—my companions—it is true, were led by nobler lights; but as for me, it was much as I told Eleanor—my affairs were so regulated that they would go on uninterruptedly in my absence; I should be no worse off for going, and if I returned, letting alone the renown of the thing, my Uncle Paul's donation was to be appropriated; every thing then was assured, and we stood possessed of lucky lives. If I had any keen or eager desire of search, any purpose to aid the growth of the world or to penetrate the secrets of its formation, as indeed I think I must have had, I did not at that time know any thing about it. But I was to learn that death and stillness have no kingdom on this globe, and that even in the extremest bitterness of cold and ice perpetual interchange and motion is taking place. So we went, all sails set on favourable winds, bounding over blue sea, skirting frowning coasts, and ever pushing our way up into the dark mystery of the North.

I shall not delay here to tell of Danish posts and the hospitality of summer settlements in their long afternoon of arctic daylight; nor will I weary you with any description of the succulence of the radishes that grew under the panes of glass in the Governor's scrap of moss and soil, scarcely of more size than a lady's parlour fernery, and which seemed to our dry mouths full of all the earth's cool juices—but advance, as we ourselves hastened to do, while that chill and crystalline sun shone, up into the ice-cased dens and caverns of the Pole. By the time that the long, blue twilight fell, when the rough and rasping cold sheathed all the atmosphere, and the great stars pricked themselves out on the heavens like spears' points, the *Albatross* was hauled up for winter-quarters, banked and boarded, heaved high on fields of ice; and all her inmates, during the wintry dark, led the life that prepared them for further exploits in higher latitudes the coming year, learning the dialects of the Esquimaux, the tricks of the seal and walrus, making long explorations with the dogs and Glipnu, their master, breaking ourselves in for business that had no play about it.

Then, at last, the August suns set us free again; inlets of tumultuous water traversed the great ice-floes; the *Albatross*, refitted, ruffled all her plumage and spread her wings once more for the North—for the secret that sat there domineering all its substance.

It was a year since we had heard from home; but who staid to think of that while our keel spurned into foam the sheets of steely seas, and day by day brought us nearer to the hidden things we sought? For myself I confess that, now so close to the end as it seemed, curiosity and research absorbed every other faculty; Eleanor might be mouldering back to the parent earth—I could not stay to meditate on such a possibility; my Uncle Paul's donation might enrich itself with gold-dust instead of the gathered dust of idle days—it was nothing to me. I had but one thought, one ambition, one desire in those days—the discovery of the clear seas and open passage. I endured all our hardships as if they had been luxuries: I made light of scurvy, banqueted off train-oil, and met that cold for which there is no language framed, and which might be a new element; or which, rather, had seemed in that long night like the vast void of ether beyond the uttermost star, where was neither air nor light nor heat, but only bitter negation and emptiness. I was hardly conscious of my body; I was only a concentrated search in myself.

The recent explorers had announced here, in the neighbourhood of where our third summer at last found us, the existence of an immense space of clear water. One even declared that he had seen it.

My Uncle Paul had pronounced the declaration false, and the sight an impossibility. The North he believed to be the breeder of icebergs, an ever-welling fountain of cold; the great glaciers there forever form, forever fall; the ice-packs line the gorges from year to year unchanging; peaks of volcanic rock drop their frozen mantles like a scale only to display the fresher one beneath. The whole region, said he, is Plutonic, blasted by a primordial convulsion of the great forces of creation; and though it may be a few miles nearer to the central fires of the earth, allowing that there are such things, yet that would not in itself detract from the frigid power of its sunless solitudes, the more especially when it is remembered that the spinning of the earth, while in its first plastic material, which gave it greater circumference and thinness of shell at its equator, must have thickened the shell correspondingly at the poles; and the character of all the waste and wilderness there only signifies the impenetrable wall between its surface and centre, through which wall no heat could enter or escape. The great rivers, like the White and the Mackenzie, emptying to the north of the continents, so far from being enough in themselves to form any body of ever fresh and flowing water, can only pierce the opposing ice-fields in narrow streams and bays and inlets as they seek the Atlantic and the Pacific seas. And as for the theory of the currents of water heated in the tropics and carried by the rotary motion of the planet to the Pole, where they rise and melt the ice-floes into this great supposititious sea, it is simply an absurdity on the face of it, he argued, when you remember that warm water being in its nature specifically lighter than cold it would have risen to the surface long before it reached there. No, thought my Uncle Paul, who took nothing for granted; it is as I said, an absurdity on the face of it; my nephew shall prove it, and I stake half the earnings of my life upon it.

To tell the truth, I thought much the same as he did; and now that such a mere trifle of distance intervened, between me and the proof, I was full of a feverish impatience that almost amounted to insanity.

We had proceeded but a few days, coasting the crushing capes of rock that every where seemed to run out in a diablerie of tusks and horns to drive us from the region that they warded, now cruising through a runlet of blue water just wide enough for our keel, with silver reaches of frost stretching away into a ghastly horizon—now plunging upon tossing seas, the sun wheeling round and round, and never sinking from the strange, weird sky above us, when again to our look-out a glimmer in the low horizon told its awful tale—a sort of smoky lustre like that which might ascend from an army of spirits— the fierce and fatal spirits tented on the terrible field of the ice-floe.

We were alone, our single little ship speeding ever upward in the midst of that untravelled desolation. We spoke seldom to one another, oppressed with the sense of our situation. It was a loneliness that seemed more than a death in life, a solitude that was supernatural. Here and now it was clear water; ten hours later and we were caught in the teeth of the cold, wedged in the ice that had advanced upon us and surrounded us, fettered by another winter in latitudes where human life had never before been supported.

We found, before the hands of the dial had taught us the lapse of a week, that this would be something not to be endured. The sun sank lower every day behind the crags and silvery horns; the heavens grew to wear a hue of violet, almost black, and yet unbearably dazzling; as the notes of our voices fell upon the atmosphere they assumed a metallic tone, as if the air itself had become frozen from the beginning of the world and they tinkled against it; our sufferings had mounted in their intensity till they were too great to be resisted.

It was decided at length—when the one long day had given place to its answering night, and in the jet-black heavens the stars, like knobs of silver, sparkled so large and close upon us that we might have grasped them in our hands—that I should take a sledge with Glipnu and his dogs, and see if there were any path to the westward by which, if the *Albatross* were forsaken, those of her crew that remained might follow it, and find an escape to safety. Our path was on a frozen sea; if we discovered land we did not know that the foot of man had ever trodden it; we could hope to find no *caché* of snow-buried food—neither fish nor game lived in this desert of ice that was so devoid of life in any shape as to seem dead itself. But, well provisioned, furred to the eyes, and essaying to nurse some hopefulness of heart, we set out on our way through this Valley of Death, relieving one another, and travelling day and night.

Still night and day to the west rose the black coast, one interminable height; to the east extended the sheets of unbroken ice; sometimes a huge glacier hung pendulous from the precipice; once we saw, by the starlight, a white, foaming, rushing river arrested and transformed to ice in its flight down that steep. A south wind began to blow behind us; we travelled on the ice; three days, perhaps, as days are measured among men, had passed, when we found that we made double progress, for the ice travelled too; the whole field, carried by some northward-bearing current, was afloat; it began to be crossed and cut by a thousand crevasses; the cakes, an acre each, tilted up and down, and made wide waves with their ponderous plashing in the black body of the sea; we could hear them grinding distantly in the clear dark against the coast, against each other. There was no retreat—there was no advance; we were on the ice, and the ice was breaking up. Suddenly we rounded a tongue of the primeval rock, and recoiled before a narrow gulf—one sharp shadow, as deep as despair, as full of aguish fears. It was just wide enough for the sledge to span. Glipnu made the dogs leap; we could be no worse off if they drowned. They touched the opposite block; it careened; it went under; the sledge went with it; I was left alone where I had stood. Two dogs broke loose, and scrambled up beside me; Glipnu and the others I never saw again. I sank upon the ice; the dogs crouched beside me; sometimes I think they saved my brain from total ruin, for without them I could not have withstood the enormity of that loneliness, a loneliness that it was impossible should be broken—floating on and on with that vast journeying company of spectral ice. I had food enough to support life for several days to come, in the pouch at my belt; the dogs and I shared it—for, last as long as it would, when it should be gone there was only death before us—no reprieve— sooner or later that; as well sooner as later—the living terrors of this icy hell were all about us, and death could be no worse.

Still the south wind blew, the rapid current carried us, the dark skies grew deep and darker, the lanes and avenues between the stars were crowded with forebodings—for the air seemed full of a new power, a strange and invisible influence, as if a king of unknown terrors here held his awful state. Sometimes the dogs stood up and growled and bristled their shaggy hides; I, prostrate on the ice, in all my frame was stung with a universal tingle. I was no longer myself. At this moment my blood seemed to sing and bubble in my veins; I grew giddy with a sort of delirious and inexplicable ecstasy; with another moment unutterable horror seized me; I was plunged and weighed down with a black and suffocating load, while evil things seemed to flap their wings in my face, to breathe in my mouth, to draw my soul out of my body and carry it careering through the frozen realm of that murky heaven, to restore it with a shock of agony. Once as I lay there, still floating, floating northward, out of the dim dark rim of the water-world, a lance of piercing light shot up the zenith; it divided the heavens like a knife; they opened out in one blaze, and the fire fell sheetingly down before my face—cold fire, curdingly cold—light robbed of heat, and set free in a preternatural anarchy of the elements; its fringes swung to and fro before my face, pricked it with flaming spiculæ, dissolving in a thousand colours that spread every where over the low field, flashing, flickering, creep- ing, reflecting, gathering again in one long serpentine line of glory that wavered in slow convolutions across the cuts and crevasses of the ice, wreathed ever nearer, and, lifting its head at last, became nothing in the darkness but two great eyes like glowing coals, with which it stared me to a stound, till I threw myself face down to hide me in the ice; and the whining, bristling dogs cowered backward, and were dead.

I should have supposed myself to be in the region of the magnetic pole of the sphere, if I did not know that I had long since left it behind me. My pocket-compass had become entirely useless, and every scrap of metal that I had about me had become a loadstone. The very ice, as if it were congealed from water that held large quantities of iron in solution; iron escaping from whatever solid land there was beneath or around, the Plutonic rock that such a region could have alone veined and seamed with metal. The very ice appeared to have a magnetic quality; it held me so that I changed my position upon it with difficulty, and, as if it established a battery by the aid of the singular atmosphere above it, frequently sent thrills quivering through and through me till my flesh seemed about to resolve into all the jarring atoms of its original constitution; and again soothed me, with a velvet touch, into a state which, if it were not sleep, was at least haunted by visions that I dare not believe to have been realities, and from which I always awoke with a start to find myself still floating, floating. My watch had long since ceased to beat. I felt an odd persuasion that I had died when that stood still, and only this slavery of the magnet, of the cold, this power that locked every thing in invisible fetters and let nothing loose again, held my soul still in the bonds of my body. Another idea, also, took possession of me, for my mind was open to whatever visitant chose to enter, since utter despair of safety or release had left it vacant of a hope or fear. These enormous days and nights, swinging in their arc six months long, were the pendulum that dealt time in another measure than that dealt by the sunlight of lower zones; they told the time of what interminable years, the years of what vast generations far beyond the span that covered the age of the primeval men of Scripture—they measured time on this gigantic and enduring scale for what wonderful and mighty beings, old as the everlasting hills, as destitute as they of mortal sympathy, cold and inscrutable, handling the two-edged javelins of frost and magnetism, and served by all the unknown polar agencies. I fancied that I saw their far-reaching cohorts, marshalling and manœuvring at times in the field of an horizon that was boundless, the glitter of their spears and casques, the sheen of their white banners; and again, sitting in fearful circle with their phantasmagoria they shut and hemmed me in and watched me writhe like a worm before them.

I had a fancy that the perpetual play of magnetic impulses here gradually disintegrated myself to any further fear, I cowered beneath the stare of those dead and icy eyes. Slowly we rounded, and ever rounded; the inside, on which my place was, moving less slowly than the outer circle of the sheeted mass in its viscid flow; and as we moved, by some fate my eye was caught by the substance on which this figure sat. It was no figure at all now, but a bare jag of rock rising in the centre of this solid whirlpool, and carrying on its summit something which held a light that not one of these icy freaks, pranking in the dress of gems and flowers, had found it possible to assume. It was a thing so real, so genuine, my breath became suspended; my heart ceased to beat; my brain, that had been a lump of ice, seemed to move in its skull; hope, that had deserted me, suddenly sprung up like a second life within me; the old passion was not dead, if I was. It rose stronger than life or death or than myself. If I could but snatch that mass of moonstone, that inestimable wealth! It was nothing deceptive, I declared to myself. What more natural home could it have than this region, thrown up here by the old Plutonic powers of the planet, as the same substance in smaller shape was thrown up on the peaks of the Mount St. Gothard, when the Alpine aiguilles first sprang into the day? There it rested, limpid with its milky pearl, casting out flakes of flame and azure, of red and leaf-green light, and holding yet a sparkle of silver in the reflections and refractions of its inner axis—the splendid Turk's-eye of the lapidaries, the cousin of the water-opal and the girasole, the precious essence of feldspar. Could I break it, I would find clusters of great hemitrope crystals. Could I obtain it, I should have a jewel in that mass of moonstone such as the world never saw! The throne of Jemschid could not cast a shadow beside it.

Then the bitterness of my fate overwhelmed me. Here, with this treasure of a kingdom, this jewel that could not be priced, this wealth beyond an Emperor's—and here only to die! My stolid apathy vanished, old thoughts dominated once more, old habits, old desires. I thought of Eleanor then in her warm, sunny home, the blossoms that bloomed around her, the birds that sang, the cheerful evening fires, the longing thoughts for one who never came, who never was to come. But I would! I cried, where human voice had never cried before. I would return! I would take this treasure with me! I would not be defrauded! Should not I, a man, conquer this inanimate blind matter? I reached out my hands to seize it. Slowly it receded—slowly, and less slowly; or was the motion of the ice still carrying me onward? Had we encircled this apex? and were we driving out into the open and uncovered North, and so down the seas and out to the open main of black water again? If so—if I could live through it—I must have this thing!

I rose, and as well as I could, with my cramped and stiffened limbs, I moved to go back for it. It was useless; the current that carried us was growing invincible, the gaping gulfs of the outer seas were sucking us toward them. I fell; I scrambled to my feet; I would still have gone back, but, as I attempted it, the ice whereon I was inclined ever so slightly, tipped more boldly, gave way, and rose in a billow, broke, and piled over on another mass beneath. Then the cavern was behind us, and I comprehended that this ice-stream, having doubled its central point, now in its outward movement encountered the still incoming body, and was to pile above and pass over it, the whole expanse bending, cracking, breaking, crowding, and compressing, till its rearing tumult made bergs more mountainous than the offshot glaciers of the Greenland continent, that should ride safely down to crumble in the surging seas below. As block after block of the rent ice rose in the air, lighted by the blue and bristling aurora-points, toppled and mounted higher, it seemed to me that now indeed I was battling with those elemental agencies in the dreadful fight I had desired—one man against the might of matter. I sprang from that block to another; I gained my balance on a third, climbing, shouldering, leaping, struggling, holding with my hands, catching with my feet, crawling, stumbling, tottering, rising high and higher with the mountain ever making underneath; a power unknown to my foes coming to my aid, a blessed rushing warmth that glowed on all the surface of my skin, that set the blood to racing in my veins, that made my heart beat with newer hope, sink with newer despair, rise buoyant with new determination. Except when the shaft of light pierced the shivering sky I could not see or guess the height that I had gained. I was vaguely aware of chasms that were bottomless, of precipices that opened on them, of pinnacles rising round me in aerial spires, when suddenly the shelf, on which I must have stood, yielded, as if it were pushed by great hands, swept down a steep incline like an avalanche, stopped half-way, but sent me flying on, sliding, glancing, like a shooting-star, down, down the slippery side, breathless, dizzy, smitten with blistering pain by awful winds that whistled by me, far out upon the level ice below that tilted up and down again with the great resonant plash of open water, and conscious for a moment that I lay at last upon a fragment that the mass behind urged on, I knew and I remembered nothing more.

Faces were bending over me when I opened my eyes again, rough, uncouth, and bearded faces, but no monsters of the pole. Whalemen rather, smelling richly of train-oil, but I could recall nothing in all my life one fraction so beautiful as they; the angels on whom I hope to open my eyes when Death has really taken me will scarcely seem sights more blest than did those rude whalers of the North Pacific Sea. The North Pacific Sea—for it was there that I was found, explain it how you may—whether the *Albatross* had pierced farther to the west than her sailing-master knew, and had lost her reckoning with a disordered compass-needle under new stars—or whether I had really been the sport of the demoniac beings of the ice, tossed by them from zone to zone in a dozen hours. The whalers, real creatures enough, had discovered me on a block of ice, they said; nor could I, in their opinion, have been many days undergoing my dreadful experience, for there was still food in my wallet when they opened it. They would never believe a word of my story, and so far from regarding me as one who had proved the Northwest Passage in my own person, they considered me a mere idle maniac, as uncomfortable a thing to have on shipboard as a ghost or a dead body, wrecked and unable to account for myself, and gladly transferred me to a homeward-bound Russian man-of-war, whose officers afforded me more polite but quite as decided scepticism. I have never to this day found any one who believed my story when I told it—so you can take it for what it is worth. Even my Uncle Paul flouted it, and absolutely refused to surrender the sum on whose expectation I had taken ship; while my old ancestor, who hung peeling over the hall fire, dropped from his frame in disgust at the idea of one of his hard-cash descendants turning romancer. But all I know is that the *Albatross* never sailed into port again, and that if I open my knife today and lay it on the table it will wheel about till the tip of its blade points full at the North Star.

I have never found any one to believe me, did I say? Yes, there is one—Eleanor never doubted a word of my narration, never asked me if cold and suffering had not shaken my reason. But then, after the first recital, she has never been willing to hear another word about it, and if I ever allude to my lost treasure or the possibility of instituting search for it, she asks me if I need more lessons to be content with the treasure that I have, and gathers up her work and gently leaves the room. So that, now I speak of it so seldom, if I had not told the thing to you it might come to pass that I should forget altogether the existence of my mass of moonstone. My mass of moonshine, old Paul calls it. I let him have his say; he can not have that nor any thing else much longer; but when all is done I recall Galileo and I mutter to myself, "*Per simuove*—it *was* a mass of moonstone! With these eyes I saw it, with these hands I touched it, with this heart I longed for it, with this will I mean to have it yet!"

THE CAPTAIN OF THE "POLESTAR"

Arthur Conan Doyle

Six years before he introduced the world to Sherlock Holmes in 1886, Arthur Conan Doyle (1859–1930) embarked on "the first real outstanding adventure" of his life, spending seven months in the Arctic as surgeon on the whaling ship, the *Hope*, aged only twenty and still a medical student in Edinburgh. It was an experience that left a lasting impact. As Doyle recalls in his autobiography *Memories and Adventures* (1924), the "peculiar other-world feeling of the Arctic regions" is "so singular that if you have once been there the thought of it haunts you all your life". There are undoubtedly traces of the stereotypical allure of the Romantic North in Doyle's descriptions of the scenes he encountered on the *Hope*. "It is a region of purity", he notes, "of white ice and of blue water, with no human dwelling within a thousand miles to sully the freshness of the breeze which blows across the ice-fields": a "region of romance" where you "stand on the very brink of the unknown".

"The Captain of the 'Polestar'" appeared in *Temple Bar* in 1883 with Doyle's Arctic travels still fresh in his mind. The story forms an interesting companion piece to Hogg's "The Surpassing Adventures of Allan Gordon". Both feature an irascible ship's captain. Both form part of the literary history of Scottish whaling, and neither story devotes much attention to whales (though Doyle describes the "dangerously fascinating" business of harpooning in some detail in *Memories and Adventures*). Where Doyle's story differs from Hogg's is in its emphasis on the supernatural, a theme that preoccupied Doyle for much of his life and which led him to participate in numerous séances and other experiments in the paranormal.

SEPTEMBER 11th.—Lat. 81° 40' N.; long. 2° E. Still lying-to amid enormous ice-fields. The one which stretches away to the north of us, and to which our ice-anchor is attached, cannot be smaller than an English county. To the right and left unbroken sheets extend to the horizon. This morning the mate reported that there were signs of pack ice to the southward. Should this form of sufficient thickness to bar our return, we shall be in a position of danger, as the food, I hear, is already running somewhat short. It is late in the season, and the nights are beginning to reappear. This morning I saw a star twinkling just over the fore-yard, the first since the beginning of May. There is considerable discontent among the crew, many of whom are anxious to get back home to be in time for the herring season, when labour always commands a high price upon the Scotch coast. As yet their displeasure is only signified by sullen countenances and black looks, but I heard from the second mate this afternoon that they contemplated sending a deputation to the captain to explain their grievance. I much doubt how he will receive it, as he is a man of fierce temper, and very sensitive about anything approaching to an infringement of his rights. I shall venture after dinner to say a few words to him upon the subject. I have always found that he will tolerate from me what he would resent from any other member of the crew. Amsterdam Island, at the north-west corner of Spitzbergen, is visible upon our starboard quarter—a rugged line of volcanic rocks, intersected by white seams, which represent glaciers. It is curious to think that at the present moment there is probably no human being nearer to us than the Danish settlements in the south of Greenland—a good nine hundred miles as the crow flies. A captain takes a great responsibility upon himself when he risks his vessel under such circumstances. No whaler has ever remained in these latitudes till so advanced a period of the year.

9 p.m.—I have spoken to Captain Craigie, and though the result has been hardly satisfactory, I am bound to say that he listened to what I had to say very quietly and even deferentially. When I had finished he put on that air of iron determination which I have frequently observed upon his face, and paced rapidly backwards and forwards across the narrow cabin for some minutes. At first I feared that I had seriously offended him, but he dispelled the idea by sitting down again, and putting his hand upon my arm with a gesture which almost amounted to a caress. There was a depth of tenderness too in his wild dark eyes which surprised me considerably. "Look here, Doctor," he said, "I'm sorry I ever took you—I am indeed—and I would give fifty pounds this minute to see you standing safe upon the Dundee quay. It's hit or miss with me this time. There are fish to the north of us. How dare you shake your head, sir, when I tell you I saw them blowing from the masthead?"—this in a sudden burst of fury, though I was not conscious of having shown any signs of doubt. "Two-and-twenty fish in as many minutes as I am a living man, and not one under ten foot.* Now, Doctor, do you think I can leave the country when there is only one infernal strip of ice between me

---

* A whale is measured among whalers not by the length of its body, but by the length of its whalebone.

and my fortune? If it came on to blow from the north tomorrow we could fill the ship and be away before the frost could catch us. If it came on to blow from the south—well, I suppose the men are paid for risking their lives, and as for myself it matters but little to me, for I have more to bind me to the other world than to this one. I confess that I am sorry for *you*, though. I wish I had old Angus Tait who was with me last voyage, for he was a man that would never be missed, and you—you said once that you were engaged, did you not?"

"Yes," I answered, snapping the spring of the locket which hung from my watch-chain, and holding up the little vignette of Flora.

"Curse you!" he yelled, springing out of his seat, with his very beard bristling with passion. "What is your happiness to me? What have I to do with her that you must dangle her photograph before my eyes?" I almost thought that he was about to strike me in the frenzy of his rage, but with another imprecation he dashed open the door of the cabin and rushed out upon deck, leaving me considerably astonished at his extraordinary violence. It is the first time that he has ever shown me anything but courtesy and kindness. I can hear him pacing excitedly up and down overhead as I write these lines.

I should like to give a sketch of the character of this man, but it seems presumptuous to attempt such a thing upon paper, when the idea in my own mind is at best a vague and uncertain one. Several times I have thought that I grasped the clue which might explain it, but only to be disappointed by his presenting himself in some new light which would upset all my conclusions. It may be that no human eye but my own shall ever rest upon these lines, yet as a psychological study I shall attempt to leave some record of Captain Nicholas Craigie.

A man's outer case generally gives some indication of the soul within. The captain is tall and well-formed, with dark, handsome face, and a curious way of twitching his limbs, which may arise from nervousness, or be simply an outcome of his excessive energy. His jaw and whole cast of countenance is manly and resolute, but the eyes are the distinctive feature of his face. They are of the very darkest hazel, bright and eager, with a singular mixture of recklessness in their expression, and of something else which I have sometimes thought was more allied with horror than any other emotion. Generally the former predominated, but on occasions, and more particularly when he was thoughtfully inclined, the look of fear would spread and deepen until it imparted a new character to his whole countenance. It is at these times that he is most subject to tempestuous fits of anger, and he seems to be aware of it, for I have known him lock himself up so that no one might approach him until his dark hour was passed. He sleeps badly, and I have heard him shouting during the night, but his cabin is some little distance from mine, and I could never distinguish the words which he said.

This is one phase of his character, and the most disagreeable one. It is only through my close association with him, thrown together as we are day after day, that I have observed it. Otherwise he is an agreeable companion, well-read and entertaining, and as gallant a seaman as ever trod a deck. I shall not easily forget the way in which he handled the ship when we were caught by a gale among the loose ice at the beginning of April. I have never seen him so cheerful, and even hilarious, as he was that night, as he paced backwards and forwards upon the bridge amid the flashing of the lightning and the howling of the wind. He has told me several times that the thought of death was a pleasant one to him, which is a sad thing for a young man to say; he cannot be much more than thirty, though his hair and moustache are already slightly grizzled. Some great sorrow must have overtaken him and blighted his whole life. Perhaps I should be the same if I lost my Flora—God knows! I think if it were not for her that I should care very little whether the wind blew from the north or the south tomorrow. There, I hear him come down the companion, and he has locked himself up in his room, which shows that he is still in an unamiable mood. And so to bed, as old Pepys would say, for the candle is burning down (we have to use them now since the nights are closing in), and the steward has turned in, so there are no hopes of another one.

September 12th.—Calm, clear day, and still lying in the same position. What wind there is comes from the south-east, but it is very slight. Captain is in a better humour, and apologised to me at breakfast for his rudeness. He still looks somewhat distrait, however, and retains that wild look in his eyes which in a Highlander would mean that he was "fey"—at least so our chief engineer remarked to me, and he has some reputation among the Celtic portion of our crew as a seer and expounder of omens.

It is strange that superstition should have obtained such mastery over this hard-headed and practical race. I could not have believed to what an extent it is carried had I not observed it for myself. We have had a perfect epidemic of it this voyage, until I have felt inclined to serve out rations of sedatives and nerve-tonics with the Saturday allowance of grog. The first symptom of it was that shortly after leaving Shetland the men at the wheel used to complain that they heard plaintive cries and screams in the wake of the ship, as if something were following it and were unable to overtake it. This fiction has been kept up during the whole voyage, and on dark nights at the beginning of the seal-fishing it was only with great difficulty that men could be induced to do their spell. No doubt what they heard was either the creaking of the rudder-chains, or the cry of some passing sea-bird. I have been fetched out of bed several times to listen to it, but I need hardly say that I was never able to distinguish anything unnatural. The men, however, are so absurdly positive upon the subject that it is hopeless to argue with them. I mentioned the matter to the captain once, but to my surprise he took it very gravely, and indeed appeared to be considerably disturbed by what I told him. I should have thought that he at least would have been above such vulgar delusions.

All this disquisition upon superstition leads me up to the fact that Mr. Manson, our second mate, saw a ghost last night—or, at least, says that he did, which of course is the same thing. It is quite refreshing to have some new topic of conversation after the eternal routine of bears and whales which has served us for so many months. Manson swears the ship is haunted, and that he would not stay in her a day if he had any other place to go to. Indeed the fellow is honestly frightened, and I had to give him some chloral and bromide of potassium this morning to steady him down. He seemed quite indignant when I suggested that he had been having an extra glass the night before, and I was obliged to pacify him by keeping as grave a countenance as possible during his story, which he certainly narrated in a very straightforward and matter-of-fact way.

"I was on the bridge," he said, "about four bells in the middle watch, just when the night was at its darkest. There was a bit of a moon, but the clouds were blowing across it so that you couldn't see far from the ship. John M'Leod, the harpooner, came aft from the fo'c'sle-head and reported a strange noise on the starboard bow. I went forrard and we both heard it, sometimes like a bairn crying and sometimes like a wench in pain. I've been seventeen years to the country and I never heard seal, old or young, make a sound like that. As we were standing there on the fo'c'sle-head the moon came out from behind a cloud, and we both saw a sort of white figure moving across the ice-field in the same direction that we had heard the cries. We lost sight of it for a while, but it came back on the port bow, and we could just make it out like a shadow on the ice. I sent a hand aft for the rifles, and M'Leod and I went down on to the pack, thinking that maybe it might be a bear. When we got on the ice I lost sight of M'Leod, but I pushed on in the direction where I could still hear the cries. I followed them for a mile or maybe more, and then running round a hummock I came right on to the top of it standing and waiting for me seemingly. I don't know what it was. It wasn't a bear, anyway. It was tall and white and straight, and if it wasn't a man nor a woman, I'll stake my davy it was something worse. I made for the ship as hard as I could run, and precious glad I was to find myself aboard. I signed articles to do my duty by the ship, and on the ship I'll stay, but you don't catch me on the ice again after sundown."

That is his story, given as far as I can in his own words. I fancy what he saw must, in spite of his denial, have been a young bear erect upon its hind legs, an attitude which they often assume when alarmed. In the uncertain light this would bear a resemblance to a human figure, especially to a man whose nerves were already somewhat shaken. Whatever it may have been, the occurrence is unfortunate, for it has produced a most unpleasant effect upon the crew. Their looks are more sullen than before, and their discontent more open. The double grievance of being debarred from the herring fishing and of being detained in what they choose to call a haunted vessel may lead them to do something rash. Even the harpooners, who are the oldest and steadiest among them, are joining in the general agitation.

Apart from this absurd outbreak of superstition, things are looking rather more cheerful. The pack which was forming to the south of us has partly cleared away, and the water is so warm as to lead me to believe that we are lying in one of those branches of the gulfstream which run up between Greenland and Spitzbergen. There are numerous small Medusæ and sea-lemons about the ship, with abundance of shrimps, so that there is every possibility of "fish" being sighted. Indeed one was seen blowing about dinner-time, but in such a position that it was impossible for the boats to follow it.

September 13th.—Had an interesting conversation with the chief mate, Mr. Milne, upon the bridge. It seems that our captain is as great an enigma to the seamen, and even to the owners of the vessel, as he has been to me. Mr. Milne tells me that when the ship is paid off, upon returning from a voyage, Captain Craigie disappears, and is not seen again until the approach of another season, when he walks quietly into the office of the company, and asks whether his services will be required. He has no friend in Dundee, nor does anyone pretend to be acquainted with his early history. His position depends entirely upon his skill as a seaman, and the name for courage and coolness which he had earned in the capacity of mate, before being entrusted with a separate command. The unanimous opinion seems to be that he is not a Scotchman, and that his name is an assumed one. Mr. Milne thinks that he has devoted himself to whaling simply for the reason that it is the most dangerous occupation which he could select, and that he courts death in every possible manner. He mentioned several instances of this, one of which is rather curious, if true. It seems that on one occasion he did not put in an appearance at the office, and a substitute had to be selected in his place. That was at the time of the last Russian and Turkish War. When he turned up again next spring he had a puckered wound in the side of his neck which he used to endeavour to conceal with his cravat. Whether the mate's inference that he had been engaged in the war is true or not I cannot say. It was certainly a strange coincidence.

The wind is veering round in an easterly direction, but is still very slight. I think the ice is lying closer than it did yesterday. As far as the eye can reach on every side there is one wide expanse of spotless white, only broken by an occasional rift or the dark shadow of a hummock. To the south there is the narrow lane of blue water which is our sole means of escape, and which is closing up every day. The captain is taking a heavy responsibility upon himself. I hear that the tank of potatoes has been finished, and even the biscuits are running short, but he preserves the same impassable countenance, and spends the greater part of the day at the crow's nest, sweeping the horizon with his glass. His manner is very variable, and he seems to avoid my society, but there has been no repetition of the violence which he showed the other night.

7.30 p.m.—My deliberate opinion is that we are commanded by a madman. Nothing else can account for the extraordinary vagaries of Captain Craigie. It is fortunate that I have kept this journal of our voyage, as it will serve to justify us in case we have to put him under any sort of restraint, a step which I should only consent to as a last resource. Curiously enough it was he himself who suggested lunacy and not mere eccentricity as the secret of his strange conduct. He was standing upon the bridge about an hour ago, peering as usual through his glass, while I was walking up and down the quarter-deck. The majority of the men were below at their tea, for the watches have not been regularly kept of late. Tired of walking, I leaned against the bulwarks, and admired the mellow glow cast by the sinking sun upon the great ice-fields which surround us. I was suddenly aroused from the reverie into which I had fallen by a hoarse voice at my elbow, and starting round I found that the captain had descended and was standing by my side. He was staring out over the ice with an expression in which horror, surprise, and something approaching to joy were contending for the mastery. In spite of the cold, great drops of perspiration were coursing down his forehead, and he was evidently fearfully excited. His limbs twitched like those of a man upon the verge of an epileptic fit, and the lines about his mouth were drawn and hard.

"Look!" he gasped, seizing me by the wrist, but still keeping his eyes upon the distant ice, and moving his head slowly in a horizontal direction, as if following some object which was moving across the field of vision. "Look! There, man, there! Between the hummocks! Now coming out from behind the far one! You see her—you *must* see her! There still! Flying from me, by God, flying from me—and gone!"

He uttered the last two words in a whisper of concentrated agony which shall never fade from my remembrance. Clinging to the ratlines he endeavoured to climb up upon the top of the bulwarks as if in the hope of obtaining a last glance at the departing object. His strength was not equal to the attempt, however, and he staggered back against the saloon skylights, where he leaned panting and exhausted. His face was so livid that I expected him to become unconscious, so lost no time in leading him down the companion, and stretching him upon one of the sofas in the cabin. I then poured him out some brandy, which I held to his lips, and which had a wonderful effect upon him, bringing the blood back into his white face and steadying his poor shaking limbs. He raised himself up upon his elbow, and looking round to see that we were alone, he beckoned to me to come and sit beside him.

"You saw it, didn't you?" he asked, still in the same subdued awesome tone so foreign to the nature of the man.

"No, I saw nothing."

His head sank back again upon the cushions. "No, he wouldn't without the glass," he murmured. "He couldn't. It was the glass that showed her to me, and then the eyes of love—the eyes of love. I say, Doc, don't let the steward in! He'll think I'm mad. Just bolt the door, will you!"

I rose and did what he had commanded.

He lay quiet for a while, lost in thought apparently, and then raised himself up upon his elbow again, and asked for some more brandy.

"You don't think I am, do you, Doc?" he asked, as I was putting the bottle back into the after-locker. "Tell me now, as man to man, do you think that I am mad?"

"I think you have something on your mind," I answered, "which is exciting you and doing you a good deal of harm."

"Right there, lad!" he cried, his eyes sparkling from the effects of the brandy. "Plenty on my mind—plenty! But I can work out the latitude and the longitude, and I can handle my sextant and manage my logarithms. You couldn't prove me mad in a court of law, could you, now?" It was curious to hear the man lying back and coolly arguing out the question of his own sanity.

"Perhaps not," I said; "but still I think you would be wise to get home as soon as you can, and settle down to a quiet life for a while."

"Get home, eh?" he muttered, with a sneer upon his face. "One word for me and two for yourself, lad. Settle down with Flora—pretty little Flora. Are bad dreams signs of madness?"

"Sometimes," I answered.

"What else? What would be the first symptoms?"

"Pains in the head, noises in the ears, flashes before the eyes, delusions—"

"Ah! what about them?" he interrupted. "What would you call a delusion?"

"Seeing a thing which is not there is a delusion."

"But she *was* there!" he groaned to himself. "She *was* there!" and rising, he unbolted the door and walked with slow and uncertain steps to his own cabin, where I have no doubt that he will remain until tomorrow morning. His system seems to have received a terrible shock, whatever it may have been that he imagined himself to have seen. The man becomes a greater mystery every day, though I fear that the solution which he has himself suggested is the correct one, and that his reason is affected. I do not think that a guilty conscience has anything to do with his behaviour. The idea is a popular one among the officers, and, I believe, the crew; but I have seen nothing to support it. He has not the air of a guilty man, but of one who has had terrible usage at the hands of fortune, and who should be regarded as a martyr rather than a criminal.

The wind is veering round to the south tonight. God help us if it blocks that narrow pass which is our only road to safety! Situated as we are on the edge of the main Arctic pack, or the "barrier" as it is called by the whalers, any wind from the north has the effect of shredding out the ice around us and allowing our escape, while a wind from the south blows up all the loose ice behind us, and hems us in between two packs. God help us, I say again!

September 14th.—Sunday, and a day of rest. My fears have been confirmed, and the thin strip of blue water has disappeared from the southward. Nothing but the great motionless ice-fields around us, with their weird hummocks and fantastic pinnacles. There is a deathly silence over their wide expanse which is horrible. No lapping of the waves now, no cries of seagulls or straining of sails, but one deep universal silence in which the murmurs of the seamen, and the creak of their boots upon the white shining deck, seem discordant and out of place. Our only visitor was an Arctic fox, a rare animal upon the pack, though common enough upon the land. He did not come near the ship, however, but after surveying us from a distance fled rapidly across the ice. This was curious conduct, as they generally know nothing of man, and being of an inquisitive nature, become so familiar that they are easily captured. Incredible as it may seem, even this little incident produced a bad effect upon the crew. "Yon puir beastie kens mair, ay, an' sees mair nor you nor me!" was the comment of one of the leading harpooners, and the others nodded their acquiescence. It is vain to attempt to argue against such puerile superstition. They have made up their minds that there is a curse upon the ship, and nothing will ever persuade them to the contrary.

The captain remained in seclusion all day except for about half an hour in the afternoon, when he came out upon the quarter-deck. I observed that he kept his eye fixed upon the spot where the vision of yesterday had appeared, and was quite prepared for another outburst, but none such came. He did not seem to see me, although I was standing close beside him. Divine service was read as usual, by the chief engineer. It is a curious thing that in whaling vessels the Church of England Prayer-book is always employed, although there is never a member of that Church among either officers or crew. Our men are all Roman Catholics or Presbyterians, the former predominating. Since a ritual is used which is foreign to both, neither can complain that the other is preferred to them, and they listen with all attention and devotion, so that the system has something to recommend it.

A glorious sunset, which made the great fields of ice look like a lake of blood. I have never seen a finer and at the same time more weird effect. Wind is veering round. If it will blow twenty-four hours from the north all will yet be well.

September 15th.—Today is Flora's birthday. Dear lass! it is well that she cannot see her boy, as she used to call me, shut up among the ice-fields with a crazy captain and a few weeks' provisions. No doubt she scans the shipping list in the *Scotsman* every morning to see if we are reported from Shetland. I have to set an example to the men and look cheery and unconcerned; but God knows, my heart is very heavy at times.

The thermometer is at nineteen Fahrenheit today. There is but little wind, and what there is comes from an unfavourable quarter. Captain is in an excellent humour; I think he imagines he has seen some other omen or vision, poor fellow, during the night, for he came into my room early in the morning, and stooping down over my bunk, whispered, "It wasn't a delusion, Doc; it's all right!" After breakfast he asked me to find out how much food was left, which the second mate and I proceeded to do. It is even less than we had expected. Forward they have half a tank full of biscuits, three barrels of salt meat, and a very limited supply of coffee beans and sugar. In the after-hold and lockers there are a good many luxuries, such as tinned salmon, soups, haricot mutton, etc., but they will go a very short way among a crew of fifty men. There are two barrels of flour in the store-room, and an unlimited supply of tobacco. Altogether there is about enough to keep the men on half rations for eighteen or twenty days—certainly not more. When we reported the state of things to the captain, he ordered all hands to be piped, and addressed them from the quarter-deck. I never saw him to better advantage. With his tall, well-knit figure, and dark animated face, he seemed a man born to command, and he discussed the situation in a cool, sailor-like way which showed that while appreciating the danger he had an eye for every loophole of escape.

"My lads," he said, "no doubt you think I brought you into this fix, if it is a fix, and maybe some of you feel bitter against me on account of it. But you must remember that for many a season no ship that comes to the country has brought in as much oil-money as the old *Polestar*, and every one of you has had his share of it. You can leave your wives behind you in comfort, while other poor fellows come back to find their lassies on the parish. If you have to thank me for the one you have to thank me for the other, and we may call it quits. We've tried a bold venture before this and succeeded, so now that we've tried one and failed we've no cause to cry out about it. If the worst comes to the worst, we can make the land across the ice, and lay in a stock of seals which will keep us alive until the spring. It won't come to that, though, for you'll see the Scotch coast again before three weeks are out. At present every man must go on half rations, share and share alike, and no favour to any. Keep up your hearts and you'll pull through this as you've pulled through many a danger before." These few simple words of his had a wonderful effect upon the crew. His former unpopularity was forgotten, and the old harpooner whom I have already mentioned for his superstition, led off three cheers, which were heartily joined in by all hands.

September 16th.—The wind has veered round to the north during the night, and the ice shows some symptoms of opening out. The men are in a good humour in spite of the short allowance upon which they have been placed. Steam is kept up in the engine-room, that there may be no delay should an opportunity for escape present itself. The captain is in exuberant spirits, though he still retains that wild "fey" expression which I have already remarked upon. This burst of cheerfulness puzzles me more than his former gloom. I cannot understand it. I think I mentioned in an early part of this journal that one of his oddities is that he never permits any person to enter his cabin, but insists upon making his own bed, such as it is, and performing every other office for himself. To my surprise he handed me the key today and requested me to go down there and take the time by his chronometer while he measured the altitude of the sun at noon. It is a bare little room, containing a washing-stand and a few books, but little else in the way of luxury, except some pictures upon the walls. The majority of these are small cheap oleographs, but there was one water-colour sketch of the head of a young lady which arrested my attention. It was evidently a portrait, and not one of those fancy types of female beauty which sailors particularly affect. No artist could have evolved from his own mind such a curious mixture of character and weakness. The languid, dreamy eyes, with their drooping lashes, and the broad, low brow, unruffled by thought or care, were in strong contrast with the clean-cut, prominent jaw, and the resolute set of the lower lip. Underneath it in one of the corners was written, "M.B., æt. 19." That anyone in the short space of nineteen years of existence could develop such strength of will as was stamped upon her face seemed to me at the time to be well-nigh incredible. She must have been an extraordinary woman. Her features have thrown such a glamour over me that, though I had but a fleeting glance at them, I could, were I a draughtsman, reproduce them line for line upon this page of the journal. I wonder what part she has played in our captain's life. He has hung her picture at the end of his berth, so that his eyes continually rest upon it. Were he a less reserved man I should make some remark upon the subject. Of the other things in his cabin there was nothing worthy of mention—uniform coats, a camp-stool, small looking-glass, tobacco-box, and numerous pipes, including an oriental hookah—which, by the by, gives some colour to Mr. Milne's story about his participation in the war, though the connection may seem rather a distant one.

11.20 p.m.—Captain just gone to bed after a long and interesting conversation on general topics. When he chooses he can be a most fascinating companion, being remarkably well-read, and having the power of expressing his opinion forcibly without appearing to be dogmatic. I hate to have my intellectual toes trod upon. He spoke about the nature of the soul, and sketched out the views of Aristotle and Plato upon the subject in a masterly manner. He seems to have a leaning for metempsychosis and the doctrines of Pythagoras. In discussing them we touched upon modern spiritualism, and I made some joking allusion to the impostures of Slade, upon which, to my surprise, he warned me most impressively against confusing the innocent with the guilty, and argued that it would be as logical to brand Christianity as an error because Judas, who professed that religion, was a villain. He shortly afterwards bade me good night and retired to his room.

The wind is freshening up, and blows steadily from the north. The nights are as dark now as they are in England. I hope tomorrow may set us free from our frozen fetters.

September 17th.—The Bogie again. Thank Heaven that I have strong nerves! The superstition of these poor fellows, and the circumstantial accounts which they give, with the utmost earnestness and self-conviction, would horrify any man not accustomed to their ways. There are many versions of the matter, but the sum-total of them all is that something uncanny has been flitting round the ship all night, and that Sandie M'Donald of Peterhead and "lang" Peter Williamson of Shetland saw it, as also did Mr. Milne on the bridge—so, having three witnesses, they can make a better case of it than the second mate did. I spoke to Milne after breakfast, and told him that he should be above such nonsense, and that as an officer he ought to set the men a better example. He shook his weather-beaten head ominously, but answered with characteristic caution, "Mebbe, aye, mebbe na, Doctor," he said, "I didna ca' it a ghaist. I canna' say I preen my faith in sea-bogles an' the like, though there's a mony as claims to ha' seen a' that and waur. I'm no easy feared, but maybe your ain bluid would run a bit cauld, mun, if instead o' speerin' aboot it in daylicht ye were wi' me last night, an' seed an awfu' like shape, white an' gruesome, whiles here, whiles there, an' it greetin' and ca'ing in the darkness like a bit lambie that hae lost its mither. Ye would na' be sae ready to put it a' doon to auld wives' clavers then, I'm thinkin'." I saw it was hopeless to reason with him, so contented myself with begging him as a personal favour to call me up the next time the spectre appeared—a request to which he acceded with many ejaculations expressive of his hopes that such an opportunity might never arise.

As I had hoped, the white desert behind us has become broken by many thin streaks of water which intersect it in all directions. Our latitude today was 80° 52" N., which shows that there is a strong southerly drift upon the pack. Should the wind continue favourable it will break up as rapidly as it formed. At present we can do nothing but smoke and wait and hope for the best. I am rapidly becoming a fatalist. When dealing with such uncertain factors as wind and ice a man can be nothing else. Perhaps it was the wind and sand of the Arabian deserts which gave the minds of the original followers of Mahomet their tendency to bow to kismet.

These spectral alarms have a very bad effect upon the captain. I feared that it might excite his sensitive mind, and endeavoured to conceal the absurd story from him, but unfortunately he overheard one of the men making an allusion to it, and insisted upon being informed about it. As I had expected, it brought out all his latent lunacy in an exaggerated form. I can hardly believe that this is the same man who discoursed philosophy last night with the most critical acumen and coolest judgement. He is pacing backwards and forwards upon the quarter-deck like a caged tiger, stopping now and again to throw out his hands with a yearning gesture, and stare impatiently out over the ice. He keeps up a continual mutter to himself, and once he called out, "But a little time, love—but a little time!" Poor fellow, it is sad to see a gallant seaman and accomplished gentleman reduced to such a pass, and to think that imagination and delusion can cow a mind to which real danger was but the salt of life. Was ever a man in such a position as I, between a demented captain and a ghost-seeing mate? I sometimes think I am the only really sane man aboard the vessel—except perhaps the second engineer, who is a kind of ruminant, and would care nothing for all the fiends in the Red Sea so long as they would leave him alone and not disarrange his tools.

The ice is still opening rapidly, and there is every probability of our being able to make a start tomorrow morning. They will think I am inventing when I tell them at home all the strange things that have befallen me.

12 p.m.—I have been a good deal startled, though I feel steadier now, thanks to a stiff glass of brandy. I am hardly myself yet, however, as this handwriting will testify. The fact is, that I have gone through a very strange experience, and am beginning to doubt whether I was justified in branding everyone on board as madmen because they professed to have seen things which did not seem reasonable to my understanding. Pshaw! I am a fool to let such a trifle unnerve me; and yet, coming as it does after all these alarms, it has an additional significance, for I cannot doubt either Mr. Manson's story or that of the mate, now that I have experienced that which I used formerly to scoff at.

After all it was nothing very alarming—a mere sound, and that was all. I cannot expect that anyone reading this, if anyone ever should read it, will sympathise with my feelings, or realise the effect which it produced upon me at the time. Supper was over, and I had gone on deck to have a quiet pipe before turning in. The night was very dark—so dark that, standing under the quarter-boat, I was unable to see the officer upon the bridge. I think I have already mentioned the extraordinary silence which prevails in these frozen seas. In other parts of the world, be they ever so barren, there is some slight vibration of the air—some faint hum, be it from the distant haunts of men, or from the leaves of the trees or the wings of the birds, or even the faint rustle of the grass that covers the ground. One may not actively perceive the sound, and yet if it were withdrawn it would be missed. It is only here in these Arctic seas that stark, unfathomable stillness obtrudes itself upon you all in its gruesome reality. You find your tympanum straining to catch some little murmur, and dwelling eagerly upon every accidental sound within the vessel. In this state I was leaning against the bulwarks when there arose from the ice almost directly underneath me a cry, sharp and shrill, upon the silent air of the night, beginning, as it seemed to me, at a note such as prima donna never reached, and mounting from that ever higher and higher until it culminated in a long wail of agony, which might have been the last cry of a lost soul. The ghastly scream is still ringing in my ears. Grief, unutterable grief, seemed to be expressed in it, and a great longing, and yet through it all there was an occasional wild note of exultation. It shrilled out from close beside me, and yet as I glared into the darkness I could discern nothing. I waited some little time, but without hearing any repetition of the sound, so I came below, more shaken than I have ever been in my life before. As I came down the companion I met Mr. Milne coming up to relieve the watch. "Weel, Doctor," he said, "maybe that's auld wives' clavers tae? Did ye no hear it skirling? Maybe that's a supersteetion? What d'ye think o't noo?" I was obliged to apologise to the honest fellow, and acknowledge that I was as puzzled by it as he was. Perhaps tomorrow things may look different. At present I dare hardly write all that I think. Reading it again in days to come, when I have shaken off all these associations, I should despise myself for having been so weak.

September 18th.—Passed a restless and uneasy night, still haunted by that strange sound. The captain does not look as if he had had much repose either, for his face is haggard and his eyes bloodshot. I have not told him of my adventure of last night, nor shall I. He is already restless and excited, standing up, sitting down, and apparently utterly unable to keep still.

A fine lead appeared in the pack this morning, as I had expected, and we were able to cast off our ice-anchor, and steam about twelve miles in a west-sou'-westerly direction. We were then brought to a halt by a great floe as massive as any which we have left behind us. It bars our progress completely, so we can do nothing but anchor again and wait until it breaks up, which it will probably do within twenty-four hours, if the wind holds. Several bladder-nosed seals were seen swimming in the water, and one was shot, an immense creature more than eleven feet long. They are fierce, pugnacious animals, and are said to be more than a match for a bear. Fortunately they are slow and clumsy in their movements, so that there is little danger in attacking them upon the ice.

The captain evidently does not think we have seen the last of our troubles, though why he should take a gloomy view of the situation is more than I can fathom, since everyone else on board considers that we have had a miraculous escape, and are sure now to reach the open sea.

"I suppose you think it's all right now, Doctor?" he said, as we sat together after dinner.

"I hope so," I answered.

"We mustn't be too sure—and yet no doubt you are right. We'll all be in the arms of our own true loves before long, lad, won't we? But we mustn't be too sure—we mustn't be too sure."

He sat silent a little, swinging his leg thoughtfully backwards and forwards. "Look here," he continued; "it's a dangerous place this, even at its best—a treacherous, dangerous place. I have known men cut off very suddenly in a land like this. A slip would do it sometimes—a single slip, and down you go through a crack, and only a bubble on the green water to show where it was that you sank. It's a queer thing," he continued with a nervous laugh, "but all the years I've been in this country I never once thought of making a will—not that I have anything to leave in particular, but still when a man is exposed to danger he should have everything arranged and ready—don't you think so?"

"Certainly," I answered, wondering what on earth he was driving at.

"He feels better for knowing it's all settled," he went on. "Now if anything should ever befall me, I hope that you will look after things for me. There is very little in the cabin, but such as it is I should like it to be sold, and the money divided in the same proportion as the oil-money among the crew. The chronometer I wish you to keep yourself as some slight remembrance of our voyage. Of course all this is a mere precaution, but I thought I would take the opportunity of speaking to you about it. I suppose I might rely upon you if there were any necessity?"

"Most assuredly," I answered; "and since you are taking this step, I may as well—"

"You! you!" he interrupted. "*You're* all right. What the devil is the matter with *you*? There, I didn't mean to be peppery, but I don't like to hear a young fellow, that has hardly began life, speculating about death. Go up on deck and get some fresh air into your lungs instead of talking nonsense in the cabin, and encouraging me to do the same."

The more I think of this conversation of ours the less do I like it. Why should the man be settling his affairs at the very time when we seem to be emerging from all danger? There must be some method in his madness. Can it be that he contemplates suicide? I remember that upon one occasion he spoke in a deeply reverent manner of the heinousness of the crime of self-destruction. I shall keep my eye upon him, however, and though I cannot obtrude upon the privacy of his cabin, I shall at least make a point of remaining on deck as long as he stays up.

Mr. Milne pooh-poohs my fears, and says it is only the "skipper's little way." He himself takes a very rosy view of the situation. According to him we shall be out of the ice by the day after tomorrow, pass Jan Meyen two days after that, and sight Shetland in little more than a week. I hope he may not be too sanguine. His opinion may be fairly balanced against the gloomy precautions of the captain, for he is an old and experienced seaman, and weighs his words well before uttering them.

The long-impending catastrophe has come at last. I hardly know what to write about it. The captain is gone. He may come back to us again alive, but I fear me—I fear me. It is now seven o'clock of the morning of the 19th of September. I have spent the whole night traversing the great ice-floe in front of us with a party of seamen in the hope of coming upon some trace of him, but in vain. I shall try to give some account of the circumstances which attended upon his disappearance. Should anyone ever chance to read the words which I put down, I trust they will remember that I do not write from conjecture or from hearsay, but that I, a sane and educated man, am describing accurately what actually occurred before my very eyes. My inferences are my own, but I shall be answerable for the facts.

The captain remained in excellent spirits after the conversation which I have recorded. He appeared to be nervous and impatient, however, frequently changing his position, and moving his limbs in an aimless choreic way which is characteristic of him at times. In a quarter of an hour he went upon deck seven times, only to descend after a few hurried paces. I followed him each time, for there was something about his face which confirmed my resolution of not letting him out of my sight. He seemed to observe the effect which his movements had produced, for he endeavoured by an overdone hilarity, laughing boisterously at the very smallest of jokes, to quiet my apprehensions.

After supper he went on to the poop once more, and I with him. The night was dark and very still, save for the melancholy soughing of the wind among the spars. A thick cloud was coming up from the north-west, and the ragged tentacles which it threw out in front of it were drifting across the face of the moon, which only shone now and again through a rift in the wrack. The captain paced rapidly backwards and forwards, and then seeing me still dogging him, he came across and hinted that he thought I should be better below—which, I need hardly say, had the effect of strengthening my resolution to remain on deck.

I think he forgot about my presence after this, for he stood silently leaning over the taffrail and peering out across the great desert of snow, part of which lay in shadow, while part glittered mistily in the moonlight. Several times I could see by his movements that he was referring to his watch, and once he muttered a short sentence, of which I could only catch the one word "ready." I confess to having felt an eerie feeling creeping over me as I watched the loom of his tall figure through the darkness, and noted how completely he fulfilled the idea of a man who is keeping a tryst. A tryst with whom? Some vague perception began to dawn upon me as I pieced one fact with another, but I was utterly unprepared for the sequel.

By the sudden intensity of his attitude I felt that he saw something. I crept up behind him. He was staring with an eager questioning gaze at what seemed to be a wreath of mist, blown swiftly in a line with the ship. It was a dim nebulous body, devoid of shape, sometimes more, sometimes less apparent, as the light fell on it. The moon was dimmed in its brilliancy at the moment by a canopy of thinnest cloud, like the coating of an anemone.

"Coming, lass, coming," cried the skipper, in a voice of unfathomable tenderness and compassion, like one who soothes a beloved one by some favour long looked for, and as pleasant to bestow as to receive.

What followed happened in an instant. I had no power to interfere. He gave one spring to the top of the bulwarks, and another which took him on to the ice, almost to the feet of the pale misty figure. He held out his hands as if to clasp it, and so ran into the darkness with outstretched arms and loving words. I still stood rigid and motionless, straining my eyes after his retreating form, until his voice died away in the distance. I never thought to see him again, but at that moment the moon shone out brilliantly through a chink in the cloudy heaven, and illuminated the great field of ice. Then I saw his dark figure already a very long way off, running with prodigious speed across the frozen plain. That was the last glimpse which we caught of him—perhaps the last we ever shall. A party was organised to follow him, and I accompanied them, but the men's hearts were not in the work, and nothing was found. Another will be formed within a few hours. I can hardly believe I have not been dreaming, or suffering from some hideous nightmare, as I write these things down.

7.30 p.m.—Just returned dead beat and utterly tired out from a second unsuccessful search for the captain. The floe is of enormous extent, for though we have traversed at least twenty miles of its surface, there has been no sign of its coming to an end. The frost has been so severe of late that the overlying snow is frozen as hard as granite, otherwise we might have had the footsteps to guide us. The crew are anxious that we should cast off and steam round the floe and so to the southward, for the ice has opened up during the night, and the sea is visible upon the horizon. They argue that Captain Craigie is certainly dead, and that we are all risking our lives to no purpose by remaining when we have an opportunity of escape. Mr. Milne and I have had the greatest difficulty in persuading them to wait until tomorrow night, and have been compelled to promise that we will not under any circumstances delay our departure longer than that. We propose therefore to take a few hours' sleep, and then to start upon a final search.

September 20th, evening.—I crossed the ice this morning with a party of men exploring the southern part of the floe, while Mr. Milne went off in a northerly direction. We pushed on for ten or twelve miles without seeing a trace of any living thing except a single bird, which fluttered a great way over our heads, and which by its flight I should judge to have been a falcon. The southern extremity of the ice-field tapered away into a long narrow spit which projected out into the sea. When we came to the base of this promontory, the men halted, but I begged them to continue to the extreme end of it, that we might have the satisfaction of knowing that no possible chance had been neglected.

We had hardly gone a hundred yards before M'Donald of Peterhead cried out that he saw something in front of us, and began to run. We all got a glimpse of it and ran too. At first it was only a vague darkness against the white ice, but as we raced along together it took the shape of a man, and eventually of the man of whom we were in search. He was lying face downwards upon a frozen bank. Many little crystals of ice and feathers of snow had drifted on to him as he lay, and sparkled upon his dark seaman's jacket. As we came up some wandering puff of wind caught these tiny flakes in its vortex, and they whirled up into the air, partially descended again, and then, caught once more in the current, sped rapidly away in the direction of the sea. To my eyes it seemed but a snowdrift, but many of my companions averred that it started up in the shape of a woman, stooped over the corpse and kissed it, and then hurried away across the floe. I have learned never to ridicule any man's opinion, however strange it may seem. Sure it is that Captain Nicholas Craigie had met with no painful end, for there was a bright smile upon his blue pinched features, and his hands were still outstretched as though grasping at the strange visitor which had summoned him away into the dim world that lies beyond the grave.

We buried him the same afternoon with the ship's ensign around him, and a thirty-two pound shot at his feet. I read the burial service, while the rough sailors wept like children, for there were many who owed much to his kind heart, and who showed now the affection which his strange ways had repelled during his lifetime. He went off the grating with a dull, sullen splash, and as I looked into the green water I saw him go down, down, down until he was but a little flickering patch of white hanging upon the outskirts of eternal darkness. Then even that faded away, and he was gone. There he shall lie, with his secret and his sorrows and his mystery all still buried in his breast, until that great day when the sea shall give up its dead, and Nicholas Craigie come out from among the ice with the smile upon his face, and his stiffened arms outstretched in greeting. I pray that his lot may be a happier one in that life than it has been in this.

I shall not continue my journal. Our road to home lies plain and clear before us, and the great ice-field will soon be but a remembrance of the past. It will be some time before I get over the shock produced by recent events. When I began this record of our voyage I little thought of how I should be compelled to finish it. I am writing these final words in the lonely cabin, still starting at times and fancying I hear the quick nervous step of the dead man upon the deck above me. I entered his cabin tonight, as was my duty, to make a list of his effects in order that they might be entered in the official log. All was as it had been upon my previous visit, save that the picture which I have described as having hung at the end of his bed had been cut out of its frame, as with a knife, and was gone. With this last link in a strange chain of evidence I close my diary of the voyage of the *Polestar*.

[Note by Dr. John M'Alister Ray, senior.—I have read over the strange events connected with the death of the captain of the *Polestar*, as narrated in the journal of my son. That everything occurred exactly as he describes it I have the fullest confidence, and, indeed, the most positive certainty, for I know him to be a strong-nerved and unimaginative man, with the strictest regard for veracity. Still, the story is, on the face of it, so vague and so improbable, that I was long opposed to its publication. Within the last few days, however, I have had independent testimony upon the subject which throws a new light upon it. I had run down to Edinburgh to attend a meeting of the British Medical Association, when I chanced to come across

Dr. P——, an old college chum of mine, now practising at Saltash, in Devonshire. Upon my telling him of this experience of my son's, he declared to me that he was familiar with the man, and proceeded, to my no small surprise, to give me a description of him, which tallied remarkably well with that given in the journal, except that he depicted him as a younger man. According to his account, he had been engaged to a young lady of singular beauty residing upon the Cornish coast. During his absence at sea his betrothed had died under circumstances of peculiar horror.]

SKULE SKERRY

John Buchan

John Buchan (1875–1940) is best known as the novelist who gave the world the Richard Hannay series, including the enduring classic of wartime espionage *The Thirty-Nine Steps* (1915). Buchan's writing is considerably richer and more diverse than the Hannay adventures suggest, however, encompassing biography, history, poetry and a number of works of supernatural fiction. As well as a much-loved author, Buchan was throughout his career a public figure, as a colonial administrator, MP and, at the time of his death, Governor General of Canada. It was while serving as Governor General that Buchan wrote his last—and best—novel, the sombre, mystical story of Canada's Northwest Territories *Sick Heart River* (published posthumously in 1940) that articulates both the romantic allure and "secret madness" of the North. For Buchan, the ends of the Earth were an idea as much as a place. As Buchan concluded in his book of geographical mysteries *The Last Secrets* (1923), quoting Fridtjof Nansen, "the history of Polar exploration is a single mighty manifestation of the power of the Unknown over the mind of man".

"Skule Skerry" is taken from the 1928 volume of short stories *The Runagates Club*, a cycle of tales told by prominent (fictional) members of British society gathered around the table of a gentleman's club. This is the tale told by the ornithologist Anthony Hurrell. Like much of Buchan's writing, it is characterised by a detailed and tender depiction of the natural world, mixed in with a dose of Gothic horror. With the action of the story unfolding at 61° latitude in the west of the Orkneys, this is the most southerly of the northerly stories, though it is one with its narrative gaze set firmly out towards the "icy tides" that deliver a narrative climax arriving from much further north.

Who's there, besides foul weather?

King Lear.

Mr. Anthony Hurrell was a small man, thin to the point of emaciation, but erect as a ramrod and wiry as a cairn terrier. There was no grey in his hair, and his pale far-sighted eyes had the alertness of youth, but his lean face was so wrinkled by weather that in certain lights it looked almost venerable, and young men, who at first sight had imagined him their contemporary, presently dropped into the "sir" reserved for indisputable seniors. His actual age was, I believe, somewhere in the forties. He had inherited a small property in Northumberland, where he had accumulated a collection of the rarer wildfowl, but much of his life had been spent in places so remote that his friends could with difficulty find them on the map. He had written a dozen ornithological monographs, was joint editor of the chief modern treatise on British birds, and had been the first man to visit the *tundras* of the Yenisei. He spoke little and that with an agreeable hesitation, but his ready smile, his quick interest, and the impression he gave of having a fathomless knowledge of strange modes of life, made him a popular and intriguing figure among his friends. Of his doings in the War he told us nothing; what we knew of them—and they were sensational enough in all conscience—we learned elsewhere. It was Nightingale's story which drew him from his customary silence. At the dinner following that event he made certain comments on current explanations of the supernormal. "I remember once," he began, and before we knew he had surprised us by embarking on a tale.

He had scarcely begun before he stopped. "I'm boring you," he said deprecatingly. "There's nothing much in the story... You see, it all happened, so to speak, inside my head... I don't want to seem an egotist..."

"Don't be an ass, Tony," said Lamancha. "Every adventure takes place chiefly inside the head of somebody. Go on. We're all attention."

"It happened a good many years ago," Hurrell continued, "when I was quite a young man. I wasn't the cold scientist then that I fancy I am today. I took up birds in the first instance chiefly because they fired what imagination I possess. They fascinated me, for they seemed of all created things the nearest to pure spirit—those little beings with a normal temperature of 125°. Think of it. The goldcrest, with a stomach no bigger than a bean, flies across the North Sea! The curlew sandpiper, which breeds so far north that only about three people have ever seen its nest, goes to Tasmania for its holidays! So I always went bird-hunting with a queer sense of expectation and a bit of a tremor, as if I was walking very near the boundaries of the things we are not allowed to know. I felt this especially in the migration season. The small atoms, coming God knows whence and going God knows whither, were sheer mystery—they belonged to a world built in different dimensions from ours. I don't know what I expected, but I was always waiting for something, as much in a flutter as a girl at her first ball. You must realise that mood of mine to understand what follows.

"One year I went to the Norland Islands for the spring migration. Plenty of people do the same, but I had the notion to do something a little different. I had a theory that migrants go north and south on a fairly narrow road. They have their corridors in the air as clearly defined as a highway, and keep an inherited memory of these corridors, like the stout conservatives they are. So I didn't go to the Blue Banks or to Noop or to Hermaness or any of the obvious places, where birds might be expected to make their first landfall.

"At that time I was pretty well read in the sagas, and had taught myself Icelandic for the purpose. Now it is written in the Saga of Earl Skuli, which is part of the Jarla Saga or Saga of the Earls, that Skuli, when he was carving out his earldom in the Scots islands, had much to do with a place called the Isle of the Birds. It is mentioned repeatedly, and the saga-man has a lot to say about the amazing multitude of birds there. It couldn't have been an ordinary gullery, for the Northmen saw too many of these to think them worth mentioning. I got it into my head that it must have been one of the alighting places of the migrants, and was probably as busy a spot today as in the eleventh century. The saga said it was near Halmarsness, and that is on the west side of the island of Una, so to Una I decided to go. I fairly got that Isle of Birds on the brain. From the map it might be any one of a dozen skerries under the shadow of Halmarsness.

"I remember that I spent a good many hours in the British Museum before I started, hunting up the scanty records of those parts. I found—I think it was in Adam of Bremen—that a succession of holy men had lived on the isle, and that a chapel had been built there and endowed by Earl Rognvald, which came to an end in the time of Malise of Strathearn. There was a bare mention of the place, but the chronicler had one curious note. 'Insula Avium,' ran the text, 'quæ est ultima insula et proximo, Abysso.' I wondered what on earth he meant. The place was not ultimate in any geographical sense, neither the farthest north nor the farthest west of the Norlands. And what was the 'abyss'? In monkish Latin the word generally means

Hell—Bunyan's Bottomless Pit—and sometimes the grave; but neither meaning seemed to have much to do with an ordinary sea skerry.

"I arrived at Una about eight o'clock in a May evening, having been put across from Voss in a flit-boat. It was a quiet evening, the sky without clouds but so pale as to be almost grey, the sea grey also but with a certain iridescence in it, and the low lines of the land a combination of hard greys and umbers, cut into by the harder white of the lighthouse. I can never find words to describe that curious quality of light that you get up in the North. Sometimes it is like looking at the world out of deep water—Farquharson used to call it 'milky,' and one saw what he meant. Generally it is a sort of essence of light, cold and pure and distilled, as if it were reflected from snow. There is no colour in it, and it makes thin shadows. Some people find it horribly depressing—Farquharson said it reminded him of a churchyard in the early morning where all his friends were buried—but personally I found it tonic and comforting. But it made me feel very near the edge of the world.

"There was no inn, so I put up at the post-office, which was on a causeway between a freshwater loch and a sea voe, so that from the doorstep you could catch brown trout on one side and sea-trout on the other. Next morning I set off for Halmarsness, which lay five miles to the west over a flat moorland all puddled with tiny lochans. There seemed to be nearly as much water as land. Presently I came to a bigger loch under the lift of ground which was Halmarsness. There was a gap in the ridge through which I looked straight out to the Atlantic, and there in the middle distance was what I knew instinctively to be my island.

"It was perhaps a quarter of a mile long, low for the most part, but rising in the north to a grassy knoll beyond the reach of any tides. In parts it narrowed to a few yards' width, and the lower levels must often have been awash. But it was an island, not a reef, and I thought I could make out the remains of the monkish cell. I climbed Halmarsness, and there, with nesting skuas swooping angrily about my head, I got a better view. It was certainly my island, for the rest of the archipelago were inconsiderable skerries, and I realised that it might well be a resting-place for migrants, for the mainland cliffs were too thronged with piratical skuas and other jealous fowl to be comfortable for weary travellers.

"I sat for a long time on the headland looking down from the three hundred feet of basalt to the island half a mile off—the last bit of solid earth between me and Greenland. The sea was calm for Norland waters, but there was a snowy edging of surf to the skerries which told of a tide rip. Two miles farther south I could see the entrance to the famous Roost of Una, where, when tide and wind collide, there is a wall like a house, so that a small steamer cannot pass it. The only sign of human habitation was a little grey farm in the lowlands toward the Roost, but the place was full of the evidence of man—a herd of Norland ponies, each tagged with its owner's name—grazing sheep of the piebald Norland breed—a broken barbed-wire fence that drooped over the edge of the cliff. I was only an hour's walk from a telegraph office, and a village which got its newspapers not more than three days late. It was a fine spring noon, and in the empty bright land there was scarcely a shadow... All the same, as I looked down at the island I did not wonder that it had been selected for attention by the saga-man and had been reputed holy. For it had an air of concealing something, though it was as bare as a billiard-table. It was an intruder, an irrelevance in the picture, planted there by some celestial caprice. I decided forthwith to make my camp on it, and the decision, inconsequently enough, seemed to me to be something of a venture.

"That was the view taken by John Ronaldson, when I talked to him after dinner. John was the post-mistress's son, more fisherman than crofter, like all Norlanders, a skilful sailor and an adept at the dipping lug, and noted for his knowledge of the western coast. He had difficulty in understanding my plan, and when he identified my island he protested.

"'Not Skule Skerry!' he cried. 'What would take ye there, man? Ye'll get a' the birds ye want on Halmarness and a far better bield. Ye'll be blawn away on the skerry, if the wund rises.'

"I explained to him my reasons as well as I could, and I answered his fears about a gale by pointing out that the island was sheltered by the cliffs from the prevailing winds, and could be scourged only from the south, south-west, or west, quarters from which the wind rarely blew in May. 'It'll be cauld,' he said, 'and wat.' I pointed out that I had a tent and was accustomed to camping. 'Ye'll starve'—I expounded my proposed methods of commissariat. 'It'll be an ill job getting ye on and off'—but after cross-examination he admitted that ordinarily the tides were not difficult, and that I could get a row-boat to a beach below the farm I had seen—its name was Sgurravoe. Yet when I had said all this he still raised objections, till I asked him flatly what was the matter with Skule Skerry.

"'Naebody gangs there,' he said gruffly.

"'Why should they?' I asked. 'I'm only going to watch the birds.'

"But the fact that it was never visited seemed to stick in his throat and he grumbled out something that surprised me. 'It has an ill name,' he said. But when I pressed him he admitted that there was no record of shipwreck or disaster to account for the ill name. He repeated the words 'Skule Skerry' as if they displeased him. 'Folk dinna gang near it. It has aye had an ill name. My grandfather used to say that the place wasna canny.'

"Now your Norlander has nothing of the Celt in him, and is as different from the Hebridean as a Northumbrian from a Cornishman. They are a fine, upstanding, hard-headed race, almost pure Scandinavian in blood, but they have as little poetry in them as a Manchester radical. I should have put them down as utterly free from superstition, and, in all my many visits to the islands I have never yet come across a folk-tale—hardly even a historical legend. Yet here was John Ronaldson, with his weather-beaten face and stiff chin and shrewd blue eyes, declaring that an innocent-looking island 'wasna canny,' and showing the most remarkable disinclination to go near it.

"Of course all this only made me keener. Besides, it was called Skule Skerry, and the name could only come from Earl Skuli; so it was linked up authentically with the oddments of information I had collected in the British Museum—the Jarla Saga and Adam of Bremen and all the rest of it. John finally agreed to take me over next morning in his boat, and I spent the rest of the day in collecting my kit. I had a small E.P. tent, and a Wolseley valise and half a dozen rugs, and, since I had brought a big box of tinned stuffs from the Stores, all I needed was flour and meal and some simple groceries. I learned that there was a well on the island, and that I could count on sufficient driftwood for my fire, but to make certain I took a sack of coals and another of peats. So I set off next day in John's boat, ran with the wind through the Roost of Una when the tide was right, tacked up the coast, and came to the skerry early in the afternoon.

"You could see that John hated the place. We ran into a cove on the east side, and he splashed ashore as if he expected to have his landing opposed, looking all the time sharply about him. When he carried my stuff to a hollow under the knoll which gave a certain amount of shelter, his head was always twisting round. To me the place seemed to be the last word in forgotten peace. The swell lipped gently on the reefs and the little pebbled beaches, and only the babble of gulls from Halmarsness broke the stillness.

"John was clearly anxious to get away, but he did his duty by me. He helped me to get the tent up, found a convenient place for my boxes, pointed out the well and filled my water bucket, and made a zareba of stones to protect my camp on the Atlantic side. We had brought a small dinghy along with us, and this was to be left with me, so that when I wanted I could row across to the beach at Sgurravoe. As his last service he fixed an old pail between two boulders on the summit of the knoll, and filled it with oily waste, so that it could be turned into a beacon.

"'Ye'll maybe want to come off,' he said, 'and the boat will maybe no be there. Kindle your flare, and they'll see it at Sgurravoe and get the word to me, and I'll come for ye though the Muckle Black Silkie himsel' was hunkerin' on the skerry.'

"Then he looked up and sniffed the air. 'I dinna like the set of the sky,' he declared. 'It's a bad weatherhead. There'll be mair wund than I like in the next four and twenty hours.'

"So saying, he hoisted his sail and presently was a speck on the water towards the Roost. There was no need for him to hurry, for the tide was now wrong, and before he could pass the Roost he would have three hours to wait on this side of the Mull. But the man, usually so deliberate and imperturbable, had been in a fever to be gone.

"His departure left me in a curious mood of happy loneliness and pleasurable expectation. I was left solitary with the seas and the birds. I laughed to think that I had found a streak of superstition in the granite John. He and his Muckle Black Silkie! I knew the old legend of the North which tells how the Finns, the ghouls that live in the deeps of the ocean, can on occasion don a seal's skin and come to land to play havoc with mortals. But *diablerie* and this isle of mine were worlds apart. I looked at it as the sun dropped, drowsing in the opal-coloured tides, under a sky in which pale clouds made streamers like a spectral *aurora borealis,* and I thought that I had stumbled upon one of those places where Nature seems to invite one to her secrets. As the light died the sky was flecked as with the roots and branches of some great nebular tree. That would be the 'weatherhead' of which John Ronaldson had spoken.

"I set my fire going, cooked my supper, and made everything snug for the night. I had been right in my guess about the migrants. It must have been about ten o'clock when they began to arrive—after my fire had died out and I was smoking my last pipe before getting into my sleeping-bag. A host of fieldfares settled gently on the south part of the skerry. A faint light lingered till after midnight, but it was not easy to distinguish the little creatures, for they were aware of my presence and did not alight within a dozen yards of me. But I made out bramblings and buntings and what I thought was the Greenland wheatear; also jack snipe and sanderling; and I believed from their cries that the curlew sandpiper and the whimbrel were there. I went to sleep in a state of high excitement, promising myself a fruitful time on the morrow.

"I slept badly, as one often does one's first night in the open. Several times I woke with a start under the impression that I was in a boat rowing swiftly with the tide. And every time I woke I heard the flutter of myriad birds, as if a velvet curtain was being slowly switched along an oak floor. At last I fell into deeper sleep, and when I opened my eyes it was full day.

"The first thing that struck me was that it had got suddenly colder. The sky was stormily red in the east, and masses of woolly clouds were banking in the north. I lit my fire with numbed fingers and hastily made tea. I could see the nimbus of seafowl over Halmarsness, but there was only one bird left on my skerry. I was certain from its forked tail that it was a Sabine's gull, but before I got my glass out it was disappearing into the haze towards the north. The sight cheered and excited me, and I cooked my breakfast in pretty good spirits.

"That was literally the last bird that came near me, barring the ordinary shearwaters and gulls and cormorants that nested round about Halmarsness. (There was not one single nest of any sort on the island. I had heard of that happening before in places which were regular halting grounds for migrants.) The travellers must have had an inkling of the coming weather and were waiting somewhere well to the south. For about 9 o'clock it began to blow. Great God, how it blew! You must go to the Norlands if you want to know what wind can be. It is like being on a mountain-top, for there is no high ground to act as a wind-break. There was no rain, but the surf broke in showers and every foot of the skerry was drenched with it. In a trice Halmarsness was hidden, and I seemed to be in the centre of a maelstrom, choked with scud and buffeted on every side by swirling waters.

"Down came my tent at once. I wrestled with the crazy canvas and got a black eye from a pole, but I managed to drag the ruins into the shelter of the zareba which John had built, and tumble some of the bigger boulders on it. There it lay, flapping like a sick albatross. The water got into my food boxes, and soaked my fuel, as well as every inch of my clothing... I had looked forward to a peaceful day of watching and meditation, when I could write up my notes; and instead I spent a morning like a Rugger scrum. I might have enjoyed it, if I hadn't been so wet and cold, and could have got a better lunch than some clammy mouthfuls out of a tin. One talks glibly about being 'blown off' a place, generally an idle exaggeration—but that day I came very near the reality. There were times when I had to hang on for dear life to one of the bigger stones to avoid being trundled into the yeasty seas.

"About two o'clock the volume of the storm began to decline, and then for the first time I thought about the boat. With a horrid sinking of the heart I scrambled to the cove where we had beached it. It had been drawn up high and dry, and its painter secured to a substantial boulder. But now there was not a sign of it except a ragged rope-end round the stone. The tide had mounted to its level, and tide and wind had smashed the rotten painter. By this time what was left of it would be tossing in the Roost.

"This was a pretty state of affairs. John was due to visit me next day, but I had a cold twenty-four hours ahead of me. There was of course the flare he had left me, but I was not inclined to use this. It looked like throwing up the sponge and confessing that my expedition had been a farce. I felt miserable, but obstinate, and, since the weather was clearly mending, I determined to put the best face on the business, so I went back to the wreckage of my camp, and tried to tidy up. There was still far too much wind to do anything with the tent, but the worst of the spindrift had ceased, and I was able to put out my bedding and some of my provender to dry. I got a dry jersey out of my pack, and, as I was wearing fisherman's boots and oilskins, I managed to get some slight return of comfort. Also at last I succeeded in lighting a pipe. I found a corner under the knoll which gave me a modicum of shelter, and I settled myself to pass the time with tobacco and my own thoughts.

"About three o'clock the wind died away completely. That I did not like, for a dead lull in the Norlands is often the precursor of a new gale. Indeed, I never remembered a time when some wind did not blow, and I had heard that when such a thing happened people came out of their houses to ask what the matter was. But now we had the deadest sort of calm. The sea was still wild and broken, the tides raced by like a mill-stream, and a brume was gathering which shut out Halmarsness—shut out every prospect except a narrow circuit of grey water. The cessation of the racket of the gale made the place seem uncannily quiet. The present tumult of the sea, in comparison with the noise of the morning, seemed no more than a mutter and an echo.

"As I sat there I became conscious of an odd sensation. I seemed to be more alone, more cut off, not only from my fellows but from the habitable earth, than I had ever been before. It was like being in a small boat in mid-Atlantic—but worse, if you understand me, for that would have been loneliness in the midst of a waste which was nevertheless surrounded and traversed by the works of man, whereas now I felt that I was clean outside man's ken. I had come somehow to the edge of that world where life is, and was very close to the world which has only death in it.

"At first I do not think there was much fear in the sensation—chiefly strangeness, but the kind of strangeness which awes without exciting. I tried to shake off the mood, and got up to stretch myself. There was not much room for exercise, and as I moved with stiff legs along the reefs I slipped into the water, so that I got my arms wet. It was cold beyond belief—the very quintessence of deathly Arctic ice, so cold that it seemed to sear and bleach the skin.

"From that moment I date the most unpleasant experience of my life. I became suddenly the prey of a black depression, shot with the red lights of terror. But it was not a numb terror, for my brain was acutely alive... I had the sense to try to make tea, but my fuel was still too damp, and the best I could do was to pour half the contents of my brandy flask into a cup and swallow the stuff. That did not properly warm my chilled body, but—since I am a very temperate man—it speeded up my thoughts instead of calming them. I felt myself on the brink of a childish panic.

"One thing I thought I saw clearly—the meaning of Skule Skerry. By some alchemy of nature, at which I could only guess, it was on the track by which the North exercised its spell, a cableway for the magnetism of that cruel frozen Uttermost, which man might penetrate but could never subdue or understand. Though the latitude was only 61°, there were folds of tucks in space, and this isle was the edge of the world. Birds knew it, and the old Northmen, who were primitive beings like the birds, knew it. That was why an inconsiderable skerry had been given the name of a conquering Jarl. The old Church knew it, and had planted a chapel to exorcise the demons of darkness. I wondered what sights the hermit, whose cell had been on the very spot where I was cowering, had seen in the winter dusks.

"It may have been partly the brandy acting on an empty stomach, and partly the extreme cold, but my brain, in spite of my efforts to think rationally, began to run like a dynamo. It is difficult to explain my mood, but I seemed to be two persons—one a reasonable modern man trying to keep sane and scornfully rejecting the fancies which the other, a cast-back to something elemental, was furiously spinning. But it was the second that had the upper hand... I felt myself loosed from my moorings, a mere waif on uncharted seas. What is the German phrase? *Urdummheit*—Primal Idiocy? That is what was the matter with me. I had fallen out of civilisation into the Outlands and was feeling their spell... I could not think, but I could remember, and what I had read of the Norse voyagers came back to me with horrid persistence. They had known the outland terrors—the Sea Walls at the world's end, the Curdled Ocean with its strange beasts. Those men did not sail north as we did, in steamers, with modern food and modern instruments, huddled into crews and expeditions. They had gone out almost alone, in brittle galleys, and they had known what we could never know.

"And then, I had a shattering revelation. I had been groping for a word and I suddenly got it. It was Adam of Bremen's '*proxima Abysso.*' This island was next door to the Abyss, and the Abyss was that blanched world of the North which was the negation of life.

"That unfortunate recollection was the last straw. I remember that I forced myself to get up and try again to kindle a fire. But the wood was still too damp, and I realised with consternation that I had very few matches left, several boxes having been ruined that morning. As I staggered about I saw the flare which John had left for me, and had almost lit it. But some dregs of manhood prevented me—I could not own defeat in that babyish way—I must wait till John Ronaldson came for me next morning. Instead I had another mouthful of brandy, and tried to eat some of my sodden biscuits. But I could scarcely swallow; this infernal cold, instead of rousing hunger, had given me only a raging thirst.

"I forced myself to sit down again with my face to the land. You see, every moment I was becoming more childish. I had the notion—I cannot call it a thought—that down the avenue from the North something terrible and strange might come. My nervous state must have been pretty bad, for though I was cold and empty and weary I was scarcely conscious of physical discomfort. My heart was fluttering like a scared boy's; and all the time the other part of me was standing aside and telling me not to be a damned fool... I think that if I had heard the rustle of a flock of migrants I might have pulled myself together, but not a blessed bird had come near me all day. I had fallen into a world that killed life, a sort of Valley of the Shadow of Death.

"The brume spoiled the long northern twilight, and presently it was almost dark. At first I thought that this was going to help me, and I got hold of several of my half-dry rugs, and made a sleeping-place. But I could not sleep, even if my teeth had stopped chattering, for a new and perfectly idiotic idea possessed me. It came from a recollection of John Ronaldson's parting words. What had he said about the Black Silkie—the Finn who came out of the deep and hunkered on this skerry? Raving mania! But on this lost island in the darkening night, with icy tides lapping about me, was any horror beyond belief?

"Still, the sheer idiocy of the idea compelled a reaction. I took hold of my wits with both hands and cursed myself for a fool. I could even reason about my folly. I knew what was wrong with me. I was suffering from *panic*—a physical affection produced by natural causes, explicable, though as yet not fully explained. Two friends of mine had once been afflicted with it; one in a lonely glen in the Jotunheim, so that he ran for ten miles over stony hills till he found a saeter and human companionship: the other in a Bavarian forest, where both he and his guide tore for hours through the thicket till they dropped like logs beside a highroad. This reflection enabled me to take a pull on myself and to think a little ahead. If my troubles were physical then there would be no shame in looking for the speediest cure. Without further delay I must leave this God-forgotten place.

"The flare was all right, for it had been set on the highest point of the island, and John had covered it with a peat. With one of my few remaining matches I lit the oily waste, and a great smoky flame leapt to heaven.

"If the half-dark had been eery, this sudden brightness was eerier. For a moment the glare gave me confidence, but as I looked at the circle of moving water evilly lit up all my terrors returned... How long would it take John to reach me? They would see it at once at Sgurravoe—they would be on the look-out for it—John would not waste time, for he had tried to dissuade me from coming—an hour—two hours at the most...

"I found I could not take my eyes from the waters. They seemed to flow from the north in a strong stream, black as the heart of the elder ice, irresistible as fate, cruel as hell. There seemed to be uncouth shapes swimming in them, which were more than the flickering shadows from the flare... Something portentous might at any moment come down that river of death... Someone...

"And then my knees gave under me and my heart shrank like a pea, for I saw that the someone had come.

"He drew himself heavily out of the sea, wallowed for a second, and then raised his head and, from a distance of five yards, looked me blindly in the face. The flare was fast dying down, but even so at that short range it cast a strong light, and the eyes of the awful being seemed to be dazed by it. I saw a great dark head like a bull's—an old face wrinkled as if in pain—a gleam of enormous broken teeth—a dripping beard—all formed on other lines than God has made mortal creatures. And on the right of the throat was a huge scarlet gash. The thing seemed to be moaning, and then from it came a sound—whether of anguish or wrath I cannot tell—but it seemed to be the cry of a tortured fiend.

"That was enough for me. I pitched forward in a swoon, hitting my head on a stone, and in that condition three hours later John Ronaldson found me.

"They put me to bed at Sgurravoe with hot earthenware bottles, and the doctor from Voss next day patched up my head and gave me a sleeping draught. He declared that there was little the matter with me except shock from exposure, and promised to set me on my feet in a week.

"For three days I was as miserable as a man could be, and did my best to work myself into a fever. I had said not a word about my experience, and left my rescuers to believe that my only troubles were cold and hunger, and that I had lit the flare because I had lost the boat. But during these days I was in a critical state. I knew that there was nothing wrong with my body, but I was gravely concerned about my mind.

"For this was my difficulty. If that awful thing was a mere figment of my brain then I had better be certified at once as a lunatic. No sane man could get into such a state as to see such portents with the certainty with which I had seen that creature come out of the night. If, on the other hand, the thing was a real presence, then I had looked on something outside natural law, and my intellectual world was broken in pieces. I was a scientist, and a scientist cannot admit the supernatural. If with my eyes I had beheld the monster in which Adam of Bremen believed, which holy men had exorcised, which even the shrewd Norlanders shuddered at as the Black Silkie, then I must burn my books and revise my creed. I might take to poetry or theosophy, but I would never be much good again at science.

"On the third afternoon I was trying to doze, and with shut eyes fighting off the pictures which tormented my brain. John Ronaldson and the farmer of Sgurravoe were talking at the kitchen door. The latter asked some question, and John replied—

"'Aye, it was a wall-ross and nae mistake. It cam ashore at Gloop Ness and Sandy Fraser hae gotten the skin of it. It was deid when he found it, but no long deid. The puir beast would drift south on some floe, and it was sair hurt, for Sandy said it had a hole in its throat ye could put your nieve in. There hasna been a wall-ross come to Una since my grandfather's day.'

"I turned my face to the wall and composed myself to sleep. For now I knew that I was sane, and need not forswear science."

THE THIRD INTERNE

Idwal Jones

Idwal Jones (1887–1964) was born in Wales, but spent the majority of his life in the US after his parents relocated to Pennsylvania in 1902. In 1918 Jones was drawn to California by the gold rush and after stints as a prospector and rancher made a living from writing, initially as a journalist, before broadening out to fiction and later screenwriting. His work, as the *New York Times* put it in Jones's obituary, was characterised by a "vast vocabulary, a turn for humour and a haunting sense of magic".

"The Third Interne" was published in *Weird Tales*, the seminal US pulp magazine that introduced the world to H. P. Lovecraft's Cthulhu mythos and its many imitations. *Weird Tales* contains a number of stories on Arctic and Antarctic themes (see also Leahy's and Ferguson's stories in this volume), though Lovecraft's classic Antarctic story "At the Mountains of Madness" was rejected. Jones's story is set in Yarmolinsk Prison at the edge of the Arctic Circle in Russia. The location appears to be fictional; it may well be that Jones concocted his setting from the name of his contemporary Avrahm Yarmolinsky, a prominent translator and academic in New York. As a tale of mad science and the far north, "The Third Interne" carries an echo of Mary Shelley's *Frankenstein*. In this lineage, it's not the land (and sea and ice) itself that holds the horror, but rather its function as a place outside the established limits of civilisation where darker enterprises might secretly unfold.

Doctor Alexis Garshin poured himself a glass of wine, sank deep into his leathern armchair, and watched the hearth-flames through the haze of an excellent cigar. Outside, the wind howled morosely like a thief. A blizzard had come up from the tundra, and it was plastering the windows with gobbets of snow. Certainly, Yarmolinsk Prison, near the Arctic line, was the most desolate the little Government inspector had yet visited. A man could very well go mad in the solitude. But its chief, Doctor Melchior Pashev, found it a heaven: nobody to trouble him, all the time he wanted to carry on his researches in biology, a fair salary, and little to do; for the prison and its hospital rarely held more than a dozen souls, beyond the staff of five. Garshin, a neurologist himself, admired him greatly.

Pashev had just gone out, to visit a dying trapper up the river a way, excusing himself for leaving his guest so hastily, but he would return in an hour, and dinner would keep. A bleak night, and Garshin shuddered at the idea of facing that howling wind, with snow in his teeth. Himself, he rather loved comfort. But a restful hour would do him good, and there was nobody afoot in this wing of the prison.

The door opened. A young man entered—a pallid, tousle-haired young man, with the burning eyes of a fanatic. A theological student, Garshin thought.

"Good evening, sir," said Garshin. "Doctor Pashev has gone out for an hour."

"He is gone for ever," said the young man, closing the door. "He is never coming back."

"Indeed?" queried Garshin. "I might even say, you surprize me."

"Now is my opportunity to give word to humanity, to the outside world, from which I have been a prisoner for two years," began the young man, drawing up a chair and fixing his eyes on Garshin. "Listen to me:

"I am the third interne. There were two, and the woman, Katerina Ivanovna. We came here from the University of Astrakhan, where a small band of us had devoted ourselves to the study of the brain and the nervous system. Our God was the great Pavlov, promulgator of the theory of the conditioned reflex. He received us once, and we stayed with him a month. Then we left, because we had discovered a far greater scientific man than he—Doctor Melchior Pashev, the brilliant worker in neurology.

"You probably know nothing about him, for you must be an engineer. I can see that, because your face is not hard. Sir, with all due respect to you, you are an infant in learning compared to Pashev. He is as aloof as an icy summit of the Alps; he dwells in the realm of pure brain; human beings are nothing to him but matter to dissect. He would immolate his own mother on the altar of science. But he is a master. Pavlov, Einstein, Metchnikoff—not one of these is worthy to latch his shoes or fetch in his shaving-water.

"We read at Astrakhan his report on the spinal accessory nerve, proving that it not only controls the motor fibres of the larynx but some of the fibres of the heart as well. This is only a trifle in the vast researches of the man, who became at once the most renowned thinker in the world.

"Pavlov's experiments on dogs were child's play, sir. Pashev began where Pavlov left off, and went to an astronomical height beyond him. He cut off the head of a mastiff, and kept it alive, functioning beautifully, for three years. It barked, drank water, blinked its eyes with affection, and showed all the normal reactions of a canine, save that it had no body.

"Our enthusiasm when we read of this knew no bounds. It made us delirious with admiration. Here was a genius on the track of the larger synthesis, who would crack open the last secrets of life, make himself the mightiest genius that ever was born. We would go to him and beg him to take us on as his apprentices. The two friends, Benno and Nicolai Suvorin, my fiancée, who was Katerina Ivanovna, and myself.

"So we pooled our funds, borrowed money right and left and came here to Yarmolinsk, half starved, weary and more dead than alive, and he took us in. An epidemic of bubonic plague had decimated the province, all the nurses and internes in this hospital had died, and so had Doctor Plotkin, Pashev's assistant. He died right in the chair you are sitting in. Don't start, sir. It all happened three years ago.

"We began working. We tended the sick, swept the wards, buried the dead, did all the menial work that came to hand; and at night studied in the dissecting-room, working with the great man himself. It was Katerina Ivanovna, with whom I was in love, and I who worked out with him the theory, first proposed by the learned Bengali, Professor Gobind Lal, that the ganglia send out their own impulses.

"I know I am obscure, sir, but you will never know how indefatigably we toiled, like slaves, devotedly, eager to serve the man we idolised, feeling rewarded enough that he tolerated us about him.

"But Katerina was devoted to me, also. We had our plans. After two years we were to go to Moscow and start up in practise as specialists on the brain. Renown and fortune would be ours. I would be professor at Moscow University, Katerina my assistant, and we would care for nothing but each other, our science and music. Katerina was a fine pianist, and kept her skill fresh, practising an hour a day before she went to her routine in the ward, which was as early as five in the morning.

"We mastered that dog's head. Pashev had now gone beyond that, and was having success in keeping alive the head of a chimpanzee. His device was most ingenious. The head was mounted on a glass base. The facial, auditory, ocul-motor nerves—all the nerves of the head were given stimuli and nourishment by a fine series of magnetic networks, terminating in a cell-box. The circulatory system was kept going by a delicate motor and pump. And to crown all, there was Pashev's masterpiece, a chain of ganglia, made of rubber and platinum, which took the place of the spinal cord.

"That chimpanzee's head roared, opened its mouth, blinked at the light, winced at a mirror flash or the prick of a pin. It was as alive as mine. Nicolai and Benno, bereft of all interest in life save this tremendous achievement, worshipped Pashev more than ever. They bowed to him, shrinking in awe. It went far beyond idolatry.

"One day they came to him and pleaded. 'You cannot find out by the head of an anthropoid ape what the conscious brain is doing. If it were a man's head, it could talk back to you. Think of the service such a head would do for pure science!'

"'Well?' said Pashev.

"'We offer ourselves to you for experimentation.'

*

178

"They meant it. Even Pashev was moved, touched almost to tears of joy at the offer. He tried to dissuade them, spoke to them for nearly five minutes. But they were insistent. They had no relatives, no ties of any kind, no love for anything but science. So Pashev agreed. The decapitation was done in the operating-room. The heads were immediately removed to glass bases, the severed edges cauterised, and the wires and arterial tubes and ganglia fibres, already prepared, were attached.

"Where was I? Sir, I fell ill of a brain fever and was confined for three weeks. The horror of it was too much for me. That was my way of escape, swooning to the floor when I learned Pashev had agreed to do this favour for Nicolai and Benno, my friends.

"I recovered, but it was weeks and weeks before I was myself, and I had fears that I should go mad. Insanity has long been a matter of interest to me, sir. But, as I said, my health and mental poise returned, with reason unshaken.

"What hurt me was the horror, the contempt with which Katerina now viewed me. She regarded me as a renegade to science, a coward, a pitiful wretch, unfit to love. It was another blow to me, but you never know the depth of a woman's forgiveness, and in time she loved me again.

"So we had rather a happy life, sometimes radiantly happy, especially when of a winter evening—the nights are long here at Yarmolinsk, sir—she would play on the piano for us, a little Schubert or a folk-song of our Astrakhan land. Pashev had a vulnerable spot in his armour: he was susceptible to the charms of music, and he would listen to Katerina play or sing, listen to her by the hour, elbows on his knee, his eyes fixed on her lovely face. I believe, sir, that all scientific men should cultivate one of the arts, else their imagination becomes atrophied. Darwin, to the end of his days, never ceased to regret that he had lost all taste for poetry. I have always admired Einstein for his devotion to the violin. And Professor Gobind Lal for his delight in painting little water-colours.

"I sometimes imagined the two were in love—merely a fancy of mine, but it shadowed my spirits often, though it went as swiftly as it came. Pashev, my idol, was beyond such weakness, and Katerina was loyal to me.

"It was my task to minister to the two heads, to see that the pumps and the cells were functioning as they should. You, as an engineer, sir, will appreciate the importance of my task. It was Pashev who made all the notes, who conversed with Nicolai and Benno, holding to their barely-moving lips a microphone attached to a device strapped to his ears. They spoke of how they felt, what their reactions were to heat and cold, to the prick of a pin, the flash of a mirror. They spoke only of matters of laboratory interest; for them the rest of the world did not exist. Were they happy, you ask? I presume so. They were like souls that had attained Nirvana, beyond good and evil, beyond all feeling save response to sensory stimuli by eye, ear and the nerves of the skin.

"'They never did have much imagination,' Pashev said once, coldly, as if disappointed. 'A woman, now—ah, what help one could get out of a woman!'

"Katerina spoke at once. With the light of a fanatical devotion for an ideal in her eyes she spoke to Pashev, offering herself; nay, insisting that he decapitate her and add one more chapter to his great work on the sensory reactions of the head *sans corpus*. I froze with horror, then went mad again. I can still see the pity on the face of the doctor, the joy and pride of the master whose pupil has come up to his highest expectations.

"For weeks I was ill, lost to the world, and when I returned, feeble, to my work, Katerina was gone. Her body was gone, but her head was on the heavy glass shelf, alongside that of Nicolai.

"You look horror-stricken, sir, and I can well understand how you feel. Light your cigar. See, your hand is shaking. Perhaps you now get an inkling of the hell I have lived through, and the bitter disillusion of my life when I found that my idol was a fiend, a demon out of the bottomless pit.

"Every night I say good-bye to the heads of the only human beings I ever loved. Why did my heart turn against Pashev? Ah, I must tell you. But don't stare at me so, your frighten me. I was in the laboratory alone one night, going through with a candle, when I heard a voice. It was Katerina's.

"'Coward!' she was saying. 'Coward! Here we all are but you. Ah, what a fool you were, and blind! I loved only Doctor Pashev. He seduced me the very night I came.'

"I fled past them with the candle, gibbering, my head turned so I shouldn't see the pity in the eyes of Nicolai and Benno, who knew the truth all along. And upstairs I wondered what they were saying to each other in the darkness. I heard them laugh! A laugh of contempt!"

"My dear friend, here I am!" In the doorway stood Doctor Pashev, tall, benevolent and smiling, his fur coat whitened with snow.

"I am happy to tell you the trapper will pull through, after all."

The pallid young man had risen, then fell to the floor in a convulsion. It was an attack, Garshin observed, of hystero-epilepsy, an interesting case. Pashev stooped at once and carried the victim out of the room. When he returned, the Government inspector said to him, firmly:

"Doctor Pashev, you must allow me to go into your laboratory for a minute."

"Certainly. There is the door, to the left."

Garshin entered and moved to the heavy glass mantelpiece. It held nothing but three skulls, which he lifted curiously. He could find no tubes nor wires nor any attachment. They were old, dust-covered, marked with ink, as if they had been kept there for years and years. He left the laboratory, thoughtful. The tale was naught but a figment of the imagination.

"I suppose," said Pashev, lighting a cigarette, "that poor fellow has been telling you some weird story about heads and some woman he loved, eh?"

"Yes. He had me on edge for an hour. I don't think I was ever so frightened in my life. Reminded me I had nerves, after all."

"He tells the story well," said Pashev, sadly, "because he has told it often—to everyone who comes here. It is rather pitiful. He came here three years ago with two youths, friends of his, and a young woman that he loved, to assist me during that distressful outbreak of the plague. The three died inside of a week. The shock to him was permanent. But he is harmless, and quite a help to me in the laboratory."

A servant entered with a large tray.

"Ah, here comes our belated dinner," said Pashev. "Let us sit down. There's nothing like a sledge-ride to give a fillip to one's appetite. Pigeons and claret! We do ourselves well, here. Your health, my dear friend!"

IQSINAQTUTALIK PIQTUQ: THE HAUNTED BLIZZARD

Aviaq Johnston

Aviaq Johnston (1992–) is an Inuk writer from Nunavut, Canada's most northerly territory, which extends up to around five hundred miles of the North Pole. Johnston is best known for her young adult fiction inspired by traditional Inuit storytelling, most notably the award-winning *Those Who Run in the Sky* (2017), which relates the adventures of the shaman Pitu, "lost in the world of the spirits" following a snowstorm.

"Iqsinaqtutalik Piqtuq: The Haunted Blizzard" forms part of an anthology of Arctic horror stories titled *Taaqtumi*, meaning "In the Dark" in Inuktitut, one of Canada's main Inuit languages. Indigenous horror more broadly has started to receive serious critical attention in North America. In many cases there is a strong link between the Indigenous experience of historical trauma and the narrative tropes of horror fiction. As the Tuscarora First Nations writer Alicia Eliot notes, "many non-Indigenous horror writers depict situations that Indigenous people have already weathered—such as apocalyptic viral outbreaks that decimate whole populations". There are also notable connections between Indigenous folklore and horror. Inuit stories are full of menacing creatures and spectral entities, as part of a rich tradition of orature that also has a practical function in providing cautionary tales for children growing up in extreme conditions.

"Iqsinaqtutalik Piqtuq: The Haunted Blizzard" takes place in the modern world of the Canadian Arctic, but explores older and deeper energies in the land and air.

The wind blows without mercy against the building, making the students chatter with excitement. We ignore the teacher and run to the big, turquoise-trimmed windows. Looking outside, we see the telltale signs of a blizzard: the growing snowdrifts, the snow blowing across the ground, people struggling to walk against the wind. We also see—well, *don't* see is more accurate—other signs of the blizzard. Buildings and landmarks missing on the horizon as the approaching storm obscures them in its white and violent embrace.

There is a high-pitched *beep*, then the PA system crackles as the voice of the school secretary comes out alternating languages from Inuktitut to English. "Due to the sudden change in weather, school is cancelled until further notice. For students with older siblings at the high school, you must wait to be picked up before leaving. Please notify a parent or guardian once you arrive safely at home!"

Anything that our teacher may have said is lost as all thirty of us exclaim in delight and rush out of the classroom to get our jackets on and leave. Within moments, I am bundled up into my snow pants, my winter boots, and the parka my auntie made for me this year.

A stampede of students storms out of the school from all exits. I am among the grade sevens, the last grade before we move on to the high school uptown. We are at that age where we are old enough to leave the school on our own, even if we have a sibling at the high school.

We burst from the recess door where a playground is protected by the u-shape of the school's courtyard. We usually call it the kindergarten playground because it is safer and easier for teachers to watch as they shiver in their Canada Goose parkas. The day is already darkening, as we barely have sunlight for more than a couple hours in the winter. A twilight has taken its place in the sky.

The playground is nearly abandoned as the younger kids in lower grades wait inside for their parents or siblings to pick them up, and other older kids leave through other exits with more direct paths home. We older kids run in haphazard directions, excited to go home to do whatever we want: watch TV without parental or sibling intervention, eat all the snacks left in the fridge or cupboards, sneak around to see what our parents might be hiding in their bedrooms.

The wind blows sharp snow pellets against my face. It stings my eyes, but my body is filled with such jubilance that I don't care. Ulii, Nita, and I all run toward our section of town together. We live near the breakwater on the shoreline, the *iksarvik*. Our houses are all close enough together that we can get most of the way home before splitting up.

Ulii is the first to separate. Her brother is smoking a cigarette on their porch, bundled into a shabby coat. He must be freezing. He isn't wearing gloves or mitts, and as Ulii arrives at the steps, we can hear him berating her for no reason, as he always does.

The storm continues to thicken as Nita and I keep trudging home. We stopped running just outside the playground, our excitement dwindling, and we are now leaning forward into the wind. Our heads are turned to the ground, our hands holding onto the fur trim of our hoods to keep the wind from blowing them off our heads. We slide from the middle of the road where the wind is strongest to walkways between houses where there is more cover.

We reach Nita's house next. Its humble frame is surrounded by hunting equipment strewn across the ground. The equipment had been tied onto her grandfather's *qamutiik*, but the wind has loosened the grip of the rope, and the tools are being swept away. Her grandfather's husky is bundled into a ball on the porch to stay warm.

Nita's grandmother is staring out the window, waiting for her arrival. Once she spots us outside, she rushes to open the door.

"*Atii, tuavi!*" she calls out in Inuktitut. She can't speak English. "Come on, hurry up!" is what she said.

Nita rushes up the stairs and I continue on my way home, but her grandmother calls out to me again. "Inu!" she calls. "Stay with us! It's too dangerous... this storm is full of bad things!"

"I'm okay, Grandmother!" I answer in Inuktitut. Having grown up copying Nita, I call her Grandmother, too. "I will be home soon!" I tell her.

She keeps calling after me, but I've gone too far. The wind distorts and carries her words away.

I walk around a mound of snow built up by snowploughs. The wind rests for a second, and I finally look up from the path I know by heart. I can see my house from here, elevated a metre off the ground on stilts drilled deep into the permafrost.

In the fleeting quiet, something feels wrong. I stop walking for a moment and look at the path ahead of me. Everything seems normal. I look behind, and there's nothing—

Wait.

There's a shadow.

Something squeals from my throat and I start running. The wind soon picks up speed and sharpens, piercing my ears as I run.

I remember what Nita's grandmother shouted at me, and I want to kick myself for not listening. Her voice echoes in my mind. *This storm is full of bad things.*

There are blizzards all year long. Sometimes they come only once a month, but often they come more frequently. Sometimes they destroy things in town, blow the doors and roofs off buildings, cover tracks in the snow that hunters need to follow on their way home, and bury precious equipment until the snow melts in the summer.

This blizzard is different though. Elders tell us stories about blizzards all the time, about their danger and about the things they do to our homes and our people. Once in a while in Inuktitut class, an elder will tell us about a storm that fits itself in among the others. Once in a long time—years and decades in between—this blizzard comes back. It roams through our land, bringing something with it. The elders never tell us what it brings; ghosts or creatures or perhaps it is simply the shadow that I caught a glimpse of in that second. They just say to find shelter and to never be alone.

This storm is full of bad things. She had tried to warn me.

I am running, but barely moving. The path behind my house feels like it's turning into a tunnel as the wind picks up again, and I'm fighting against the air.

I hazard another look back, and the shadow is still there. It looks like a person. It's following me, but the wind is slowing it down, too.

Finally I am close enough that I can touch the side of my house. Reaching the stairs, my feet finally have traction and I climb up the steps as quickly as I can. I lock the door as I make it inside, flicking on the porch light.

A gust of wind howls up the stairs outside. There are no windows in the porch, so I can't see if the shadow has followed me here. I'm too scared to move as I lean against the door, hoping the lock and my weight can keep me safe and secure. The house is empty and dark.

Ring! Ring! Ring!

The phone rings from the living room. I'm still stuck in the porch, frozen.

What was it?

The phone keeps ringing until the answering machine picks it up. After the beep, I hear my mother's voice. "*Panik?* Call me when you get home, okay? I'm stuck at work. The weather is too bad outside."

My mom's voice makes me feel safe again, so I head to the living room still wearing all my outdoor clothing. I flick on each light I pass: the hallway, the kitchen, the living room.

I dial my mom's office number. She answers on the first ring. "Panik?" she says.

"Hi *Anaana*," I say.

"Are you home?" she asks, but she gives me no time to answer because she already knows I'm home. She saw our phone number on the caller ID. "Inu, are you alone? *Ataata* is going to try to get home, but he has to wait for everyone to leave so he can lock up at work."

"Yeah, I'm alone." I tell her.

"Okay," she says. The wind is booming against the house. It's getting harder to hear her voice. "You have to stay inside; it's too dangerous. I already heard that the roof of the Northern is being blown off."

"Yup. Anaana?"

"Huh?" Anaana says, her relief at knowing I'm home safe has changed her apprehension to disinterest.

"I think I saw something when I was coming here," I say frantically. "There was a shadow and—"

"It was just someone trying to walk home in the blizzard, Inu." My mom's voice sounds frustrated. She sighs. "You and your imagination."

"I really saw it!" I say.

"*Taima*. That's enough." Her frustration thickens in her voice. "I'm already worried as it is. Ataata will be home soon."

"Okay," I say, but my stomach is sinking into my knees and my chest feels like it is being pushed down and squeezed tight. "Bye."

"I love you, Panik," she says before she hangs up the phone, all the way at the other end of our island town.

My mother doesn't know. She's too grown up to remember the scary parts of our land. The scary things that hide around us. She thinks that the land is nothing more than the science of the space around us, environment and nature. She thinks this is all that lives outside.

For some reason, elders and children know more than adults do, and I wonder why that is. They act like they know everything, as if everything has an explanation. At some point in their lives they forget the stories children are told, dismissing them as fairy tales and myths. They think that the scary women in the ice aren't real, or that the little folk that you can only see at sunset are just imaginary, or that giants never roamed the earth. Just like all adults, my mother has forgotten all those things the elders had passed down.

But... maybe it does make sense that it was just another person walking home in the blizzard. *Maybe* that makes sense.

I may have been confused. In my memory, I see a tall human-shaped figure, with long limbs, long hair, made entirely of blackness, of shadow.

But maybe my mom is right.

With my growing calm, I decide that my mom was probably right. My dad will be home soon anyway, and if adults are too blind to see the scary things around us, then maybe the scary things can't see adults either.

I turn on the TV and sit on the floor. Kids cartoons come on the screen. I don't even like them, but I don't want to change the channel. The cartoon is full of bright and vibrant colours, and I am beginning to forget the shadows I have seen.

Before long, the blizzard winds tear against the house, and suddenly, I am in darkness.

Power outage.

In the quiet I notice something. Utter silence. The wind outside isn't booming anymore. Through the open curtains I can see the gusting wind, but I can't hear its howling cries. In the silence, I notice a different sound emerge. A small, yet frantic sound. A clinking from somewhere inside the house.

Slowly, the sound of the wind picks back up and the small sound is lost in the noise.

Something seems wrong again. The hair stands up on the back of my neck and I look around, trying to find where the clinking noise is coming from. But I can't.

I look back to the TV and see myself reflected in the dim light coming through the window. The kitchen is visible in the TV's reflection as well, and for a moment I don't pay attention to it. The electricity always goes out for a bit during a blizzard. It's normal enough. I look back at the TV, willing it to turn back on...

Until I realise that there is a shape in the kitchen window. A shadow peering in.

The power comes back on, the lights shining bright as they return. Slowly, I look back to the kitchen window, but I don't see anything. I stand up and walk toward the hallway.

I look back at the door, brow furrowed and heart racing. For a moment, I don't seem to know what is wrong as I look at the dark porch. The winds are blowing as loud as ever, the noise deafening, but normal.

But...

Didn't I turn on the porch light?

I feel the breath catch in my throat, no more air coming in or out. I scream and run down the hall to my parents' bedroom, the farthest from the porch.

The door to their room is open and I am about to run straight inside, but something catches my attention. Staring past the room, to the back door that we never use, something is different about it. It's been closed and locked shut for years.

The doorknob is shaking, turning back and forth with urgency. That was the frantic little noise I had heard when the power was out. Whatever is outside, it is trying to come in through the door.

I am stranded. Maybe there is more than one of what I've seen, at both the door and the window? And somehow it turned off the porch light?

So... is it already inside?

I turn around and run toward the one bathroom in my house. There are no windows in there and it is the only room inside the house that locks. I slam the door shut, locking it.

But when I turn away from the door and see the shower curtain drawn, my heart stops. Neither I nor my parents ever leave the shower curtain splayed across the tub. Tears fall freely from my eyes.

I am stuck.

Truthfully, I don't know why I'm crying, sobbing, screaming in such terror. I don't know why the shower curtain is scaring me so. I don't know what hides on the other side.

Darkness extends out from behind the curtain, it dims the light to almost nothing. The wind is shaking my house violently, as if in a hurricane, a tornado, a flood, an avalanche. I can't see anything in the darkness, I can just feel the floor shaking beneath me as I crumple down, trembling as hard as the shaking house.

A voice I have never heard before speaks, scratchy and hoarse, "*Qanuikkavit?*" it says. "What's wrong?"

"*Anigit! Avani!*" I cry into its darkness. "Get out! Go away!"

A laugh echoes out, "*Qanuikkavit?*" It keeps asking.

There is a scratching noise, metal against metal, as the shower curtain is pushed aside.

SOUTH

A SECRET OF THE SOUTH POLE

Hamilton Drummond

Hamilton Drummond (1857–1935) is a little-known writer mainly of historical fiction, often with a supernatural twist. Apart from a steady stream of reviews of his fiction in the periodical press in the late nineteenth and early twentieth centuries, little material is available on his life today beyond the fact that he was born in Ireland and possibly buried in Tonbridge.

"A Secret of the South Pole", published in the *Windsor Magazine* in 1901, is a nautical mystery that draws on a long tradition of stories—factual, fictional and somewhere in between—about ghost ships: vessels adrift on the ocean without any (living) human inhabitants. In the annals of polar literature, Samuel Taylor Coleridge's "The Rime of the Ancient Mariner" (1798) provides one of the most notable spectral ships. After the mariner and his crew escape from Antarctic's "land of mist and snow", they are overjoyed to see a sail, only to discover a "naked hulk" on which DEATH and DEATH-IN-LIFE are busy playing dice. Poe's 1833 short story "MS Found in a Bottle" (1833) offers a similar scenario when the narrator arrives on board a weird ship with a crew, who, even if they are alive, are "utterly unconscious of his presence" and surrounded by "scattered mathematical instruments of the most quaint and obsolete construction". There is also a longstanding (unsubstantiated) legend of a ship, the *Jenny*, found by a whaler in the Drake Passage (north of Antarctica's South

Shetland Islands), with the Captain still sitting at his desk writing in his log, some seventeen years after his death. "A Secret of the South Pole" uses the trope of the derelict ship to play on the menace and mysteriousness long associated with southerly latitudes.

All Sloppleton knew him as "Cap'n Towson," and if I had my own suspicions that quartermaster, with a third mate's certificate, was nearer the mark, I kept my opinion to myself. The fiction—if it was a fiction—was an innocent one, and none of his making, nor, indeed, any business of mine.

The only claims I ever heard him urge were those of seamanship and experience. Of the first I am no judge, a ten-foot punt being the largest craft I have ever navigated; but the frank deference shown him by the fishermen and longshore sailor-folk argued that his claim was just. That he was a deep-water seaman I am certain; not simply because of his familiarity with sundry foreign ports of which I also had some knowledge, but there was that depth in the eye, that set and grave immobility of face, which are born of dealing with Nature in the bulk. The serious gravity of the sea begets itself in those who do business continually in great waters.

As to his experience, I have only himself as witness; but even when large allowance has been made for amplification and the imagination which is the gift of the sea, I hold the evidence to be sufficient. Those of my friends to whom I have retold his tales have not scrupled to call him liar, and certainly his stories were at times largely capable of disbelief. But for my part I always found it hard to doubt him; he was so circumstantial, so fluent, so calmly level, so credulous of himself. There was no assertiveness, no subtle doubt lurking in an appeal for belief, but just a quiet assurance that disarmed incredulity. Your habitual liar has a way of calling the gods to witness that is in itself suspicious. With Towson there was none of that. The thing was so because it was so. It was as if Galileo said the sun moved because it moved, and not all the Pope Urbans in the world could make it a lie.

Still, at times I almost had my doubts, and was inclined to think he had missed his generation and was a survival of the Arabian Nights. For instance, he had one story of a tidal wave, the precedent hollow of which burrowed so deep that it laid bare—but that is not the present story, and so may be left aside. Only, even with it, as Cap'n Towson told the tale, I declare I saw the oozy sludge of the sea's foundations creep up and up the hissing crystal surface of the watery mountain, until its foul and slimy blackness stained it to its summit. A lie? Well, maybe so—maybe so; but then, you did not hear Cap'n Towson tell the story, and I did. More truth lies in the way a thing is told than most men suppose, which is a subtle saying and needs some thinking out. We had become very good friends, we two, especially during ten days' wet weather.

Sloppleton is not a cheerful place in a grey drizzle, and a man wearies of the smell of twist tobacco and stale beer held in suspense in the atmosphere of the local taproom. These ten days, therefore, were mostly spent by the open window of my diggings, our boot heels on the wooden bench which lay by the wall, and ourselves sunk as far in the comfort of two armchairs as the hard padding of the shiny horsehair would permit.

But once—it was on the afternoon of the tenth day—a straggle of sunshine tempted us out into the sloppy road, and when the downpour recommenced, Cap'n Towson's cottage was the nearest shelter, and there we retreated. It was not the first time I had been his guest, and so the collected treasures of his seafaring life were more or less familiar. There were the usual birds of gay plumage under glass shades, the uncouth seashells, the fretted sprays of coral, the dreary conventional specimens which serve to keep green the memory of the retired merchant seaman. A ship's model was placed above the doorway, its spars awry, its thread ropes snapped and tangled. Over the mantelpiece there gaped a set of shark's jaws, topped by the blade of a swordfish, and perched on the carefully dusted Bible was the figure of a nodding mandarin.

They were all so obviously the matter-of-course possessions of such a man that I had never given them a second look; but now, as Cap'n Towson absented himself to hunt up the ingredients of a friendly grog, I wandered aimlessly round the room and took stock of its stale curiosities. One thing only struck me as an oddity, and that by reason of its inconsequence rather than its strangeness, and at it I was staring when Cap'n Towson returned with his liquid hospitality carefully balanced in the depths of a soup-plate; not, be it understood, what he would have called "awash," but I take it trays were at a premium.

"Ah!" said he, setting down the plate with a clang that drove the little mandarin into a passion of affirmation, "you're a deep one, you are. There you are at the Koe—I—nore first thing. That's the gem o' the whole kit, that is. I've always said I'll give the whole shanty to the man that tells me what it is, an' now's your chance, for what I say I stick to."

"It's a bit dark, Cap'n," I began.

"Oh! have all the light on the subject you can," and he chuckled as if at a joke. "I'll pull the blind up. There, what do you make of it now?"

To be frank, I didn't make much. It was an irregular, flattish fragment, perhaps two inches square, and slightly curved inwards at top and bottom. A stout thread held it in place against a piece of millboard, and the whole was framed and glazed like a picture. In colour it was greyish blue, and its surface smooth but dull. There was neither inscription nor mark upon it that I could see.

"Well?" and he shook me by the elbow with a kind of good-humoured, triumphant impatience. "Well?"

Tilting it so that the light—dim at the best, for the rain was coming down heavier than ever—fell upon it, I bent down and then drew back, in the approved fashion of a critic who is at a loss for an opinion and yet fears to show his ignorance.

"It is—that is to say, it looks like—metal?"

Cap'n Towson smacked his thigh noisily.

"The shanty's safe for this time. Guess again, mate."

But I shook my head. What was the use of guessing. There was no doubt that Cap'n Towson's mystery went beyond the mere composition of the fragment he preserved so carefully, and I said as much.

"You're right, sir; an' by gum! them that goes down to the sea in ships see mortal queer things. Now, there isn't a museum in the whole country has the equal to that scrapple of shucks there. Metal, says you? Well, maybe 'tis; then again, maybe it's glass, maybe it's pottery, an' maybe it's somethin' of all three, that we folks on our side of the world know nothin' about. I give you my word I don't know, and I never met the man as could tell me. That's a bit o' the South Pole, that is!" and again he chuckled, but checked himself. "But, by gum! it was no laughing matter. When I die, I'm a-goin' to leave it to the British Museum. I s'pose they'll pound it to bits to see what it's made of. Even then they won't be any the wiser, an' there's no more where that came from—at least, I hope not, if what I think came in it. We've trouble enough in the world without that. Well, let 'em pound. When that day comes I won't care. Mix your grog, an' I'll tell you how I came by it."

In the soup-plate were two long tumblers pushed one into the other, a small jug of water, and a bottle of rum three-parts full. Separating the tumblers, he handed me one, laid his thick, stumpy fingers round his own so that their lower line encircled the curve of the bottom, and filled the glass until the spirit rose level above the upper line of his forefinger. Then he handed me the bottle, and added about an equal quantity of water.

"Strict measure's my motter, Mr. Ward, strict measure. Then a man never drinks too much nor too little; the first is brutal and the second beastly. Here's luck! Now, sir, you'd best sit down, and—yes, I'll fill it again. In a manner, d'ye see, there's two yarns in it, and I'm not so sure where to begin. At the beginning? Easy said an' seems reasonable, but I ain't no circus rider. To spin two yarns at once is about as bad as to straddle a couple of barebacked horses. Sooner or later they'll part company, and then where are you? No, I'll drop the barque *Julia K. Anderson*, five weeks out from 'Frisco and bound round the Horn, much as she dropped me, and that's without so much as a 'By your leave,' an' begin where she left off with three of us—Tobias Clark, Joe Brady, an' myself—adrift in the Pacific. I was a fo'c'sle band those days, Mr. Ward, and I'm not ashamed of it. Why should I? It's a noble calling is the sea, and I reckon England sucks her Empire out o' the salt water. The fo'c'sle isn't the poop-deck, I know, an' there are some that sneer at a sailorman's ignorance; but mostly the fo'c'sle knows as much as the fo'c'sle wants to, and when I say we were about 110° West and 5° South, you'll know we were half distance between the Marquesas and the Galapagos. Thanks be to goodness! the ocean stood to her name, an' with the Line so near we had no cold to grumble at. How did we get there, an' in an open boat? Now, sir, that's the other yarn, and I'll tell it any day in the week; but what I'm talkin' of now is that sliver o' potsherd there in the frame, an' the sooner I get to it the sooner I'll be done.

"Bein' there, there was two things we might do, make east to the mainland or west to the islands, an' the drift o' the current settled it for us. No man of sense swots more in the tropics than he can help, and when God Almighty sets the sea drifting," and he raised his hand reverently as if in a salute, "why, it's only a fool that doesn't say 'Amen' an' be thankful. That means, d'ye see, we headed for the islands.

"A day an' a night we had made our westing, an' with the sudden coming o' the morning Brady woke me up.

"'Glory be!' says he, shaking me, 'the trip's over afore it's begun, an' good luck go with it! Look ye there!'

"With that I sat up, blinking an' gaping, for I had been sound as a top, an' my eyes were still glued with sleep, till he slewed me round an' pointed astern. 'Whoo-oop!' says be, dancing an' laughing an' crying all in one, like the mad Irishman he was; 'if that isn't the makings of land, oh! call me Bull.'

"By that I had my knee on the after thwart an' was staring east with my hands as telescope. The sun was up, an' a point or two to the north, so that the black spot was plain enough, being no more than live miles away, maybe four, the shimmer o' the sea in the sun makin' it hard to guess. Too plain, for I turns to Brady and says to him, sudden-like—

"'Bull!'

"My word! Mr. Ward, you should ha' seen his jaw drop, though at first he didn't catch on. "'What d'ye mean? Who's ye callin' names?'

"'What I say. Bull! Bull-calf, if ye like it better, an' a darned sight too good for ve. Don't you know a derelict when you see her?'

"By this time Clark had crawled out o' the bows, an' was on his hands an' knees between us, leaning over the starn.

"'Irish is right, an' Irish is wrong,' says he, 'which is a way them Irish have, an' makes it so hard to know when you've got 'em. She's a blamed hulk, that's what she is sure enough; but I guess'—Clark was a New Yorker—'I guess she's sound enough, for she rides high, an' a tight hulk is better'n a crank cockleshell any day in the week.'

"But that didn't satisfy Brady. Not that he kicked. No, sir, Brady was no fool till his fourth tot o' rum, but as he laid himself to his oar—me steerin'—I saw his face was sort o' vacant-like; an' he was mutterin', 'Bull, Bull,' slowly an' softly to himself, like a man tryin' to get the grip o' somethin' that beat him. It's not often a man gives himself away as badly as Brady did.

"Well, sir, as I say, I was steerin', an' little by little as the hulk bulked agin the sky, I liked its looks less an' less. 'Twasn't that it had no masts an' was as bare o' bulwarks as a canal barge. That was right enough in a derelict, an' I'd seen it from the first, though Brady in his hot haste had missed that they were missin'. No, it wasn't that the decks were swept as clean as if they'd been whittled bare with a jackknife, but it was the unchancy look of her.

"Such a craft I never saw in all my days. She was driftin' portside on, an' as she rose on the sky she was more like a brace o' narrow, two-storey cottages gone awash than a decent ship. High an' rounded at the bows, high an' rounded at the starn, an' low in the waist, with no kind of elbow room between the two. She had great square windows for ports, an' except for the ragged stumps o' two masts she was naked as a shell. There wasn't so much as a twisted end of a stay stickin' out from the side.

"When she was a little less'n a quarter of a mile off, I sang out, an' we lay to an' took stock.

"My! but her hull was smooth! The old man o' the 'Frisco hooker had been a bully for holystonin', but *Julia K.* never had her decks polished like the side walls an' gable ends o' them cottages; no, sir. Their smoothness was past words, an' fairly beat me; but Clark, the Yank, twigged it in a wink. I reckon he'd done some whalin' in his time.

"'Ice,' says he, 'an' whips of ice at that.'

"'Begorrah!' chips in Brady, with a grin. 'I hope she's some aboard. I could do with a bit in the grog this weather.'

"But neither Clark nor me laughed. The uncanny lumpishness of the thing bothered me.

"'Blame me if ever I saw such a craft,' says I.

"'Haven't ye?' says Brady. 'Well, faith! I have, or a half wan, anyhow. It was high an' dry on the Kerry coast, an' they do say it was there afore Crom'ell's time, bad cess to him!'"

"Ah! Cap'n Towson," interrupted I. "I have it now. She was Spanish."

"Maybe, sir, maybe. What we saw afterwards might ha' been Spanish, but Spain never made that mossel o' shucks there in the frame. Call her Spanish, Mr. Ward, though it makes no odds.

"What I've figured out is this. She went bust, say, 40° West an' the same North, an' the south-east arm o' the Gulf Stream bore her past the Azores, west o' the Cape Verdes, and so into the Guinea Channel. Then she got south into the Equatorial current, an' drifted west until the flow splits on San Roque, when down she came south again until she caught the Antarctic drift, an' crawled away east on the 40th parallel. Somewhere near Saint Paul's a wind took her, and away she went into the ice, where Clark made out she lay two hundred years an' more. Long or short, it's there, to the best o' my belief, that bit o' china-metal went aboard of her; though that, like the reckoning I've laid out for her, is nothin' better than guesswork. It's mighty little we know of what goes on in the pack-ice 'way south, an' one thing's sure, in the ice she was. The pulpy sleekness of her timbers proved that. For a while we sat eyeing her, then says Clark—

"'A corpse, boys, that's what she is—a corpse.'

"'A corpse that doesn't want no buryin',' answers Brady. 'Leastways, not till we've done with her. Here, skipper, give us a tot o' rum all round, an' let's go aboard. I've had as much of a half-inch plank as is good for me health.'

"But Clark had a word to say. 'She's a hundred years old, maybe two, maybe three; happen she's rotten.'

"'Rotten yourself!' cried Brady, swirling the boat round with a dash of his oar; 'look, how she floats. I'm for boarding her, anyhow. Sixteen hundred miles in an open boat, when I can have a sound bottom under me and a deck overhead? Not likely! Put your back in it, mate.'

"'Put your back in it,' said I, an' no more passed until we were squarely alongside the hulk. Still, for all Brady's talk, the more I saw, the less I liked. If it was as old as Clark said, then it must be the devil's own ship, surely, or it would have gone under long before. Then, again, Clark might be wrong, an' when I came to think of it that was worse. So there I hung in the wind, betwixt an' between it is an' it isn't. But Brady had no doubts.

"'Saints be good to us!' said he cheerfully, an' standing up on the thwart he gripped the edge of the port an' looked in—the upper port, you understand; the under one was close on the water's edge an' tight battened. Then 'Saints be good to us!' he said again, but as if he had more need of the goodness, an' wasn't so sure it was to be had for the asking.

"The sea was as calm as a lake, but where there's such a vast o' water there's always a rise an' fall. Not much of a swing it wasn't, but enough to tilt the port now up an inch or two, an' now down.

"'Well?' said Clark. 'Well?'

"But it wasn't until the hull had swung two or three times that Brady answered.

"'The skylight's covered over, but I'm thinking Davy Jones is aboard, for I see what's like a bundle o' clothes on the floor. Best shin up an' whip the tarpaulin off.'

"'If one shins up,' says I, 'we all shin up. We stick together, whether here or there.'

"'All it is,' says Brady, an' up he climbs, with the painter round the crook of his arm.

"The port gave him a foothold, an' from there he could get a grip o' the edge o' the deck; but, all the same, it was no easy job. Once on deck, he made the rope fast round the stump o' the mast, so that me an' Clark had an easy road.

"The sea takes a man to many a queer spot, Mr. Ward, but never to a queerer than that old hulk. Where we stood was more like the round top of a tower than a ship's deck, an' though I'm no more a coward than another, I'd have no stomach for a gale o' wind on such a craft. But the colour was queerer than the build. 'Twas all a greyish-white, smooth as an egg an' spongy like sodden cork, so spongy that our boots left the print o' the big nails clear up to the flat o' the sole, an' where Clark's was split at the heel there was the split showin' sharp an' clean with every tramp.

"'Ice,' says he again. 'Ice, an' freezin' an' thawin' and dryin' and soakin' an' freezin'. That's what that means.'

"The only part of the deck where we stood that wasn't as flush as the palm o' your hand was the skylight. It ran up the middle o' the poop an' was longish an' low. I reckon it served as a seat in the days the old scow wasn't a corpse. Brady was right when he said it was covered over, but 'twasn't with tarpaulins. Maybe they didn't have tarpaulins in those days. If not, they had what was as good, four or five, or perhaps eight or ten thicknesses o' canvas and blankets, but so matted that no man could tell which was one an' which was t'other, the rain an' the spray an' the wind an' the sun had beat them so solid. Tags o' cordage hangin' from the rings at the sides showed how they had been lashed, but the ropes had wore out long before, an' what held them in their place was a criss-cross o' chain, stout enough once maybe, but rusted to the fineness of a weddin' ring. The whole was a dirty, washed-out grey, the colour somethin' of a wasp's nest, an' the most corpse-like thing in the whole corpse ship.

"'Ice,' says Clark again, with a nod of his head at the skylight; 'all that was to keep the cold out; an' by gum! I guess they wanted it, every scrap!'

"'Then they don't want it no more,' says Brady. 'Be the Holy Fly! it's hot enough here. Let's have it off, bullies!'

"The chains were little better than streaks o' rust, an' so snapped with the first tug, but I tell you, Mr. Ward, that tug gave me the shivers. It was ghastly to think they hadn't been handled for maybe more than three hundred years, an' that the beggars who strained them were lyin' down below with mighty little on but their bones; but when it came to rippin' off the rotten canvas, that was ghastlier still. I give you my word it was like strippin' the dead, an' even now there are times when I lie awake o' nights that I can hear the soft rastle o' the rip o' the stuff; an' when I hear it, the skin of my back creeps an' I go cold down the spine.

"There was a grating, under the canvas, and glass under the grating, all covered thick with a woolly, soft dust like you get in the corners o' your pockets. The glass an' grating were both set in a frame, but the wood had shrunk with the heat. It stuck a bit, but no more than was natural, an' rather as if somethin' was suckin' at the glass. The edges seemed free enough, an', except for the suckin' back, it lifted out as easy as say 'Knife.' A bar of iron, still pretty stout, ran along the middle o' the skylight from end to end, holdin' the back o' the frame in place. Laying the glazed grating down on the deck, we looked inside.

"All that," said Cap'n Towson, breaking off suddenly, "all that is nothin'—at least, no more than any man might come across in five years' cruisin' over God's waters; but what came after was queer, mighty queer, that I'll admit.

"What with the portholes an' the open skylight, an' the sun blazing above, the cabin was as plain to be seen as the palm o' your hand. My word! but it was spick an' span. Of course, there was the raffle of odds an' ends lyin' round loose, for I take it sailormen were just sailormen three hundred years ago, an' had their easy-going ways much as they have now, but there warn't no dust to speak of. I tell you, Mr. Ward, that took my breath. All these years o' travel an' no dust to show for them! Why, you can't leave a cuddy a week but you could write your name on the chair backs. Yes, that bothered me; but what bothered me worse was to see a slim, queer-shaped bottle standin' on end on the table right under my nose, an' half full o' some brownish stuff. Now, what business had a bottle to be end up after jogging half round the world, an' rocked by Heaven only knows what gales o' wind? A slim, crank thing it was, too. We don't have the like of it nowadays, an' more's the pity it got broke. An' what business had the liquor lyin' in it all them years, an' never dryin' up? That, as Clark would say, rattled me, an' small wonder. It was a creepy thing to come on all of a sudden, an' in such a ghost of a craft, but there was more besides it. By the bottle was a tin platter, bright enough, so bright y'd say a cloth had wiped it the day before, an' on the platter was a lump o' ship's bread. It was like nothin' in the way o' hard tuck I ever saw, but ship's bread it was, an' no mistake. I tell you that staggered me. The bottle maybe was fixed somehow, an' the platter maybe was fixed; but what fixed a lump o' crusty, slippy hard tuck all these hundred years, an' the hulk driftin', driftin', through who knows what rastle an' tumble of seas? I don't know that Clark or Brady took notice. I reckon they were huntin' after the heaps o' clothes Irish had seen through the port, an' when I saw them peerin' an' stretchin' their necks I quit shiverin' an' followed their wake. Nor were the bundles far to seek. Three o' them there were, all the length but twice the girth o' a common man, so that when Clark said 'Ice' for the fourth time, I guess he was about right. You can bet it knows how to freeze south of 80°!

"They were bunched in a heap by the cuddy door, an' must have had three suits apiece on them; thin in the legs, with no breeches to speak of, puffed at the hips, an' with great heavy cloaks. The door was fast shut, an' I could see a thick bar across it, the ends fallin' into sockets beyond the posts, as if to stand against hard pressure.

"'For bears an' such vermin,' says Clark, who caught my eye. 'I guess them three was all that was left o' the ship's crew, an' so good people was scarce. The rest was in Kingdom Come.'

"I reckon he was about right, but I didn't answer. I was tryin' to puzzle it out for myself, an' the way they lay told a talc. They were all head-on to the door; they were all flat on their faces, with their arms stretched out an' their fingers clawin' at the floor. That meant they were makin' a bolt for the open when somethin' dropped them in their tracks, dropped them sudden an' dropped them sure. Just so, but what? what? That's what I asked myself, an' maybe the answer was that one held what looked like a crumple o' paper in his hand—whitey yellow it was; an' on the floor, a foot or two from their big boots, was a mash o' bluey grey stuff. That there stuck in the frame was the biggest mossel left, the rest was stamped into grit. They had no hats on—maybe they'd rolled off when they tumbled—an' their hair was longer than was common even for an old-time sailorman; but their ears peeped through the wisps, an' the shape o' them, an' the shape o' their hands, was as plump an' good as if they were havin' no more than a dog's snooze till the bo'sun whistled. I said as much to Clark.

"'Bo'sun?' says he; 'I guess Davy Jones was the last bo'sun that piped them to quarters. Tell you what, Towson; see that bluey grit there, an' what's in the chap's hand? I'll lay a dollar they picked up somethin' in the ice that scared them to death, an' it was in that smashed grit!'

"Maybe he was right. In my own belief the thing had been some kind of a hollow case, with more in it than what that hand gripped. Some kind of a gas, maybe, or fluid that turned to gas, an' in the turnin'—but, there, it's all guesswork.

"'When it comes to bettin',' says Brady, 'I'll bet I'm goin' below; an' as the door's battened, here's my road!'

"Leaning forward, he gripped the iron bar with his left hand, an' caught a grab o' the edge o' the skylight with his right to hoist himself up. But as his fingers closed inwards over the ledge he flung himself back with a yell.

"'Preserve us! What's that?'

"Then he stood starin', his great mouth wide open an' droppin' at the corners. 'Twas all one as if he'd seen a ghost.

"'Shucks!' says Clark. 'did ye never face a dead man before? That kind can't hurt ye.'

"'Ever face a dead man? Aye, did I,' answers Brady, the Irish in him flarin' up; 'an' if ye give me any more o' yer lip, I'll be facin' another, an' mighty quick, too. Who said dead men?—though, be the hokey! 'twas all the feel of a corpse.'

"'Then why don't ye go down!'

"For answer Brady leant one hand on the bar as before and bent cautiously forward. The other hand he rested on the outer edge o' the skylight, an' I took notice he didn't put as much as a tip of his finger across the rim. Down he lowered himself, slowly down, down, down, like as if he was goin' to drink, until his face was level with the bar an' the edge o' the wood. Then, as it dipped below the line, he jumped back like before.

"'None o' yer tricks, Clark!' he yelled.

"'Tricks!' says Clark. 'Is the fool gone mad?'

"'Didn't ye slop somethin' cowld an' wet in me face?'

"'You're crazed,' says Clark, 'clean crazed. Where would I get anythin' cold or wet in such a swelter o' heat? No one stirred a finger. Here, I'll go below.'

"Sittin' on the edge o' the wood, he gripped the bar, slewed himself round, an' made as if to drop his legs through the skylight; but all of a sudden he stopped, an' I heard him gasp.

"'By gum!' says he, an' his face went white. 'That's queer—that's darned queer!'

"'What's the matter, Clark?' said Brady, jeerin' him. 'Why don't ye go down? Is it the dead men y're feared of? Sure, men like them can't hurt ye. God rest their sowls!' he added solemnly.

"But Clark never heeded him except to say, 'I'm sorry I spoke, Irish.' An' the fashion he said it, subdued and puzzled-like, meant more than the words, though it wasn't Clark's way to climb down. He was a New Yorker, you remember, and that kind mostly hangs on to their crow, right or wrong. From Brady he turned to me.

"'Lay your hand alongside my leg—will ye, Towson?—an' tell me what's got me.'

"Then I noticed that, instead of his feet dangling this way an that, as a man's mostly do, they hung stiff an' cramped-like.

"'Got you?' says I; 'what could get you? Are you pullin' my leg?'

"'No,' says he, speakin' very quietly an' with a weak twist of his mouth, 'but there's somethin' pullin' mine—leastways, holdin' it. Feel along of me, as I told you, an', for Heaven's sake, hurry!'

"With that I stretched my arm down, palm out, slowly, slowly, the way I'd seen Brady move—though for the life o' me I couldn't have told why, for there was nothin' to see—an', like him, I went hack with a jump an' a yell. There, just below the line o' the frame, where there was nothin', nothin' at all but clear air an' sunshine, was a cold spongy clamminess, like dry, soft ice—ice that was a thin, dry jelly, an' that sank under the hand like dough.

"'Why don't ye go down,' says Brady again, 'why don't ye go down, ye Yankee coward? Is it the dead you're feared of!'

"That stung Clark. Curious, isn't it! Call a man a cur, an' he grins, or maybe ruffles up a bit; but call him an English cur, an' he'll shake the life out of you! To couple Yank with coward was too much for Clark, an' Heaven keep me from ever seein' again the sight I saw then!

"'Who's coward?' says he. 'Don't talk so much, Irish. Coward yourself, an' come on if you dare! All hands below!'

"Gripping the bar in front, he swung off an' let himself drop with a thrust up that partly turned him round. For a breath he hung as if upon nothin'; but I reckon he hadn't fairly let go the bar when he'd have given the world an' all for a fresh hold. Down he floundered, not straight as a man should, but as if he was drownin' an' drownin' in cold pitch that sucked him in by inches. That the stuff, whatever it was, gripped him close, I know, for I saw his clothes run up his leg an' leave it bare; an' that he repented his foolhardiness I know, for up flew one hand to catch at the bar, up with a wild swing—an' missed it, gritting it with his finger-nails; an' out flew the other, clutchin' at the wooden ledge, but missed it, too.

"'Help! Help!' he screamed, with a sob, throwing his head back.

"His eyes caught mine as he went under, though to me an' Brady it was just that his open mouth was below the line o' the skylight. But under he was, for the scream stopped short with a choked gurgle, though his mouth gaped an' his jaw wagged like as if he was chewin' on somethin' soft.

"Up to that we had stood scared and staring; but as he screamed, our sense came back, an' we plunged forward, grabbing at his hands. But if he was late, so were we. He had slipped past reach, an', as we watched, we saw him light on the table slowly and greasily, an' paw at it vaguely with his feet. For a minute he swayed there, his big sea-boots makin' no noise on the wood, an' his arms beating the air with cramped jerks, like as if somethin' held his hands. Then he staggered an' rolled sideways to the floor, where he lay on his back, twelve feet away, giving us stare for stare, an' we no more able to help him than if he was fifty fathoms under the sea. As many men as you've fingers I've seen drown, but never one like that; yet drown he did, if I know what drownin' means! God have mercy upon him, for it was an awful end! Three great pants he gave—pants like to split his chest; then he lay quiet, an', as the hulk rocked to the heave o' the swell, the sunshine through the port played backwards an' forwards across his face without so much as a flaw in its light.

"Brady pulled himself together first. After we'd failed to catch Clark's hands, he had leaned over the skylight, dry sobbin' an' prayin' like a mother by a cradle; but at last he shook himself, as a dog might comin' out o' water.

"'I'm goin' down, Towson,' says he.

"'Down?' cried I. 'Down? Why, man, it's death! Do you see yonder?'

"'Arrah, then! have I eyes? Isn't it that that takes me down? How far off's the table?'

"'Seven feet, be it more or less,' says I, wonderin' if I had a madman on my hands next. What's your notion?'

"'My notion is, the air's froze—not with cowld, but with somethin' that was in what's smashed on the floor there. My notion is the cuddy was caulked as tight as a captain's gig, an' when the poor divils broke whatever it was, they found sudden death, for the air must have gone solid in a wink. See how they broke for the door an' missed it. That's my notion, an' I'm goin' to hack the air outen her.'

"Well, sir, hack it out he did, but the bottle went smash, an' the bread turned to dust the minute the fresh air struck it. So did the three poor souls, all but their bare bones, an' their queer clothes crumbled at the touch like burnt paper, so that all that was left was the bit o' stuff you see in the frame there. That's the yarn, an' maybe Irish was right. They say folks can turn air to water now, why not to solid? For we don't know everything our side the world, for all our cocksure ways. There's a powerful deal goes on beyond 80° South that we know nothin' at all about, an' that's the fact."

IN AMUNDSEN'S TENT

John Martin Leahy

The writing career of John Martin Leahy (1886–1967) appears to have been relatively brief. He produced three novels and a handful of short stories from 1924–28 before fading into literary obscurity as he pursued a career with the Northwest Cooperage Company, a barrel-making firm in Leahy's native Washington State. Leahy's fiction taps into the early twentieth century's recurrent fascination with lost worlds. At a time when Earth's geographical mysteries were beginning to seem exhausted, fiction and film derived considerable energy from finding ways to rediscover—or reinvent—the planet's strangeness. The function of the poles as portals to other worlds forms the basis for Leahy's third novel *The Living Death*, in which a group of adventurers find a "subterranean route" from Antarctica to the "Gardens of Paradise", a "vision of fairyland" and the "abode of monsters". (We will see something of this tradition of the verdant poles in Sophie Wenzel Ellis's "Creatures of the Light").

"In Amundsen's Tent" is the last of Leahy's published works (though his second novel *Drome* was republished in 1952 featuring Leahy's own cover art). It follows a number of the same characters that featured in *The Living Death* and takes as its premise the 1911 race between Roald Amundsen and Robert Falcon Scott to be the first person to reach the South Pole (Amundsen would win and Scott would never return). Rather than a lost world narrative, "In

Amundsen's Tent" is more in the line of cryptofiction, another notable polar genre in which the narrative drama emerges from an encounter with a weird being on the cusp of zoology and the occult. As such, Leahy's story represents a notable precursor to John W. Campbell's classic Antarctic alien novella *Who Goes There?*, first published in *Astounding Science Fiction* in 1938 and adapted for the big screen in 1951 and 1982.

"Inside the tent, in a little bag, I left a letter, addressed to H.M. the King, giving information of what he (sic) had accomplished... Besides this letter, I wrote a short epistle to Captain Scott, who, I assumed, would be the first to find the tent."

CAPTAIN AMUNDSEN: *The South Pole.*

"We have just arrived at this tent, 2 miles from our camp, therefore about 1½ miles from the pole. In the tent we find a record of five Norwegians having been here, as follows:

Roald Amundsen
Olav Olavson Bjaaland
Hilmer Hanssen
Sverre H. Hassel
Oscar Wisting

16 DEC. 1911.

* * *

"Left a note to say I had visited the tent with companions."

CAPTAIN SCOTT: HIS LAST JOURNAL.

"Travellers," says Richard A. Proctor, "are sometimes said to tell marvellous stories; but it is a noteworthy fact that, in nine cases out of ten, the marvellous stories of travellers have been confirmed."

Certainly no traveller ever set down a more marvellous story than that of Robert Drumgold. This record I am at last giving to the world, with my humble apologies to the spirit of the hapless explorer for withholding it so long. But the truth is that Eastman, Dahlstrom and

I thought it the work of a mind deranged; little wonder, forsooth, if his mind had given way, what with the fearful sufferings which he had gone through and the horror of that fate which was closing in upon him.

What was it, that *thing* (if thing it was) which came to him, the sole survivor of the party which had reached the Southern Pole, thrust itself into the tent and, issuing, left but the severed head of Drumgold there?

Our explanation at the time, and until recently, was that Drumgold had been set upon by his dogs and devoured. Why, though, the flesh had not been stripped from the head was to us an utter mystery. But that was only one of the many things that were utter mysteries.

But now we know—or feel certain—that this explanation was as far from the truth as that desolate, ice-mangled spot where he met his end is from the smiling, flower-spangled regions of the tropics.

Yes, we thought that the mind of poor Robert Drumgold had given way, that the horror in Amundsen's tent and that thing which came to Drumgold there in his own—we thought all was madness only. Hence our suppression of this part of the Drumgold manuscript. We feared that the publication of so extraordinary a record might cast a cloud of doubt upon the real achievements of the Sutherland expedition.

But of late our ideas and beliefs have undergone a change that is nothing less than a metamorphosis. This metamorphosis, it is scarcely necessary to say, was due to the startling discoveries made in the region of the Southern Pole by the late Captain Stanley Livingstone, as confirmed and extended by the expedition conducted by Darwin Frontenac. Captain Livingstone, we now learn, kept his real discovery, what with the doubts and derision which met him on his return to the world, a secret from every living soul but two—Darwin

Frontenac and Bond McQuestion. It is but now, on the return of Frontenac, that we learn how truly wonderful and amazing were those discoveries made by the ill-starred captain. And yet, despite the success of the Frontenac expedition, it must be admitted that the mystery down there in the Antarctic is enhanced rather than dissipated. Darwin Frontenac and his companions saw much; but we know that there are things and beings down there that they did not see. The Antarctic—or, rather, part of it—has thus suddenly become the most interesting and certainly the most fearful area on this globe of ours.

So another marvellous story told—or, rather, only partly told—by a traveller has been confirmed. And here are Eastman and I preparing to go once more to the Antarctic to confirm, as we hope, another story—one eery and fearful as any ever conceived by any romanticist.

And to think that it was ourselves, Eastman, Dahlstrom and I, who made the discovery! Yes, it was we who entered the tent, found there the head of Robert Drumgold and the pages whereon he had scrawled his story of mystery and horror. To think that we stood there, in the very spot where it had been, and thought the story but as the baseless fabric of some madman's vision!

How vividly it all rises before me again—the white expanse, glaring, blinding in the untempered light of the Antarctic sun; the dogs straining in the harness, the cases on the sleds, long and black like coffins; our sudden halt as Eastman fetched up in his tracks, pointed and said, "Hello! What's that?"

A half-mile or so off to the left, some object broke the blinding white of the plains.

"*Nunatak*, I suppose," was my answer.

"Looks to me like a cairn or a tent," Dahlstrom said.

"How on earth," I queried, "could a tent have got down here in 87° 30' south? We are far from the route of either Amundsen or Scott."

"H'm," said Eastman, shoving his amber-coloured glasses up onto his forehead that he might get a better look, "I wonder. Jupiter Ammon, Nels," he added, glancing at Dahlstrom, "I believe that you are right."

"It certainly," Dahlstrom nodded, "looks like a cairn or a tent to me. I don't think it's a *nunatak*."

"Well," said I, "it would not be difficult to put it to the proof."

"And that, my hearties," exclaimed Eastman, "is just what we'll do! We'll soon see what it is—whether it is a cairn, a tent, or only a *nunatak*."

The next moment we were in motion, heading straight for that mysterious object there in the middle of the eternal desolation of snow and ice.

"Look there!" Eastman, who was leading the way, suddenly shouted. "See that? It *is* a tent!"

A few moments, and I saw that it was indeed so. But who had pitched it there? What were we to find within it?

I could never describe those thoughts and feelings which were ours as we approached that spot. The snow lay piled about the tent to a depth of four feet or more. Near by, a splintered ski protruded from the surface—and that was all.

And the stillness! The air, at the moment, was without the slightest movement. No sounds but those made by our movements, and those of the dogs, and our own breathing, broke that awful silence of death.

"Poor devils!" said Eastman at last. "One thing, they certainly pitched their tent well."

The tent was supported by a single pole, set in the middle. To this pole three guy-lines were fastened, one of them as taut as the day its stake had been driven into the surface. But this was not all: a half-dozen lines, or more, were attached to the sides of the tent. There it had stood for we knew not how long, bidding defiance to the fierce winds of that terrible region.

Dahlstrom and I each got a spade and began to remove the snow. The entrance we found unfastened but completely blocked by a couple of provision-cases (empty) and a piece of canvas. "How on earth," I exclaimed, "did those things get into that position?"

"The wind," said Dahlstrom. "And, if the entrance had not been blocked, there wouldn't have been any tent here now; the wind would have split and destroyed it long ago."

"H'm," mused Eastman. "The wind did it, Nels—blocked the place like that? I wonder."

The next moment we had cleared the entrance. I thrust my head through the opening. Strangely enough, very little snow had drifted in. The tent was dark green, a circumstance which rendered the light within somewhat weird and ghastly—or perhaps my imagination contributed not a little to that effect.

"What do you see, Bill?" asked Eastman. "What's inside?"

My answer was a cry, and the next instant I had sprung back from the entrance.

"What is it, Bill?" Eastman exclaimed. "Great heaven, what is it, man?"

"A head!" I told him.

"A head?"

"A human head!"

He and Dahlstrom stooped and peered in. "What is the meaning of this?" Eastman cried. "A severed human head!"

Dahlstrom dashed a mittened hand across his eyes.

"Are we dreaming?" he exclaimed.

"'Tis no dream, Nels," returned our leader. "I wish to heaven it was. A head! A human head!"

"Is there nothing more?" I asked.

"Nothing. No body, not even stripped bone—only that severed head. Could the dogs—"

"Yes?" queried Dahlstrom.

"Could the dogs have done this?"

"Dogs!" Dahlstrom said. "This is not the work of dogs."

We entered and stood looking down upon that grisly remnant of mortality.

"It wasn't dogs," said Dahlstrom.

"Not dogs?" Eastman queried. "What other explanation is there—except cannibalism?"

Cannibalism! A shudder went through my heart. I may as well say at once, however, that our discovery of a good supply of pemmican and biscuit on the sled, at that moment completely hidden by the snow, was to show us that that fearful explanation was not the true one. The dogs! That was it, that was the explanation—even though what the victim himself had set down told us a very different story. Yes, the explorer had been set upon by his dogs and devoured. But there were things that militated against that theory. Why had the animals left that head—in the frozen eyes (they were blue eyes) and upon the frozen features of which was a look of horror that sends a shudder through my very soul even now? Why, the head did not have even the mark of a single fang, though it appeared to have been *chewed* from the trunk. Dahlstrom, however, was of the opinion that it had been *hacked* off.

And there, in the man's story, in the story of Robert Drumgold, we found another mystery—a mystery as insoluble (if it was true) as the presence here of his severed head. There the story was, scrawled in lead-pencil across the pages of his journal. But what were we to make of a record—the concluding pages of it, that is—so strange and so dreadful?

But enough of this, of what we thought and of what we wondered. The journal itself lies before me, and I now proceed to set down the story of Robert Drumgold in his own words. Not a word, not a comma shall be deleted, inserted or changed.

Let it begin with his entry for January the 3rd, at the end of which day the little party was only fifteen miles (geographical) from the Pole.

Here it is.

Jan. 3.—Lat. of our camp 89° 45' 10". Only fifteen miles more, and the Pole is ours—unless Amundsen or Scott has beaten us to it, or both. But it will be ours just the same, even though the glory of discovery is found to be another's. What shall we find there?

All are in fine spirits. Even the dogs seem to know that this is the consummation of some great achievement. And a thing that is a mystery to us is the interest they have shown this day in the region before us. Did we halt, there they were gazing and gazing straight south and sometimes sniffing and sniffing. What does it mean?

Yes, in fine spirits all—dogs as well as we three men. Everything is auspicious. The weather for the last three days has been simply glorious. Not once, in this time, has the temperature been below minus 5. As I write this, the thermometer shows one degree above. The blue of the sky is like that of which painters dream, and, in that blue, tower cloud formations, violet-tinged in the shadows, that are beautiful beyond all description. If it were possible to forget the fact that nothing stands between ourselves and a horrible death save the meagre supply of food on the sleds, one could think he was in some fairyland—a glorious fairyland of white and blue and violet.

A fairyland? Why has that thought so often occurred to me? Why have I so often likened this desolate, terrible region to fairyland? Terrible? Yes, to human beings it is terrible—frightful beyond all words. But, though so unutterably terrible to men, it may not be so in reality. After all, are all things, even of this earth of ours, to say nothing of the universe, made for man—this being (a godlike spirit in the body of a quasi-ape) who, set in the midst of wonders, leers and slavers in madness and hate and wallows in the muck of a thousand lusts? May there not be other beings—yes, even on this very earth of ours—more wonderful—yes, and more terrible too—than he?

Heaven knows, more than once, in this desolation of snow and ice, I have seemed to feel their presence in the air about us—nameless entities, disembodied, *watching* things.

Little wonder, forsooth, that I have again and again thought of these strange words of one of America's greatest scientists, Alexander Winchell:

"Nor is incorporated rational existence conditioned on warm blood, nor on any temperature which does not change the forms of matter of which the organism may be composed. There may be intelligences corporealised after some concept not involving the processes of ingestion, assimilation and reproduction. Such bodies would not require daily food and warmth. They might be lost in the abysses of the ocean, or laid up on a stormy cliff through the tempests of an arctic winter, or plunged in a volcano for a hundred years, and yet retain consciousness and thought."

All this Winchell tells us is conceivable, and he adds:

"Bodies are merely the local fitting of intelligence to particular modifications of universal matter and force."

And these entities, nameless things whose presence I seem to feel at times—are they benignant beings or things more fearful than even the madness of the human brain ever has fashioned?

But, then, I must stop this. If Sutherland or Travers were to read what I have set down here, they would think that I was losing my senses or would declare me already insane. And yet, as there is a heaven above us, it seems that I do actually believe that this frightful place knows the presence of beings other than ourselves and our dogs—things which we cannot see but which are watching us.

Enough of this.

Only fifteen miles from the Pole. Now for a sleep and on to our goal in the morning. Morning! There is no morning here, but day unending. The sun now rides as high at midnight as it does at midday. Of course, there is a change in altitude, but it is so slight as to be imperceptible without an instrument.

But the Pole! Tomorrow the Pole! What will we find there? Only an unbroken expanse of white, or—

Jan. 4.—The mystery and horror of this day—oh, how could I ever set that down? Sometimes, so fearful were those hours through which we have just passed, I even find myself wondering if it wasn't all only a dream. A dream! I would to heaven that it had been but a dream! As for the end—I must keep such thoughts out of my head.

Got under way at an early hour. Weather more wondrous than ever. Sky an azure that would have sent a painter into ecstasies. Cloud-formations indescribably beautiful and grand. The going, however, was pretty difficult. The place a great plain stretching away with a monotonous uniformity of surface as far as the eye could reach. A plain never trod by human foot before? At length, when our dead reckoning showed that we were drawing near to the Pole, we had the answer to that. Then it was that the keen eyes of Travers detected some object rising above the blinding white of the snow.

On the instant Sutherland had thrust his amber glasses up onto his forehead and had his binoculars to his eyes.

"Cairn!" he exclaimed, and his voice sounded hollow and very strange. "A cairn or a—*tent*. Boys, they have beaten us to the Pole!"

He handed the glasses to Travers and leaned, as though a sudden weariness had settled upon him, against the provision-cases on his sled.

"Forestalled!" said he. "Forestalled!"

I felt very sorry for our brave leader in those, his moments of terrible disappointment, but for the life of me I did not know what to say. And so I said nothing.

At that moment a cloud concealed the sun, and the place where we stood was suddenly involved in a gloom that was deep and awful. So sudden and pronounced, indeed, was the change that we gazed about us with curious and wondering looks. Far off to the right and to the left, the plain blazed white and blinding. Soon, however, the last gleam of sunshine had vanished from off it. I raised my look up to the heavens. Here and there edges of cloud were touched as though with the light of wrathful golden fire. Even then, however, that light was fading. A few minutes, and the last angry gleam of the sun had vanished. The gloom seemed to deepen about us every moment. A curious haze was concealing the blue expanse of the sky overhead. There was not the slightest movement in the gloomy and weird atmosphere. The silence was heavy, awful, the silence of the abode of utter desolation and of death.

"What on earth are we in for now?" said Travers.

Sutherland moved from his sled and stood gazing about into the eerie gloom.

"Queer change, this!" said he. "It would have delighted the heart of Doré."

"It means a blizzard, most likely," I observed. "Hadn't we better make camp before it strikes us? No telling what a blizzard may be like in this awful spot."

"Blizzard?" said Sutherland. "I don't think it means a blizzard, Bob. No telling, though. Mighty queer change, certainly. And how different the place looks now, in this strange gloom! It is surely weird and terrible—that is, it certainly looks weird and terrible."

He turned his look to Travers.

"Well, Bill," he asked, "what did you make of it?"

He waved a hand in the direction of that mysterious object the sight of which had so suddenly brought us to a halt. I say in the direction of the object, for the thing itself was no longer to be seen.

"I believe it is a tent," Travers told him.

"Well," said our leader, "we can soon find out what it is—cairn or tent, for one or the other it must certainly be."

The next instant the heavy, awful silence was broken by the sharp crack of his whip.

"Mush on, you poor brutes!" he cried. "On we go to see what is over there. Here we are at the South Pole. Let us see who has beaten us to it."

But the dogs didn't want to go on, which did not surprise me at all, because, for some time now, they had been showing signs of some strange, inexplicable uneasiness. What had got into the creatures, anyway? For a time we puzzled over it; then we *knew*, though the explanation was still an utter mystery to us. They were *afraid*. Afraid? An inadequate word, indeed. It was fear, stark, terrible, that had entered the poor brutes. But whence had come this inexplicable fear? That also we soon knew. The thing they feared, whatever it was, was in that very direction in which we were headed!

A cairn, a tent? What did this thing mean?

"What on earth is the matter with the critters?" exclaimed Travers. "Can it be that—"

"It's for us to find out what it means," said Sutherland.

Again we got in motion. The place was still involved in that strange, weird gloom. The silence was still that awful silence of desolation and of death.

Slowly but steadily we moved forward, urging on the reluctant, fearful animals with our whips.

At last Sutherland, who was leading, cried out that he saw it. He halted, peering forward into the gloom, and we urged our teams up alongside his.

"It must be a tent," he said.

And a tent we found it to be—a small one supported by a single bamboo and well guyed in all directions. Made of drab-coloured gabardine. To the top of the tent-pole another had been lashed. From this, motionless in the still air, hung the remains of a small Norwegian flag and, underneath it, a pennant with the word "Fram" upon it. Amundsen's tent!

What should we find inside it? And what was the meaning of that—the strange way it bulged out on one side?

The entrance was securely laced. The tent, it was certain, had been here for a year, all through the long Antarctic night; and yet, to our astonishment, but little snow was piled up about it, and most of this was drift. The explanation of this must, I suppose, be that, before the air currents have reached the Pole, almost all the snow has been deposited from them.

For some minutes we just stood there, and many, and some

of them dreadful enough, were the thoughts that came and went. Through the long Antarctic night! What strange things this tent could tell us had it been vouchsafed the power of words! But strange things it might tell us, nevertheless. For what was that inside, making the tent bulge out in so unaccountable a manner? I moved forward to feel of it there with my mittened hand, but, for some reason that I cannot explain, of a sudden I drew back. At that instant one of the dogs whined—the sound so strange and the terror of the animal so unmistakable that I shuddered and felt a chill pass through my heart. Others of the dogs began to whine in that mysterious manner, and all shrank back cowering from the tent.

"What does it mean?" said Travers, his voice sunk almost to a whisper. "Look at them. It is as though they are imploring us to— keep away."

"To keep away," echoed Sutherland, his look leaving the dogs and fixing itself once more on the tent.

"Their senses," said Travers, "are keener than ours. They already know what we can't know until we see it."

"See it!" Sutherland exclaimed. "I wonder. Boys, what are we going to see when we look into that tent? Poor fellows! They reached the Pole. But did they ever leave it? Are we going to find them in there dead?"

"Dead?" said Travers with a sudden start. "The dogs would never act that way if 'twas only a corpse inside. And, besides, if that theory was true, wouldn't the sleds be here to tell the story? Yet look around. The level uniformity of the place shows that no sled lies buried here."

"That is true," said our leader. "What *can* it mean? What *could* make that tent bulge out like that? Well, here is the mystery before us, and all we have to do is unlace the entrance and look inside to solve it."

He stepped to the entrance, followed by Travers and me, and began to unlace it. At that instant an icy current of air struck the place and the pennant above our heads flapped with a dull and ominous sound. One of the dogs, too, thrust his muzzle skyward, and a deep and long-drawn howl arose. And while the mournful, savage sound yet filled the air, a strange thing happened.

Through a sudden rent in that gloomy curtain of cloud, the sun sent a golden, awful light down upon the spot where we stood. It was but a shaft of light, only three or four hundred feet wide, though miles in length, and there we stood in the very middle of it, the plain on each side involved in that weird gloom, now denser and more eery than ever in contrast to that sword of golden fire which thus so suddenly had been flung down across the snow.

"Queer place this!" said Travers. "Just like a beam lying across a stage in a theatre."

Travers' simile was a most apposite one, more so than he perhaps ever dreamed himself. That place was a stage, our light the wrathful fire of the Antarctic sun, ourselves the actors in a scene stranger than any ever beheld in the mimic world.

For some moments, so strange was it all, we stood there looking about us in wonder and perhaps each one of us in not a little secret awe.

"Queer place, all right!" said Sutherland. "But—"

He laughed a hollow, sardonic laugh. Up above, the pennant flapped and flapped again, the sound of it hollow and ghostly. Again rose the long-drawn, mournful, fiercely sad howl of the wolf-dog.

"But," added our leader, "we don't want to be imagining things, you know."

"Of course not," said Travers.

"Of course not," I echoed.

A little space, and the entrance was open and Sutherland had thrust head and shoulders through it.

I don't know how long it was that he stood there like that. Perhaps it was only a few seconds, but to Travers and me it seemed rather long.

"What is it?" Travers exclaimed at last. "What do you see?"

The answer was a scream—the horror of that sound I can never forget—and Sutherland came staggering back and, I believe, would have fallen had we not sprung and caught him.

"What is it?" cried Travers. "In God's name, Sutherland, what did you see?"

Sutherland beat the side of his head with his hand, and his look was wild and horrible.

"What is it?" I exclaimed. "What did you see in there?"

"I can't tell you—I can't! Oh, oh, I wish that I had never seen it! Don't look! Boys, don't look into that tent—unless you are prepared to welcome madness, or worse."

"What gibberish is this?" Travers demanded, gazing at our leader in utter astonishment. "Come, come, man! Buck up. Get a grip on yourself. Let's have an end to this nonsense. Why should the sight of a dead man, or dead men, affect you in this mad fashion?"

"Dead men?" Sutherland laughed, the sound wild, maniacal.

"Dead men? If 'twas only that! Is this the South Pole? Is this the earth, or are we in a nightmare on some other planet?"

"For heaven's sake," cried Travers, "come out of it! What's got into you? Don't let your nerves go like this."

"A dead man?" queried our leader, peering into the face of Travers. "You think I saw a dead man? I wish it was only a dead man. Thank God, you two didn't look!"

On the instant Travers had turned.

"Well," said he, "I am going to look!"

But Sutherland cried out, screamed, sprang after him and tried to drag him back.

"It would mean horror and perhaps madness!" cried Sutherland. "Look at me. Do you want to be like me?"

"No!" Travers returned. "But I am going to see what is in that tent."

He struggled to break free, but Sutherland clung to him in a frenzy of madness.

"Help me, Bob!" Sutherland cried.

"Hold him back, or we'll all go insane."

But I did not help him to hold Travers back, for, of course, it was my belief that Sutherland himself was insane. Nor did Sutherland hold Travers. With a sudden wrench, Travers was free. The next instant he had thrust head and shoulders through the entrance of the tent.

Sutherland groaned and watched him with eyes full of unutterable horror.

I moved toward the entrance, but Sutherland flung himself at me with such violence that I was sent over into the snow. I sprang to my feet full of anger and amazement.

"What the hell," I cried, "is the matter with you, anyway? Have you gone crazy?"

The answer was a groan, horrible beyond all words of man, but that sound did not come from Sutherland. I turned. Travers was staggering away from the entrance, a hand pressed over his face, sounds that I could never describe breaking from deep in his throat. Sutherland, as the man came staggering up to him, thrust forth an arm and touched Travers lightly on the shoulder. The effect was instantaneous and frightful. Travers sprang aside as though a serpent had struck at him, screamed and screamed yet again.

"There, there!" said Sutherland gently. "I told you not to do it. I tried to make you understand, but—but you thought that I was mad."

"It can't belong to this earth!" moaned Travers.

"No," said Sutherland. "That horror was never born on this planet of ours. And the inhabitants of earth, though they do not know it, can thank God Almighty for that."

"But it is *here*!" Travers exclaimed. "How did it come to this awful place? And where did it come from?"

"Well," consoled Sutherland, "it is dead—it must be dead."

"Dead? How do we know that it is dead? And don't forget this: it didn't come here alone!"

Sutherland started. At that moment the sunlight vanished, and everything was once more involved in gloom.

"What do you mean?" Sutherland asked. "Not alone? How do you know that it did not come alone?"

"Why, it is there *inside* the tent; but the entrance was laced—from the *outside*!"

"Fool, fool that I am!" cried Sutherland a little fiercely. "Why didn't I think of that? Not alone! Of course it was not alone!"

He gazed about into the gloom, and I knew the nameless fear and horror that chilled him to the very heart, for they chilled me to my very own.

Of a sudden arose again that mournful, savage howl of the wolf-dog. We three men started as though it was the voice of some ghoul from hell's most dreadful corner.

"Shut up, you brute!" gritted Travers. "Shut up, or I'll brain you!"

Whether it was Travers' threat or not, I do not know; but that howl sank, ceased almost on the instant. Again the silence of desolation and of death lay upon the spot. But above the tent the pennant stirred and rustled, the sound of it, I thought, like the slithering of some repulsive serpent.

"What did you see in there?" I asked them.

"Bob—Bob," said Sutherland, "don't ask us that."

"The thing itself," said I, turning, "can't be any worse than this mystery and nightmare of imagination."

But the two of them threw themselves before me and barred my way.

"No!" said Sutherland firmly. "You must not look into that tent, Bob. You must not see that—that—I don't know what to call it. Trust us; believe us, Bob! 'Tis for your sake that we say that you must not do it. We, Travers and I, can never be the same men again—the brains, the souls of us can never be what they were before we saw *that*!"

"Very well," I acquiesced. "I can't help saying, though, that the whole thing seems to me like the dream of a madman."

"That," said Sutherland, "is a small matter indeed. Insane? Believe that it is the dream of a madman. Believe that we are insane. Believe that you are insane yourself. Believe anything you like. Only *don't look*!"

"Very well," I told them. "I won't look. I give in. You two have made a coward of me."

"A coward?" said Sutherland. "Don't talk nonsense, Bob. There are some things that a man should never know; there are some things that a man should never see; that horror there in Amundsen's tent is—both!"

"But you said that it is dead."

Travers groaned. Sutherland laughed a little wildly.

"Trust us," said the latter; "believe us, Bob. 'Tis for your sake, not for our own. For that is too late now. We have seen it, and you have not."

For some minutes we stood there by the tent, in that weird gloom, then turned to leave the cursed spot. I said that undoubtedly Amundsen had left some records inside, that possibly Scott had reached the Pole, and visited the tent, and that we ought to secure any such mementoes. Sutherland and Travers nodded, but each declared that he would not put his head through the entrance again for all the wealth of Ormus and of Ind—or words to that effect. We must, they said, get away from the awful place—get back to the world of men with our fearful message.

"You won't tell me what you saw," I said, "and yet you want to get back so that you can tell it to the world."

"We aren't going to tell the world what we saw," answered Sutherland. "In the first place, we couldn't, and, in the second place, if we could, not a living soul would believe us. But we can warn people, for that thing in there did not come alone. Where is the other one—or the others?"

"Dead, too, let us hope!" I exclaimed.

"Amen!" said Sutherland. "But maybe, as Bill says, it isn't dead. Probably—"

Sutherland paused, and a wild, indescribable look came into his eyes.

"Maybe it—*can't die!*"

"Probably," said I nonchalantly, yet with secret disgust and with poignant sorrow.

What was the use? What good would it do to try to reason with a couple of madmen? Yes, we must get away from this spot, or they would have me insane, too. And the long road back? Could we ever make it now? And what *had* they seen? What unimaginable horror was there behind that thin wall of gabardine? Well, whatever it was, it was real. Of that I could not entertain the slightest doubt.

Real? Real enough to wreck, virtually instantaneously, the strong brains of two strong men. But—were my poor companions really mad, after all?

"Or maybe," Sutherland was saying, "the other one, or the others, went back to Venus or Mars or Sirius or Algol, or hell itself, or wherever they came from, to get more of their kind. If that is so, heaven have pity on poor humanity! And, if it or they are still here on this earth, then sooner or later—it may be a dozen years, it may be a century—but sooner or later the world will know it, know it to its woe and to its horror. For they, if living, or if gone for others, will come again."

"I was thinking—" began Travers, his eyes fixed on the tent.

"Yes?" Sutherland queried.

"—that," Travers told him, "it might be a good plan to empty the rifle into that thing. Maybe it isn't dead; maybe it can't die—maybe it only *changes*. Probably it is just hibernating, so to speak."

"If so," I laughed, "it will probably hibernate till doomsday."

But neither one of my companions laughed.

"Or," said Travers, "it may be a demon, a ghost materialised. I can't say incarnated."

"A ghost materialised!" I exclaimed. "Well, may not every man or woman be just that? Heaven knows, many a one acts like a demon or a fiend incarnate."

"They may be," nodded Sutherland. "But that hypothesis doesn't help us any here."

"It may help things some," said Travers, starting toward his sled.

A moment or two, and he had got out the rifle.

"I thought," said he, "that nothing could ever take me back to that entrance. But the hope that I may—"

Sutherland groaned.

"It isn't earthly, Bill," he said hoarsely. "It's a nightmare. I think we had better go now."

Travers was going—straight toward the tent.

"Come back, Bill!" groaned Sutherland. "Come back! Let us go while we can."

But Travers did not come back. Slowly he moved forward, rifle thrust out before him, finger on the trigger. He reached the tent, hesitated a moment, then thrust the rifle-barrel through. As fast as he could work trigger and lever, he emptied the weapon into the tent—into that horror inside it.

He whirled and came back as though in fear the tent was about to spew forth behind him all the legions of foulest hell.

What was that? The blood seemed to freeze in my veins and heart as there arose from out the tent a sound—a sound low and throbbing—a sound that no man ever had heard on this earth—one that I hope no man will ever hear again.

A panic, a madness seized upon us, upon men and dogs alike, and away we fled from that cursed place.

The sound ceased. But again we heard it. It was more fearful, more unearthly, soul-maddening, hellish than before.

"Look!" cried Sutherland. "Oh, my God, *look at that!*"

The tent was barely visible now. A moment or two, and the curtain of gloom would conceal it. At first I could not imagine what had made Sutherland cry out like that. Then I saw it, in that very moment before the gloom hid it from view. The tent was moving! It swayed, jerked like some shapeless monster in the throes of death, like some nameless thing seen in the horror of nightmare or limned on the brain of utter madness itself.

And that is what happened there; that is what we saw. I have set it down at some length and to the best of my ability under the truly awful circumstances in which I am placed. In these hastily scrawled pages is recorded an experience that, I believe, is not surpassed by the wildest to be found in the pages of the most imaginative romanticist. Whether the record is destined ever to reach the world, ever to be scanned by the eye of another—only the future can answer that.

I will try to hope for the best. I cannot blink the fact, however, that things are pretty bad for us. It is not only this sinister, nameless mystery from which we are fleeing—though heaven knows that is horrible enough—but it is the *minds* of my companions. And, added to that, is the fear for my own. But there, I must get myself in hand. After all, as Sutherland said, I didn't see it. I must not give way. We must somehow get our story to the world, though we may have for our reward only the mockery of the world's unbelief, its scoffing—the world, against which is now moving, gathering, a menace more dreadful than any that ever moved in the fevered brain of any prophet of woe and blood and disaster.

We are a dozen miles or so from the Pole now. In that mad dash away from that tent of horror, we lost our bearings and for a time, I fear, went panicky. The strange, eery gloom denser than ever. Then came a fall of fine snow-crystals, which rendered things worse than ever. Just when about to give up in despair, chanced upon one of our beacons. This gave us our bearings, and we pressed on to this spot.

Travers has just thrust his head into the tent to tell us that he is sure he saw something moving off in the gloom. Something moving! This must be looked into.

(If Robert Drumgold could only have left as full a record of those days which followed as he had of that fearful 4th of January! No man can ever know what the three explorers went through in their struggle to escape that doom from which there was no escape—a doom the mystery and horror of which perhaps surpass in gruesomeness what the most dreadful Gothic imagination ever conceived in its utterest abandonment to delirium and madness.)

Jan. 5.—Travers *had* seen something, for we, the three of us, saw it again today. Was it that horror, that thing not of this earth, which they saw in Amundsen's tent? We don't know what it is. All we know is that it is something that moves. God have pity on us all—and on every man and woman and child on this earth of ours if this thing is what we fear!

6th.—Made 25 mi. today—20 yesterday. Did not see it today. *But heard it.* Seemed near—once, in fact, as though right over our heads. But that must have been imagination. Effect on dogs most terrible. Poor brutes! It is as horrible to them as it is to us. Sometimes I think even more. Why is it following us?

7th.—Two of dogs gone this morning. One or another of us on guard all "night". Nothing seen, not a sound heard, yet the animals have vanished. Did they desert us? We say that is what happened but each man of us knows that none of us believes it. Made 18 mi. Fear that Travers is going mad.

8th.—Travers gone! He took the watch last night at 12, relieving Sutherland. That was the last seen of Travers—the last that we shall ever see. No tracks—not a sign in the snow. Travers, poor Travers, gone! Who will be the next?

Jan. 9.—Saw it again! Why does it let us see it like this—sometimes? Is it that horror in Amundsen's tent? Sutherland declares that it is not—that it is something more hellish. But then S. is mad now—mad—mad—mad. If I wasn't sane, I could think that it all was only imagination. *But I saw it!*

Jan. 11.—Think it is the 11th but not sure. I can no longer be sure of anything—save that I am alone and that it is watching me. Don't know how I know, for I cannot see it. But I do know—it is watching me. It is always watching. And sometime it will come and get me—as it got Travers and Sutherland and half of the dogs.

Yes, today must be the 11th. For it was yesterday—surely it was only yesterday—that it took Sutherland. I didn't see it take him, for a fog had come up, and Sutherland—he would go on in the fog—was so slow in following that the vapour hid him from view. At last when he didn't come, I went back. But S. was gone—man, dogs, sled, everything was gone. Poor Sutherland! But then he was mad. Probably that was why it took him. Has it spared me because I am yet sane? S. had the rifle. Always he clung to that rifle—as though a bullet could save him from what we saw! My only weapon is an axe. But what good is an axe?

Jan. 13.—Maybe it is the 14th. I don't know. What does it matter? Saw it *three* times today. Each time it was closer. Dogs still whining about tent. There—that horrible hellish sound again. Dogs still now. That sound again. But I dare not look out. The axe.

Hours later. Can't write any more.

Silence. Voices—I seem to hear voices. But that sound again.

Coming nearer. At entrance now—now—

CREATURES OF THE LIGHT

Sophie Wenzel Ellis

Sophie Wenzel Ellis (1893–1984) was an author of pulp fiction whose imagination was particularly drawn to a combination of weird science and strange bodies. "The White Wizard" (1929), for instance, is an "eerie tale of the jungles of South America and a scientist who robbed the dead brains of the world's master-minds"; "Slaves of the Dust" (1930), relates a story of a rat with a "man's head and face", again set in South America. "The Dwellers in the House" (1933) concerns a man who "changed bodies at will and perpetuated his ego throughout the ages".

"Creatures of the Light", published in *Astounding Tales of Super Science* in 1930, contains many of Ellis's favourite motifs: science on the brink of the supernatural in a remote, mysterious world. The story's focus on eugenics shows Ellis engaging with a key controversy in the US. 1924 had seen the state of Virginia pass the "Eugenical Sterilization Act"; 1926 saw the establishment of the American Eugenics Society. "The Creatures of the Light" is part of the backlash against this bleak direction in US politics. In setting her drama in the Far South, Ellis is unwittingly participating in what would become a recurrent association between Antarctica and the political right. A Nazi whaling mission to acquire oil for margarine in 1938–39 has formed the flimsy basis for decades of conspiracy mongering about a secret Nazi fortress beneath the ice where Hitler continued the Third

Reich, in some accounts with the help of those other stereotypical Antarctic denizens: extra-terrestrials.

I n a night club of many lights and much high-pitched laughter, where he had come for an hour of forgetfulness and an execrable dinner, John Northwood was suddenly conscious that Fate had begun shuffling the cards of his destiny for a dramatic game.

First, he was aware that the singularly ugly and deformed man at the next table was gazing at him with an intense, almost excited scrutiny. But, more disturbing than this, was the scowl of hate on the face of another man, as handsome as this other was hideous, who sat in a far corner hidden behind a broad column, with rude elbows on the table, gawking first at Northwood and then at the deformed, almost hideous man.

Northwood's blood chilled over the expression on the handsome, fair-haired stranger's perfectly carved face. If a figure in marble could display a fierce, unnatural passion, it would seem no more eldritch than the hate in the icy blue eyes.

It was not a new experience for Northwood to be stared at: he was not merely a good looking young fellow of twenty-five, he was scenery, magnificent and compelling. Furthermore, he had been in the public eye for years, first as a precocious child and, later, as a brilliant young scientist. Yet, for all his experience with hero worshippers to put an adamantine crust on his sensibilities, he grew warm-eared under the gaze of these two strangers—this hunchback with a face like a grotesque mask in a Greek play, this other who, even handsomer than himself, chilled the blood queerly with the cold perfection of his godlike masculine beauty.

Northwood sensed something familiar about the hunchback. Somewhere he had seen that huge, round, intelligent face splattered with startling features. The very breadth of the man's massive brow was not altogether unknown to him, nor could Northwood look into the mournful, near-sighted black eyes without trying to recall when and where he had last seen them.

But this other of the marble-perfect nose and jaw, the blond, thick-waved hair, was totally a stranger, whom Northwood fervently hoped he would never know too well.

Trying to analyse the queer repugnance that he felt for this handsome, boldly staring fellow, Northwood decided: "He's like a newly-made wax figure endowed with life."

Shivering over his own fantastic thought, he again glanced swiftly at the hunchback, who he noticed was playing with his coffee, evidently to prolong the meal.

One year of calm-headed scientific teaching in a famous old eastern university had not made him callous to mysteries. Thus, with a feeling of high adventure, he finished his supper and prepared to go. From the corner of his eye, he saw the hunchback leave his seat, while the handsome man behind the column rose furtively, as though he, too, intended to follow.

Northwood was out in the dusky street about thirty seconds, when the hunchback came from the foyer. Without apparently noticing Northwood, he hailed a taxi. For a moment, he stood still, waiting for the taxi to pull up at the curb. Standing thus, with the street light limning every unnatural angle of his twisted body and every queer abnormality of his huge features, he looked almost repulsive.

On his way to the taxi, his thick shoulder jostled the younger man. Northwood felt something strike his foot, and, stooping in the crowded street, picked up a black leather wallet.

"Wait!" he shouted as the hunchback stepped into the waiting taxi.

But the man did not falter. In a moment, Northwood lost sight of him as the taxi moved away.

He debated with himself whether or not he should attempt to follow. And while he stood thus in indecision, the handsome stranger approached him.

"Good evening to you," he said curtly. His rich, musical voice, for all its deepness, held a faint hint of the tremulous, birdlike notes heard in the voice of a young child who has not used his vocal chords long enough for them to have lost their exquisite newness.

"Good evening," echoed Northwood, somewhat uncertainly. A sudden aura of repulsion swept coldly over him. Seen close, with the brilliant light of the street directly on his too perfect face, the man was more sinister than in the café. Yet Northwood, struggling desperately for a reason to explain his violent dislike, could not discover why he shrank from this splendid creature, whose eyes and flesh had a new, fresh appearance rarely seen except in very young boys.

"I want what you picked up," went on the stranger.

"It isn't yours!" Northwood flashed back. Ah! that effluvium of hatred which seemed to weave a tangible net around him!

"Nor is it yours. Give it to me!"

"You're insolent, aren't you?"

"If you don't give it to me, you will be sorry." The man did not raise his voice in anger, yet the words whipped Northwood with almost physical violence. "If he knew that I saw everything that happened in there—that I am talking to you at this moment—he would tremble with fear."

"But you can't intimidate me."

"No?" For a long moment, the cold blue eyes held his contemptuously. "No? I can't frighten you—you worm of the Black Age?"

Before Northwood's horrified sight, he vanished; vanished as though he had turned suddenly to air and floated away.

The street was not crowded at that time, and there was no pressing group of bodies to hide the splendid creature. Northwood gawked stupidly, mouth half open, eyes searching wildly everywhere. The man was gone. He had simply disappeared, in this sane, electric-lighted street.

Suddenly, close to Northwood's ear, grated a derisive laugh. "I can't frighten you?" From nowhere came that singularly young-old voice.

As Northwood jerked his head around to meet blank space, a blow struck the corner of his mouth. He felt the warm blood run over his chin.

"I could take that wallet from you, worm, but you may keep it, and see me later. But remember this—the thing inside never will be yours."

The words fell from empty air.

For several minutes, Northwood waited at the spot, expecting another demonstration of the abnormal, but nothing else occurred. At last, trembling violently, he wiped the thick moisture from his forehead and dabbed at the blood which he still felt on his chin.

But when he looked at his handkerchief, he muttered:

"Well, I'll be jiggered!"

The handkerchief bore not the slightest trace of blood.

*

Under the light in his bedroom, Northwood examined the wallet. It was made of alligator skin, clasped with a gold signet that bore the initial M. The first pocket was empty; the second yielded an object that sent a warm flush to his face.

It was the photograph of a gloriously beautiful girl, so seductively lovely that the picture seemed almost to be alive. The short, curved upper lip, the full, delicately voluptuous lower, parted slightly in a smile that seemed to linger in every exquisite line of her face. She looked as though she had just spoken passionately, and the spirit of her words had inspired her sweet flesh and eyes.

Northwood turned his head abruptly and groaned, "Good Heavens!"

He had no right to palpitate over the picture of an unknown beauty. Only a month ago, he had become engaged to a young woman whose mind was as brilliant as her face was plain. Always he had vowed that he would never marry a pretty girl, for he detested his own masculine beauty sincerely.

He tried to grasp a mental picture of Mary Burns, who had never stirred in him the emotion that this smiling picture invoked. But, gazing at the picture, he could not remember how his fiancée looked.

Suddenly the picture fell from his fingers and dropped to the floor on its face, revealing an inscription on the back. In a bold, masculine hand, he read: "Your future wife."

"Some lucky fellow is headed for a life of bliss," was his jealous thought.

He frowned at the beautiful face. What was this girl to that hideous hunchback? Why did the handsome stranger warn him, "*The thing inside never will be yours?*"

Again he turned eagerly to the wallet.

In the last flap he found something that gave him another surprise: a plain white card on which a name and address were written by the same hand that had penned the inscription on the picture.

EMIL MUNDSON, PH. D.,
44½ INDIAN COURT

Emil Mundson, the electrical wizard and distinguished scientific writer, friend of the professor of science at the university where Northwood was an assistant professor; Emil Mundson, whom, a week ago, Northwood had yearned mightily to meet.

Now Northwood knew why the hunchback's intelligent, ugly face was familiar to him. He had seen it pictured as often as enterprising news photographers could steal a likeness from the over-sensitive scientist, who would never sit for a formal portrait.

Even before Northwood had graduated from the university where he now taught, he had been avidly interested in Emil Mundson's fantastic articles in scientific journals. Only a week ago, Professor Michael had come to him with the current issue of New Science, shouting excitedly:

"Did you read this, John, this article by Emil Mundson?" His shaking, gnarled old fingers tapped the open magazine.

Northwood seized the magazine and looked avidly at the title of the article, "Creatures of the Light."

"No, I haven't read it," he admitted. "My magazine hasn't come yet."

"Run through it now briefly, will you? And note with especial care the passages I have marked. In fact, you needn't bother with anything else just now. Read this—and this—and this." He pointed out pencilled paragraphs. Northwood read:

> Man always has been, always will be a creature of the light. He is forever reaching for some future point of perfected evolution which, even when his most remote ancestor was a fish creature composed of a few cells, was the guiding power that brought him up from the first stinking sea and caused him to create gods in his own image.
>
> It is this yearning for perfection which sets man apart from all other life, which made him *man* even in the rudimentary stages of his development. He was man when he wallowed in the slime of the new world and yearned for the air above. He will still be man when he has evolved into that glorious creature of the future whose body is deathless and whose mind rules the universe.

Professor Michael, looking over Northwood's shoulder, interrupted the reading:

"*Man always has been man*," he droned emphatically. "That's not original with friend Mundson, of course; yet it is a theory that has not received sufficient investigation." He indicated another marked paragraph. "Read this thoughtfully, John. It's the crux of Mundson's thought."

Northwood continued:

> Since the human body is chemical and electrical, increased knowledge of its powers and limitations will enable us to work with Nature in her sublime but infinitely slow processes of human evolution. We need not wait another fifty thousand

years to be godlike creatures. Perhaps even now we may be standing at the beginning of the splendid bridge that will take us to that state of perfected evolution when we shall be Creatures who have reached the Light.

Northwood looked questioningly at the professor. "Queer, fantastic thing, isn't it?"

Professor Michael smoothed his thin, grey hair with his dried-out hand. "Fantastic?" His intellectual eyes behind the thick glasses sought the ceiling. "Who can say? Haven't you ever wondered why all parents expect their children to be nearer perfection than themselves, and why is it a natural impulse for them to be willing to sacrifice themselves to better their offspring?" He paused and moistened his pale, wrinkled lips. "Instinct, Northwood. We Creatures of the Light know that our race shall reach that point in evolution when, as perfect creatures, we shall rule all matter and live forever." He punctuated the last words with blows on the table.

Northwood laughed drily. "How many thousands of years are you looking forward, Professor?"

The professor made an obscure noise that sounded like a smothered sniff. "You and I shall never agree on the point that mental advancement may wipe out physical limitations in the human race, perhaps in a few hundred years. It seems as though your profound admiration for Dr. Mundson would win you over to this pet theory."

"But what sane man can believe that even perfectly developed beings, through mental control, could overcome Nature's fixed laws?"

"We don't know! We don't know!" The professor slapped the magazine with an emphatic hand. "Emil Mundson hasn't written this article for nothing. He's paving the way for some announcement that will startle the scientific world. I know him. In the same manner he gave out veiled hints of his various brilliant discoveries and inventions long before he offered them to the world."

"But Dr. Mundson is an electrical wizard. He would not be delving seriously into the mysteries of evolution, would he?"

"Why not?" The professor's wizened face screwed up wisely. "A year ago, when he was back from one of those mysterious long excursions he takes in that weirdly different aircraft of his, about which he is so secretive, he told me that he was conducting experiments to prove his belief that the human brain generates electric current, and that the electrical impulses in the brain set up radioactive waves that some day, among other miracles, will make thought communication possible. Perfect man, he says, will perform mental feats which will give him complete mental domination over the physical."

Northwood finished reading and turned thoughtfully to the window. His profile in repose had the straight-nosed, full-lipped perfection of a Greek coin. Old, wizened Professor Michael, gazing at him covertly, smothered a sigh.

"I wish you knew Dr. Mundson," he said. "He, the ugliest man in the world, delights in physical perfection. He would revel in your splendid body and brilliant mind."

Northwood blushed hotly. "You'll have to arrange a meeting between us."

"I have." The professor's thin, dry lips pursed comically. "He'll drop in to see you within a few days."

And now John Northwood sat holding Dr. Mundson's card and the wallet which the scientist had so mysteriously dropped at his feet.

*

Here was high adventure, perhaps, for which he had been singled out by the famous electrical wizard. While excitement mounted in his blood, Northwood again examined the photograph. The girl's strange eyes, odd in expression rather than in size or shape, seemed to hold him. The young man's breath came quicker.

"It's a challenge," he said softly. "It won't hurt to see what it's all about." His watch showed eleven o'clock. He would return the wallet that night. Into his coat pocket he slipped a revolver. One sometimes needed weapons in Indian Court.

He took a taxi, which soon turned from the well-lighted streets into a section where squalid houses crowded against each other, and dirty children swarmed in the streets in their last games of the day.

Indian Court was little more than an alley, dark and evil smelling. The chauffeur stopped at the entrance and said:

"If I drive in, I'll have to back out, sir. Number forty-four and a half is the end house, facing the entrance."

"You've been here before?" asked Northwood.

"Last week I drove the queerest bird here—a fellow as good-looking as you, who had me follow the taxi occupied by a hunchback with a face like Old Nick." The man hesitated and went on haltingly: "It might sound goofy, mister, but there was something funny about my fare. He jumped out, asked me the charge, and, in the moment I glanced at my taxi-meter, he disappeared. Yes, sir. Vanished, owing me four dollars, six bits. It was almost ghostlike, mister."

Northwood laughed nervously and dismissed him. He found his number and knocked at the dilapidated door. He heard a sudden movement in the lighted room beyond, and the door opened quickly.

Dr. Mundson faced him.

"I knew you'd come!" he said with a slight Teutonic accent. "Often I'm not wrong in sizing up my man. Come in."

Northwood cleared his throat awkwardly. "You dropped your wallet at my feet, Dr. Mundson. I tried to stop you before you got away, but I guess you did not hear me."

He offered the wallet, but the hunchback waved it aside.

"A ruse, of course," he confessed. "It just was my way of testing what your Professor Michael told about you—that you are extraordinarily intelligent, virile, and imaginative. Had you sent the wallet to me, I should have sought elsewhere for my man. Come in."

Northwood followed him into a living room evidently recently furnished in a somewhat hurried manner. The furniture, although rich, was not placed to best advantage. The new rug was a trifle crooked on the floor, and the lamp shades clashed in colour with the other furnishings.

Dr. Mundson's intense eyes swept over Northwood's tall, slim body.

"Ah, you're a man!" he said softly. "You are what all men would be if we followed Nature's plan that only the fit shall survive. But modern science is permitting the unfit to live and to mix their defective beings with the developing race!" His huge fist gesticulated madly. "Fools! Fools! They need me and perfect men like you."

"Why?"

"Because you can help me in my plan to populate the earth with a new race of godlike people. But don't question me too closely now. Even if I should explain, you would call me insane. But watch; gradually I shall unfold the mystery before you, so that you will believe."

He reached for the wallet that Northwood still held, opened it with a monstrous hand, and reached for the photograph. "She shall bring you love. She's more beautiful than a poet's dream."

A warm flush crept over the young man's face.

"I can easily understand," he said, "how a man could love her, but for me she comes too late."

"Pooh! Fiddlesticks!" The scientist snapped his fingers. "This girl was created for you. That other—you will forget her the moment you set eyes on the sweet flesh of this Athalia. She is an houri from Paradise—a maiden of musk and incense." He held the girl's photograph toward the young man. "Keep it. She is yours, if you are strong enough to hold her."

Northwood opened his card case and placed the picture inside, facing Mary's photograph. Again the warning words of the mysterious stranger rang in his memory: "*The thing inside never will be yours.*"

"Where to," he said eagerly; "and when do we start?"

"To the new Garden of Eden," said the scientist, with such a beatific smile that his face was less hideous. "We start immediately. I have arranged with Professor Michael for you to go."

Northwood followed Dr. Mundson to the street and walked with him a few blocks to a garage where the scientist's motor car waited.

"The apartment in Indian Court is just a little eccentricity of mine," explained Dr. Mundson. "I need people in my work, people whom I must select through swift, sure tests. The apartment comes in handy, as tonight."

Northwood scarcely noted where they were going, or how long they had been on the way. He was vaguely aware that they had left the city behind, and were now passing through farms bathed in moonlight.

At last they entered a path that led through a bit of woodland. For half a mile the path continued, and then ended at a small, enclosed field. In the middle of this rested a queer aircraft. Northwood knew it was a flying machine only by the propellers mounted on the top of the huge ball-shaped body. There were no wings, no birdlike hull, no tail.

"It looks almost like a little world ready to fly off into space," he commented.

"It is just about that." The scientist's squat, bunched-out body, settled squarely on long, thin, straddled legs, looked gnomelike in the moonlight. "One cannot copy flesh with steel and wood, but one can make metal perform magic of which flesh is not capable. My sun-ship is not a mechanical reproduction of a bird. It is—but, climb in, young friend."

Northwood followed Dr. Mundson into the aircraft. The moment the scientist closed the metal door behind them, Northwood was instantly aware of some concealed horror that vibrated through his nerves. For one dreadful moment, he expected some terrific agent of the shadows that escaped the electric lights to leap upon him. And this was odd, for nothing could be saner than the globular interior of the aircraft, divided into four wedge-shaped apartments.

Dr. Mundson also paused at the door, puzzled, hesitant.

"Someone has been here!" he exclaimed. "Look, Northwood! The bunk has been occupied—the one in this cabin I had set aside for you."

He pointed to the disarranged bunk, where the impression of a head could still be seen on a pillow.

"A tramp, perhaps."

"No! The door was locked, and, as you saw, the fence around this field was protected with barbed wire. There's something wrong. I felt it on my trip here all the way, like someone watching me in the dark. And don't laugh! I have stopped laughing at all things that seem unnatural. You don't know what is natural."

Northwood shivered. "Maybe someone is concealed about the ship."

"Impossible. Me, I thought so, too. But I looked and looked, and there was nothing."

All evening Northwood had burned to tell the scientist about the handsome stranger in the Mad Hatter Club. But even now he shrank from saying that a man had vanished before his eyes.

Dr. Mundson was working with a succession of buttons and levers. There was a slight jerk, and then the strange craft shot up, straight as a bullet from a gun, with scarcely a sound other than a continuous whistle.

"The vertical rising aircraft perfected," explained Dr. Mundson. "But what would you think if I told you that there is not an ounce of gasoline in my heavier-than-air craft?"

"I shouldn't be surprised. An electrical genius would seek for a less obsolete source of power."

In the bright flare of the electric lights, the scientist's ugly face flushed. "The man who harnesses the sun rules the world. He can make the desert places bloom, the frozen poles balmy and verdant. You, John Northwood, are one of the very few to fly in a machine operated solely by electrical energy from the sun's rays."

"Are you telling me that this airship is operated with power from the sun?"

"Yes. And I cannot take the credit for its invention." He sighed. "The dream was mine, but a greater brain developed it—a brain that may be greater than I suspect." His face grew suddenly graver.

A little later Northwood said: "It seems that we must be making fabulous speed."

"Perhaps!" Dr. Mundson worked with the controls. "Here, I've cut her down to the average speed of the ordinary airplane. Now you can see a bit of the night scenery."

Northwood peeped out the thick glass porthole. Far below, he saw two tiny streaks of light, one smooth and stationery, the other wavering as though it were a reflection in water.

"That can't be a lighthouse!" he cried.

The scientist glanced out. "It is. We're approaching the Florida Keys."

"Impossible! We've been travelling less than an hour."

"But, my young friend, do you realise that my sun-ship has a speed of over one thousand miles an hour, how much over I dare not tell you?"

Throughout the night, Northwood sat beside Dr. Mundson, watching his deft fingers control the simple-looking buttons and levers. So fast was their flight now that, through the portholes, sky and earth looked the same: dark grey films of emptiness. The continuous weird whistle from the hidden mechanism of the sun-ship was like the drone of a monster insect, monotonous and soporific during the long intervals when the scientist was too busy with his controls to engage in conversation.

For some reason that he could not explain, Northwood had an aversion to going into the sleeping apartment behind the control room. Then, towards morning, when the suddenly falling temperature struck a biting chill throughout the sun ship, Northwood, going into the cabin for fur coats, discovered why his mind and body shrank in horror from the cabin.

After he had procured the fur coats from a closet, he paused a moment, in the privacy of the cabin, to look at Athalia's picture.

Every nerve in his body leaped to meet the magnetism of her beautiful eyes. Never had Mary Burns stirred emotion like this in him. He hung over Mary's picture, wistfully, hoping almost prayerfully that he could react to her as he did to Athalia; but her pale, over-intellectual face left him cold.

"Cad!" he ground out between his teeth. "Forgetting her so soon!"

The two pictures were lying side by side on a little table. Suddenly an obscure noise in the room caught his attention. It was more vibration than noise, for small sounds could scarcely be heard above the whistle of the sun-ship. A slight compression of the air against his neck gave him the eery feeling that someone was standing close behind him. He wheeled and looked over his shoulder. Half ashamed of his startled gesture, he again turned to his pictures. Then a sharp cry broke from him.

Athalia's picture was gone.

He searched for it everywhere in the room, in his own pockets, under the furniture. It was nowhere to be found.

In sudden, overpowering horror, he seized the fur coats and returned to the control room.

Dr. Mundson was changing the speed.

"Look out the window!" he called to Northwood.

The young man looked and started violently. Day had come, and now that the sun-ship was flying at a moderate speed, the ocean beneath was plainly visible; and its entire surface was covered with broken floes of ice and small, ragged icebergs. He seized a telescope and focused it below. A typical polar scene met his eyes: penguins strutted about on cakes of ice, a whale blowing in the icy water.

"A part of the Antarctic that has never been explored," said Dr. Mundson; "and there, just showing on the horizon, is the Great Ice Barrier." His characteristic smile lighted the morose black eyes. "I am enough of the dramatist to wish you to be impressed with what I shall show you within less than an hour. Accordingly, I shall make a landing and let you feel polar ice under your feet."

After less than a minute's search, Dr. Mundson found a suitable place on the ice for a landing, and, with a few deft manipulations of the controls, brought the sun-ship swooping down like an eagle on its prey.

For a long moment after the scientist had stepped out on the ice, Northwood paused at the door. His feet were chained by a strange reluctance to enter this white, dead wilderness of ice. But Dr. Mundson's impatient, "Ready?" drew from him one last glance at the cosy interior of the sun-ship before he, too, went out into the frozen stillness.

They left the sun-ship resting on the ice like a fallen silver moon, while they wandered to the edge of the Barrier and looked at the grey, narrow stretch of sea between the ice pack and the high cliffs of the Barrier. The sun of the commencing six-months' Antarctic day was a low, cold ball whose slanted rays struck the ice with blinding whiteness. There were constant falls of ice from the Barrier, which thundered into the ocean amid great clouds of ice smoke that lingered like wraiths around the edge. It was a scene of loneliness and waiting death.

"What's that?" exclaimed the scientist suddenly.

Out of the white silence shrilled a low whistle, a familiar whistle. Both men wheeled toward the sun-ship.

Before their horrified eyes, the great sphere jerked and glided up, and swerved into the heavens.

*

Up it soared; then, gaining speed, it swung into the blue distance until, in a moment, it was a tiny star that flickered out even as they watched.

Both men screamed and cursed and flung up their arms despairingly. A penguin, attracted by their cries, waddled solemnly over to them and regarded them with manlike curiosity.

"Stranded in the coldest spot on earth!" groaned the scientist.

"Why did it start itself, Dr. Mundson!" Norwood narrowed his eyes as he spoke.

"It didn't!" The scientist's huge face, red from cold, quivered with helpless rage. "Human hands started it."

"What! Whose hands?"

"*Ach*! Do I know?" His Teutonic accent grew more pronounced, as it always did when he was under emotional stress. "Somebody whose brain is better than mine. Somebody who found a way to hide away from our eyes. *Ach, Gott*! Don't let me think!"

His great head sank between his shoulders, giving him, in his fur suit, the grotesque appearance of a friendly brown bear.

"Doctor Mundson," said Northwood suddenly, "did you have an enemy, a man with the face and body of a pagan god—a great, blond creature with eyes as cold and cruel as the ice under our feet?"

"Wait!" The huge round head jerked up. "How do you know about Adam? You have not seen him, won't see him until we arrive at our destination."

"But I have seen him. He was sitting not thirty feet from you in the Mad Hatter's Club last night. Didn't you know? He followed me to the street, spoke to me, and then—" Northwood stopped. How could he let the insane words pass his lips?

"Then, what? Speak up!"

*

Northwood laughed nervously. "It sounds foolish, but I saw him vanish like that." He snapped his fingers.

"*Ach, Gott!*" All the ruddy colour drained from the scientist's face. As though talking to himself, he continued:

"Then it is true, as he said. He has crossed the bridge, He has reached the Light. And now he comes to see the world he will conquer—came unseen when I refused my permission."

He was silent for a long time, pondering. Then he turned passionately to Northwood.

"John Northwood, kill me! I have brought a new horror into the world. From the unborn future, I have snatched a creature who has reached the Light too soon. Kill me!" He bowed his great, shaggy head.

"What do you mean, Dr. Mundson: that this Adam has arrived at a point in evolution beyond this age?"

"Yes. Think of it! I visioned godlike creatures with the souls of gods. But, Heaven help us, man always will be man; always will lust for conquest. You and I, Northwood, and all others are barbarians to Adam. He and his kind will do what men always do to barbarians—conquer and kill."

"Are there more like him?" Northwood struggled with a smile of unbelief.

"I don't know. I did not know that Adam had reached a point so near the ultimate. But you have seen. Already he is able to set aside what we call natural laws."

Northwood looked at the scientist closely. The man was surely mad—mad in this desert of white death.

"Come!" he said cheerfully. "Let's build an Eskimo snow house. We can live on penguins for days. And who knows what may rescue us?"

For three hours the two worked at cutting ice blocks. With snow for mortar, they built a crude shelter which enabled them to rest out of the cold breath of the spiral polar winds that blew from the south.

Dr. Mundson was sitting at the door of their hut, moodily pulling at his strong, black pipe. As though a fit had seized him, he leaped up and let his pipe fall to the ice.

"Look!" he shouted. "The sun-ship!"

It seemed but a moment before the tiny speck on the horizon had swept overhead, a silver comet on the greyish-blue polar sky. In another moment it had swooped down, eaglewise, scarcely fifty feet from the ice hut.

Dr. Mundson and Northwood ran forward. From the metal sphere stepped the stranger of the Mad Hatter Club. His tall, straight form, erect and slim, swung toward them over the ice.

"Adam!" shouted Dr. Mundson. "What does this mean? How dare you!"

Adam's laugh was like the happy demonstration of a boy. "So? You think you still are master? You think I returned because I reverenced you yet?" Hate shot viciously through the freezing blue eyes. "You worm of the Black Age!"

Northwood shuddered. He had heard those strange words addressed to himself scarcely more than twelve hours ago.

Adam was still speaking: "With a thought I could annihilate you where you are standing. But I have use for you. Get in." He swept his hand to the sun-ship.

Both men hesitated. Then Northwood strode forward until he was within three feet of Adam. They stood thus, eyeing each other, two splendid beings, one blond as a Viking, the other dark and vital.

"Just what is your game?" demanded Northwood.

The icy eyes shot forth a gleam like lightning. "I needn't tell you, of course, but I may as well let you suffer over the knowledge." He curled his lips with superb scorn. "I have one human weakness. I want Athalia." The icy eyes warmed for a fleeting second. "She is anticipating her meeting with you—bah! The taste of these women of the Black Age! I could kill you, of course; but that would only inflame her. And so I take you to her, thrust you down her throat. When she sees you, she will fly to me." He spread his magnificent chest.

"Adam!" Dr. Mundson's face was dark with anger. "What of Eve?"

"Who are you to question my actions? What a fool you were to let me, whom you forced into life thousands of years too soon, grow more powerful than you! Before I am through with all of you petty creatures of the Black Age, you will call me more terrible than your Jehovah! For see what you have called forth from unborn time."

He vanished.

Before the startled men could recover from the shock of it, the vibrant, too-new voice went on:

"I am sorry for you, Mundson, because, like you, I need specimens for my experiments. What a splendid specimen you will be!" His laugh was ugly with significance. "Get in, worms!"

Unseen hands cuffed and pushed them into the sun-ship.

Inside, Dr. Mundson stumbled to the control room, white and drawn of face, his great brain seemingly paralysed by the catastrophe.

"You needn't attempt tricks," went on the voice. "I am watching you both. You cannot even hide your thoughts from me."

And thus began the strange continuation of the journey. Not once, in that wild half-hour's rush over the polar ice clouds, did they see Adam. They saw and heard only the weird signs of his presence:

a puffing cigar hanging in midair, a glass of water swinging to unseen lips, a ghostly voice hurling threats and insults at them.

Once the scientist whispered: "Don't cross him; it is useless. John Northwood, you'll have to fight a demigod for your woman!"

Because of the terrific speed of the sun-ship, Northwood could distinguish nothing of the topographical details below. At the end of half-an-hour, the scientist slowed enough to point out a tall range of snow-covered mountains, over which hovered a play of coloured lights like the *aurora australis*.

"Behind those mountains," he said, "is our destination."

Almost in a moment, the sun-ship had soared over the peaks. Dr. Mundson kept the speed low enough for Northwood to see the splendid view below.

In the giant cup formed by the encircling mountain range was a green valley of tropical luxuriance. Stretches of dense forest swept half up the mountains and filled the valley cup with tangled verdure. In the centre, surrounded by a broad field and a narrow ring of woods, towered a group of buildings. From the largest, which was circular, came the auroralike radiance that formed an umbrella of light over the entire valley.

"Do I guess right," said Northwood: "that the light is responsible for this oasis in the ice?"

"Yes," said Dr. Munson. "In your American slang, it is canned sunshine containing an overabundance of certain rays, especially the Life Ray, which I have isolated." He smiled proudly. "You needn't look startled, my friend. Some of the most common things store sunlight. On very dark nights, if you have sharp eyes, you can see the radiance given off by certain flowers, which many naturalists say is trapped sunshine. The familiar nasturtium and the marigold opened for me the way to hold sunshine against the long polar night, for they taught me how to apply the Einstein theory of bent light. Stated simply, during the polar night, when the sun is hidden over the rim of the world, we steal some of his rays; during the polar day we concentrate the light."

"But could stored sunshine alone give enough warmth for the luxuriant growth of those jungles?"

"An overabundance of the Life Ray is responsible for the miraculous growth of all life in New Eden. The Life Ray is Nature's most powerful force. Yet Nature is often niggardly and paradoxical in her use of her powers. In New Eden, we have forced the powers of creation to take ascendency over the powers of destruction."

At Northwood's sudden start, the scientist laughed and continued: "Is it not a pity that Nature, left alone, requires twenty years to make a man who begins to die in another ten years? Such waste is not tolerated in New Elden, where supermen are younger than babes and—"

"Come, worms; let's land."

It was Adam's voice. Suddenly he materialised, a blond god, whose eyes and flesh were too new.

They were in a world of golden skylight, warmth and tropical vegetation. The field on which they had landed was covered with a velvety green growth of very soft, fine-bladed grass, sprinkled with tiny, star-shaped blue flowers. A balmy, sweet-scented wind, downy as the breeze of a dream, blew gently along the grass and tingled against Northwood's skin refreshingly. Almost instantly he had the sensation of perfect well being, and this feeling of physical perfection was part of the ecstasy that seemed to pervade the entire valley. Grass and breeze and golden skylight were saturated with a strange ether of joyousness.

At one end of the field was a dense jungle, cut through by a road that led to the towering building from which, while above in the sun-ship, they had seen the golden light issue.

From the jungle road came a man and a woman, large, handsome people, whose flesh and eyes had the sinister newness of Adam's. Even before they came close enough to speak, Northwood was aware that while they seemed of Adam's breed, they were yet unlike him. The difference was psychical rather than physical; they lacked the aura of hate and horror that surrounded Adam. The woman drew Adam's head down and kissed him affectionately on both cheeks.

Adam, from his towering height, patted her shoulder impatiently and said: "Run on back to the laboratory, grandmother. We're following soon. You have some new human embryos, I believe you told me this morning."

"Four fine specimens, two of them being your sister's twins."

"Splendid! I was sure that creation had stopped with my generation. I must see them." He turned to the scientist and Northwood. "You needn't try to leave this spot. Of course I shall know instantly and deal with you in my own way. Wait here."

He strode over the emerald grass on the heels of the woman.

Northwood asked: "Why does he call that girl grandmother?"

"Because she is his ancestress." He stirred uneasily. "She is of the first generation brought forth in the laboratory, and is no different from you or I, except that, at the age of five years, she is the ancestress of twenty generations."

"My God!" muttered Northwood.

268

"Don't start being horrified, my friend. Forget about so-called natural laws while you are in New Eden. Remember, here we have isolated the Life Ray. But look! Here comes your Athalia!"

Northwood gazed covertly at the beautiful girl approaching them with a rarely graceful walk. She was tall, slender, round-bosomed, narrow-hipped, and she held her lovely body in the erect poise of splendid health. Northwood had a confused realisation of uncovered bronzy hair, drawn to the back of a white neck in a bunch of short curls; of immense soft black eyes; lips the colour of blood, and delicate, plump flesh on which the golden skylight lingered graciously. He was instantly glad to see that while she possessed the freshness of young girlhood; her skin and eyes did not have the horrible newness of Adam's.

When she was still twenty feet distant, Northwood met her eyes and she smiled shyly. The rich, red blood ran through her face; and he, too, flushed.

She went to Dr. Mundson and, placing her hands on his thick shoulders, kissed him affectionately.

"I've been worried about you, Daddy Mundson." Her rich contralto voice matched her exotic beauty. "Since you and Adam had that quarrel the day you left, I did not see him until this morning, when he landed the sun-ship alone."

"And you pleaded with him to return for us?"

"Yes." Her eyes drooped and a hot flush swept over her face.

Dr. Mundson smiled. "But I'm back now, Athalia, and I've brought some one whom I hope you will be glad to know."

Reaching for her hand, he placed it simply in Northwood's.

"This is John, Athalia. Isn't he handsomer than the pictures of him which I televisioned to you? God bless both of you."

He walked ahead and turned his back.

*

A magical half hour followed for Northwood and Athalia. The girl told him of her past life, how Dr. Mundson had discovered her one year ago working in a New York sweat shop, half dead from consumption. Without friends, she was eager to follow the scientist to New Eden, where he promised she would recover her health immediately.

"And he was right, John," she said shyly. "The Life Ray, that marvellous energy ray which penetrates to the utmost depths of earth and ocean, giving to the cells of all living bodies the power to grow and remain animate, has been concentrated by Dr. Mundson in his stored sunshine. The Life Ray healed me almost immediately."

Northwood looked down at the glorious girl beside him, whose eyes already fluttered away from his like shy black butterflies. Suddenly he squeezed the soft hand in his and said passionately:

"Athalia! Because Adam wants you and will get you if he can, let us set aside all the artificialities of civilisation. I have loved you madly ever since I saw your picture. If you can say the same to me, it will give me courage to face what I know lies before me."

Athalia, her face suddenly tender, came closer to him.

"John Northwood, I love you."

Her red lips came temptingly close; but before he could touch them, Adam suddenly pushed his body between him and Athalia. Adam was pale, and all the icyness was gone from his blue eyes, which were deep and dark and very human. He looked down at Athalia, and she looked up at him, two handsome specimens of perfect manhood and womanhood.

"Fast work, Athalia!" The new vibrant voice was strained. "I was hoping you would be disappointed in him, especially after having been wooed by me this morning. I could take you if I wished, of course; but I prefer to win you in the ancient manner. Dismiss him!" He jerked his thumb over his shoulder in Northwood's direction.

Athalia flushed vividly and looked at him almost compassionately. "I am not great enough for you, Adam. I dare not love you."

Adam laughed, and still oblivious of Northwood and Dr. Mundson, folded his arms over his breast. With the golden skylight on his burnished hair, he was a valiant, magnificent spectacle.

"Since the beginning of time, gods and archangels have looked upon the daughters of men and found them fair. Mate with me, Athalia, and I, fifty thousand years beyond the creature Mundson has selected for you, will make you as I am, the deathless overlord of life and all nature."

He drew her hand to his bosom.

For one dark moment, Northwood felt himself seared by jealousy, for, through the plump, sweet flesh of Athalia's face, he saw the red blood leap again. How could she withhold herself from this splendid superman?

But her answer, given with faltering voice, was the old, simple one: "I have promised him, Adam. I love him." Tears trembled on her thick lashes.

"So! I cannot get you in the ancient manner. Now I'll use my own."

He seized her in his arms, crushed her against him, and, laughing over her head at Northwood, bent his glistening head and kissed her on the mouth.

There was a blinding flash of blue electric sparks—and nothing else. Both Adam and Athalia had vanished.

*

Adam's voice came in a last mocking challenge: "I shall be what no other gods before me have been—a good sport. I'll leave you both to your own devices, until I want you again."

White-lipped and trembling, Northwood groaned: "What has he done now?"

Dr. Mundson's great head drooped. "I don't know. Our bodies are electric and chemical machines; and a super intelligence has discovered new laws of which you and I are ignorant."

"But Athalia..."

"She is safe; he loves her."

"Loves her!" Northwood shivered. "I cannot believe that those freezing eyes could ever look with love on a woman."

"Adam is a man. At heart he is as human as the first man-creature that wallowed in the new earth's slime." His voice dropped as though he were musing aloud. "It might be well to let him have Athalia. She will help to keep vigour in the new race, which would stop reproducing in another few generations without the injection of Black Age blood."

"Do you want to bring more creatures like Adam into the world?" Northwood flung at him. "You have tampered with life enough, Dr. Mundson. But, although Adam has my sympathy. I'm not willing to turn Athalia over to him."

"Well said! Now come to the laboratory for chemical nourishment and rest under the Life Ray."

They went to the great circular building from whose highest tower issued the golden radiance that shamed the light of the sun, hanging low in the north-east.

"John Northwood," said Dr. Mundson, "with that laboratory, which is the centre of all life in New Eden, we'll have to whip Adam. He gave us what he called a 'sporting chance' because he knew that he is able to send us and all mankind to a doom more terrible than hell. Even now we might be entering some hideous trap that he has set for us."

They entered by a side entrance and went immediately to what Dr. Mundson called the Rest Ward. Here, in a large room, were ranged rows of cots, on many of which lay men basking in the deep orange flood of light which poured from individual lamps set above each cot.

"It is the Life Ray!" said Dr. Mundson reverently. "The source of all growth and restoration in Nature. It is the power that bursts open the seed and brings forth the shoot, that increases the shoot into a giant tree. It is the same power that enables the fertilised ovum to develop into an animal. It creates and recreates cells almost instantly; accordingly, it is the perfect substitute for sleep. Stretch out, enjoy its power; and while you rest, eat these nourishing tablets."

Northwood lay on a cot, and Dr. Mundson turned the Life Ray on him. For a few minutes a delicious drowsiness fell upon him, producing a spell of perfect peace which the cells of his being seemed to drink in. For another delirious, fleeting space, every inch of him vibrated with a thrilling sensation of freshness. He took a deep, ecstatic breath and opened his eyes.

"Enough," said Dr. Mundson, switching off the Ray. "After three minutes of rejuvenation, you are commencing again with perfect cells. All ravages from disease and wear have been corrected."

Northwood leaped up joyously. His handsome eyes sparkled, his skin glowed. "I feel great! Never felt so good since I was a kid."

A pleased grin spread over the scientist's homely face. "See what my discovery will mean to the world! In the future we shall all go to the laboratory for recuperation and nourishment. We'll have almost twenty-four hours a day for work and play."

*

He stretched out on the bed contentedly. "Some day, when my work is nearly done, I shall permit the Life Ray to cure my hump."

"Why not now?"

Dr. Mundson sighed. "If I were perfect, I should cease to be so overwhelmingly conscious of the importance of perfection." He settled back to enjoyment of the Life Ray.

A few minutes later, he jumped up, alert as a boy. "*Ach*! That's fine. Now I'll show you how the Life Ray speeds up development and produces four generations of humans a year."

With restored energy, Northwood began thinking of Athalia. As he followed Dr. Mundson down a long corridor, he yearned to see her again, to be certain that she was safe. Once he imagined he felt a gentle, soft-fleshed touch against his hand, and was disappointed not to see her walking by his side. Was she with him, unseen? The thought was sweet.

Before Dr. Mundson opened the massive bronze door at the end of the corridor, he said:

"Don't be surprised or shocked over anything you see here, John Northwood. This is the Baby Laboratory."

They entered a room which seemed no different from a hospital ward. On little white beds lay naked children of various sizes, perfect, solemn-eyed youngsters and older children as beautiful as animated statues. Above each bed was a small Life Ray projector. A white-capped nurse went from bed to bed.

"They are recuperating from the daily educational period," said the scientist. "After a few minutes of this they will go into the growing room, which I shall have to show you through a window. Should you and I enter, we might be changed in a most extraordinary manner." He laughed mischievously. "But, look, Northwood!"

*

He slid back a panel in the wall, and Northwood peered in through a thick pane of clear glass. The room was really an immense outdoor arena, its only carpet the fine-bladed grass, its roof the blue sky cut in the middle by an enormous disc from which shot the aurora of trapped sunshine which made a golden umbrella over the valley. Through openings in the bottom of the disc poured a fine rain of rays which fell constantly upon groups of children, youths and young girls, all clad in the merest scraps of clothing. Some were dancing, others were playing games, but all seemed as supremely happy as the birds and butterflies which fluttered about the shrubs and flowers edging the arena.

"I don't expect you to believe," said Dr. Mundson, "that the oldest young man in there is three months old. You cannot see visible changes in a body which grows as slowly as the human being, whose normal period of development is twenty years or more. But I can give you visible proof of how fast growth takes place under the full power of the Life Ray. Plant life, which, even when left to nature, often develops from seed to flower within a few weeks or months, can be seen making its miraculous changes under the Life Ray. Watch those gorgeous purple flowers over which the butterflies are hovering."

Northwood followed his pointing finger. Near the glass window through which they looked grew an enormous bank of resplendent violet coloured flowers, which literally enshrouded the entire bush with their royal glory. At first glance it seemed as though a violent wind were snatching at flower and bush, but closer inspection proved that the agitation was part of the plant itself. And then he saw that the movements were the result of perpetual composition and growth.

*

He fastened his eyes on one huge bud. He saw it swell, burst, spread out its passionate purple velvet, lift the broad flower face to the light for a joyous minute. A few seconds later a butterfly lighted airily to sample its nectar and to brush the pollen from its yellow dusted wings. Scarcely had the winged visitor flown away than the purple petals began to wither and fall away, leaving the seed pod on the stem. The visible change went on in this seed pod. It turned rapidly brown, dried out, and then sent the released seeds in a shower to the rich black earth below. Scarcely had the seeds touched the ground than they sent up tiny green shoots that grew larger each moment. Within ten minutes there was a new plant a foot high. Within half an hour, the plant budded, blossomed, and cast forth its own seed.

"You understand?" asked the scientist. "Development is going on as rapidly among the children. Before the first year has passed, the youngest baby will have grandchildren; that is, if the baby tests out fit to pass its seed down to the new generation. I know it sounds absurd. Yet you saw the plant."

"But Doctor," Northwood rubbed his jaw thoughtfully, "Nature's forces of destruction, of tearing down, are as powerful as her creative powers. You have discovered the ultimate in creation and upbuilding. But perhaps—oh, Lord, it is too awful to think!"

"Speak, Northwood!" The scientist's voice was impatient.

"It is nothing!" The pale young man attempted a smile. "I was only imagining some of the horror that could be thrust on the world if a supermind like Adam's should discover Nature's secret of death and destruction and speed it up as you have sped the life force."

"*Ach Gott!*" Dr. Mundson's face was white. "He has his own laboratory, where he works every day. Don't talk so loud. He might be listening. And I believe he can do anything he sets out to accomplish."

Close to Northwood's ear fell a faint, triumphant whisper: "Yes, he can do anything. How did you guess, worm?"

It was Adam's voice.

"Now come and see the Leyden jar mothers," said Dr. Mundson. "We do not wait for the child to be born to start our work."

He took Northwood to a laboratory crowded with strange apparatus, where young men and women worked. Northwood knew instantly that these people, although unusually handsome and strong, were not of Adam's generation. None of them had the look of newness which marked those who had grown up under the Life Ray.

"They are the perfect couples whom I combed the world to find," said the scientist. "From their eugenic marriages sprang the first children that passed through the laboratory. I had hoped," he hesitated and looked sideways at Northwood, "I had dreamed of having the children of you and Athalia to help strengthen the New Race."

A wave of sudden disgust passed over Northwood.

"Thanks," he said tartly. "When I marry Athalia, I intend to have an old-fashioned home and a Black Age family. I don't relish having my children turned into—experiments."

"But wait until you see all the wonders of the laboratory! That is why I am showing you all this."

Northwood drew his handkerchief and mopped his brow. "It sickens me, Doctor! The more I see, the more pity I have for Adam—and the less I blame him for his rebellion and his desire to kill and to rule. Heavens! What a terrible thing you have done, experimenting with human life."

"Nonsense! Can you say that all life—all matter—is not the result of scientific experiment? Can you?" His black gaze made Northwood uncomfortable. "Buck up, young friend, for now I am going to show

277

you a marvellous improvement on Nature's bungling ways—the Leyden jar mother." He raised his voice and called, "Lilith!"

The woman whom they had met on the field came forward.

"May we take a peep at Lona's twins?" asked the scientist. "They are about ready to go to the growing dome, are they not?"

"In five more minutes," said the woman. "Come see."

She lifted one of the black velvet curtains that lined an entire side of the laboratory and thereby disclosed a globular jar of glass and metal, connected by wires to a dynamo. Above the jar was a Life Ray projector. Lilith slid aside a metal portion of the jar, disclosing through the glass underneath the squirming, kicking body of a baby, resting on a bed of soft, spongy substance, to which it was connected by the navel cord.

"The Leyden jar mother," said Dr. Mundson. "It is the dream of us scientists realised. The human mother's body does nothing but nourish and protect her unborn child, a job which science can do better. And so, in New Eden, we take the young embryo and place it in the Leyden jar mother, where the Life Ray, electricity, and chemical food shortens the period of gestation to a few days."

At that moment a bell under the Leyden jar began to ring. Dr. Mundson uncovered the jar and lifted out the child, a beautiful, perfectly formed boy, who began to cry lustily.

"Here is one baby who'll never be kissed," he said. "He'll be nourished chemically, and, at the end of the week, will no longer be a baby. If you are patient, you can actually see the processes of development taking place under the Life Ray, for babies develop very fast."

Northwood buried his face in his hands. "Lord! This is awful. No childhood; no mother to mould his mind! No parents to watch over him, to give him their tender care!"

"Awful, fiddlesticks! Come see how children get their education, how they learn to use their hands and feet so they need not pass through the awkwardness of childhood."

He led Northwood to a magnificent building whose façade of white marble was as simply beautiful as a Greek temple. The side walls, built almost entirely of glass, permitted the synthetic sunshine to sweep from end to end. They first entered a library, where youths and young girls poured over books of all kinds. Their manner of reading mystified Northwood. With a single sweep of the eye, they seemed to devour a page, and then turned to the next. He stepped closer to peer over the shoulder of a beautiful girl. She was reading "Euclid's Elements of Geometry," in Latin, and she turned the pages as swiftly as the other girl occupying her table, who was devouring "Paradise Lost."

Dr. Mundson whispered to him: "If you do not believe that Ruth here is getting her Euclid, which she probably never saw before today, examine her from the book; that is, if you are a good enough Latin scholar."

Ruth stopped her reading to talk to him, and, in a few minutes, had completely dumbfounded him with her pedantic replies, which fell from lips as luscious and unformed as an infant's.

"Now," said Dr. Mundson, "test Rachael on her Milton. As far as she has read, she should not misquote a line, and her comments will probably prove her scholarly appreciation of Milton."

Word for word, Rachael was able to give him "Paradise Lost" from memory, except the last four pages, which she had not read. Then, taking the book from him, she swept her eyes over these pages, returned the book to him, and quoted copiously and correctly.

*

Dr. Mundson gloated triumphantly over his astonishment. "There, my friend. Could you now be satisfied with old-fashioned children who spend long, expensive years in getting an education? Of course, your children will not have the perfect brains of these, yet, developed under the Life Ray, they should have splendid mentality.

"These children, through selective breeding, have brains that make everlasting records instantly. A page in a book, once seen, is indelibly retained by them, and understood. The same is true of a lecture, of an explanation given by a teacher, of even idle conversation. Any man or woman in this room should be able to repeat the most trivial conversation days old."

"But what of the arts, Dr. Mundson? Surely even your supermen and women cannot instantly learn to paint a masterpiece or to guide their fingers and their brains through the intricacies of a difficult musical composition."

"No?" His dark eyes glowed. "Come see!"

Before they entered another wing of the building, they heard a violin being played masterfully.

Dr. Mundson paused at the door.

"So that you may understand what you shall see, let me remind you that the nerve impulses and the coordinating means in the human body are purely electrical. The world has not yet accepted my theory, but it will. Under superman's system of education, the instantaneous records made on the brain give immediate skill to the acting parts of the body. Accordingly, musicians are made over night."

He threw open the door. Under a Life Ray projector, a beautiful, Junoesque woman was playing a violin. Facing her, and with eyes fastened to hers, stood a young man, whose arms and slender fingers mimicked every motion she made. Presently she stopped playing and handed the violin to him. In her own masterly manner, he repeated the score she had played.

"That is Eve," whispered Dr. Mundson. "I had selected her as Adam's wife. But he does not want her, the most brilliant woman of the New Race."

Northwood gave the woman an appraising look. "Who wants a perfect woman? I don't blame Adam for preferring Athalia. But how is she teaching her pupil?"

"Through thought vibration, which these perfect people have developed until they can record permanently the radioactive waves of the brains of others."

Eve turned, caught Northwood's eyes in her magnetic blue gaze, and smiled as only a goddess can smile upon a mortal she has marked as her own. She came toward him with outflung hands.

"So you have come!" Her vibrant contralto voice, like Adam's, held the birdlike, broken tremulo of a young child's. "I have been waiting for you, John Northwood."

Her eyes, as blue and icy as Adam's, lingered long on him, until he flinched from their steely magnetism. She slipped her arm through his and drew him gently but firmly from the room, while Dr. Mundson stood gaping after them.

They were on a flagged terrace arched with roses of gigantic size, which sent forth billows of sensuous fragrance. Eve led him to a white marble seat piled with silk cushions, on which she reclined her superb body, while she regarded him from narrowed lids.

"I saw your picture that he televisioned to Athalia," she said. "What a botch Dr. Mundson has made of his mating." Her laugh rippled like falling water. "I want you, John Northwood!"

Northwood started and blushed furiously. Smile dimples broke around her red, humid lips.

"Ah, you're old-fashioned!"

Her large, beautiful hand, fleshed more tenderly than any woman's hand he had ever seen, went out to him appealingly. "I can bring you amorous delight that your Athalia never could offer in her few years of youth. And I'll never grow old, John Northwood."

She came closer until he could feel the fragrant warmth of her tawny, ribbon bound hair pulse against his face. In sudden panic he drew back.

"But I am pledged to Athalia!" tumbled from him. "It is all a dreadful mistake, Eve. You and Adam were created for each other."

"Hush!" The lightning that flashed from her blue eyes changed her from seductress to angry goddess. "Created for each other! Who wants a made-to-measure lover?"

The luscious lips trembled slightly, and into the vivid eyes crept a suspicion of moisture. Eternal Eve's weapons! Northwood's handsome face relaxed with pity.

"I want you, John Northwood," she continued shamelessly. "Our love will be sublime." She leaned heavily against him, and her lips were like a blood red flower pressed against white satin. "Come, beloved, kiss me!"

Northwood gasped and turned his head. "Don't, Eve!"

"But a kiss from me will set you apart from all your generation, John Northwood, and you shall understand what no man of the Black Age could possibly fathom."

Her hair had partly fallen from its ribbon bandage and poured its fragrant gold against his shoulder.

"For God's sake, don't tempt me!" he groaned. "What do you mean?"

"That mental and physical and spiritual contact with me will temporarily give you, a three-dimension creature, the power of the new sense, which your race will not have for fifty thousand years."

White-lipped and trembling, he demanded: "Explain!"

Eve smiled. "Have you not guessed that Adam has developed an additional sense? You've seen him vanish. He and I have the sixth sense of Time Perception—the new sense which enables us to penetrate what you of the Black Age call the Fourth Dimension. Even you whose mentalities are framed by three dimensions have this sixth sense instinct. Your very religion is based on it, for you believe that in another life you shall step into Time, or, as you call it, eternity." She leaned closer so that her hair brushed his cheek. "What is eternity, John Northwood? Is it not keeping forever ahead of the Destroyer? The future is eternal, for it is never reached. Adam and I, through our new sense which comprehends Time and Space, can vanish by stepping a few seconds into the future, the Fourth Dimension of Space. Death can never reach us, not even accidental death, unless that which causes death could also slip into the future, which is not yet possible."

"But if the Fourth Dimension is future Time, why can one in the third dimension feel the touch of an unseen presence in the Fourth Dimension—hear his voice, even?"

"Thought vibration. The touch is not really felt nor the voice heard: they are only imagined. The radioactive waves of the brain of even you Black Age people are swift enough to bridge Space and Time. And it is the mind that carries us beyond the third dimension."

*

Her red mouth reached closer to him, her blue eyes touched hidden forces that slept in remote cells of his being. "You are going into Eternal Time, John Northwood, Eternity without beginning or end. You understand? You feel it? Comprehend it? Now for the contact—kiss me!"

Northwood had seen Athalia vanish under Adam's kiss. Suddenly, in one mad burst of understanding, he leaned over to his magnificent temptress.

For a split second he felt the sweet pressure of baby-soft lips, and then the atoms of his body seemed to fly asunder. Black chaos held him for a frightful moment before he felt, sanity return.

He was back on the terrace again, with Eve by his side. They were standing now. The world about him looked the same, yet there was a subtle change in everything.

Eve laughed softly. "It is puzzling, isn't it? You're seeing everything as in a mirror. What was left before is now right. Only you and I are real. All else is but a vision, a dream. For now you and I are existing one minute in future time, or, more simply, we are in the Fourth Dimension. To everything in the third dimension, we are invisible. Let me show you that Dr. Mundson cannot see you."

They went back to the room beyond the terrace. Dr. Mundson was not present.

"There he goes down the jungle path," said Eve, looking out of a window. She laughed. "Poor old fellow. The children of his genius are worrying him."

They were standing in the recess formed by a bay window. Eve picked up his hand and laid it against her face, giving him the full, blasting glory of her smiling blue eyes.

Northwood, looking away miserably, uttered a low cry. Coming over the field beyond were Adam and Athalia. By the trimming on the blue dress she wore, he could see that she was still in the Fourth Dimension, for he did not see her as a mirror image.

A look of fear leaped to Eve's face. She clutched Northwood's arm, trembling.

"I don't want Adam to see that I have passed you beyond," she gasped. "We are existing but one minute in the future. Always Adam and I have feared to pass too far beyond the sweetness of reality. But now, so that Adam may not see us, we shall step five minutes into what-is-yet-to-be. And even he, with all his power, cannot see into a future that is more distant than that in which he exists."

She raised her humid lips to his. "Come, beloved."

Northwood kissed her. Again came the moment of confusion, of the awful vacancy that was like death, and then he found himself and Eve in the laboratory, following Adam and Athalia down a long corridor. Athalia was crying and pleading frantically with Adam. Once she stopped and threw herself at his feet in a gesture of dramatic supplication, arms outflung, streaming eyes wide open with fear.

Adam stooped and lifted her gently and continued on his way, supporting her against his side.

Eve dug her fingers into Northwood's arm. Horror contorted her face, horror mixed with rage.

"My mind hears what he is saying, understands the vile plan he has made, John Northwood. He is on his way to his laboratory to destroy not only you and most of these in New Eden, but me as well. He wants only Athalia." Striding forward like an avenging goddess, she pulled Northwood after her.

"Hurry!" she whispered. "Remember, you and I are five minutes in the future, and Adam is only one. We are witnessing what will occur four minutes from now. We yet have time to reach the laboratory before him and be ready for him when he enters. And because he will have to go back to Present Time to do his work of destruction, I will be able to destroy him. Ah!"

Fierce joy burned in her flashing blue eyes, and her slender nostrils quivered delicately. Northwood, peeping at her in horror, knew that no mercy could be expected of her. And when she stopped at a certain door and inserted a key, he remembered Athalia. What if she should enter with Adam in Present Time?

They were inside Adam's laboratory, a huge apartment filled with queer apparatus and cages of live animals. The room was a strange paradox. Part of the equipment, the walls, and the floor was glistening with newness, and part was moulding with extreme age. The powers of disintegration that haunt a tropical forest seemed to be devouring certain spots of the room. Here, in the midst of bright marble, was a section of wall that seemed as old as the pyramids. The surface of the stone had an appalling mouldiness, as though it had been lifted from an ancient graveyard where it had lain in the festering ground for unwholesome centuries.

Between cracks in this stained and decayed section of stone grew fetid moss that quivered with the microscopic organisms that infest age-rotten places. Sections of the flooring and woodwork also reeked with mustiness. In one dark, webby corner of the room lay a pile of bleached bones, still tinted with the ghastly greys and pinks of putrefaction. Northwood, overwhelmingly nauseated, withdrew his eyes from the bones, only to see, in another corner, a pile of worm-eaten clothing that lay on the floor in the outline of a man.

Faint with the reek of ancient mustiness, Northwood retreated to the door, dizzy and staggering.

"It sickens you," said Eve, "and it sickens me also, for death and decay are not pleasant. Yet Nature, left to herself, reduces all to this. Every grave that has yawned to receive its pray hides corruption no less shocking. Nature's forces of creation and destruction forever work in partnership. Never satisfied with her composition, she destroys and starts again, building, building towards the ultimate of perfection. Thus, it is natural that if Dr. Mundson isolated the Life Ray, Nature's supreme force of compensation, isolation of the Death Ray should closely follow. Adam, thirsting for power, has succeeded. A few sweeps of his unholy ray of decomposition will undo all Dr. Mundson's work in this valley and reduce it to a stinking holocaust of destruction. And the time for his striking has come!"

She seized his face and drew it toward her. "Quick!" she said. "We'll have to go back to the third dimension. I could leave you safe in the fourth, but if anything should happen to me, you would be stranded forever in future time."

She kissed his lips. In a moment, he was back in the old familiar world, where right is right and left is left. Again the subtle change wrought by Eve's magic lips had taken place.

Eve went to a machine standing in a corner of the room.

"Come here and get behind me, John Northwood. I want to test it before he enters."

Northwood stood behind her shoulder.

"Now watch!" she ordered. "I shall turn it on one of those cages of guinea pigs over there."

She swung the projector around, pointed it at the cage of small, squealing animals, and threw a lever. Instantly a cone of black mephitis shot forth, a loathsome, bituminous stream of putrefaction that reeked of the grave and the cesspool, of the utmost reaches of decay before the dust accepts the disintegrated atoms. The first touch of seething, pitchy destruction brought screams of sudden agony from the guinea pigs, but the screams were cut short as the little animals fell in shocking, instant decay. The very cage which imprisoned them shrivelled and retreated from the hellish, devouring breath that struck its noisome rot into the heart of the wood and the metal, reducing both to revolting ruin.

Eve cut off the frightful power, and the black cone disappeared, leaving the room putrid with its defilement.

"And Adam would do that to the world," she said, her blue eyes like electric-shot icicles. "He would do it to you, John Northwood—and to me!" Her full bosom strained under the passion beneath.

"Listen!" She raised her hand warningly. "He comes! The destroyer comes!"

A hand was at the door. Eve reached for the lever, and, the same moment, Northwood leaned over her imploringly.

"If Athalia is with him!" he gasped. "You will not harm her?"

A wild shriek at the door, a slight scuffle, and then the doorknob was wrenched as though two were fighting over it.

"For God's sake, Eve!" implored Northwood. "Wait! Wait!"

"No! She shall die, too. You love her!"

Icy, cruel eyes cut into him, and a new-fleshed hand tried to push him aside. The door was straining open. A beloved voice shrieked. "John!"

Eve and Northwood both leaped for the lever. Under her tender white flesh she was as strong as a man. In the midst of the struggle, her red, humid lips approached his—closer. Closer. Their merest

288

pressure would thrust him into Future Time, where the laboratory and all it contained would be but a shadow, and where he would be helpless to interfere with her terrible will.

He saw the door open and Adam stride into the room. Behind him, lying prone in the hall where she had probably fainted, was Athalia. In a mad burst of strength he touched the lever together with Eve.

The projector, belching forth its stinking breath of corruption swung in a mad arc over the ceiling, over the walls—and then straight at Adam.

Then, quicker than thought, came the accident. Eve, attempting to throw Northwood off, tripped, fell half over the machine, and, with a short scream of despair, dropped into the black path of destruction.

Northwood paused, horrified. The Death Ray was pointed at an inner wall of the room, which, even as he looked, crumbled and disappeared, bringing down upon him dust more foul than any obscenity the bowels of the earth might yield. In an instant the black cone ate through the outer parts of the building, where crashing stone and screams that were more horrible because of their shortness followed the ruin that swept far into the fair reaches of the valley.

The paralysing odour of decay took his breath, numbed his muscles, until, of all that huge building, the wall behind him and one small section of the room by the doorway alone remained whole. He was trying to nerve himself to reach for the lever close to that quiet formless thing still partly draped over the machine, when a faint sound in the door electrified him. At first, he dared not look, but his own name, spoken almost in a gasp, gave him courage.

Athalia lay on the floor, apparently untouched.

He jerked the lever violently before running to her, exultant with the knowledge that his own efforts to keep the ray from the door had saved her.

"And you're not hurt!" He gathered her close.

"John! I saw it get Adam." She pointed to a new mound of mouldy clothes on the floor. "Oh, it is hideous for me to be so glad, but he was going to destroy everything and everyone except me. He made the ray projector for that one purpose."

Northwood looked over the pile of putrid ruins which a few minutes ago, had been a building. There was not a wall left intact.

"His intention is accomplished, Athalia," he said sadly. "Let's get out before more stones fall."

In a moment they were in the open. An ominous stillness seemed to grip the very air—the awful silence of the polar wastes which lay not far beyond the mountains.

"How dark it is, John!" cried Athalia. "Dark and cold!"

"The sunshine projector!" gasped Northwood. "It must have been destroyed. Look, dearest! The golden light has disappeared."

"And the warm air of the valley will lift immediately. That means a polar blizzard." She shuddered and clung closer to him. "I've seen Antarctic storms, John. They're death."

Northwood avoided her eyes. "There's the sun-ship. We'll give the ruins the once over in case there are any survivors; then we'll save ourselves."

Even a cursory examination of the mouldy piles of stone and dust convinced them that there could be no survivors. The ruins looked as though they had lain in those crumbling piles for centuries. Northwood, smothering his repugnance, stepped among them—among the green, slimy stones and the unspeakable revolting débris, staggering back and faint and shocked when he came upon dust that was once human.

"God!" he groaned, hands over eyes. "We're alone, Athalia! Alone in a charnel house. The laboratory housed the entire population, didn't it?"

"Yes. Needing no sleep nor food, we did not need houses. We all worked here, under Dr. Mundson's generalship, and, lately under Adam's, like a little band of soldiers fighting for a great cause."

"Let's go to the sun-ship, dearest."

"But Daddy Mundson was in the library," sobbed Athalia. "Let's look for him a little longer."

Sudden remembrance came to Northwood. "No, Athalia! He left the library. I saw him go down the jungle path several minutes before I and Eve went to Adam's laboratory."

"Then he might be safe!" Her eyes danced. "He might have gone to the sun-ship."

Shivering, she slumped against him. "Oh, John! I'm cold."

Her face was blue. Northwood jerked off his coat and wrapped it around her, taking the intense cold against his unprotected shoulders. The low, grey sky was rapidly darkening, and the feeble light of the sun could scarcely pierce the clouds. It was disturbing to know that even the summer temperature in the Antarctic was far below zero.

"Come, girl," said Northwood gravely. "Hurry! It's snowing."

They started to run down the road through the narrow strip of jungle. The Death Ray had cut huge swathes in the tangle of trees and vines, and now areas of heaped débris, livid with the colours of recent decay, exhaled a mephitic humidity altogether alien to the snow that fell in soft, slow flakes. Each hesitated to voice the new fear: had the sun-ship been destroyed?

By the time they reached the open field, the snow stung their flesh like sharp needles, but it was not yet thick enough to hide from them a hideous fact.

The sun-ship was gone.

It might have occupied one of several black, foul areas on the green grass, where the searching Death Ray had made the very soil putrefy, and the rocks crumble into shocking dust.

Northwood snatched Athalia to him, too full of despair to speak. A sudden terrific flurry of snow whirled around them, and they were almost blown from their feet by the icy wind that tore over the unprotected field.

"It won't be long," said Athalia faintly. "Freezing doesn't hurt, John, dear."

"It isn't fair, Athalia! There never would have been such a marriage as ours. Dr. Mundson searched the world to bring us together."

"For scientific experiment!" she sobbed. "I'd rather die, John. I want an old-fashioned home, a Black Age family. I want to grow old with you and leave the earth to my children. Or else I want to die here now under the kind, white blanket the snow is already spreading over us." She drooped in his arms.

Clinging together, they stood in the howling wind, looking at each other hungrily, as though they would snatch from death this one last picture of the other.

Northwood's freezing lips translated some of the futile words that crowded against them. "I love you because you are not perfect. I hate perfection!"

"Yes. Perfection is the only hopeless state, John. That is why Adam wanted to destroy, so that he might build again."

They were sitting in the snow now, for they were very tired. The storm began whistling louder, as though it were only a few feet above their heads.

"That sounds almost like the sun-ship," said Athalia drowsily.

"It's only the wind. Hold your face down so it won't strike your flesh so cruelly."

"I'm not suffering. I'm getting warm again." She smiled at him sleepily.

Little icicles began to form on their clothing, and the powdery snow frosted their uncovered hair.

Suddenly came a familiar voice: "*Ach Gott!*"

Dr. Mundson stood before them, covered with snow until he looked like a polar bear.

"Get up!" he shouted. "Quick! To the sun-ship!"

He seized Athalia and jerked her to her feet. She looked at him sleepily for a moment, and then threw herself at him and hugged him frantically.

"You're not dead?"

Taking each by the arm, he half dragged them to the sun-ship, which had landed only a few feet away. In a few minutes he had hot brandy for them.

While they sipped greedily, he talked, between working the sun-ship's controls.

"No, I wouldn't say it was a lucky moment that drew me to the sun-ship. When I saw Eve trying to charm John, I had what you American slangists call a hunch, which sent me to the sun-ship to get it off the ground so that Adam couldn't commandeer it. And what is a hunch but a mental penetration into the Fourth Dimension?" For a long moment, he brooded, absent-minded. "I was in the air when the black ray, which I suppose is Adam's deviltry, began to destroy everything it touched. From a safe elevation I saw it wreck all my work." A sudden spasm crossed his face. "I've flown over the entire valley. We're the only survivors—thank God!"

"And so at last you confess that it is not well to tamper with human life?" Northwood, warmed with hot brandy, was his old self again.

"Oh, I have not altogether wasted my efforts. I went to elaborate pains to bring together a perfect man and a perfect woman of what Adam called our Black Age." He smiled at them whimsically.

"And who can say to what extent you have thus furthered natural evolution?" Northwood slipped his arm around Athalia. "Our children might be more than geniuses, Doctor!"

Dr. Mundson nodded his huge, shaggy head gravely.

"The true instinct of a Creature of the Light," he declared.

BRIDE OF THE ANTARCTIC

Mordred Weir

Mordred Weir is one of the many pen names of Amelia Reynolds Long (1904–1978), an American writer whose reputation was based mainly on a series of mystery novels, and (like Sophie Wenzel Ellis) a number of contributions to 1920s and 30s pulp magazines. The most notable of these is "The Thought Monster" (1930) from *Weird Tales*: "a goose-flesh story of the sudden and frightful deaths caused by a strange creature in a panic-stricken village" which formed the basis for the 1958 film *Fiend Without a Face*.

Published in 1939 in *Strange Stories*, "Bride of the Antarctic" provides an interesting contribution to the gender history of polar exploration and its fictional representation. While the Arctic and Antarctic wildernesses are often conceived as places of macho self-realisation—the intrepid explorer battling against the elements to prove his heroism and virility—"Bride of the Antarctic" is one of several stories in this collection that critiques the patriarchal poles. Think of how Allan Gordon in James Hogg's story ends up relying on a female bear, or the way that Harriet Prescott Spofford focuses on male failure. "Bride of the Antarctic" was written not long after the Danish-Norwegian explorer Caroline Mikkelsen became the first woman to take part in an Antarctic expedition in 1935 (although there are accounts that place Māori women explorers on an Antarctic island much earlier); the story's premise is the stereotypical assumption that the poles are no place for a woman. "Bride of the Antarctic" may not be an explicit feminist call to arms, but it does show the story's male adventurers as haunted by the spectres of their own misogynist world-views.

The three of us who were to spend the long Antarctic night in the little camp on the coast of Victoria Land stood on the edge of the shelf ice and watched the hull of the *Stormy Petrel* slip further and further into the distance. Finally, seen through the ghostly shroud of the sea-mist, she appeared more like a mirage than a real ship. Then, because we could not bear the moment when she should fade from our sight entirely, we turned back to the huge bonfire which we had built as a kind of parting salute to her.

The wood for that bonfire had been discovered when the crew of the *Petrel* were helping to lay the foundations for the shack in which we were to spend the winter making weather observations. It had consisted of a number of old boxes and casks, most of them broken and battered by the Antarctic blizzards that had passed over them. They were the derelict remains of a former camp that had occupied the spot.

Farrell had pointed to some half obliterated letters on one of the boxes.

"Remains of the Howell Expedition," he had observed. "I knew their camp was around here somewhere."

A shiver that was not due to the polar cold had passed over Farrell and he had added grimly: "I hope we have better luck than they did."

Everyone knew about the ill-fated Howell Expedition, and about Mad Bill Howell, its leader and organiser, who had forced his young and beautiful wife to accompany him upon a project that would tax the stamina of even the stoutest men. When the ship had sailed away, leaving Howell, his wife, and fourteen others upon that lonely wasteland of perpetual snow and ice, the girl had cried and begged to go back with it; but Howell had strangely, stubbornly refused.

What his motive was, nobody ever knew. Some said it was jealousy; others, that it was sheer, inhuman love of wanton cruelty. But in any case, he was bound and determined that the girl should remain a prisoner there in the barren fastness of the southern pole, condemned to undergo its harrowing torture of cold and darkness along with himself.

That winter had been hard, even for the Antarctic; and the ship returning to pick them up in the spring was almost two months late in reaching them. When at last it succeeded in forcing its way through the pressure ice and dropping anchor in the little cove upon which the camp had been situated, its crew beheld only a few snow-covered mounds, like forsaken graves, where its buildings should have been.

At first sight it looked as though the entire company had perished; then from an opening in one of the mounds, they saw two gaunt, bedraggled figures emerge and come running toward them. The two were Captain Howell and the cook, Jim Witherspoon. All the others, including Gloria Howell, had died during the long winter night.

Both men collapsed upon being taken aboard ship; but Jim Witherspoon had talked in his delirium, and some of the things he had said were awful. He babbled of how the subzero cold had set in; a cold for whose unexpected intensity the expedition had been unprepared. He told how the first man had died, and his body, placed in a packing-case, had been buried in a shallow grave in the ice. Then had followed another and another, while those who remained grew a little more crazed each day by the horror and the cold. And through it all, Gloria Howell had ironically gone on living.

Last of all, Witherspoon raved about one hideous time toward the end of the polar night, when the girl, unable to endure the torment longer, had cried aloud for warmth and light, and Mad Bill Howell, her husband, in a fit of savage rage...

But that part was the nightmare of delirium, of course. Not even such a sadistic monster as Captain Howell would have turned a human creature, stripped naked, out into the merciless cold of the Antarctic blizzard!

After the return to America, Howell had disappeared completely from the public eye, and even from the ken of his friends. Considering what he must have had on his conscience, even discounting the cook's ravings, it was no wonder.

Thoughts something like this were flitting through my mind as I watched my two companions, Farrell and Murdock, heap more wood upon the fire. They worked with an almost feverish activity; and somehow I got the impression that they were labouring to be rid of the last material remains of that other, ill-fated camp.

At last Farrell, with a mighty heave of his broad shoulders, tossed the last box upon the fire. It was a narrow, oblong packing-case nearly six feet in length; and it must have been unusually heavy, for it landed with a dull, sullen thud that sent the hot embers scattering and sizzling upon the snow.

For a while we stood watching the leaping flames, our forms and faces seen in wavy focus through the alternating layers of hot and cold air. Farrell as was his habit, kept up a running chatter upon inconsequential matters, while Murdock, always taciturn and aloof, watched the dancing sparks through half closed, brooding eyes, as though he saw in them some reflection of his own secret thoughts.

We were not prepared for what followed, although we should have been.

As the fire burned low to its final embers, a ghastly, rounded object appeared. It was a grinning human skull, blackened by the fire, with eye-sockets and jaws filled with glowing coals!

Farrell let out a sharp exclamation, like a yelp, and jumped back. Murdock's breath whistled in his throat, and his figure stiffened like a dog's does at scent of danger. I saw that we had been burning not just a box but a coffin, and said so. We abandoned the remains of the fire to the extinguishing force of the elements.

The shack in which we were to spend the long months of the Antarctic night was snug enough, but small for the occupancy of three men, measuring barely twelve feet in any of its dimensions. Beneath it was a kind of cellar formed by the laying of the foundations, and entered by a trapdoor in the floor, to be used principally for the disposal of refuse. In the roof was a second trap, reached by a rope ladder. This would serve as a means of entrance and egress when the snows buried our ordinary door.

Murdock lit the big hurricane lamp that hung from the rafters, for the red rim of the sun was already low upon the northern horizon, and set about preparing supper. When it was ready, we ate it in silence, our minds busy with many things.

At last Farrell who never could hold his tongue at the proper time, spoke.

"Did you see it?" he asked.

"See what?" I inquired when Murdock did not speak.

"That last box. It was a coffin."

"Needless to say," I muttered hoping to discourage this line of conversation.

"It was some poor devil from the Howell Expedition," Farrell rattled on. "There must be others around here."

Murdock looked up. There was a strange, cold light in his eyes, like the reflection of the sun upon the ice. "Shut up," he growled savagely.

Farrell mumbled something half resentfully, and began to fill his pipe. After that, the subject was dropped.

In the weeks that followed, the Antarctic night settled down upon us. The penguins left for the coastal islands, taking with them the last vestige of sociability that the frozen polar continent possessed. Occasionally, with our sounding instruments we could hear the seals stirring under the ice; but ordinarily there was no sound but the snapping and groaning of the frost as everything froze more solidly.

Finally even this ceased; we were in a world of intersteller silence disturbed only by the periodic howling of the Antarctic blizzards. The night had descended upon us.

By the end of the first month, the blackness was complete even at midday. Strange stars hung from an ebon sky, so large that their apparent nearness was frightening. The snow was already half way up our windows; and we had to go daily to the roof to remove it from the trapdoor and to clear the ventilator shafts.

One day a strange light appeared at the tops of the windows. Pulling on our furs and face-masks, we climbed to the roof, and beheld the black vault of the sky split with waving banners of red and green light.

The Aurora Australis!

In the vivid, unearthly glare, we could see the white crags of the Admiralty Range, at whose feet we crouched; and in the distance, rising above them, the steep, black sides of Mt. Erebus, a lazy cloud of grey ash drifting about his crater, like the smoke from a funeral pyre. The sight was like a harbinger of evil; and we crept back into the house and fastened the trap above us.

It was shortly after this that the noises began.

Mere whisperings at first, they were audible only when we had settled down in our bunks for our hours of sleep. Then gradually they became louder, like ghostly fingers scratching to get in; and always they brought with them a feeling of melancholy, weighing our spirits down with a sense of cold dread and foreboding.

Murdock grew more and more silent and morose, as if he were brooding over something; while even the talkative Farrell was depressed. As for myself, I set about being cheerful with a determination that was almost ferocious.

"Did you hear it last night, sir?" Farrell put the question unexpectedly, looking up from the meteorological reports he was writing.

"You mean the house creaking?" I asked, while Murdock watched both of us from his bunk.

"No sir; the voice."

"Nonsense!" I was deliberately scornful. "What you heard was the timbers creaking under the weight of snow on the roof."

"But it came from *under* the house sir." Farrell was annoyingly persistent. "And it was a voice. Murdock heard it, too."

I turned to Murdock. "What did you hear?"

He looked at me out of moody eyes that reflected the lantern light glassily. "I heard—what he says," he muttered.

I rose and pulled on my furs; then, with a withering look at my two companions, I climbed the ladder to the roof. I had to be alone for a while, in order to think clearly.

There *had* been a sound that night; a very human-like sound. But it had been *only* a sound; not a voice.

In the days that followed, the house seemed to grow colder. It had always been draughty about the floor and in the night when the fire in the stove was allowed to burn down to a mere bed of glowing coals, the temperature would drop to something that I shiver even now to think about. But now the cold was different. It was no longer the mere absence of heat; it was a positive, sentient force, creeping into our sleeping-bags at night and weaving icy fingers about our hearts.

Worse still, although none of us spoke of it, we were all listening for the voice. Although no verbal agreement had been made, it was tacitly understood that it should not be mentioned again among us.

This had a strange effect. As time passed, we found ourselves talking less and less to one another, fearful lest someone should forget. But always we were listening—listening.

And then one night it came.

We were in our bunks, each pretending to the others that he slept. Suddenly the room was cold; colder even than it had been before, than it had ever been. The dim lamp that hung from the rafters flickered, and its light took on a weird, greenish hue, like burning sea-salt. We sat up in our bunks and looked at one another, our dilated eyes crying out that all of us had heard.

From the cellar under our house had come a queer dull sound, like the sudden expulsion of air from a container previously sealed.

Something was moving down there, something that was trying to get out. And there was only one way out; the trapdoor in the floor!

In spite of the cold, I felt the sweat start upon my forehead, while my mouth and throat became dry as parchment. I forced myself to reach for the revolver that hung upon the wall beside me; then, by a supreme effort of will, I climbed out of my sleeping-bag.

My legs were trembling under me as I took the few steps to the trapdoor. Gripping the revolver in my right hand, I slipped back the bolt with my left, and began to lift the trap. It came upward with a sort of heave, as if something was pushing from beneath.

The screams from the two men in the bunks came simultaneously. Something was rising through the open trap; something that looked like a thick, white mist! It got into my eyes and throat, blinding and choking me. With the last ounce of strength that remained in me, I slammed the trapdoor down and scrambled back into my bunk.

But it was too late. Something was in the room with us. It had come up through the open trap, and was taking form out of the mist. We saw it take shape. Afterwards, Farrell and I tried to tell each other that what we had seen had been a trick of the light and the damp air let up from the cellar; but we both knew that the thing had assumed the almost nude form of a woman draped in a long white bridal veil. Or was it a shroud?

The figure swayed forward, the curves of its white body gleaming through the veil, its arms outstretched. It glided toward the corner where Murdock cowered in his bunk, but it did not touch him. In stead, it floated toward the ceiling, and disappeared through the roof.

Murdock rose from his bunk like a man hypnotised. Without stopping to put on his furs, he climbed the ladder and began to push open the trap in the roof.

"Murdock, you fool! Come back!" I croaked. "You'll be frozen to death out there!"

Only a hissing flurry of snowflakes answered me. Then the trap fell shut with a dull, heavy thud…

When the *Stormy Petrel* returned for us in the spring, we had to report the loss of one man.

"Poor devil!" the captain said when he had heard our story. "I guess coming back to this spot was too much for him. He probably didn't know you'd locate here when he signed up."

"Why, what do you mean?" I asked. "What had the place to do with it?"

"Oh, I forgot," he replied. "We didn't find out who he really was until after we'd left you here. He was Captain Howell, leader of the Howell Expedition. You remember."

After that I was not surprised when, in dismantling the house, a coffin containing the frozen body of Gloria Howell was discovered in our cellar.

1943

GHOST

Henry Kuttner

Henry Kuttner (1915–1958) was a prolific author who made his name in the pulp magazines of the 1930s, publishing his first story while still a teenager. Kuttner was a byword for versatility; according to *Startling Stories*, Kuttner "has written stark psychological stories, howling slapstick, keen-edged satire, nimble-witted farce and spine-chilling shockers". He published under a number of pseudonyms (the *New York Times* in his obituary counted sixteen) and collaborated extensively with his wife Catherine Lucille Moore, herself one of the most noted science-fiction writers of her generation. Given that he wrote over 200 stories, not to mention over a dozen novels, it is hardly surprising that Kuttner landed on polar themes from time to time, especially since he was a correspondent of H. P. Lovecraft and a contributor to the Cthulhu mythos which often looked to the ends of the earth. Among his polar (and subpolar) stories is the 1947 novel *The Power and the Glory* that tells of a "treasure beyond imagining" on an Alaskan peak.

"Ghost", published in *Astounding Science-Fiction* in 1943, illustrates Kuttner's longstanding interest in psychoanalysis. As the horror writer Robert Bloch (author of the novel that would become Hitchcock's *Psycho*) phrased it, Kuttner was concerned in his fiction with "delving into the deepest and darkest dreams of all, that murkiest of mysteries which is the mortal mind". The polar worlds have often carried the burden in literature of functioning as the screen on which the terrors and fantasies of the unconscious might be projected. "Ghost" is somewhat different in its orientation as a story that locates the spectral peril less in the landscape and more in the technology of human endeavour in a way that (loosely) anticipates twenty-first century anxieties about IT and mental health.

The president of Integration almost fell out of his chair. His ruddy cheeks turned sallow, his jaw dropped, and the hard blue eyes, behind their flexolenses, lost their look of keen inquiry and became merely stupefied. Ben Halliday slowly swivelled around and stared out at the skyscrapers of New York, as though to assure himself that he was living in the Twenty-first Century and the golden age of science.

No witches, riding on broomsticks, were visible outside the window.

Only slightly reassured, Halliday turned back to the prim, grey, tight-mouthed figure across the desk. Dr. Elton Ford did not look like Cagliostro. He resembled what he was: the greatest living psychologist.

"What did you say?" Halliday asked weakly.

Ford put his fingertips together precisely and nodded. "You heard me. The answer is ghosts. Your Antarctic Integration Station is haunted."

"You're joking." Halliday sounded hopeful.

"I'm giving you my theory in the simplest possible terms. Naturally, I can't verify it without field work."

"*Ghosts!*"

The trace of a smile showed on Ford's thin lips. "Without sheets or clanking chains. This is a singularly logical sort of ghost, Mr.

Halliday. It has nothing to do with superstition. It could have existed only in this scientific age. In the Castle of Otranto it would have been absurd. Today—with your integrators—you have paved the way for hauntings. I suspect that this is the first of many, unless you take certain precautions. I believe I can solve this problem—and future ones. But the only possible method is an empirical one. I must lay the ghost, not with bell, book and candle, but through application of psychology."

Halliday was still dazed. "You believe in *ghosts*?"

"Since yesterday, I believe in a certain peculiar type of haunting. Basically, this business has nothing in common with the apparitions of folklore. But as a result of new factors, the equation equals exactly the same as ... well, the Horla, Blackwood's yarns, or even Bulwer-Lytton's 'Haunters and the Haunted'. The manifestations are the same."

"I don't get it."

"In witchcraft days a hag stirred herbs in a caldron, added a few toads and bats, and cured someone of heart disease. Today we leave out the fauna and use digitalis."

Halliday shook his head in a baffled way. "Dr. Ford. I don't quite know what to say. You must know what you're talking about—"

"I assure you that I do."

"But—"

"Listen," Ford said carefully. "Since Bronson died, you can't keep an operator at your Antarctic Station. This man—Larry Crockett—has even stayed longer than most, but he feels the phenomena, too. A dull, hopeless depression, completely passive and overpowering."

"But that station is one of the science centres of the world! Ghosts in that place?"

"It's a new sort of ghost," Ford said. "It also happens to be one of the oldest. Dangerous, too. Modern science, my dear man, has finally gone full circle and created a haunting. Now I'm going down to Antarctica and try exorcism."

"Oh, Lord." Halliday said.

The Station's *raison d'être* was the huge underground chamber known irreverently as the Brainpan. It was something out of classic history, Karnak or Babylon or Ur—high-ceilinged and completely bare except for the double row of giant pillars that flanked the walls.

These were of white plastic and insulated and each was twenty feet high, six feet in diameter, and featureless. They contained the new radioatom brains perfected by Integration. They were the integrators.

Not colloids, they consisted of mind-machines, units reacting at light-velocity speeds. They were not, strictly speaking, robots. Nor were they free brains, capable of ego-consciousness. Scientists had broken down the factors that make up the intelligent brain, created supercharged equivalents, and achieved delicate, well-functioning organisms with a fantastically high I. Q. They could be operated either singly or in circuit. The capability increased proportionately.

The integrators' chief function was that of efficiency. They could answer questions. They could solve complicated problems. They could compute a meteorite's orbit within minutes or seconds, where a trained astrophysicist would have taken weeks to get the same answer. In the swift, well-oiled world of 2030, time was invaluable. In five years the integrators had also proved themselves invaluable.

They were superbrains—but limited. They were incapable of self-adjustment, for they were without ego.

Thirty white pillars towered in the Brainpan, their radioatom brains functioning with alarming efficiency. They never made a mistake."

They were—*minds*! And they were delicate, sensitive, powerful.

*

Larry Crockett was a big red-faced Irishman with blue-black hair, and a fiery temper. Seated at dinner across from Dr. Ford, he watched dessert come out of the Automat slot and didn't care a great deal. The psychologist's keen eyes were watchful.

"Did you hear me, Mr. Crockett?"

"What? Oh, yeah. But there's nothing wrong. I just feel lousy."

"Since Bronson's death there have been six men at this post. They have all felt lousy."

"Well, living here alone, cooped up under the ice—"

"They had lived alone before at other stations. So had you."

Crockett's shrug was infinitely weary. "I dunno. Maybe I should quit, too."

"You're—afraid to stay here?"

"No. There's nothing to be afraid of."

"Not even ghosts?" Ford said.

"Ghosts? A few of those might pep up the atmosphere."

"Before you were stationed here, you were ambitious. You planned on marrying, you were working for a promotion—"

"Yeah."

"What's the matter? Lost interest?"

"You might call it that," Crockett acknowledged. "I don't see much point in ... in anything."

"Yet you're healthy. The tests I gave you show that. There's a black, profound depression in this place; I feel it myself." Ford paused. The dull weariness, lurking at the back of his mind, crept slowly forward like a gelid, languid tide. He stared around. The station was bright, modern and cheerful. Yet it did not seem so.

He went on.

"I've been studying the integrators, and find them most interesting."

Crockett didn't answer. He was looking absently at his coffee.

"Most interesting," Ford repeated. "By the way, do you know what happened to Bronson?"

"Sure. He went crazy and killed himself."

"Here."

"Right. What about it?"

"His ghost remains," Ford said.

Crockett looked up. He pushed back his chair, hesitating between a laugh and blank astonishment. Finally he decided on the laugh. It didn't sound very amused.

"Then Bronson wasn't the only crazy one," he remarked.

Ford grinned. "Let's go down and see the integrators."

Crockett met the psychologist's eyes, a faint, worried frown appearing on his face. He tapped his fingers nervously on the table.

"Down there? Why?"

"Do you mind?"

"Hell, no," Crockett said after a pause. "It's just—"

"The influence is stronger there," Ford suggested. "You feel more depressed when you are near the integrators. Am I right?"

"O. K.," Crockett muttered. "So what?"

"The trouble comes from there. Obviously."

"They're running all right. We feed in the questions and we get the right answers."

"I'm not talking about intellect," Ford pointed out. "I'm discussing emotions."

Crockett laughed shortly. "Those damn machines haven't got any emotions."

"None of their own. They can't create. All their potentialities were built into them. But listen, Crockett—you take a super-complicated thinking machine, a radioatom brain, and it's necessarily very sensitive and receptive. It's got to be. That's why you can have a thirty-unit hookup here—you're at the balancing point of the magnetic currents."

"Well?"

"Bring a magnet near a compass and what happens? The compass works on magnetism. The integrators work on—something else. And they're delicately balanced—beautifully poised."

"Are you trying to tell me they've gone mad?" Crockett demanded.

"That's too simple," Ford told him. "Madness implies flux. There are variable periods. The brains in the integrators are—well, poised, frozen within their fixed limits, irrevocably in their orbits. But they are sensitive to one thing, because they have to be. Their strength is their weakness."

"So?"

"Did you ever live with a lunatic?" Ford asked. "I'm sure you didn't. There's a certain—effect—on sensitive people. The integrators are a damn sight more mentally suggestive than a human being."

"You're talking about induced madness," Crockett said, and Ford nodded in a pleased fashion.

"An induced phase of madness, rather. The integrators can't follow the madness pattern; they're not capable of it. They're simply radioatom brains. But they're receptive. Take a blank phonograph record and play a tune—cut the wax and you'll have a disk that will repeat the same thing over and over. Certain parts of the integrators were like blank records. Intangible parts that were the corollary of a finely tuned thinking apparatus. No free will is involved. The abnormally sensitive integrators recorded a mental pattern and are reproducing. Bronson's pattern."

"So," Crockett said, "the machines have gone nuts."

"No. Lunacy implies consciousness of self. The integrators record and repeat. Which is why six operators had to leave this station."

"Well," Crockett said, "so I am. Before I go crazy, too. It's—rather nasty."

"What's it like?"

"I'd kill myself if it weren't too much trouble," the Irishman said succinctly.

Ford took out a celoflex notebook and spun the wheel. "I've a case history of Bronson here. D'you know anything about types of insanity?"

"Not much. Bronson—I used to know him. Sometimes he'd be 'way down in the dumps, and then again he'd be the life of the party."

"Did he ever mention suicide?"

"Not that I know of."

Ford nodded. "If he'd talked about it, he never would have done it. He was that type. A manic-depressive, moods of deep depression alternating with periods of elation. Early in the history of psychiatry, patients were classed in two groups; paranoia or dementia praecox. But that didn't work. There was no line of demarcation; the types overlapped. Nowadays we have manic-depressive and schizophrenic. Schizoids can't be cured; the other can. You, Mr. Crockett, are a manic-depressive type, easily influenced."

"Yeah? That doesn't mean I'm crazy, though."

Ford grinned. "Scarcely. Like everyone else, you trend in a certain direction. If you ever became insane, you would be a manic-depressive. While I would be a schizophrenic, for I'm a schizoid type. Most psychologists are: it's the outgrowth of a compensated complex, inferiority or superiority."

"You mean—"

The doctor went on; he had a purpose in explaining these matters to Crockett. Complete understanding is part of the therapy.

"Put it this way. Manic-depressives are fairly simple cases; they swing from elation to depression—a big swing, unlike the steady, quick pulse of a schizoid graph. It covers days, weeks, or months. When a manic-depressive type goes over the border, his worst period is on the descending curve—the downbeat. He sits and does nothing. He's the most acutely miserable person on earth—sometimes so unhappy he even enjoys it. Not till the upcurve is reached does he change from passive to active. That's when he breaks chairs and requires a strait jacket."

Crockett was interested now. He was applying Ford's words to himself, which was the normal reaction.

"The schizoid, on the other hand," Ford continued, "has no such simple prognosis. Anything can happen. You get the split personality, the mother fixations, and the complexes—Oedipus, return to childhood, persecution, the king complex—an infinite variety almost. A schizoid is incurable—but, luckily, a manic-depressive isn't. Our ghost here is manic-depressive."

The Irishman had lost some of his ruddy colour. "I'm beginning to get the idea."

Ford nodded. "Bronson went insane here. The integrators were profoundly receptive. He killed himself on the downbeat of his manic-depressive curve, that period of intolerable depression, and the mental explosion—the sheer concentration of Bronson's madness—impressed itself on the radioatom brains of the integrators. The phonograph record, remember. The electrical impulses from those brains keep sending out that pattern—the downbeat. And the integrators are so powerful that anyone in the station can't help receiving the impressions."

Crockett gulped and drank cold coffee. "My God! That's—horrible!"

"It's a ghost," Ford said. "A perfectly logical ghost, the inevitable result of supersensitive thinking mechanisms. And you can't use occupational therapy on an integrator."

"Cigarette? Hm-m-m." Crockett puffed smoke and scowled. "You've convinced me of one thing, doctor. I'm going to get out of here."

Ford patted the air. "If my theory is correct, there's a possible cure—by induction."

"Eh?"

"Bronson could have been cured if he'd had treatment in time. There are therapies. Now"—Ford touched his notebook—"I have built up a complete picture of Bronson's psychology. I have also located a manic-depressive who is almost a duplicate of Bronson—a very similar case history, background and character. A sick magnet can be cured by demagnetisation."

"Meanwhile," Crockett said, with a relapse into morbidity, "we have a ghost."

Nevertheless he became interested in Ford's curious theories and the man's therapies. This calm acceptance of superstitious legend—and proof!—had a fascination for the big Irishman. In Crockett's blood ran the heritage of his Celtic forbears, a mysticism tempered with a hardened toughness. He had lately found the station's atmosphere almost unendurable. Now—

The station was a self-contained unit, so that only one operator was necessary. The integrators themselves were like sealed lubrication joints; once built, they were perfect of their type, and required no repairs. Apparently nothing could go wrong with them—except, of course, induced psychic crack-up. And even that did not affect their efficiency. The intergrators continued to solve abstruse problems, and the answers were always right. A human brain would have gone completely haywire, but the radioatom brains simply fixed their manic-depressive downbeat pattern and continued to broadcast it—distressingly.

There were shadows in the station. After a few days Dr. Ford noticed those intangible, weary shadows that, vampiric, drew the life and the energy from everything. The sphere of influence extended beyond the station itself. Occasionally Crockett went topside and, muffled in his heat-unit parka, went off on dangerous hikes. He drove himself to the limits of exhaustion as though hoping to outpace the monstrous depression that crouched under the ice.

But the shadows darkened invisibly. The grey, leaden sky of the Antarctic had never depressed Crockett before; the distant mountains, gigantic ranges towering like Ymir's mythical brood, had not seemed sentient till now. They were half alive, too old, too tired to move, dully satisfied to remain stagnantly crouching on the everlasting horizon of the ice fields. As the glaciers ground down, leaden, powerful, infinitely weary, the tide of the downbeat thrust against Crockett. His healthy animal mind shrank back, failed, and was engulfed.

He fought against it, but the secret foe came by stealth and no wall could keep it out. It permeated him as by osmosis. It was treacherous and deadly.

Bronson, squatting in silence, his eyes fixed on nothing, sunk into a black pit that would prison him for eternity—Crockett pictured that and shuddered. Too often these days his thoughts went back to illogical tales he had read; M. R. James, and his predecessor Henry James; Bierce and May Sinclair and others who had written of impossible ghosts. Previously Crockett had been able to enjoy ghost stories, getting a vicarious kick out of them, letting himself, for the moment, pretend to believe in the incredible. Can such things be? "Yes," he had said, but he had not believed. Now there was a ghost in the station, and Ford's logical theories could not battle Crockett's age-old superstition-instinct.

Since hairy men crouched in caves there has been fear of the dark. The fanged carnivores roaring outside in the night have not always been beasts. Psychology has changed them; the distorted, terrible sounds spawned in a place of peril—the lonely, menacing night beyond the firelight's circle—have created trolls and werewolves, vampires and giants and women with hollow backs.

Yes—there is fear. But most of all, beating down active terror, came the passive, shrouding cloak of infinitely horrible depression.

The Irishman was no coward. Since Ford's arrival, he had decided to stay, at least until the psychologist's experiment had succeeded or failed. Nevertheless he was scarcely pleased by Ford's guest, the manic-depressive the doctor had mentioned.

William Quayle looked not at all like Bronson, but the longer he stayed, the more he reminded Crockett of the other man. Quayle was a thin, dark, intense-eyed man of about thirty, subject to fits of violent rage when anything displeased him. His cycle had a range of approximately one week. In that time he would swing from blackest depression to wild exultation. The pattern never varied. Nor did he seem affected by the ghost; Ford said that the intensity of the up-curve was so strong that it blocked the effect of the integrators' downbeat radiation.

"I have his history," Ford said. "He could have been cured easily at the sanitarium where I found him, but luckily I got my requisition in first. See how interested he's getting in plastics?"

They were in the Brainpan; Crockett was unwillingly giving the integrators a routine inspection. "Did he ever work in plastics before, Doc?" the Irishman asked. He felt like talking; silence only intensified the atmosphere that was murkiest here.

"No, but he's dexterous. The work occupies his mind as well as his hands; it ties in with his psychology. It's been three weeks, hasn't it? And Quayle's well on the road to sanity."

"It's done nothing for … for this." Crockett waved toward the white towers.

"I know. Not yet—but wait a while. When Quayle's completely cured, I think the integrators will absorb the effect of his therapy. Induction—the only possible treatment for a radioatom brain. Too bad Bronson was alone here for so long. He could have been cured if only—"

But Crockett didn't like to think about that. "How about Quayle's dreams?"

Ford chuckled. "Hocus-pocus, eh? But in this case it's justified. Quayle is troubled or he wouldn't have gone mad. His troubles show up in dreams, distorted by the censor band. I have to translate them, figuring out the symbolism by what I know of Quayle himself. His word-association tests give me quite a lot of help."

"How?"

"He's been a misfit. It stemmed from his early relationships; he hated and feared his father, who was a tyrant. Quayle as a child was made to feel he could never compete with anyone—he'd be sure to fail. He identifies his father with all his obstacles."

Crockett nodded, idly watching a vernier. "You want to destroy his feeling toward his father, is that it?"

"The idea, rather, that his father has *power*. I must prove Quayle's capabilities to himself, and also alter his attitude that his father was infallible. Religious mania is tied in, too, perhaps naturally, but that's a minor factor."

"*Ghosts!*" Crockett said suddenly. He was staring at the nearest integrator.

In the cold clarity of the fluorescents Ford followed the other man's gaze. He pursed his lips, turning to peer down the length of the great underground room, where the silent pillars stood huge and impassive.

"I know," Ford said. "Don't think I don't feel it, too. But I'm fighting the thing, Crockett. That's the difference. If I simply sat in a corner and absorbed that downbeat, it would get me. I keep active—personifying the downbeat as an antagonist." The hard, tight face seemed to sharpen. "It's the best way."

"How much longer—

"We're approaching the end. When Quayle's cured, we'll know definitely."

—Bronson, crouching in shadows, sunk in apathetic, hopeless dejection, submerged in a blind blank horror so overwhelming that thought was an intolerable and useless effort—the will to fight gone, leaving only fear, and acceptance of the stifling, encroaching dark— .

This was Bronson's legacy. Yes, Crockett thought, ghosts existed. Now, in the Twenty-first Century. Perhaps never until now. Previously ghosts had been superstition. Here, in the station under the ice, shadows hung where there were no shadows. Crockett's mind was assaulted continuously, sleeping or waking, by that fantastic haunting. His dreams were characterised by a formless, vast, unspeakable darkness that moved on him inexorably, while he tried to run on leaden feet.

But Quayle grew better.

*

Three weeks—four—five—and finally six passed. Crockett was haggard and miserable, feeling that this would be his prison till he died, that he could never leave it. But he stuck it out with dogged persistence. Ford maintained his integrity; he grew tighter, drier, more restrained. Not by word or act did he admit the potency of the psychic invasion.

But the integrators acquired personalities, for Crockett. They were demoniac, sullen, inhuman afreets crouching in the Brainpan, utterly heedless of the humans who tended them.

A blizzard whipped the icecap to turmoil; deprived of his trips topside, Crockett became more moody than ever. The automats, fully stocked, provided meals, or the three would have gone hungry. Crockett was too listless to do more than his routine duties, and Ford began to cast watchful glances in his direction. The tension did not slacken.

Had there been a change, even the slightest variation in the deadly monotony of the downbeat, there might have been hope. But the record was frozen forever in that single phase. Too hopeless and damned even for suicide, Crockett tried to keep a grip on his rocking sanity. He clung to one thought: presently Quayle would be cured, and the ghost would be laid.

Slowly, imperceptibly, the therapy succeeded. Dr. Ford, never sparing himself, tended Quayle with gentle care, guiding him toward sanity, providing himself as a crutch on which the sick man could lean. Quayle leaned heavily, but the result was satisfying.

The integrators continued to pour out their downbeat pattern— but with a difference now.

Crockett noticed it first. He took Ford down to the Brainpan and asked the doctor for his reactions.

"Reactions? Why? Do you think there's—"

"Just—feet it," Crockett said, his eyes bright. "There's a difference. Don't you get it?"

"Yeah," Ford said slowly, after a long pause. "I think so. It's hard to be sure."

"Not if both of us feel the same thing."

"That's true. There's a slackening—a cessation. Hm-m-m. What did you do today, Crockett?"

"Eh? Why—the usual. Oh, I picked up that Aldous Huxley book again."

"Which you haven't touched for weeks. It's a good sign. The power of the downbeat is slackening. It won't go on to an ascending curve, of course; it'll just die out. Therapy by induction—when I cured Quayle, I automatically cured the integrators." Ford took a long, deep breath. Exhaustion seemed to settle down on him abruptly.

"You've done it, doc," Crockett said, something like hero-worship in his eyes.

But Ford wasn't listening. "I'm tired," he muttered. "Oh, my God, I'm tired! The tension's been terrific. Fighting that damned ghost every moment... I haven't dared allow myself a sedative, even. Well, I'm going to break out the amytal now."

"What about a drink? We ought to celebrate. If—" Crockett looked doubtfully at the nearest integrator. "If you're sure."

"There's little doubt about it. No, I want my sleep. That's all!"

He took the lift and was drawn up out of sight. Left alone in the Brainpan, Crockett managed a lopsided grin. There were still shadows lurking in the distance, but they were fading.

He called the integrators an unprintable name. They remained imperturbable.

"Oh, sure," Crockett said, "you're just machines. Too damn sensitive, that's all. Ghosts! Well, from now on, I'm the boss. I'm going to invite my friends up here and have one drunken party from sunrise to sunset. And the sun doesn't set for a long time in these latitudes!"

On that cogent thought, he followed Ford. The psychologist was already asleep, breathing steadily, his face relaxed in tired lines. He looked older, Crockett thought. But who wouldn't?

The pulse was lessening; the downbeat was fading. He could almost detect the ebb. That unreasoning depression was no longer all-powerful. He was—yeah!—beginning to make plans!

"I'm going to make chile," Crockett decided. "The way that guy in El Paso showed me. And wash it down with Scotch. Even if I have to celebrate by myself, this calls for an orgy." He thought doubtfully of Quayle, and looked in on the man. But Quayle was glancing over a late novel, and waved casually at his guest.

"Hi, Crockett. Anything new?"

"N-no. I just feel good."

"So do I. Ford says I'm cured. The man's a wonder."

"He is," Crockett agreed heartily. "Anything you want?"

"Nothing I can't get for myself." Quayle nodded toward the wall automat-slot. "I'm due to be released in a few days. You've treated me like a brother Christian, but I'll be glad to get back home. There's a job waiting for me—one I can fill without trouble."

"Good. Wish I were going with you. But I've a two-year stretch up here, unless I quit or fainaigue a transfer."

"You've got all the comforts of home."

"Yeah!" Crockett said, shuddering slightly. He hurried off to prepare chile, fortifying himself with smoky-tasting, smooth whiskey. If only he wasn't jumping the gun—Suppose the downbeat hadn't been eliminated? Suppose that intolerable depression came back in all its force?

Crockett drank more whiskey. It helped.

*

Which, in itself, was cheering. Liquor intensifies the mood. Crockett had not dared touch it during the downbeat. But now he just got happier, and finished his chile with an outburst of tuneless song. There was no way of checking the psychic emanation of the integrators with any instrument, of course; yet the cessation of that deadly atmosphere had unmistakable significance.

The radioatom brains were cured. Bronson's mental explosion, with its disastrous effects, had finally run its course and been eliminated—by induction. Three days later a plane picked up Quayle and flew back northward toward South America, leaving Ford to clean up final details and make a last check up.

The atmosphere of the station had changed utterly. It was bright, cheerful, functional. The integrators no longer sat like monstrous devil-gods in a private hell. They were sleek, efficient tubes, as pleasing to the eye as a Brancusi, containing radioatom brains that faithfully answered the questions Crockett fed them. The station ran smoothly. Up above, the grey sky blasted a cleansing, icy gale upon the polar cap.

Crockett prepared for the winter. He had his books, he dug up his sketch pad and examined his water colours, and felt he could last till spring without trouble. There was nothing depressing about the station *per se*. He had another drink and wandered off on a tour of inspection.

Ford was standing before the integrators, studying them speculatively. He refused Crockett's offer of a highball.

"No, thanks. These things are all right now, I believe. The downbeat is completely gone."

"You ought to have a drink," said Crockett. "We've been through something, brother. This stuff relaxes you. It eases the letdown."

"No... I must make out my report. The integrators are such beautifully logical devices it would be a pity to have them crack up. Luckily, they won't. Now that I've proved it's possible to cure insanity by induction."

Crockett leered at the integrators. "Little devils. Look at 'em, squatting there as though butter wouldn't melt in their mouths."

"Hm-m-m. When will the blizzard let up? I want to arrange for a plane."

"Can't tell. The one before last didn't stop for a week This one—" Crockett shrugged "I'll try to find out, but I won't make any promises."

"I'm anxious to get back."

"Well—" Crockett said. He took the lift, went back to his office, and checked incoming calls, listing the questions he must feed into the integrators. One of them was important: a geological matter from the California Sub-Tech Quake Control. But it could wait till all the calls were gathered.

Crockett decided against another drink. For some reason he hadn't fulfilled his intention of getting tight; ordinary relief had proved a strong intoxicant. Now, whistling softly, he gathered the sheaf of items and started back toward the Brainpan. The station looked swell, he thought. Maybe it was the knowledge that he'd had a reprieve from a death sentence. Only it had been worse than knowledge of certain death—that damned downbeat. Ugh!

He got into the lift, a railed platform working on old-fashioned elevator principles. Magnetic lifts couldn't be used near the integrators. He pushed the button, and, looking down, saw the Brainpan beneath him, the white cylinders dwarfed by perspective.

Footsteps sounded. Turning, Crockett discovered Ford running toward him. The lift was already beginning to drop, and Crockett's fingers went hastily toward the stop stud.

He changed his mind as Ford raised his hand and exhibited a pistol. The bullet smashed into Crockett's thigh. He went staggering back till he hit the rail, and by that time Ford had leaped into the elevator, his face no longer prim and restrained, his eyes blazing with madness, and his lips wetly slack.

He yelled gibberish and squeezed the trigger again. Crockett desperately flung himself forward. The bullet missed, though he could not be sure, and his hurtling body smashed against Ford. The psychologist, caught off balance fell against the rail. As he tried to fire again Crockett, his legs buckling, sent his fist toward Ford's jaw.

The timing, the balance, were fatally right. Ford went over the rail. After a long time Crockett heard the body strike, far down.

The lift sank smoothly. The gun still lay on the platform. Crockett, groaning, began to tear his shirt into an improvised tourniquet. The wound in his thigh was bleeding badly.

The cold light of the fluorescents showed the towers of the integrators, their tops level with Crockett now, and then rising as he continued to drop. If he looked over the edge of the platform he could see Ford's body. But he would see it soon enough anyway.

It was utterly silent.

Tension, of course, and delayed reaction. Ford should have got drunk. Liquor would have made a buffer against the violent reaction from those long weeks of hell. Weeks of battling the downbeat, months in which Ford had kept himself keenly alert, visualising the menace as a personified antagonist, keying himself up to a completely abnormal pitch.

Then success, and the cessation of the downbeat. And silence, deadly, terrifying—time to relax and think.

And Ford—going mad.

He had said something about that weeks ago, Crockett remembered. Most psychologists have a tendency toward mental instability; that's why they gravitate into the field, and why they understand it.

The lift stopped. Ford's motionless body was about a yard away. Crockett could not see the man's face.

Insanity—manic-depressives are fairly simple cases. The schizophrenic are more complex. And incurable.

Incurable.

Dr. Ford was a schizoid type. He had said that, weeks ago.

And now Dr. Ford, a victim of schizophrenic insanity, had died by violence, as Bronson had died. Thirty white pillars stood in the Brainpan, cryptically impassive, and Crockett looked at them with the beginning of a slow, dull horror.

Thirty radioatom brains, supersensitive, ready to record a new pattern on the blank wax disks. Not manic-depressive this time, not the downbeat.

On the contrary, it would be uncharted, incurable schizophrenic insanity.

A mental explosion—yeah. Dr. Ford, lying there dead, a pattern of madness fixed in his brain at the moment of death. A pattern that might be anything.

Crockett watched the thirty integrators and wondered what was going on inside those gleaming white shells. He would find out before the blizzard ended, he thought, with a sick horror.

For the station was haunted again.

1946

THE POLAR VORTEX

Malcolm M. Ferguson

Malcolm M. Ferguson (1919–2011) was a librarian, antiquarian book dealer and occasional author of science fiction. His literary output is confined to six short stories written in the 1940s and early 1950s, five of them published in *Weird Tales*, shortly after he returned from military service in the Second World War. Ferguson's brief literary career included a recurrent interest in solitude. "Croatan" (1948) concerns "the sole survivor [who] seeks to express the enigmatic end of his tribe by a last tense message". "Terror Under Eridu" (1949) begins with the testimony of a "doomed man" trapped in the Temple of Ehpor, an ancient ruin guarded by the "lidded mouth-foot of a gastropod of unheard-of size" ("Mind-staggering, nightmarish thing!").

"The Polar Vortex", Ferguson's first story, treats solitude less through the formulaic pulp fiction weirdness of the vanishing tribe or the giant man-eating snail and more as a psychological experience. As such, Ferguson taps into a recurrent strand of polar literature: what would it be like to find yourself alone at the ends of the earth? Like Kuttner's "Ghost", "The Polar Vortex" is a story on the cusp of science and psychoanalysis. Here the drama is poised between astronomical observation and the inner life of its protagonist, between the night sky and the tormented mind. Like many stories in this collection, the plot unfolds against the question of money: not in this case how to make it, but rather what to do if you've got way too much of it.

Among the effects of the late Leopold Lemming, multi-millionaire turned scientist and dabbler, was a small, battered old chest containing several hundred yards of wire on which had been recorded sounds, and a two-hundred-page transcript of an experiment. Lemming had made his money in real estate, which is quite another thing from science, and in spite of his considerably advantageous investments in new scientific inventions, most people thought of Lemming as a shrewd businessman and only a dabbler in the sciences, or, as they put it, the pseudo-sciences.

This opinion continued throughout the estate's auction at the appearance of such fantastic objects as rune-hilted swords, waxen images of notables, volumes of Paracelsus, the *Book of the Dead*, and Cotton Mather, all copiously annotated in a cryptic shorthand, with now and then a vehement objection bursting into English as he disagreed with one or another of these. There were quite a number of these objects, some common, some very esoteric indeed, but all apparently appraised as to their validity. Then there were volumes on the sciences—astronomy, mathematics, physics, predominantly, all bearing this code of the modern Pepys, whose choice of objects was so strange.

The most curious acquisition made from Lemming's effects, however, was the battered old chest, which contained the manuscript in English, the dictaphone wire, and a small sheaf of notes, which turned out to be the case-book of an experiment Lemming had made in connection with his observatory at the South Pole. These effects gave evidence of a shocking ruthlessness, blindly idolatrous to the acquisition of scientific knowledge, revealing a curiously terrible experiment, which could be pieced together from the notebook Lemming used and the wire-reel—

THE CASE-BOOK OF DANIEL IMBRIFER

1 Feb.: I am opening this notebook with high hopes. I think Daniel Imbrifer will be an excellent subject. Clerk by day, student by night, he strives with the valour of Prometheus. He'll do.

And now, two years to the day since I laid the cornerstone of the glass-domed observatory at the South Magnetic Pole, I've met him in a bookstore, vastly hungering for knowledge and forasmuch as he could not buy both books and food. Just under six foot tall, raven-haired: that he was a fathomer of dark pools was reflected in his eyes. I hope to plumb the depths of those pools and stir them into a mad wrath that spews up the long-hidden debris of their deepest abysms. I want to whip up such a tidal frenzy in his mind that all surface craft will be lost, and derelict thoughts be riven from their mud-moored deeps.

But not a bit of this eagerness could be seen in my casual introduction as we both groped for the same book. In a moment he knew me from various news photos and articles. We talked, I feigning interest in several odd volumes, he unfolding forthright views on science and myth alike under my discreet probings, proving with every word to be the man I wanted for my experiment. A noble mind, full of youthful energy, impatient to storm the gates of wisdom.

*

17 Mar.: Imbrifer and I sat late in my library, and over the third highball I showed him the model of my Antarctic planetarium. I had mentioned it often—now I was ready. I explained to him that there was to be a council of scientists there, and cunningly interwove names known to him and names known only to my mind. I spoke with regret of my unsuccessful attempts to get someone who could represent the layman, since all these men had pursued their theories so long that they were blind to all others. A good pupil demands clear expression from his teacher, and often finds the weak places in an exposition I argued. With such a student we could inaugurate a series of round-table discussions, of seminars, of papers and paper-chases.

How could he be anything but impressed by this, and by the model of the sheer-glass, double-thick hemisphere in the deserted waste of the Antarctic, whose winter is a perpetual night. I dissembled the model and showed him the subterrene dynamo, the storage passageways, enough devices to insure the safety of a dozen men for a year at least.

I showed him the telescope alongside the observatory, which, even in the model, could be raised cunningly from its garage just as coastal guns are brought into place. And Imbrifer saw that the telescope could fathom the skies, recording on the deep screen before him what it probed, as if on an oversized television screen. It's a delicate machine, yet especially made to withstand cold—with the advantage that in the winter nights of the South Polar region there are a minimum of deflecting heat waves.

Imbrifer took it all in, and I've taken him in—he's hooked. I have yet to get him to take the custodianship of the place until the "conference" starts. Say a month from the time we leave him there, flying away; his eye fixed as a cyclops' on the sky. I have yet to explain to him the apparatus for projecting an artificial skyscraper in cloudy weather. Perhaps I'll leave that until he gets there.

Ah, but he's a prober—all concerned for the science of the thing; lured to look at the fascinating, and away from my magic-making skullduggery. Teasing his mind to reveal its secrets, catching himself in superstitions and intimations of mortality, and then perplexing himself with "Why?" Anon playing cat and mouse with a whim, letting it go and catching it again.

29 *Mar.*: It is agreed. Daniel Imbrifer will fly with me on the 14th of next month. I promised him the crop's cream of scientists, and so regaled him. He's to represent Everyman, or his equivalent in the Enquiring Man of Today, at this intellectual Olympiad. While most of this is secret, I have had his picture taken as "assisting me in research" and it's appearing in newspapers here and there. For one month, I told him yesterday, he is to be the sole caretaker at the polar observatory, relieving the four men now on duty there. He is to study the earth and the heavens, the vast deeps of space, and the tiny realm of man. I explained that as one goes to a foreign *country* to learn its language, here was his opportunity to study astronomy, to contemplate, with all the resources of modern science, the stars and the space between the stars. But little does he realise, storming the gates of wisdom, that this may be too much; that like no other man on earth this world will be too little with him.

Of course I've shown him that physically he will be quite safe. Physically, yes, as snug as a bug in a rug—auxiliary heating equipment, an emergency dynamo, and an oil-heating system if these should fail. A veritable anthill of tunnels stocked with more food than such a student as he was used to, rayed out, dry, cool, and air-conditioned, into the ice and frozen earth below.

14 Apr.: At the South Pole. The giant plane landed on the rough ice outside, taxiing to within 100 yards of the polished dome, which had kept its perfect sheen under the combined protection of an oil which prevents blown ice-particles from forming and piling up, an invisibly fine-veined de-icing system raying throughout the sheer glass dome, and a judicious placing of the observatory at the bottom of a shallow bowl which is perpetually scooped by the winds themselves, yet is shallow enough to give the observatory an excellent horizon.

The four caretakers, on shift for a month, greeted us enthusiastically. I have to keep them as much out of Imbrifer's way as I can, and exert all care that they pack their books and cards and magazines and games with which they passed the time and beat boredom back. I hit on the scheme of opposing such "vain frivolities" for my student-friend with a sanctimonious air that was quite out of my character.

15 Apr.: At the South Pole—or, to be technical, at the hypothetical magnetic South Pole, diametrically antipodal to the magnetic North Pole. Today I leave Daniel Imbrifer to his studies, to burn the midnight oil in the uninterrupted Antarctic night. And with problems as ponderable as the night is long.

He and I checked the observatory's apparatus—its temperature kept evenly at a chilly 58.6 degrees Fahrenheit, its air-conditioning functioning perfectly, preventing heat-waves from piling up under the dome, but creating a steady, fountain-shaped current of air, and keeping sight of the stars undistorted. And below us purred this giant dynamo with a low, even pulsing which was barely perceptible.

The lighting in the dome has been cut down to three shielded stroboscopic lights. One casts a wan light over a study table; another at the head of the bed on a goose-neck to swing over the low book-shelf; the third by the apparatus for raising the telescope. This was the extent of the furniture under the dome, and the smooth, heavy, steel floor has only the trap-door leading to the underground plant in the centre. Around this is a steel ring, flush with the floor, which will reveal its purpose to Imbrifer in a short while. I checked its mechanism, as delicate as a watch, and found that when heavy clouds obscure the heavens the electric eye will release a jetty vapour to fill the empty air-space between the inner and outer layer of glass in the dome. The ring in the floor will become a band of light, projecting on the dome's vapid black an exact replica of the heavens as they would have appeared as the earth turns. And just as readily the cunning show gives way to the real one. Perhaps this device will ignite the powder train which will set fire to Imbrifer's brain, until he feels a tottery Atlas indeed.

This device I set in motion, and yet one more.

The dictaphone, whose wires will start with every sound and stop with every silence, catching every stirring above the pounding of the pulses in the brain's turbine. So.

(Extracts from the Diary of Daniel Imbrifer.):

16 Apr.: At 1350 hours by my watch, Mr. Lemming and his four caretakers left, having instructed me thoroughly regarding the equipment I will need to use here. It is strange that there is no communication with the rest of the world, or any reception of news of any kind. I objected strongly when he started to take the radio out, but he flew into such a rage that I finally let him have his way.

He has an outline study program prepared, with questions for me to ponder. Insolvable questions categorically stated—about dwarf stars, variable stars, comets, nebulae, gravitational pulls, orbits, the origin of the Milky Way and its present direction of movement.

The bookcase contains a dozen books on astronomy, celestial navigation, and mathematics, plus a strange typescript volume containing a collection of folklore and mythology concerning man's contemplation of the heavens. Selections from Pliny, Max Mueller, Sigmund Freud, Sir James Frazer, Oswald Spengler, Dean Swift, Fiona MacLeod, Andrew Lang, Novalis, and the literature of ancient Egypt and Arabia, all showing man's perplexed fascination with the night sky.

But all my scrambling around is but the reflection of my loneliness. For immediately as the green Castor and red Pollux on the plane's wings grew dim against the less-colourful stars, loneliness rushed to my heart and took possession of my marrow. This tiny toadstool at the earth's Ultima Thule was to be my place of vigil. Well, I must stick it out now. If all goes well I can afford to try a few experiments of my own after all this.

18 Apr.: The sky being brilliant, I summoned the sentinel telescope and swept the heavens, the stars crystal dear in the Antarctic cold. Those of higher magnitude delineated as suspended in space. But what caught my eye as I followed the majestic sweep of the Milky Way across the sky was a void; an empty well in the sky—a sudden break in the spate of stars. This hole or blind spot is remarkably situated to catch the eye, being near the zenith, in the lower left quadrant of the Southern Cross. Find the Southern Cross—the cynosure of all navigators below the equator, and this void gapes before you. It is the Coalsack, gaping utterly devoid of stars from this hemisphere's most conspicuous spot.

*

20 Apr.: My calendar and my watch tell me it is the 20th of April, but my irregular hours will soon trample down the barriers between the days, since there's no daylight and dark to distinguish them. I find myself pacing the even surface of the steel floor. I linger over my meals, but the whole eating process can't be protracted over three-quarters of an hour, somehow.

I now know what the dour Scotch caretaker meant when he got wind of the fact that I was to spend a month here, alone. "It shouldn' be, mon. A young lad like ye. It's nae guid for ye to be withouten a roof. Ye canna keep yer skull's cap on withouten a roof. "Tis agin Nature and God."

And with that he took two quarts of whiskey and with finger to lips he hid them in amongst the canned food. A little later he was about to give me a pack of cards but Mr. Lemming interfered.

Mr. Lemming is a strange figure. Commonplace enough in appearance, yet how he tramples beauty and life under foot in his search for truth. Doesn't he realise that truth should be cut in chunks man can swallow? That science, unless devoted to the orientation of mankind to this world, rather than to the bedevilment of mankind for your own satisfaction and perhaps even knowledge, is a perversion. Mr. Lemming's damn-the-cost attitude is too big for this world.

I thought today that I'd at last be able to turn my thoughts to earth, at least for long enough to get my breath. But I didn't count on the genius of Mr. Lemming, who produced an image of the heavens on the dome of the observatory. It's a clever thing, throwing every detail visible to the naked eye upon the glass dome... I suppose he'd explain it as "for the guidance of the council" but I see it as an effort to sever my mental associations with the man-sized world and draw me out into the realms of space.

How little I realised when I came here. Is it really my imagination, or is Mr. Lemming trying to condition my thoughts? How? Why?

I remember a puppet-show in which a man suddenly appeared as a fearsome giant, after I had become used to the deft, graciously proportioned Lilliputians. Thus our premises of thought are altered, yet we are always human beings, not titans, nor want to be.

22 Apr.: I could not bring myself to write anything yesterday. I studied and made notes on the Southern constellations, examining the double stars all wound up in each other's fate, the dwarf stars looking what their name implies under the terrific weight of their bodies. I could not help but imagine attributes for the various stars, a childish trick firmly rooted in the mind of man.

23 Apr.: I'm still studying books on this world and this universe. I remember of a man studying the phenomenon of sleep for so long and so deeply that he inhibited himself from going to sleep—he "murdered sleep," and had to seek rest in a sanitarium.

24 Apr.: After writing the words above I went to sleep readily enough, but awoke in sudden fright, somehow startled, perhaps by a cramped position. The first tiling I saw was that baleful emptiness, the Coalsack, yawning like an ape's gape in the night. Dark in a world of dark.

25 Apr.: Tired. I had better not write. Brain fag. Sorry, Imbrifer, old boy, but the first person is not well.

26 Apr.: Today I took one of the books and went downstairs, but the lighting is bad. I could feel the stars above me if I could not see them.

It was worse, as if the fourth dimension were lurking to swallow me into thin air. I had better stand and fight like a man. If I'm going to fear anything I want to find it out before it finds me out.

(Apparently at this point the noises transcribed on the wire do not reflect alarming aberations. An inordinate amount of pacing back and forth restlessly, a good deal of talking to himself, though nothing as fascinating or understandable as the diary. Very little laughter except for a sardonic chuckle. At one point Imbrifer took to running around the observatory, but whether from nervousness or from a planned project to exercise cannot be known.)

27 Apr.: Poking around in the below-surface regions trying to consume as much time as possible making dinner, yet at the same time subconsciously speeding up, teasing myself with my bodings, when I found a covered disk in the centre of the floor inset in front of the hatch-ladder. I unscrewed the two screws that kept the cover in place and found a mariner's compass. I tripped the release on the compass, setting it in motion. The release somehow broke in doing so, but I soon overlooked this as I watched the strange action of the compass. It fluctuated, wobbled, and spun for a moment, and finally settled down to spin slowly but steadily. Deliberately and determinedly it set about to register All Points North. Around and round and round.

I suppose it sounds natural, but it was a possibility I had never anticipated. Apparently set in the centre of the building's foundation, it won't budge. It's the only compass here, too. Is this the reaction a compass should make when located as this one is? The earth's axis seems very real to me, as if it ran directly through the centre of this building. I wonder if a plumb, suspended free, would swing round instead of back and forth. I wish there were enough space to try it.

*

I've been sitting here musing for three hours now. Here is empirical evidence that I am the Man in the Mulberry Bush, and all men grope around me...

(Here is interpolated the first of the recordings from the wire, following a mad crescendo of laughter.)

"Laugh, damn you, laugh. It will steady your nerves. Now let me think this thing through. Here am I at the imaginary point around which this giant gyroscope whirls. This small compass is cogged to whirl about the same central point as does the earth, but, though concentric, it whirls faster, being somehow the centre of a smaller circle. Only at this orbit is the spin registered, since everywhere else it's off-line. Even a mile off the distance absorbs the whirl, though the compass begins to act queerly. The laws of gravitation offset all centrifugal force. Well, they do here for that matter, but there's still all that extra 'whirl' left. No, it can't be...

"Where is that whiskey the Scotchman left? Here if I can reach it... I seem to be walking all right on this dizzying disk. If only that damned compass would stop acting like a weather-cock in the centre of a cyclone. Ah, here it is...

"'Tell me why the stars do shine...' Say that's good; it's a long time since I sang that in church.

'Tell me why the stars do shine
Tell me why the ivy twines
Tell me why the sky's so blue...'

How about that ivy business? That's strange. North of the equator it spins counter-clockwise, just like a cyclone. South of the equator the vine twines clockwise, just like the cyclone. At the equator the effect is most dissipated. No crises there. But at the centre of this little 'o', this orb, it spirals to beat hell. And that, as Kipling would say, if he had been drinking, is why we have no ivy at the poles.

It's also why you don't see streamers around the South Pole come Mayday."

28 Apr.: I awoke lying across my bed, feeling rotten, fully dressed. I am not a drinking man, and feel down at the edges. But perhaps it's a good thing. This place is getting me down—and I don't mean because it's down under here, either—that's a lot of imaginary nonsense. It is, truly enough one of the poles, though, and like only one other point in the world, its antipode, its nadir, its opposite.

I feel better now. Perhaps I can study again.

29 Apr.: Today I contemplated the space between the stars, looking first at our nearest neighbour, Alpha Centaurus, and then I found (with difficulty) the external galaxy in, or rather behind, the constellation of Centaurus. This is another Milky Way—this wee haze amounts to somewhere near as much as most of the rest of our horizon's view for size. From Alpha Centaurus light is supposed to take four years and four months dragging its heels at its usual speed in a vacuum getting around to us.

2 May: My precarious equilibrium has been maintained, largely by not asking myself too many questions and by "not thinking about anything". As I spun the telescope away from a variable star I was watching, stars of the Milky Way swam across my field of vision as so many motes. Many of them are larger than our sun and several thousand light years away. And then the bottom dropped out, as it were, as if this were too much for this mechanical contraption. It registered nothing. Nothing. A blank black. I looked up. Yes, the stars still shone. But the telescope's field was a blank. Fearfully and with moist palms I turned the dial. A star appeared at the lower right corner. I spun the dial away, up and to the left. Another star appeared. Then the troupe of the Milky Way, as if the celestial ballet had started afresh. I'm afraid I whimpered at this, and fell all a-tremble, like a puppy. I had accidentally stumbled on the Coalsack, and it had taken me unawares. There is something about that celestial blind-spot that makes me want to cower in a corner, but this damned place is round.

3 May: My watch stopped when I slept. I can tell time roughly by the stars, but I might easily become confused and lose track of the days. Then I'd be afraid to reckon up for fear I'd lose a day, or a week, and have it here ahead of me. I wonder if my pulse stopped or whether it was some baleful influence here. Last night a terrible dream wrought me. A vine twined quickly out of space and seized my head. I awoke, screaming. And right above me was the lurking pit out of which the spiral spun. It seemed ages that I cowered in bed, cursing my cowardice, afraid of reality, afraid of dream.

4 May (I guess): Relief! Relief, damn Lemming! Something he hadn't thought of. A straw for me to clutch at as I whirl in the centre of this polar maelstrom.

An earthly phenomenon. One he hadn't anticipated either. He who ruled out snow and the rushing balm of a frozen death from his little study of this poor student, Daniel Imbrifer, He who created the glassy image of the heavens to taunt me; who exposed me to the gaze of the deeps, to the hypnotic pull of this vastness of space, drawing me out as oil on water, in an element equally foreign and fearsome.

The phenomenon sheds more light rather than less, the Aurora Australis. This earthly phenomenon has helped me get my feet under myself at least for long enough to learn that my mind is that of a poor earthling and should not seek to soar too far, In this assurance I have won for, though I lose my mind, I have really gained it.

Life surges back and the pulses pace for a moment more sedately. At first the Aurora Australis marched slowly in crackling white radiance, as if the atmosphere were raining manna; then in coloured energy, dancing from horizon to horizon, taking in its bounds at a Borzoi leap. Lord, once again to be an awestruck earthling and watch the hound of heaven, the leaping Loki, the frozen lightning, the shattered rainbow, energy snared and transformed by witchery, a hyperborean Ariel, an impersonalised nervousness which drives out my own. My pen flows evenly, swiftly, as this phenomenon continues, because when it dies down my energy will begin to charge and leap up.

Later: The Aurora Australis has gone, but my mind is still in the ways of men. Though alone on the night-side of the world, I know the rest is there; that the sun greets most men the world around. That work and days go on I know, that men work at the vast drop forges, at the antiquated ploughs; that they ogle the women and test their strength with other men at games; that they are often cruel, but that there will always and ultimately be beauty and a warming of the heart; and though many are killed, some will see light and humility.

Later: Perhaps I can last out the month, though I doubt it. I'm afraid to compute the time and date by celestial means. I'm afraid that time has stood still or perhaps has crept at snail's pace, as if the snail had started at the back of my skull-bone and had not yet lumped up under my hair at the top of my head—but such thoughts spin into the abysms of madness. And yet even unafflicted people use mad concepts, though they no more realise than they do the fact the earth is spinning and time speeding with it, though they see that the sun rises and sets, while I do not.

This "morning" I awoke quietly, and kept a blanket over my head until I had my wits about me. Then boldly looked out at the skies sinking into infinity, suspended in infinity. I think I can stand it today, though. I tried to make a deck of cards, but fearing I would become superstitious as luck played tricks with me. I would have embodied luck as an unseen presence behind me, fearfully pointing a skeletal hand at a card. And there is enough behind me that I have to keep driving back mentally. Sometimes obsession rides my back like a twining corpse.

I *will* choose my thoughts carefully today (today being determined as the period until I grow sufficiently tired to seek rest). I cast about me for something to do, to keep me occupied. In this calm moment I see that it is quite probable that Lemming did, wholly by design, plan to use me as his guinea pig. Since one man has willed that this be so, and since I cannot alter it, I will let this record continue as long as it will to express this emotional dispersement and end either when I'm rescued or as it will.

(From the wire dictaphone.)

"I am alone on earth.

"Once there were Adam and Eve and Pinch Me. Adam and Eve have gone off and left me here all alone. I make the world go round on course, on time. But what if I should fall asleep and it should stop, and the rest of the universe be spinning except the world?

"There's a good boy—crank the spit, If I could only really tell why I turn this world around...

"It's all in your imagination, Danny—it's all in your imagination. Damn that blasphemous compass. I'll break it, that's what I'll do, I'll get something heavy and drop it on it. This chair will do.

"There, that's better. But oh, it gapes like an empty socket! What have I done?"

(Now the diary again.)

Later: Yesterday I broke the compass. But I solved nothing by that. It still goes around in my mind. I was childish and I am just aggravating myself. I am sorry. It would be better if I left it undamaged. Then I could see that things are as they are and get a foothold on facts that are fast eluding me.

(The wire record again.)

"Eieeaaah… stop, world. Stop whirling. That ape's hairy black arm grasping the world from that ebon emptiness of the Coalsack turned inside out. Stop spinning me swivelling. Too fast. The world grasped as seaweed clenches a clam—but whirling as the ape's arm spins it, unkinking. No, no, grasping hand, pressing palm! Sweat pearled.

"It's me you want—wait—I'll stand at the nub's hub. I'll howl it down. Eiii-ah…"

NOTES OF MR. LEOPOLD LEMMING

The body of Daniel Imbrifer was found at the foot of his bed, his feet tangled in bedclothes, his skull broken on tile steel floor. He had apparently set out to stand astride this mad world. I wonder—

Fortunately I entered first, well expecting such a discovery. The crew of the ship is quite different from the one which took me away two and a half months ago. Both crews believe I left Imbrifer for only a week (though he anticipated a month's stay only), and no one knows the devices I have here—not all of them, or why. Now before they come in I will gather and put aside all the data on Imbrifer.

Here comes the pilot. I'll be shocked at my discovery, Within twenty-four hours we should leave here.

STORY SOURCES

NORTH

James Hogg, "The Surpassing Adventures of Allan Gordon" (*Tales and Sketches*, Volume I, Glasgow: Blackie and Sons, 1837).

Harriet Prescott Spofford, "The Moonstone Mass" (*Harper's Monthly*, October 1868).

Arthur Conan Doyle, "The Captain of the 'Polestar'" (*Temple Bar*, Volume 67, January 1883).

John Buchan, "Skule Skerry" (*The Runagates Club*, London: Hodder and Stoughton, 1928).

Idwal Jones, "The Third Interne" (*Weird Tales*, January 1938).

Aviaq Johnston, "Iqsinaqtutalik Piqtuq: The Haunted Blizzard" (*Taaqtumi: An Anthology of Arctic Horror Stories*, Iqaluit, Nunavut: Inhabit Media, 2019).

SOUTH

Hamilton Drummond, "A Secret of the South Pole" (*Windsor Magazine*, December 1901).

John Martin Leahy, "In Amundsen's Tent" (*Weird Tales*, January 1928).

Sophie Wenzel Ellis, "Creatures of the Light" (*Astounding Stories of Super Science*, February 1930).

Mordred Weir, "Bride of the Antarctic" (*Strange Stories*, June 1939).

Henry Kuttner, "Ghost" (*Astounding Science-Fiction*, May 1943).
Malcolm M. Ferguson, "The Polar Vortex" (*Weird Tales*, September 1946).

For more Tales of the Weird titles
visit the British Library Shop (shop.bl.uk)

We welcome any suggestions, corrections or feedback you may have, and will
aim to respond to all items addressed to the following:

The Editor (Tales of the Weird), British Library Publishing,
The British Library, 96 Euston Road, London NW1 2DB

We also welcome enquiries through our Twitter account, @BL_Publishing.